Dear Reader,

Thank you for taking the time to read my book. It has consumed me for the better part of a year and I hope you love it.
This novel contains adult content that may not be suitable
for all readers. Beyond violence and sexually explicit material,
this story also includes moments of non-consent, addiction,
and intimate partner abuse. If these topics are particularly
triggering for you, this may not be the book for you.

With love, Kristen Cari

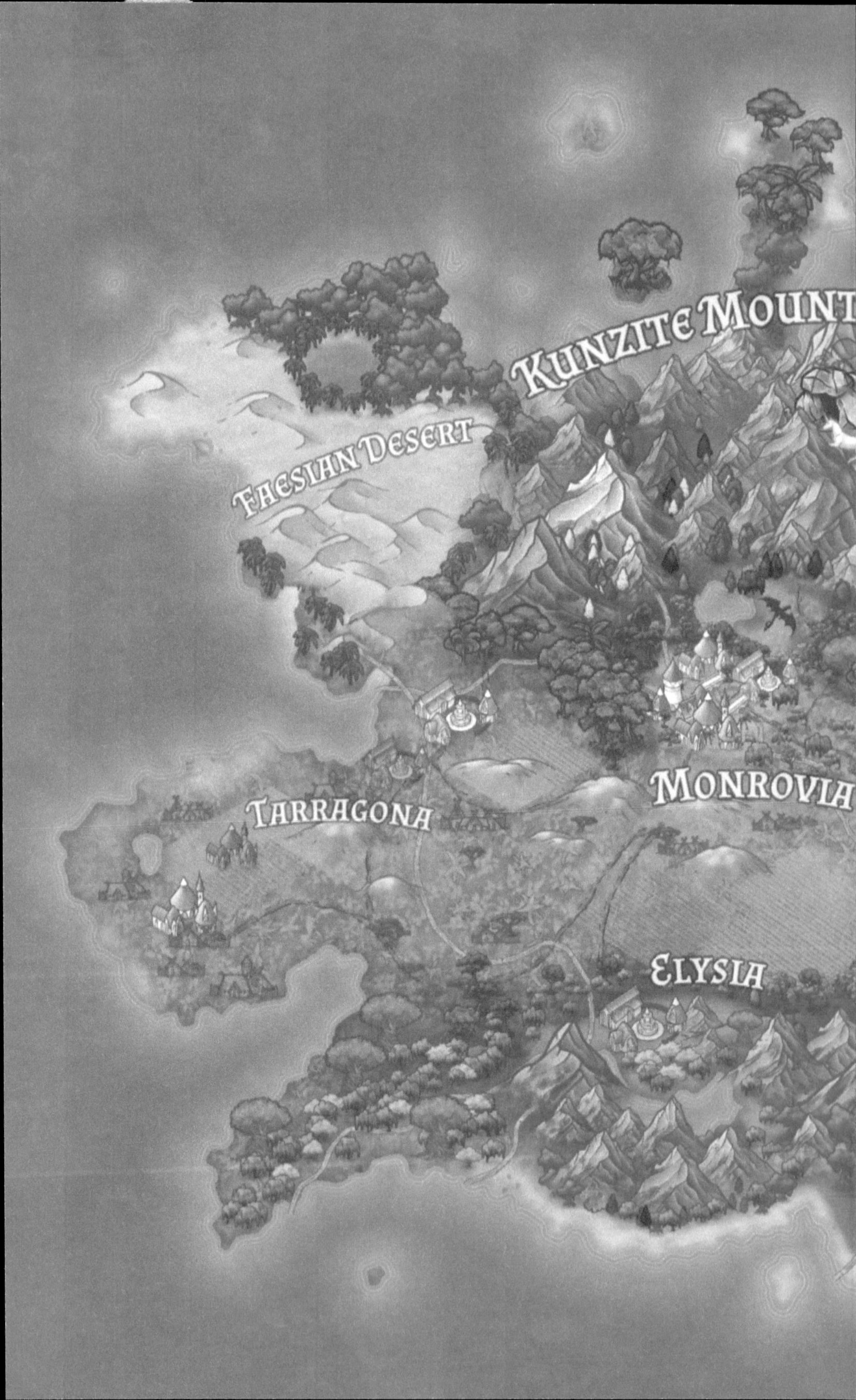

Kunzite Mount
Faesian Desert
Monrovia
Tarragona
Elysia

THE FORGOTTEN FAE
IN THE BLOOD

KRISTEN CARI

NYMERA

LAVINIA

FOOTHILL INN

MERIVALE LAKE

MONROVIA
CASTLE

GLOSSARY

AKU- SHADOW GOD, RULER OF HELL

ALYA- GODDESS OF WIND

AURELIUS- MARIGOLD'S HOME, ANCIENT FAE CITY

BEIRA- GODDESS OF ICE

CYRO- GOD OF FIRE

DRAGON- STEWARD OF ALYA

ELYSIA- SOUTHERN CITY IN NYMERA

ERADOR- HOME WORLD

HYDRA- STEWARD OF SIVO

LAVINIA- MOUNTAIN TOWN IN NYMERA

MONROVIA- CAPITAL CITY OF NYMERA

GLOSSARY

NYMERA- WORLD INHABITED BY THE FAE

PHOENIX- STEWARD OF CYRO

PNEUMA- SPIRIT ANIMAL IN ANCIENT FAE LANGUAGE

POOKA- STEWARD OF AKU, APPEARS IN FORM OF BLACK HORSE

SIVO- GOD OF WATER

SPHINX- STEWARD OF TERRA

STEWARDS OF THE GODS- MYTHOLOGICAL CREATURES OF THE GODS

TARRAGONA- WESTERN CITY IN NYMERA

TERRA- GODDESS OF EARTH

UHRA- AN AURA, THE VISUAL MANIFESTATION OF A SOUL

UNICORN- STEWARD OF BEIRA

This book is dedicated to every woman who has ever been burned, betrayed, or broken. May you rise from the ashes like the brilliant wild flower that you are. He didn't deserve you. Trust me.

IN THE
BLOOD

Kristen Cari

ONE

Wandering fingers traced the neckline of my silk bodice. I half-heartedly pushed them away, but Deric pulled me closer in protest.

"*Stop that*, I have to go soon... I-I need to get ready," I stammered as calloused hands continued to roam, leaving goosebumps in their wake.

He murmured in my ear, "You're not presenting yourself until this evening—we still have time." I felt his teeth against my throat as he nipped me playfully, before kissing his way to my mouth.

For a month now, we'd savored the rush of sneaking about. Currently, we were in an abandoned stall in the stables. His lips met mine and my resolve wavered. My body was desperate to go there, to feel his skin against mine, but I wouldn't—*couldn't*—allow it.

I groaned in self-pity as I shoved him off. "No, Deric. I came here to end this. Starting tonight, I'm a bargaining chip for the Crown. I can't afford to be debauched by my stable hand." I stepped away from him, fluffing my heavy skirts before smoothing them down.

"Marigold, please. Don't do this. Fuck the Crown—run away with me. We can pave our own path. I'll provide for you, keep you safe. I *promise* to make it worth it..." His fingers brushed along my cheek, tucking golden strands behind my ear. "The only thing that separates us is a few layers of clothing and your title. We don't need them." His blue eyes pierced right through me as he waited for my answer, while I gathered the courage to break his heart.

"You know that *I* don't care that you aren't of noble birth," I told him. "Society, on the other hand, *does*. The Queen, the advisors—they do. I'm only one person... there's nothing I can do to change the rules of an entire empire. Of course, it's tempting to shirk my responsibilities, to run away with you. But I can't. Please don't seek me out again." I didn't shy away from his gaze. He needed to understand that this was over. But his eyes... his smile... they had disarmed me. They always did.

I was a debutante, officially eligible for marriage as of this evening. There could be no more rocks thrown at my window.

Deric pulled his hand from my cheek like I'd burned him with my cold response. I hated hurting him, but a sterile slice was the kindest way to cut him. I lifted my chin and set my mouth into a thin, determined line.

"You live such a sheltered life," he said. "You have no idea what lies beyond these castle walls—what you're giving up by letting them mold you into what they want you to be. I could show you so much more—"

"I will miss this," I interrupted. "And I'll miss you. Please don't beg for something that I can't give you." I looked at him with pleading eyes. *Don't make this harder than it already is.*

"Very well. Enjoy your duty. I hope it keeps your bed warm." His face was etched in pain, so I let the jab slide. I came closer to him, allowing him time to push me away, but he didn't move as I clasped my arms around his neck.

I gave him one last kiss—a thank you for keeping my loneliness at bay... if only for a short time. It was sweet and tender, as he had been to me—always willing to take any scrap I gave him. He deserved more.

He didn't see me break down as I flew back to my gilded cage. Once I was forced to marry, my wings would be permanently clipped, and the bittersweet memories of Deric—of what could've been—would fade until forgotten.

I stood at my window, peering down at the crowded courtyard below. I tried my best to push Deric from my mind, but a melancholy dread sat hard in the pit of my stomach. He represented all the things I'd never have: Freedom, choice, love. It made me wonder... what was the point of life, if I wasn't allowed to live?

A kaleidoscope of colors danced to no particular beat, as people exited carriages, greeted each other, and made their way into Aurelius Castle.

It was May 1st—the official start of social season. It was also the day that I, and other young women, would be displayed like prized pigs ripe for the butcher at the formal Debut. A day when aristocrats came from all over the country to court each other—to judge each other.

Thea, my lady's maid, was tightening my corset while I watched the circus unfold below. I held my breath like a fat pony resisting the synch of the saddle as she pulled at the laces. A loud-trumpeting sound pierced the air as Royal blue peacocks performed their mating call on the straw-thatched roof of the stables, oblivious to the people below. They were too focused on announcing their presence to the peahens to be bothered with such trivial matters.

I noted the parallels between the heavily costumed noblemen and the birds that defied laws of survival, with their extravagant tail feathers and bright plumage. Impractical courtship rituals were not confined to one species, it seemed.

I'd been in those very stables earlier today, ending the only courtship I'd ever known. All said and done, it hadn't added up to much; a few stolen kisses, whispered conversations while we laid in the haystacks, and empty promises we both knew we couldn't keep. I'd wanted to give him all of me, but it was a risk I couldn't afford to take. My body was not mine to give away. It belonged to the Crown and always would. The thought had me clenching my jaw in simmering frustration.

A sea of vivid textiles shimmered in the sunlight below: Pink silk, blue satin, yellow chiffon. I looked for other women wearing white, closely followed by their chaperones—the other debutantes. We would present ourselves to the Queen today in a ceremony that welcomed us into society.

Deric would be mucking out stalls, while I was ogled by men with moral fiber as weak as their chins. In Aurelius, being a *gentleman* had nothing to do with gentility. I'd found that the crudest men were often the richest ones, born with so much privilege that they became aimless and cruel; as if acquiring wealth through lineage instead of labor had stunted their growth.

I was pulled out of my head when I realized Thea was talking to me. "M'lady, today is an important day for you. Society will be waiting for you to slip up. I know that parties have been difficult since your mother passed, but I have no doubt you'll shine tonight... *as long as you behave yourself.* Don't you *dare* dirty your gown before the Debut. Don't go to the stables, don't walk on any muddy trails, stay away from the lake—better yet, don't even go outside."

I held back a grin. We were a perfect pair; she enjoyed treating me like an unruly wildling, while I found endless joy in tormenting her.

She fastened my petticoat before I rushed over to my four-poster bed, where my debutante gown sat—sprawled out and freshly pressed. In a fit of impulsivity, I grabbed the dress and tossed it over my head, mussing my up-do and nearly getting tangled in the layers. I wasn't in a hurry to get to the Ball, but rather was grasping for control, wherever I could find it.

Thea waved her arms frantically, clucking at me like a puffed-up hen. Silver curls frizzed out from under her frilly mobcap, as she put her hands on her hips and glared at me. "You! You have no appreciation for my time and effort!"

I stopped moving so she could get the rest of my ensemble on. A white satin dress hugged my hourglass figure before fanning out into a bell shape around my lower half. Between the ruffles, pearls, lace trim, and tulle, I looked like an overly frosted wedding cake.

"You look lovely, dear," Thea insisted, eyes glistening. Deric would've laughed his ass off had he seen me.

I glanced in the mirror as she fixed my flattened curls. My hair was the shade of antique gold. If King Midas himself had touched my head as an infant, I would've believed it. I'd never seen the hair color on anyone else except my mother. It was my favorite feature, especially when it was free and wild with loose waves running down my back. Unfortunately, my tresses were currently being held captive in an elaborate, pinned-up coiffure that was so tight, my temples were throbbing.

Dark brown doe-eyes, thick black lashes, and a nose that gently curved down towards heart-shaped lips stared back at me as I took in my reflection. I frowned at the dusting of seasonal freckles that showed up in the warmer months, making me look younger than I was.

I was shorter and curvier than most aristocratic women, but I didn't spend much time fixating on appearances. I wasn't above it, I just found looks to be the least interesting thing about a person. Maybe I'd change my tune when I went downstairs and was swept off my feet by a line of eligible bachelors. Maybe they'd all be so charming, their looks would be the only thing to distinguish them by. I laughed out loud to keep from crying, earning a worried look from Thea.

Having observed these events for years, I knew better. Everyone at court seemed to have the same interests. Men partook in hunting, drinking and fighting, while most women gravitated towards gossip and shopping for next season's gowns. I'd tried to fit in for a while, but had finally accepted that I was simply *different*.

I yearned for novelty, for adventure. I spent most of my spare time escaping into novels that took me to faraway lands filled with pirates and dragons. If I wasn't reading, I was riding my horse, Najma. She made better company than most humans and riding was one of the few activities I was allowed to participate in.

When galloping through open fields, wind whipping my hair into knots, I could outrun the feelings that bit at my heels. I woke up most mornings with the weight of responsibility heavy on my chest. I spent most of my time learning how to fit into a role that I hadn't been born for. No amount of etiquette lessons could tame my wild spirit.

I floated through most days feeling comfortably numb, tucked away from anything considered dangerous or too exciting for a lady's delicate constitution. I could count on one hand the amount of people I cared for and who cared for me. Each gathering at the castle reminded me that sometimes the loneliest place to be was in a crowded room.

But then, I'd met Deric. It had been a slow burn of glances and accidental hand brushes until one day, as he was saddling up Najma, I'd kissed him in a moment of bravery.

I grimaced as I recalled how I'd recklessly thrown myself at him, only to break things off a short while later. It had been selfish... *impulsive*. I'd risked his job and my reputation. *It was over*, I reminded myself. We hadn't been caught. Now it was time for me to grow up and accept my fate.

We all had to play the cards we were dealt. I knew my hand could've been much worse. Some people fantasized about living in a castle and playing dress up. They wouldn't mind the mindless banter—the rules and restraints that came with being niece to the Queen. Unfortunately, I had an aversion to small talk, loathed stuffy traditions, and *hated* parties. I was indisputably ill-suited to be the successor to the throne.

I descended the stairs to the formal ballroom, searching for any familiar faces in the steadily growing crowd below. The room was ornately decorated with tapestries of cerulean blue and silver—the royal colors. Centuries worth of ancient art hung from the walls, while handwoven rugs brought warmth to the stone floors. It was always a beautiful space, but today it was breathtaking. Fresh flowers covered every surface. The smell of lilac and gardenia lingered, filling my nose with their sticky, sweet scent. The heat of the room hit me next. There were too many bodies cloistered together. I already needed fresh air.

Royal families hovered around each other like hummingbirds searching for nectar. I had no interest in pollinating, so I avoided eye contact and stuck to the shadows. I needed to find Cara. She'd act as a shield until my debut.

I made my way to the refreshments table in hopes of finding something stronger than lemonade. I was old enough to drink, but the chaperones buzzed around unmarried women like vultures scavenging for the latest scandal. Most people born into nobility considered any form of work below them; instead, they filled their time with gossip and superfluous societal rules. Ladies were allotted one glass of watered down wine at social gatherings. Men could drink as much as they wanted and be as vulgar and loud as they pleased.

Before I had the chance to find my friend, one of Queen Ophelia's personal guards appeared at my side, wearing a crisp blue uniform. "Lady Ellesmere, Queen Ophelia has requested your presence."

TWO

I strode into the opulent throne room, trying my best to look like I belonged. Portraits of long dead Kings and Queens stared lifelessly down at me. It felt as if they were judging me, hissing, "*imposter,*" as I slinked by. And they were right, I didn't belong here. I hadn't been born in the castle, but instead had been abandoned here. My father had left the night of Mama's death, never to return.

My throat tightened when I thought of him. I didn't know if he'd ever remarried, if he had other children. If he thought of me, he'd never bothered to let me know.

Ophelia had always treated me like a daughter. The only thing that came before me was her Kingdom. She'd taken the throne when King Hadrian died of a heart attack, years before I'd been born. While the council had strongly encouraged her to remarry and take a consort, she never had.

She might've been the only woman in Aurelius with any real power, and yet she was still bound to the rules of society. Like a hobbled horse, her freedom was an illusion. She believed that all people were born equal under the gods, but the mostly male council disagreed. They believed that certain people were inherently better than others—that greatness was passed down through blood. And I believed that they'd say and do anything to justify their greed.

I glanced around the room, noting the golden bronze statues of mythical creatures that lined the walls. They always caught my eye. As a child I would hide in here, staring at them for hours, pretending I was one of them.

A Sphinx, Unicorn, Dragon, Pooka, Phoenix, and Hydra all stood frozen in place, ferocious expressions on their face, as they protected the Queen. The stewards of the gods—*the Chosen Six*. They kept harmony between all beings. People occasionally prayed to them, but they were mostly just legend now, much like the gods. I bowed to the statue closest to Ophelia—a Sphinx, known for its wisdom—then towards her. I'd been performing this ritual for as long as I could remember.

"You look *angelic*, Marigold. Although, I must say, seeing you in white gives me heart palpitations after years of watching you muddy your dresses." She smiled with a twinkle in her eye.

"I haven't done that in years!" I laughed. "But you're right. White is a bold choice where I'm concerned."

"And how the years have flown by. It has been my greatest joy, watching you bloom. I'll get emotional if I think on it for too long." She, indeed, looked close to tears—an incredibly rare event. She made a point of never looking weak. I was tempted to remind her that I was the one who should be crying—that I had to go mingle with tedious twits for the rest of the evening. But I bit my tongue, because I knew she was missing my mother... as was I.

Mama had died on my tenth birthday; today was the anniversary of her death. Whenever I turned a year older, I was reminded how many years it had been since I became motherless. *Eleven.*

"I wanted to wish you a happy birthday before the festivities begin and obligation sweeps me away. I know this day, in particular, is hard for you." My aunt stepped off her throne and approached me, her cobalt velvet gown trailing behind her like a snaking river. Salt and pepper hair blended with the silver of her crown, making the sapphire gems embedded in the head-piece glow like a halo.

Rays of sunshine spilled in from large windows, highlighting her olive skin. She looked so much like Mama in this light. The same slanted brown eyes, wide smile, and oval face. She brought me in for a deep hug and whispered, "I'm so proud of you for facing your fears today."

I leaned into the embrace, soaking it in. Ophelia loved me; she'd shown it in a million tiny ways—providing for me, giving me the best education, spending quality time with me, even when she was busy. But this form of affection—*hugging*—I could count on one hand how many times this had happened. She was cerebral, often stuck in her own head.

It had been an adjustment at first, compared to my overly-affectionate, excitable mother.

Gods, I missed her warmth. Her hugs. *Her passion.*

Ophelia pulled back and took a small trinket from her pocket. "A birthday gift. This was your mother's. It's an important piece of jewelry. I've been keeping it safe until you came of age." She held up a thin gold chain. There was a single square charm that hung from it, displaying the sigil of the gods, a six-pointed star.

Six was sacred to all: we had six royal advisors, six continents, six kingdoms, and six gods. The number was believed to be lucky—blessed by the once mighty gods. Despite the crumbling temples that sat abandoned across Erador—decaying proof of dwindling faith—some customs remained.

Like most people, I rarely turned to the gods in times of need. In fact, I had a bad habit of using their names in vain. According to Thea, I'd only have myself to blame, when I was inevitably struck by lightning. Ophelia and her most faithful followers still honored them as if they were real; therefore, I could recite their names in my sleep: Sivo, God of Water. Aku, God of Shadow. Cyro, God of Fire. Beira, Goddess of Ice. Terra, Goddess of Earth. Alya, Goddess of Wind. Together, the gods ruled and protected Erador.

"Your mother wore this necklace every day until she left us. I know she'd want you to do the same. A symbol, to keep her close to you." Ophelia gave me a sad smile. She took my hand in hers, passing it to me. It was warm to the touch, as if she'd just taken it off.

I held back tears as I squeezed her tight. "Thank you for keeping it safe all these years. I remember seeing it on her. I'd assumed it had been buried with her." I turned away, not wanting to remember the details of Mama's funeral. My father hadn't attended.

She helped me clasp the necklace and centered the pendant on my chest. Her voice dropped low as she whispered, "Marigold, there are things I need to tell you... now that you've come of age—secrets I've kept to protect you and the realm. It's time you learned the truth. After the Debut, come find me and we'll go on a walk." Her brows were set in a deep furrow. "There are some secrets that not even our guards or servants can be trusted with."

I nodded in understanding and chewed on the side of my cheek, wondering what it could be. She turned back towards the throne, dismissing me in a way only a Queen could. The guards ushered me out and I released a heavy sigh before muttering to the gods, "If you *do* exist, now would be a good time to prove it. *Find me a way out of this evening.*"

I walked the perimeter of the ballroom, keeping an eye out for Cara and handing out polite smiles to familiar faces. As I glanced towards the dance floor, I tried to take steady, deep breaths. My forehead prickled with cold sweat, my hands clenched into tight fists, while I fought the instinct to lock my spine and freeze in place. *I was not a deer being hunted, for gods sakes, this was just a party. I was safe.* But my body refused to listen to my mind. The ballroom started to darken and blur and I backed against the wall to get my bearings.

Don't faint. Don't you dare faint.

The chatter would never end if I had a panic attack in the middle of the party. My mind flashed to Mama's lifeless body—*her lips tinged purple as she gasped for air.* I inhaled and exhaled rapidly, trying to catch my breath. And then I saw Cara.

My body relaxed when I recognized her black hair and cocoa complexion in the sea of nobles. I used her as my anchoring point to bring me back to the present. She was wearing a jade green dress that accentuated her lean figure. It shimmered as she swayed back and forth, trotting along the dance floor with a partner. She always looked in her element when she danced, like a gazelle leaping through tall grass. I followed their feet along the dance floor and fell into a trance. Breathing in, out, in, out...

A white-haired doctor yelled, "She's not breathing," as he checked my mother's pulse. I sat next to her, tears streaming down my cheeks as feet shuffled by. So many eyes watching—staring—doing nothing to help.

My father was on her other side, holding her hand. "Eliana..." His broken voice chanted her name over and over. We stared at each other, knowing the center of our world was gone.

I snapped out of the trance as the song ended, noting that Cara had spotted me and was making her way over. "Are you okay?" She placed her palm against my forehead. "You look like you've just seen a ghost. You're ice cold."

My hands shook as I became aware of my surroundings. I clung onto the sides of my dress in an attempt to stop the trembling.

"Let's go sit down. I'll get you a drink."

We settled ourselves in the designated wallflower section and I slowly sipped on water. We sat in silence for a few minutes before my head cleared enough to ask about the latest gossip. I needed something to distract me from the pungent smell of sweaty, overly-perfumed bodies. Not missing a beat, she told me what notable people were attending tonight and who'd been dancing together so far.

It was her second year in society. "This will be the season I find my husband," Cara insisted. I hated the idea of her marrying and moving away. She was my closest friend—my *only* friend.

If Cara was a blade of grass, deeply rooted and bending with the wind, then I was a dandelion, easily swept into infinite directions at the slightest breeze. We balanced each other well. When we were children, I perpetually had skinned knees, tangled hair, and a propensity for pushing the limits. She was often along for the ride, but only as an accomplice, never the instigator.

She was sensible until it came to love. Cara was a romantic—not an easy thing to be in high society, where people married for money and power. *"Only peasants marry for love,"* her father frequently reminded her. It hadn't deterred her. She wanted someone who saw her as more than a commodity.

She turned down two perfectly mediocre gentlemen last season. It had created tension between her and her parents. Being the oldest, in a family of daughters, Cara was under pressure to marry well. Her father was giving her one more season before he chose her husband for her. I couldn't stand the thought of her being forced into a loveless marriage. She was a rare jewel amongst flat, smooth-brained river rocks.

She'd find love; I was sure of it. Men adored her. They were drawn to her like a quill to parchment, especially once they saw her gliding across the dance floor. She was a skilled player in the game of courtship, flattering them and flirting back effortlessly, yet still able to maintain an edge of mystery.

I, on the other hand, had no natural ability at attracting the opposite sex. It didn't matter because I planned on avoiding marriage as long as possible—council be *damned*. I'd accepted the fact that an arranged marriage was unavoidable, but I refused to let them rush me into it.

"Any suitors? Proposals? Do you have your eye on anyone yet?" I flashed her a mischievous grin.

"The season started two hours ago. No one worthy of my notice... yet."

We giggled as we surveyed the room and saw several sets of eyes staring at us. We watched the crowd of dancers for several songs before I decided I couldn't keep her to myself any longer. She needed to find a husband and had no time to waste.

"What about you and the *stable boy*?" Cara nudged me playfully. My stomach sank as she unknowingly rubbed salt in the fresh wound.

"I ended it earlier today, actually. It was time." Before she could pry any deeper, I stood and said, "I hate to make you sit with your socially inept friend, when you're clearly meant to be on the dance floor. I'm going to take a walk through the gardens and get some fresh air before the Debut."

She understood everything I said, and everything I didn't say, as she squeezed my gloved hand. "I'm always here to talk. You don't have to face your hardships alone. And... I'm sorry your mother isn't here to see how gorgeous you look today." Her sincerity blurred my vision with tears that had been threatening to fall all day.

"It would be nice to have her here tonight, but I'm grateful to have you. I'll be back soon. Please cover for me if anybody asks where I am."

"I'll tell them you're powdering your nose."

"Thank you, friend." I grinned before making a beeline for the courtyard.

THREE

There were already several couples paired off, meandering along the graveled pathways. They lingered amongst the topiaries and tidy rose gardens, while chaperones trailed behind. I sipped on a stolen glass of champagne, attempting to hide in plain sight, while I passed one of several large fountains. My chaperone was otherwise-engaged and nowhere in sight. My governess, Adeline, was my assigned babysitter for the evening and currently occupied with one of the footmen. I was in no hurry to find her.

I should've stayed longer. I didn't want to let Ophelia down, but the fear that gripped me every time I got near the ballroom was paralyzing. My mother had died on the dance floor. Unbeknownst couples had waltzed around her as she fell to the floor. I couldn't be in that room now without hearing the screams from that night.

My childhood innocence had been shredded to ribbons in a matter of moments. The doctor said it was poison—someone had slipped it into her glass. One sip was all it took to shatter a family. I was supposed to be in my bedroom sleeping, but I snuck downstairs to watch the grownups dance. I'd never fully recovered from the scene I'd witnessed... from the monumental loss I experienced. No one—*nothing*—could replace the love of a mother. Especially *my* mother. She'd been sunshine personified—a living flame that glowed too bright and burnt out too soon.

She was Ophelia's only sibling and King Hadrian had been an only child. Since they had no children of their own, I was currently next in line for the throne, against all odds. I selfishly wished the Queen would remarry and try for an heir, but with her silver hair, it was likely she was past her child bearing years.

One devastating night, eleven years ago, had set me on a path I never wanted or expected; I was to be the future Queen of Aurelius. There were five other Kingdoms in Erador, but none of them wielded the power or strength of Aurelius. Every continent looked to us for cultural influence. My aunt was loving and kind, but she was also fierce and ruthless.

I didn't think I'd ever be capable of filling her shoes. My fear of crowds created an obstacle that made me a terrible prospect for a role in leadership. The flashbacks that hit me whenever I was in the ballroom were vivid enough to bring me to my knees.

I never danced in public because of it. But I was still expected to know all of the dances, and tonight the council had *highly encouraged* me to swallow my fear.

We never found out who poisoned my mother. Ophelia said it was most likely rebels trying to send a message to the royal family that we weren't untouchable. The Crown had enemies, despite its strength. There were reasons to resent us. The caste system was atrocious. Noble families gorged themselves on decadence by exploiting the masses. It was a broken system for everyone but those born into privilege.

I'd encouraged Ophelia to break the cycle, to *demand* change, but she told me I was too young to understand. There were many shades between black and white, and it was in the grey that one must rule. I hated politics.

I headed to the gardens on the north side of the courtyard, looking back to make sure no one was watching. I hurried down the path, rubbing my temple with one hand, while I slung back my glass of champagne with the other. The headache I'd been feeling since morning continued to worsen. It wrapped around my head and demanded my attention, pounding so loudly that the crunch of gravel beneath my feet wasn't enough to drown it out. In hindsight, alcohol hadn't been the best idea.

I was going to a quiet place where I could gather my thoughts. As much as I loved Cara and Ophelia, I'd never told them of my private retreat. I hadn't told Deric of this garden either, even though it would've been the perfect rendezvous location. This was *my* secret—a garden so special, I was afraid it would somehow lose its magic if I showed it to anyone else.

I'd been coming here ever since I discovered it as a wandering child. I used to go on walks by myself and pretend my mother was with me. She told me it was a place that called to people like me—a place where I could come and talk to her when I felt lonely. She was in the birds that stopped to bathe in the fountains, the butterflies that drank the nectar, and the rain that watered the flowers—a place that tied us together through space and time.

I looked up at the sky, thinking of her, before ducking under a low hanging branch that led off the garden path and onto an overgrown trail. I followed it as I took high steps over ferns, bluebells, and wood violets.

Eventually, I saw a wall of ivy. It would've been easily missed unless one knew what they were looking for. I ran my fingers along the mossy stone, and felt for the familiar latch of an old wooden door. I pushed hard with my shoulder, knowing there were vines on the other side. Even when I visited this garden daily, the ivy always grew back over the door... like it didn't want to be found.

A few more shoves and I was in. The exertion caused my skull to spark with pain. I hardly ever got headaches. It was strange one should strike so violently today, of all days. I looked through the doorway into the garden that laid before me. It always seemed to be perfectly maintained; not overly manicured, but beautifully wild. Weeds never choked out any of the perpetually blooming flowers.

Royal purple wisteria hung in clumps over the walls. Star Jasmine and lavender sprouted from the ground. Tiny white tea-roses were tucked between puffs of pink peonies. Plants didn't follow a seasonal pattern here; they grew year round, even sprouting up through snow. The garden seemed to contain a splash of magic and I didn't dare question how or why. Part of me thought this garden was *proof* that I was mad.

I picked up my skirts and collapsed against the wall across from the entrance. I breathed in and out, attempting to soothe my mind. I always felt safest in this spot, facing the door—a vantage point that lulled me into security and soon to sleep.

FOUR

*G*olden light blinded me, but I couldn't shield my eyes. My arms were frozen at my sides. I was falling, hitting the ground with a loud thud, unable to wake, unable to move. I tried to call out for help, but my mouth wouldn't form the words.

I could feel the presence of others around me, but I couldn't turn to look. Shapes and shadows flickered against a bright light. The air was heavy and humid, smelling like a sweet, summer morning. I was being pulled by an unknown force, unable to orient myself. Layers of melodic whispers echoed around me. And then... darkness swallowed me.

I startled awake, heart pounding. As I came to my senses, I was shocked to see the sun clear across the sky, hours from setting. How long had I slept? With a gasp, I remembered what day it was—where I was supposed to be. The Debut—had I missed it? Cara was going to be in trouble for covering for me—Adeline would be fired. I anxiously scanned my surroundings, wondering how I'd ended up *facing* the wall I'd been lying against.

I stood too fast, bracing myself as a wave of dizziness crashed over me. It had been too long since I'd eaten. My corset was too tight. *A wonderfully disastrous birthday, indeed.*

With some relief, I realized my headache was gone. Once the stars in my vision stopped moving, I hurdled towards the door and ran. I leapt through the brush as fast as I could, being careful not to rip my dress.

I'm an idiot. Everything Thea thinks of me is true.

I followed the hidden trail towards the gravel path, growing increasingly frantic when I couldn't find it. Perhaps my rattled brain had gone the wrong direction. Feeling disoriented, I glanced behind me, up at the pine trees, the forest floor, then towards the sky. I recognized nothing. This was a place I frequented often—I'd never gotten lost before.

I decided to backtrack and go slower this time, noting a patch of unfamiliar yellow flowers. They appeared to be *glowing*. Bending down, I examined one. How strange... they *were* glowing. Maybe new seeds had blown in on the wind from a faraway land.

As I reached down to pluck one, I heard a twig snap behind me. I whirled around, expecting to see a guard. Ophelia probably had a whole brigade out searching for me.

No one was there.

"Hello?" I called out, circling slowly. No response. I continued to search for the garden path.

Snap.

A louder crunch this time. I was not alone. Paranoia crept in. I bent down to grab a stick—a poor excuse for a weapon. I felt ridiculous, bracing myself for battle in a ball gown. If I did have to run, this monstrosity was going to weigh me down.

"Can anybody hear me?" I asked tentatively. "I've managed to lose sight of the path and would appreciate some help!"

Silence. Followed by a low growl.

I turned towards the source of the noise and saw an unrecognizable creature. It was reminiscent to a wolf, but distinctly different—distinctly *larger*. It grinned at me with long, sharp teeth that extended past its jaws. Shaggy, rust-colored fur covered its hunched body, matted in what appeared to be blood.

Its eyes were big and round with milky white centers. As the beast moved closer, I noticed that it walked with an uneven gate, as if injured or ill. I yelled, waving my weapon, but it was undeterred, moving steadily forward.

I heard another *snap*.

Turning, I saw a second set of milky eyes staring at me... and then another. I was being hunted. There were at least four of them, circling me...

inching closer. I took a moment to assess my best option for survival, then committed.

I ran towards them, yelling at the top of my lungs. I hit one with my stick, hoping my surprise attack would be enough to spook them.

And then I ran for my life.

They were yipping and howling to one another. The sound was high-pitched and haunting. They were communicating, forming a plan.

I could hear them all around me, but couldn't see them. Adrenaline pumped through me as I tried to find a tree I could climb—a spot I could hide.

The forest was thick with thorny underbrush and large roots jetting out from the ground. The trees were too tall to gain any kind of foothold. My dress was slowing me down. I wanted to rip it off, but that would take too much time.

The baying had stopped. Did that mean they were moving in for the kill? Terror hit me like a bolt of lightning.

I'd never been this deep in the forest before and recognized nothing. I tried to arc back and lose them, but could feel them gaining on me.

My heart beat wildly as my feet crunched over branches and leaves. I was so loud, so clumsy. They flew through the forest thicket like they were made for it, while I was sluggish and awkward in comparison. Such easy prey.

Was this truly how I died? In a tattered ballgown in the middle of the woods? I picked up my pace, but my dress snagged on a branch and I fell hard, rolling my ankle. I tried to stand up, but crumpled to the ground instead—panting and defeated.

I let out a string of curse words and backed myself against a tree trunk as they closed in around me. Tongues wagging, they seemed to be savoring the moment. One of them snapped at me, spittle flying from its jaws. I swung my stick and it retreated. They were waiting for me to make a mistake—to weaken. I swung my stick again.

Closing my eyes, I contemplated giving up. My breathing was strained and erratic as I struggled to suck down enough air. A sharp ache in my lungs told me I was still alive—for now. The pain would be much worse when they began tearing me apart though. Would they go for a quick kill or start with my intestines?

If I could just make it out of the forest and into the light, surely they wouldn't follow me into the open, where there was people and music. I'd never wanted to be in the middle of a crowd more. Rallying my last burst of fight, I planted my feet and snarled at my attackers.

My eyes were open, but all I saw was inky darkness, like someone had extinguished the sun. I panicked, wondering if I was somehow already dead, but then I heard a whimper... followed by six distinct snaps.

The world went silent. I couldn't see, but I could smell. Beyond the smell of bone marrow and wet dog, there was a fresh aroma of... rain and cedar. It was soothing, reminding me of the misty morning walks I used to take with my mother, back when we lived in a simple cabin in the woods.

Was I dead? Was this the after-life?

A dark haze swirled towards the sky as the forest began to reappear, dissipating faster than any natural fog. Mist twisted around me like water circling a drain, as if I was standing in the eye of a storm. My eyes re-adjusted and I saw six animals spread out around me. Their heads were bent at awkward angles, feet still twitching.

I grimaced as I took in their vacant expressions. My heart was thudding so loudly, I could barely make out the muffled voices approaching. I straightened my posture and held my weapon close to my chest, while my muscles tremored with fatigue.

A man with golden auburn hair, the color of polished bronze, appeared on horseback. The sun illuminated him through the trees as he emerged from the shadows. He was so beautiful—so god-like—that I was nearly blinded by his brilliance. I closed my eyes and then reopened them to see if I was hallucinating.

He dismounted and strode towards me, flashing a cheshire grin as he said, "I've always wanted to rescue a damsel in distress."

FIVE

I stared at the man, barely breathing.

"I'm glad we were able to get to you in time. Death by wylks would be a terrible way to go. We heard howling and then saw you thrashing through the trees. Are you alright?" He moved towards me until he was in my personal space. His green eyes were bright and curious.

I thought about hitting him with my stick, but instead I stood frozen in place.

"May I?" he asked, stopping short of touching my face. I nodded dumbly as he reached out and wiped my cheek. "You're bleeding. Were you bitten?"

My hand flew up to my face, but I felt no cut. I shook my head.

Behind him, another man emerged from the woods on a black horse. If the first man glowed like the sun, then this one was the moon and stars.

He could've been *Aku,* himself, with his shaggy dark hair and menacing gaze.

In an irritated tone, he asked, "Does she speak? Is she hurt?" He didn't bother to get off of his horse; instead he glared down at me, as if I'd somehow inconvenienced him by almost dying.

"Be nice, Raf. She looks terrified." A third voice. A red-haired man with freckles and the kindest face of the three gave me an easy smile as he trotted over on his steed.

His shining blue eyes caught my attention. They were the color of a tropical turquoise ocean—a shade I'd only seen in paintings.

The men had unfamiliar accents, which suggested they were from across the sea—from one of the Old Kingdoms: Corinthia, Rhavena, Altana, Plythe, or maybe even the deserts of Nathraza. I'd never left the continent and was unfamiliar with the different dialects, but it was common for royal members from the five other Kingdoms to join our social season.

I turned to the brunette—Raf, they'd called him. Clenching my fists, I huffed, "I speak. I somehow lost my way. And then those... those *things* attacked. I've never seen anything like them before, and so close to the castle. H-how did you create that black smoke? How did you kill them?"

I glanced down at the beasts and instantly regretted it. Adrenaline was leaving me in waves, but seeing them again caused it to spike back up. "I'm feeling rather light-headed, actually. I'd appreciate an escort back to the castle... or perhaps you could fetch the guards. I-I think I need to lie down. This is what I get for not listening to Thea..."

Raf chuckled and my wide eyes shot to him, narrowing when I realized he was *laughing at me*. "Oh, she talks alright. Now I'm wondering if she ever shuts up," he muttered to the red-head.

I sent a murderous glare in his direction, but he didn't even notice my outrage as the three men exchanged wary looks, then collectively studied me.

"You'd like an escort back to *our* castle?" The red-head smiled.

Their castle? "A-are you new guards at Aurelius Castle? I don't recognize you." My eyes darted back and forth, waiting for someone to tell me what in *Aku's hell* was going on.

"We aren't guards. We are *Princes*. And you're on private property. These are the royal woods—the *Whispering Woods*. Who are *you*?" the bronze-haired man, still standing too close, asked.

The feeling of the forest floor falling out from under me was so strong, it took all of my strength to not slide down the tree I was still backed up against.

"Aurelius? In Erador? Is this your attempt at humor?" Raf asked.

"*Yes*, Erador." I held my stick tighter. Something must've been lost in translation. Wherever I was, surely I was still in the same *world*.

"Are you... *human*?" the golden one asked, his nostrils flaring.

Was he *sniffing* me? I supposed I had gotten rather sweaty while I'd been running for my life. I took a subtle whiff. *Wait... Had he just asked if I was human?* I raised an incredulous brow. "Of course I am. Are you implying that you aren't?"

This was lunacy.

"Do we look human to you?" the freckled one asked with a grin.

I stared at them more closely, squinting. They were all unnaturally tall... and *attractive.* Two of them had pointed ears... perhaps a unique family trait?

They looked similar enough to be brothers... though, I couldn't see Raf's ears under all of his hair. And each of them had a distinct skin tone. The bronze-haired man had olive skin, the freckled one was fair, and the brunette was a sun-kissed shade of brown.

No third eyes. No fur or flippers. They looked human enough to me.

And then it hit me. *I was dreaming.* It was the only explanation.

I pinched my arm. Nothing happened.

Enough of this. I pushed off the tree and stomped past the men. Stomp is what I set out to do—limp is what I accomplished.

I brushed by the bronze-haired one. He was *beautiful.* They all were, but the way he looked at me... like a predator sizing up its prey. My pulse ramped up as I felt his eyes track me. I peered over my shoulder and batted my eye lashes at him. It was time to take control of this nightmare.

The self-proclaimed Prince jogged over, catching up quickly. He jumped in front of me, forcing me to a stop, as he gripped my forearm. My eyes flicked to the hand that dared to grab me... and then up to his face. There had been a spark—a visceral reaction when we'd touched. I jolted back as if I'd been burned, while we continued to stare at each other.

I knew this was a dream because he was *too* pretty—too symmetrical. He was *glowing* with virility. No one's teeth were that white—and the way his sharp canines hovered above his bottom lip when he grinned... it was *mesmerizing.* I'd never been attracted to *teeth* before.

This was the most vivid dream I'd ever had...

"Who *are* you?" he breathed, emerald eyes sparkling.

"The woman of your dreams," I whispered, as if in a trance. I grabbed him by the collar of his tunic, pulled him down to my level, and *kissed* him.

I'd never done anything so bold in my life... *but I was dreaming.* None of this was real.

A wave of heat washed over me as our lips touched... like a slow, inevitable flow of lava expanding to my lungs, my heart, then down to my curling toes. The force of it nearly knocked me over.

I tried to wrap my arms around his neck and deepen the kiss, but he pulled back, severing our connection. His brothers were staring at us with both disgust and amusement.

"Did you hit your head when the wylks were chasing you?" My dream lover asked with a crooked smile, resting a hand on my hip.

"I don't think so..." I said, feeling for any tender spots. My pounding headache came slamming back into me and I groaned, deciding I was ready to leave this dream. Closing my eyes and holding my breath, I concentrated.

Wake up.

Wake up, wake up, wake up!

I cracked one eye open. The men were staring at me as if I was highly volatile... and possibly insane.

"I'm not dreaming?" I asked with cold dread as I peered up at the man I'd just kissed.

"I'm afraid not," he laughed. "Why don't you come back with us? You can rest and get something to eat."

"Rest sounds good," I said weakly, feeling dizzy with embarrassment. My head was spinning so fast, I felt tipsy.

Gods, I wished I *was* drunk, then I'd at least have an excuse for my behavior.

My cheeks were on fire, making me self-conscious, which in turn made me blush harder. I didn't want to go with them; I wanted to lie down and die of humiliation, but I also didn't want to be left in the forest alone.

Feeling utterly lost and confused, I limped to his brown and black bay horse and let him hoist me onto its back. I was in such shock, I didn't even protest as I felt him slide behind me in the saddle, pressing his large, solid body against mine.

He took the reins and we began to walk through the woods, trailing behind the others. The gentle rhythm of the ride jostled us, forcing us even closer together. The inescapable friction made it difficult to forget I'd just *kissed* this perfect stranger.

He eventually settled his hands on my lap, since there was nowhere else for them to go, and I did my best to ignore them. Time seemed to move at a glacial pace as we rode on. I was almost positive that he was *purposefully* torturing me by staying silent—waiting for me to acknowledge what had transpired between us.

"What's your name?" I finally asked, desperate to break the tension.

"Do you typically kiss someone before learning their name? Or was I just in the right place at the right time?"

"I-I... I'm sorry. I don't know what came over me," I stammered.

He squeezed my thigh. "Please don't apologize. It was the highlight of my day. I'm Prince Galen Ruhn, heir to the Kingdom of Nymera." He gestured to the others ahead of us. "Those are my brothers, Louis and Rafael."

Nymera? I was certain there was no such place. *He was lying.* My stomach lurched.

"This is the part where you tell me *your* name," Galen teased.

I stared ahead, trying to decide how much truth to give him. He and his brothers had just saved me from certain death, but nothing they'd told me so far made any sense. They certainly hadn't proven themselves trustworthy.

Whoever they were, they were dressed well. They didn't look like thieves or vagabonds. All three men wore matching grey velvet tunics with green emblems over their hearts. I'd recognized the six-pointed star right away as the sigil of the gods. I reached for my mother's necklace, needing to feel it in my palm. It was a common enough symbol, but I'd never seen it used as a royal crest. It was a strange coincidence—one I wasn't ready to wrap my head around yet.

"I'm Lady Marigold of Aurelius."

"Marigold..." he drawled. "A lovely name, for an enchanting woman."

I stiffened at his compliment. Sharing a saddle designed for one meant that every time he spoke, I could feel his breath brush against my neck, eliciting tingles that I didn't want to feel. I leaned forward, trying to put space between us.

"You're truly from Erador?" he asked. "From Aurelius? But how? How did you—"

Galen stopped mid-sentence when Rafael turned around to give him a hard stare. Simultaneously, a dark fog rolled in, cooling the muggy air. The forest grew quiet and still, as if holding its breath. My heart thundered in response. The charged atmosphere felt supernatural, like the gods themselves were about to unleash a storm upon us.

A deep, humming sound vibrated at my back. I *felt* Galen's growl before I heard it. There was nothing human about it—he sounded like a mountain lion guarding its kill. I began to shake.

"We question her later—*together*," Raf snarled, baring his teeth as he changed course and trotted towards us.

"I don't take orders from you," Galen snapped back. His hand hovered on the hilt of his sword. Rafael drew a black sword from its sheath in response, pointing it menacingly at Galen—*at me*.

Hooves pounded and dust flew as Louis raced over, angling his horse to block Rafael's war path. "Knock it off, you two. The poor girl's been through enough today. We'll reconvene tomorrow morning and talk with her—together," he said, side-eyeing Galen.

I felt Galen's body tense before relaxing, then the weight of his hands as they settled back onto my lap. "Of course, brother," he said smoothly.

Rafael turned away from us, but not before shooting one last scowl at Galen.

I debated diving off the horse and running. They were going to *question* me? The Queen would have their heads! Any minute now, Ophelia's guards would find me and this entire ordeal would be over.

"You're safe. It's alright," Galen said, his mouth too close to my ear.

I sighed, leaning back into his solid chest. I'd accept my fate for now. If I closed my eyes, I could almost pretend I was riding Najma and *not* sitting in the lap of a man who'd just *roared* like a beast.

"I must ask... you know nothing of the blood curse?" Galen whispered. His brothers were now so far ahead, I could no longer see them.

"The... blood... curse?"

"And you know *nothing* of magic?" he asked with an edge to his voice.

"Magic? You mean like sleight of hand?"

"No. Never mind... We'll save it for later."

His questions raised my hackles and sent my head spinning again. Nothing made sense—nothing felt familiar. Beyond the glowing yellow flowers, there were tropical plants that looked like they belonged in a greenhouse: Blue orchids shaped like miniature paper birds, ferns that curled like fingers. Tall trees were covered in moss and lichen, their bark barely visible beneath the shades of green.

The forest was loud with chittering life. Colorful birds squawked and scattered as we walked beneath them. Dew clung to leaves and dripped down from the trees, even as sunset approached. It was difficult to tell whether the sweat that cooled my neck and trailed down my back was from nerves or humidity. Tendrils of hair fell from my pins, curling in rebellion. The longer we walked, the more evident it was that I was far from home, though I didn't understand *how*.

We eventually made it to a trail lined with fruit trees. Vibrant red fruit weighed down thin, sagging branches. My stomach growled as I gazed upon them. Something akin to a strawberry, but the size of a small melon, looked edible enough to make my mouth water.

"Are you hungry?" Galen asked when my stomach grumbled again.

I shook my head. Taking food from him wasn't a good idea for several reasons.

Galen ignored me and brought us towards the trees until we were directly beneath them. He plucked what looked to be a ripe piece of fruit, then handed it to me. "Blood berries. You can bite through the skin. Try one."

I hesitated, before deciding it wasn't worth the effort to argue. I turned in the saddle and met his gaze, sinking my teeth into the thin flesh. The skin was soft, like a peach, but the inside surprised me. It was meaty in texture and deep red in color, reminding me of... *blood*. I was so hungry, I didn't care. I began to tear into it, forgetting all sense of propriety.

"It tastes a bit like a plum," I said as sticky juice drizzled down my chin.

Galen pulled a handkerchief from somewhere and held it up to me. "I've never had a plum, but I'll take your word for it." He began dabbing at my chin, taking great care when he reached my lips... shamelessly staring at them as if under a spell. I averted my eyes, blushing at the intimate gesture.

"When I was a child, I used to sneak out to this grove and eat these until I was sick. Not much has changed; I still struggle with my self-control." His eyes darkened as they met mine. "Though... my tastes have evolved since then." He gave me a grin that showed off a dimple and I felt his charm work its way through me.

I glanced down to find a thoroughly ruined dress. The dirt-caked fabric now had red juice splatters as well. Logically, I knew the stains weren't blood, but my body responded as if they were. A cold chill seeped into my bones as I thought about how close I'd come to dying today.

"Those creatures in the woods... were they related to wolves? I've never heard of a... wylk," I mused.

"They're native to these lands. Those ones were ill. When we traveled here with our pets, new illnesses were introduced to the endemic species of this land. We try to kill the infected ones when we find them, to put them out of their misery and stop the spread of disease. That's the reason we were out in the woods today. We received several reports of a sick pack and were tracking them when we found you."

"So it was a kindness to kill them. That's a relief."

"Yes, they would've suffered had we not intervened. My father taught us to show compassion towards all living things."

"And he rules this land, I presume?"

"He died years ago, unfortunately. My mother is now in charge, along with a council of advisors."

"I'm sorry for your loss," I replied softly. "I lost mine too. He didn't die though. He just left." This day... *this man*... was making me loose-lipped.

"You experienced the loss just the same. My father was a noble leader; powerful, yet merciful. The type of King I aspire to be." He tightened his grip around my waist, shifting us into a more comfortable position.

His hard stomach muscles pressed against my back and I couldn't help but notice that he was built like a sleek warrior. How did someone even acquire a body like his? Did he spend his day carrying heavy things around?

That led me to imagine what it would feel like to be carried by him. I barely had to use my imagination, since his sizable biceps were wrapped around me, making me flood with heat. *What was wrong with me?*

"Tell me something about yourself—something not everyone knows," he said as he steered us back to the trail.

"I'm not that interesting... my life back home is tame—boring, even," I replied, evading the question.

"In the short time I've known you, I can definitively say you are *anything*, but boring." His laugh caressed the tiny hairs on the back of my neck, making my skin prickle. I squirmed in response, making him go suddenly stiff. "The verdict is still out on whether you're tame," he said, clearing his throat.

"I try to be." I smiled. "I think I have a rebellious spirit. Someone once called me a *'barn cat in a ballgown.'*" It had been Thea, earlier today.

"You held your own against those wylks with nothing but a stick, while wearing a... tent. I'd like to see a barn cat do that." He picked up the frilly fabric of my dress, scoffing. "I refuse to believe this *thing* was designed for movement of any kind. And... is it meant to *attract* the opposite sex?"

He raised a brow suspiciously before meeting my gaze and holding it. "Fascinating. It seems to be working," he said with a smirk.

Flirt. My heart began to throb throughout my whole body.

"So tell me... what does an Aurelian rebel do for fun?"

I snorted. If only he knew how little control I had over my own life. "I believe I said that I have a rebellious spirit, not that I *am* a rebel."

He gave a dissatisfied grunt. "Keeping secrets from the future King is an act of rebellion in itself, you know."

I bit my lip to keep from smiling. He wanted me to confide in him—to tell him something real—but there was no reason I should tell him my truth, especially when he was *lying* to me.

If I was smart, I'd keep my mouth shut until we arrived at our destination—just completely *stop* talking. He couldn't *force* information out of me...

I lasted less than a minute. "Fine," I sighed with exasperation. "I'm an escape artist. I like to climb out my window. I never do anything that bad... it's just nice to feel free."

His silky laugh sent another shiver down my spine. "*Rebel.* I knew it. When was the last time you snuck out?"

"Recently. I took a night swim in the lake, under the full moon."

"Sounds refreshing. Did you swim alone... or did you have company?"

"My friend, Cara, came with me."

"And is Cara a lover?" Galen asked with peaked interest.

"No... just a friend. Not that it's any of your business," I said, hyper-aware of the sweat forming between our bodies.

"Can I make it my business?" he whispered, brushing his lips against the shell of my ear.

Butterflies fluttered wildly in response. Straightening my spine, I vowed that the next time they flapped their wings, I was going to stomp them to a pulp.

I was confident Prince Charming had a knack for seducing anything that walked, and I just happened to be the current closest thing to him. I had more important things to worry about, like where we were. Not to mention, I'd *just* ended things with Deric. Hot shame washed over me.

The trail we'd been walking on opened up to a larger road as we came into a clearing. We passed walkers, riders, carts, and carriages. They were all coming or going from the gigantic white castle that loomed ahead.

Guards with grey tunics stood perfectly still outside the gatehouse, watching us approach. Each of them had a spear in hand and a green shield bearing the sigil of the gods.

They nodded to Galen as we crossed the stone bridge that led into the castle. A river rushed below us, while a sea of people mingled within the fortified walls ahead of us. It was a well-guarded fortress; it would be difficult, if not impossible, to escape. At least out the front door. I prayed it wouldn't come to that.

Several narrow towers shot up to the sky. I had to tilt my head all the way up to see them, and even then, couldn't see the tops of the pinnacles. I stared in awe at the marvel of architecture—so much larger and grander than Aurelius Castle. It must've taken centuries to build. If this was Galen's home, maybe he really was a prince.

I screamed when a large tawny-haired grizzly bear came barreling past us. In an act of self-preservation, I leaned back into Galen's chest, clinging to him. It showed no interest, just a tilt of the head in acknowledgement. I tracked it as it continued on, not believing my eyes.

"A bear! You keep *bears* as pets here?" I stammered.

Galen chuckled. "It's a good thing he didn't hear you call him a pet. All will be explained soon enough. Just stay close to me."

I believed for the first time that I was far from home. Men wore tunics that had been out of fashion for hundreds of years. Most women wore simple cotton dresses—no petticoats or corsets in sight. I must've looked ridiculous to them, buried beneath layers of tulle and lace.

A woman passed us wearing a tunic, leggings and a leather scabbard on her belt. "Women, they're wearing pants—carrying weapons. Is this typical in your Kingdom?"

"Yes, of course... It's not the same in Erador?"

I turned around to glare at him. "Why do you continue to speak of Erador as if we're somewhere else. *That's impossible.* Where are we? Who are you, really?" I demanded.

My chest tightened and I felt a wave of nausea roll through me. The stress of today had taken its toll... I was close to completely crumbling. My survival-instincts were hysterical—telling me to *do something.*

Galen stopped abruptly. We were past the gates now, inside the castle courtyard. He dismounted and took my hand, concern etched across his face. "What I'm about to tell you is the truth... as far-fetched as you may find it."

I followed his lead, carefully shifting in my heavy gown and sliding off his horse. Gripping my hips, he supported me as I landed on the ground with a soft thud. He handed the reins to a guard that had appeared out of nowhere. And then it was just us.

His mouth was set in a grim line as I fidgeted under his intense gaze. "My people used to live in Erador, but now we live here..." A deep v formed between my brows as I tried to comprehend what he was saying. "Our ancestors were led here by a world walker. She tricked us into coming to this land. She returned to Erador before closing the portal door on us. We're in a new world—we call it Nymera."

He took my hands in his as he continued, "I'm nearly positive you're telling the truth—about being from Erador. And I think you came through the door that we've been trying to access for hundreds of years. So I need to know; did you get help from a world walker... or are *you* the world walker?"

My mouth hung open, before I snapped it shut. I couldn't seem to get enough air. I inhaled in short, shallow gasps, like a fish out of water. Black spots appeared in my vision. I was about to faint.

"Breathe..." Galen murmured, rubbing gentle circles on my palms, while I broke into a cold sweat. "I need to know—are you our enemy? A spy? *Can I trust you?*"

"No. I mean... *yes!* You can trust me. I'm not a spy. I- I don't know how, but I fell asleep in my garden—in Aurelius... and woke up *here.* I don't know what a world walker is. I mean you no harm, I promise." Panic caused me to trip over my words.

"It's alright. I believe you. I'm going to need you to keep breathing though... Oxygen is still a requirement in this world." He grinned, gently holding me by my shoulders.

I felt small and insignificant in his arms—in this universe. *How? How was any of this real?*

"You're going to be a person of interest to my mother—to all of our people. The Queen is... quick to form opinions and slow to change them. It's imperative you get off on the right foot. If she finds you to be a threat, she'll lock you up and ask questions later."

I nodded solemnly. A single tear fell down my cheek and I wiped it away. I couldn't break yet. I steadied myself and took a deep breath.

He tenderly cupped my cheek in his hand as he said, "There's more, of course, but it can wait. For now, we'll tell my mother we rescued you in the woods—that you have amnesia after hitting your head and don't know how you ended up in our forest. Once you've had some time to rest, we'll tell her the truth." He lifted my chin with his pointer finger until I was looking into his eyes. The smile he gave me made me feel a little less alone.

"Why are you helping me?" I asked. Fire blazed behind his eyes and it scared me.

"You told me you're the woman of my dreams... and I'd like to find out if that's true," he said with a wink. "Welcome to Monrovia Castle."

Six

I am in a different world, I said to myself over and over, trying to comprehend the impossible. We entered the interior of the castle, but it was as if the outdoors had followed us in.

Large glass windows and skylights flooded the entryway with light, bouncing off pure white stone. Climbing plants scaled the walls, forming a labyrinth of vines and flowers. Stained-glass windows created a rainbow light-effect on our skin as we passed under them. There was a gentle buzzing in the air that made me feel awake, giddy... intoxicated. One word came to mind: *Magic*.

Trees flanked us on either side, growing right out of terra-cotta stone floors. They stretched towards the high ceilings, making it feel like we were in the middle of a bright and airy forest. Birds sailed overhead, flying back and forth between the trees. Their songs floated through the air together in harmony. And their feathers... they shimmered with every color of the rainbow as they flitted around us: Teal parrots with bright yellow chests, white ones with pink crests on their head, and a large red bird that looked like it was made of flame.

I'd never seen the wild brought indoors like this, even the art that covered the walls showcased nature's beauty with oil paintings and murals of animals and landscapes. There were no stuffy portraits of ancestors... no dusty tapestries. Everything was full of *life*.

Galen watched me as I took in my surroundings. For some odd reason, he looked captivated—almost in awe—as if I wasn't a filthy, nervous wreck.

When we passed a mirror, I decided I must've been reading him wrong, because I was in rare form, indeed. There were leaves in my unkempt hair and smears of blood where there should have been cuts. Where there *had* been cuts. How had they healed so fast?

My ankle was feeling better too, although I was milking the pain to stay close to the Prince. Did this world allow one to heal at an unnaturally fast rate? Something to ask Galen when there were less eyes on us, because currently there were guards *everywhere*; they lined the hallways and trailed behind us as they stared and whispered.

"Would it be possible to freshen up before meeting the Queen?" I asked. "I wouldn't want to offend her in my current state."

"Ah, there will be time for that soon... Unfortunately, the Queen has been alerted to your presence and she's waiting. It's never a good idea to keep her waiting." He threw me an apologetic glance before guiding me towards a set of gilded double doors.

It was all happening so fast. Shouldn't a Prince understand the importance of appearances? It was difficult to feel prepared when I looked like a creature he'd pulled from a bog.

The heavily guarded doors swung open, and we were pushed into a tropical jungle. I tripped over a tree root that darted straight out of the marble floor and Galen didn't miss a beat—catching me, then gripping me more firmly.

A warm mist settled over my skin, adding to my confusion, as I tried to figure out how we'd ended up back in the forest. I peered up, gawking. The ceiling was completely made of glass. It was the only feature that told me we were indoors.

A firm tug from Galen had me moving again—towards the Queen who was waiting for us on an elevated Dais. She sat in a chair that looked more like a gnarled tree stump than a throne.

An array of exotic plants framed the walk way. Some tucked themselves between exposed tree roots, others twisted up mossy trunks. Vines hung from tree branches in stringy tendrils, while water trickled down rock walls. Everywhere I looked, there was something new to feast my eyes on.

Plants that I'd seen as drawings in scientific journals exploded around us, like vibrant fireworks: Red bromeliads, banana trees bearing ripe fruit, fanned out monsteras, and birds of paradise.

Giant fig trees stretched higher than I could fathom—their trunks wider than five of me combined. They didn't simply grow *up*, but also webbed across the floor. Their roots looked like massive hands, reaching, clawing, *slithering* towards us, before rising up into... *were those snake heads?*

I fought my impulse to run as I studied the wooden snake totems that lined the aisle. Each sculpture reared up, as if ready to strike, while jewels the size of my fist sat in hollow eye sockets that sparkled with malice.

Our feet clicked on the jade marble as rushing water grew louder, sounding as tranquil as a nest of hissing serpents. I wanted to cover my ears, close my eyes, and curl into the fetal position.

What god had I pissed off to end up in this situation? All of them?

I glanced towards a line of soldiers when I heard a low growl. There were wolves and monstrous cats sitting amongst uniformed men and women. They stood perfectly still, but I had no doubt that one whistle would send them sprinting over.

"Her Majesty, Queen Sylvia. You may bow and pay her your respect," a uniformed herald announced. I bowed as the Queen looked down on us from her platform.

I could feel Galen's mother staring at me. I lifted my head, meeting powder-blue eyes. Her angular face was set in a pucker that negated any inner beauty, though she looked young enough to be his sister. I was taken aback, but concealed my surprise. Obsidian black hair and pale skin contrasted sharply with her son's golden features. A dark red lipstick leeched any remaining color from her cheeks.

Dressed in a pale silver gown, in a more provocative style than I was accustomed to, she showed off ample cleavage on her otherwise thin frame. The fabric draped and twisted, reminding me of the flora that surrounded us.

Her skirts splayed out around her, extending past a throne that appeared to be weaved from dried vines and mahogany branches. Gold flecks shimmered on dark wood, shining like starlight. The chair looked alive, as if one of its vines might lash out and wrap around my neck at any moment. However, it was not the throne that scared me, but the snake that sat in it, watching me through cold, narrowed slits.

"I was informed that you found a stray puppy wandering our property," the Queen drawled to Galen, looking bored. "And why exactly did you find it appropriate to bring her into my home? *Please* don't tell me you want to keep her. You should know by now that humans don't make good pets, Prince Galen."

I clenched my jaw as she spoke. *They really weren't humans.* I felt Galen's hand on my lower back, steadying me, as I trembled.

I peeked over at him. He was glaring at her with thinly-veiled hostility. "This is Marigold. She's in need of food, rest, and medical attention. Wylks found her before we did—she was almost their dinner. She injured herself during the attack and doesn't remember how she ended up in our forest. I'd like to offer her one of our guest rooms while she recovers."

"Marigolds... such pretty little flowers," the Queen said as we locked eyes. "Although personally, I've never cared for them. They aren't to my taste. Too *cheerful,* too bright... for something so short-lived. I find such obstinance, *obnoxious.*" She flicked her eyes down to where Galen was touching me.

I was in a foul mood. My ribs ached, my lungs burned—I wanted to light this corset on *fire.* And now a strange woman was slinging insults at me. Was I supposed to just roll over and take this?

"Mother—" Galen said through gritted teeth. She flashed her eyes at him and he corrected himself. "*Queen Sylvia...* Please, let her rest tonight. She'll be of interest to you. Trust me."

They exchanged a heated look.

"I must admit, I *am* curious to know how a dirty little human managed to bewitch my son." She curled her lip at me, as if I was a mud-caked piglet that belonged in a pen.

My fists clenched, but instead of releasing my rage, I swallowed it. It went down like hot tar. I curtsied to the Queen and asked sweetly, "You find me *bewitching,* Your Grace?"

Her head snapped to me, eyes narrowing. "Did you grow up in a cave or are you just extremely stupid? Speak to me again without permission and it'll be the last thing you do." My heart was in my throat as she flippantly said, "Now thank me for my hospitality and be gone."

I bowed, tail between my legs. "Thank you, Your Grace."

"Prince Galen, show her to a room in the guest wing," Sylvia sighed. "She's your responsibility. Make sure she doesn't go anywhere without a chaperone. Understood?" He nodded. "I expect a full explanation, sooner rather than later. Do *not* keep me waiting."

I was in shock, shivering from a deep chill in my bones. There was no fight left in me. I yearned to be a child and cry in my mother's arms until my tears ran dry. How had my life changed so drastically in a matter of hours? For the second time today, I felt as if I was falling, but this time there was no dream to wake up from.

Did Deric know I was missing yet? Ophelia would be worried sick by now. The entire fleet of guards was probably out hunting for me.

I stayed close to Galen, following him past guarded sections of the castle, as we padded through long, silent corridors. We turned so many times, I eventually gave up memorizing the way.

Oil lamps lit dark hallways with an amber glow as evening approached. They flickered against marble statues and ivy that seemingly grew out of thin air. Decor that felt lively in the daylight had turned ominous in the dancing shadows of dusk.

This castle was a complicated maze that I'd need to learn if I planned to escape. I wanted to put as much distance between myself and the Queen of Nymera as possible. I'd never met anyone more terrifying than Galen's mother. I pitied the woman who ended up with her for a mother-in-law.

We stopped in front of a door and Galen unlocked it with an old-fashioned key he pulled from his pocket. "After you," he said, following behind me and shutting the door.

I looked around the cozy, understated room, relieved it wasn't a prison cell. The walls were covered in a delicate, floral wallpaper. Plants hung from the ceiling and spilled from large ceramic pots. A limestone fireplace covered in hand-carved rosettes sat across from a large feather bed with a fluffed-up white duvet. Had I not been filthy, I would've fallen into it, flat on my face, not caring what the Prince thought.

Galen watched me take in my surroundings. "The maids will be by shortly to draw you a bath and bring you dinner. Do you want me to ring for a healer as well?"

"Thank you. And no, I'm fine. Just... tired," I said with a shiver.

Tired didn't begin to cover it. I was consumed with dread and loneliness... fear and worry. I was confused. And *angry*. But he was the last person I wanted to confide in. He was the one who brought me here—to his mother, who'd compared me to a *dog*.

But he'd also saved my life and kept me safe... found me a place to sleep. My mind was rattled and I couldn't tell which way was up. Was he friend or foe? Or something else entirely?

"Do you want to know more about who we are? Or would you rather wait until morning?" he asked. "You look like you're about to fall over from exhaustion."

He was observant—too observant. He appeared to be just a few years older than me, but he carried himself like he'd seen and done it all. And today he'd seen me at my most vulnerable... completely unraveled and at his mercy. And now there was nowhere to run, nowhere to hide.

"If it's all the same to you, I'd like to be done with surprises for now. My brain might melt out of my ears if my mind is blown one more time," I rambled.

Part of me wanted him to leave me be, so I could reflect on the strangest day of my life. Another part was scared to be alone.

So we stood in silence. It was so quiet that I could hear him breathing. He stared at the fire, hands in his pockets, back turned to me. Was it my imagination or was there an invisible tension beginning to grow?

Why wasn't he leaving?

I stood awkwardly between the bed and door, chewing on my lip, rocking back on my heels. I fidgeted with my fingers, staring at the dirt embedded under my nails. How long was he just going to stand there? I was about to tear this dress off whether he left or not.

I cleared my throat. "Well... thank you for every—"

My words were cut off as Galen dashed to my side, spinning me faster than humanly possible. He pushed me against the door in the next motion and pinned my hands above my head. I looked up at him, keen on an explanation, bracing myself for his next move.

"You're going to be trouble, aren't you?" he murmured, looking down at my lips that were set in a startled O-shape. I could smell his cologne of cloves and smoke, like a warm fire on a cold autumn day. His eyes shined with an emotion I couldn't read, while my heart began to thud erratically. I was a rabbit caught in his snare.

"*What* are you?" he asked. We stared at each other. I opened my mouth to speak, but before I could, he kissed me.

And like a fool, *I kissed him back.*

SEVEN

His kisses started off soft and searching, like warm drops of rain along my lips, my cheeks, my neck. Then his mouth was hovering over mine, tracing along the seam of my lips, requesting permission to enter.

I opened for him and was flooded with sensation as he teased his tongue against mine. Sparks exploded down my spine, all the way to my toes. I felt wobbly as both limbs and willpower went lax.

He knew what he was doing, and he was something *real* to cling to. So strong, so solid... as solid as the door I was pressed against. My wrists were shackled under one large hand, while the other held my waist. I was hungry, *starving* for a touch I didn't know I needed until now.

This was madness. How had things escalated so quickly?

He was a Prince, who was used to getting what he wanted—that's how.

He scraped his teeth along the delicate skin of my throat, then licked his way down to my collar bone. I was sweaty and dirty, but he didn't seem to care, licking me like an ice cream cone. And I was *melting*.

I gripped his hard biceps, anchoring myself to him to keep from floating away. After another slow-burning kiss, I shoved him off.

"What-Why-*Who*... do you think you are, kissing a stranger like that!" I demanded, trying to pull myself together. I rubbed goosebumps away, crossing my arms in an attempt to create a boundary between us.

He let out a a slow exhale, running his hands through his fiery auburn locks. His eyes were glazed over, making him look more animal than man. "You're so sweet. I can still taste blood berry juice on you, but you... *you are sweeter*," he breathed, taking a step closer.

"Stay," I said, pointing a finger at him, as if he was a dog and not a *Prince*.

His mouth tugged into a smirk and he lifted his hands, feigning innocence. "I should apologize, but I've been thinking about that kiss in the woods all day. It was... rushed. It felt important that you knew how I really wanted to kiss you. I thought my brothers would've found it rather distasteful if I took you against a tree."

"It's... it's alright. Just don't let it happen again," I said, lifting my chin up in an attempt to salvage any shred of dignity.

I was not myself. It was difficult to feel so many things at once. I'd kissed two men in one day, did that make me a terrible person? This day *had* felt more like a week, a month, *a year,* but that was no excuse for my behavior.

"Things will change tomorrow when you know more about me—when I know more about you. I just wanted one real kiss before who we are... complicates things." The sincerity of his words struck deep, settling somewhere deep in my belly. Tomorrow would be a day for truths. Today... today I could still pretend this was a dream.

"It's my birthday," I said quietly, peering down at my brown shoes that had been white hours earlier.

"Today? How old are you?" He cocked his head like a dog waiting for a bone.

"Twenty-one. I was supposed to be presented to society today... at my Debut, if that equivalent exists here."

"I believe it does, more or less. I'm sorry you missed it... to be thrown to the wolves." He took my hand and ran a finger along the sensitive skin of my wrist.

"Not all of the wolves were terrible," I said, biting my lip.

He bent down and gave me a peck on the cheek before whispering, "Happy birthday."

The maids arrived shortly after Galen left. They brought in countless buckets of water for the over-sized copper tub in the washroom. There was no indoor plumbing in this world. Nymera seemed to be a couple hundred years behind Erador in both fashion and function.

They set out a towel, a crisp white nightgown, and a covered dinner plate on a small corner table before dismissing themselves. And then I was alone.

I was starving, making it difficult to decide between a bath or food first. I chose to bathe. A cold soak would simply not do after a day like today. I scrubbed the dirt and blood off my skin first, using the oils and soap they'd left. I washed my hair next, massaging it with Eucalyptus shampoo. The scent filled my nose and I sighed in pleasure. This fragrance was a luxury where I was from. I cupped my hands and breathed it in. It tingled with its cooling effects and gave me a moment of zen I'd been desperate for since this morning.

This was the second worst day of my life, but it hadn't been completely terrible... Galen's emerald eyes were branded into the back of my mind. I closed my lids and laid back against the tub's headrest, letting myself ponder our kiss.

He'd been brazen. I should've slapped him. Instead I'd melted into him, backbone and all. What did that say about me? Was I so desperate for connection, for passion, that I'd grown reckless? Or was I just so upside down and sideways that it felt as if my actions didn't have consequences? I'd have to face him tomorrow. I'd have to face all of it tomorrow.

Once I was clean, I lifted the cover on my dinner plate and almost cried with relief when I saw pita bread, cheese, fruit, and a side of greens. It was strange how similar this world was to mine. They spoke the same language, ate the same food. We'd originated from the same place, but... *they weren't human*. I tried not to linger on what that meant. Soon enough, I'd have answers.

When my head hit the pillow, exhaustion pulled me into a deep, dream-filled stupor.

The Queen was crying on her throne. My mother was with her, comforting her.

"We knew it would happen today. We couldn't keep her from her destiny," my mother said, pacing in front of the Queen before coming to stand by her side.

"She's not ready. I wish I'd had a chance to tell her more before she left. If they find out who she is—what she is—you know what they'll do." Ophelia, who never slouched, was hunched over, elbows on her knees, hands covering her eyes. I'd never seen her look so... normal.

I tried to run up to them, but I was stuck in place as an observer. My arms ached to hold my mother. Her gold hair fell wild over her shoulders. She was magnificent.

"It's not something one can truly be ready for. We just have to trust that the gods are watching over her. I'll be watching over her too." My mother bent down in front of the Queen and took her hands. "Ready the armies. Stock the castle. We don't know how this will play out. Find the others."

The Queen looked up from her hands and rolled back her shoulders, steeling herself against the coming storm. "I will. I'll be ready. Keep her safe."

My mother nodded before bursting into flames.

Light streamed through my windows as the morning sun crested over lavender mountains. I jumped out of bed like I'd been sleeping with spiders. My skin crawled as I accepted that I wasn't in my own bedroom. It really wasn't a dream—I was in another world.

I ran to the window and looked at my surroundings. I had a view of the gardens, the forest, and the mountains beyond. They were *purple*—looking like bruised mighty giants, passed out after a fist fight.

The gardens were different from the structured, pruned ones I was used to. It appeared they were mostly functional, growing food and herbs. There were also wild flowers that flourished where spanning lawns should've been. Bumble bees and other pollinators bounced along a symphony of flora, working diligently. It comforted me to know that even in this strange place, I was surrounded by familiar sights.

Perhaps with the right perspective, this could be seen as the adventure of a lifetime. I'd been praying for something that would uproot me from my life, and here I was... so very far from home. A prisoner, yes, but I was already used to feeling caged.

Here, I was a nobody. They didn't know that I was the heir to a throne, as far as I knew. I was oddly giddy from it—or maybe I was feeling giddy from *someone* rather than *something*... But then I remembered the Queen and how much she seemed to hate humans, and I felt heavy and hopeless once more.

A knock at the door startled me. Two maids strolled in, weighed down by armfuls of clothing. "Good morning, Miss. Or... um, what should I call you?" A waif-like woman asked with a polite smile.

I smiled timidly. "Thea, my Lady's Maid, calls me M'Lady. You can call me Marigold, if you'd like."

Her forehead creased. "Lady? Miss, I don't mean to be rude... but Her Grace mentioned you were a... *human.*" She whispered the last word, as if it was a shameful secret.

My eyes grew round as I realized my error. I should've assumed that humans in this world wouldn't have status or titles. The Queen had made it clear that we were inferior to... to whatever *they* were.

"Oh, yes, of course. Marigold is fine," I said with a tight smile.

The woman side-eyed me with curiosity, then smiled. "Lovely to meet you, Marigold. I'm Lusha. We've brought some dresses. It looks like most of them should fit with a few quick alterations. May I?" She had a brush in one hand and held up a dress in the other.

I ushered her forward, sitting down at the vanity, and Lusha began to work. The other woman, who hadn't acknowledged me, busied herself by organizing my wardrobe.

Lusha whispered near my ear, "Don't bother with Tildy. She's as cold as *Beira*. It's not personal. She did grow up with human friends, but working in the castle as long as she has... she's forgotten how to talk to humans. I told her it's no different than talking to anyone else."

She caught my eye in the mirror and made a face, rolling her eyes, then gave me a warm grin. My shoulders relaxed. She was being kind when she didn't have to be.

"You have beautiful hair," Lusha said as she brushed it out. "It shines like liquid gold."

"Thank you," I said, glancing at her reflection. She had soft blue eyes and long, straight strawberry-blonde hair. It was pinned half back, showing off delicate, pointed ears. All the staff I'd seen so far had similar ears. Lusha was a whole head taller than me, which also seemed to be the norm—that and sharp, elongated canine teeth. Their fangs were beautiful, if not baleful.

I let out a shaky breath. I'd been treated well thus far. I was a guest. If they were going to hurt me, they already would have—at least that's what I was going to tell myself. And Galen didn't seem to hate humans, even if his mother did.

Lusha plaited my hair out of my face, tying it back into the same style she was wearing. Tildy dressed me in a simple sage green gown that had been tailored for someone much taller than me, but I didn't mind. It was still a vast improvement to my usual attire.

The dress wrapped around my curves, tied around my ribs, and draped down in light, silky layers. I could move so easily. The Wylks wouldn't have stood a chance if I'd been wearing *this*.

By the time I was ready, my stomach had twisted in on itself. I'd hoped Galen might come to my room and escort me down, but instead a dark-haired guard with a pallid complexion was sent. Robert, a man of few words and even fewer facial expressions. He frowned as I followed behind him, responding to my questions with one-word answers.

"How long have you worked here?"

"Fifty years," he said gruffly. *Fifty years?* He didn't even look fifty years old.

"Do you have a family?"

"None of your concern, Miss."

"Have you ever escorted a human to breakfast before?"

He gave me an affronted look that silenced me.

Robert opened the double doors onto a veranda. There was an oversized pergola that offered shade above a large wooden table. Vines climbed along the beams and weaved through the lattice. Ripe bunches of purple grapes hung low and heavy.

If there were grapes, then there was wine... a blessing from *Terra* herself. Would they water my wine here? Something told me no. Galen took me to my room unescorted last night—that led me to believe they were less rigid in this court. He could've left me compromised and my reputation destroyed, had our actions been observed in Aurelius.

It appeared that I was the only one concerned with keeping my virtue intact in this world. If last night had been a test, assessing my inherent propriety, then I'd undoubtedly failed with flying colors. Perhaps that's why Thea always synched my corset so tight... I was less likely to become distracted by the opposite sex, if I was occupied with the task of simply trying to *breathe.*

Maybe she'd been on to something, because at this moment, I couldn't help but notice the beautiful faces that sat around the table. I inhaled a gluttonous amount of oxygen as my heart began to thud unevenly. Three Princes and no Queen... I exhaled in relief.

I could feel Galen watching me as I took a seat across from him and avoided eye contact, feeling shy under the harsh morning sun. "My mother takes her breakfast in her room. You can relax. Although, I must warn you... my brothers' table manners might be equally offensive," he said.

I finally met his gaze and was greeted with a sultry smile that sent heat to the places he'd kissed last night. His brothers were sitting a few seats down. Rafael was reading a book and barely looked up to greet me, while Louis gave a huge grin and dragged his chair closer, making the stone of the terrace screech in protest.

"How did you sleep?" Louis asked between mouthfuls of food.

"Better than expected, thank you. I'm quite nervous to talk with you all, to be honest. I'd prefer to skip any pleasantries and dive right in, if that's alright with you," I said to no one in particular.

Rafael flicked his eyes up from his book. "You should eat first. Your appetite might be gone after you've heard what we have to say." I didn't appreciate him telling me what to do, especially when it took the wind out of my sails. In my stomach's current state, I wasn't even sure I could keep anything down.

"Here." Galen offered me a biscuit with jam. "Eat this and then we won't keep you waiting any longer."

My eyes darted between them as I ripped off a piece of biscuit in a notably unladylike bite. I narrowed my eyes towards Raf who was buried in his book and didn't notice.

We continued eating in awkward silence until I finished, washing my food down with a swig of herbal tea. The taste was unfamiliar and my heart sank. What if they'd poisoned or drugged it—added something that would make me speak more candidly? I set the cup down and didn't take another sip.

"Done!" I declared, more chipper than I felt.

Galen glanced towards his brothers and said, "I'll start." He studied me as I tapped my foot and drummed my fingers on my water glass. "It's alright, you aren't in any danger."

"Yet." Rafael's eyebrows rose as he spoke, but he still didn't tear his gaze from his book.

I tried to ignore the remark, gulping down my worry with a sip of water, then motioned for Galen to continue.

"As you know, our people aren't human... but we *are* originally from Erador, which makes it difficult to comprehend how you haven't heard of our kind... We're faeries. *Fae*, for short. Some humans think we're elves. We've also been accused of being vampires."

"Which we're *not*," Louis emphasized, curling his lip in disgust.

I'm not sure what I expected, but it wasn't that. *Faeries?* Weren't they supposed to be small and winged? I thought about voicing that question, but decided it might be offensive to three men who stood around six and a half feet tall.

"I've heard mention of faeries in fables and bedtime stories, and we've had occasional complaints of vampires from civilians, but I never thought there was validity to the claims." I paused to gather my thoughts, furrowing my brow. "What makes a faerie different than a human?"

"We're similar enough to mate with one another," Raf said, glancing away from his book and straight into my eyes.

My cheeks went hot at the implication of his statement, paired with the intensity of his gaze. His mouth curved into a smile, but not a particularly friendly one as he continued, "Faeries have stronger senses. Faster reflexes. Longer lives. We can heal from most injuries as well, and much more quickly than humans."

I thought of my scratches from yesterday that had disappeared within hours and swallowed hard.

"We can also wield magic," Rafael said, causing me to drop my jaw. "Fae have the ability to harness elemental energy, manipulate matter, heal the sick and wounded... Each faerie has abilities unique to them."

"Most of us can shift into an animal form too," Galen added.

Stunned, it took me a moment to find my voice. I studied their expressions and accepted that this wasn't a joke. I drank an entire glass of water, dabbing the corners of my mouth with a napkin, before finally speaking. "Show me," I said, challenging Galen with a hard stare.

EIGHT

Galen snapped his fingers and a small flame appeared, hovering above his upturned fingers. It grew higher and higher, until it almost touched the pergola above us. He switched it off with another snap.

I turned to Rafael. He hesitated for a moment, then held out his hand as a small seed appeared. Within seconds, the seed grew from a sprout, to a bud, to a blooming *black* rose. He handed it to me. It felt *real*. The petals were silky and the thorns so sharp, I pricked my finger as I ran it along the stem.

I should've known that a gift from him would be booby-trapped. A small drop of blood appeared and I sucked my thumb to remove it. The brothers looked at me with interest.

I glanced down at my thumb to find the wound had already sealed over. The rose unexpectedly turned to black dust in my hands, causing fine powder to sieve between my fingers and onto my plate.

"I have the power to create. And destroy," he said indifferently, shrugging his shoulders, while I blinked at him in disbelief.

Galen rolled his eyes. "You just can't resist showing off around pretty girls, can you, brother?"

Rafael glared at him. Louis laughed and leaned over to take the empty glass I'd been drinking from. He hovered his hand over it and water streamed down from his fingers. He handed it back. It was icy cold in my hands. The water looked clear... drinkable.

Setting it aside, I asked, "And you can shift into animals?" My mind drifted to the grizzly bear I'd seen in the streets yesterday. Gears slowly turned as I tried to connect what I'd seen with what they were telling me.

"Our shifting forms will be revealed on our terms. It's impolite to ask a faerie what their *pneuma* is," Rafael replied coolly.

His attitude was getting tedious. And so was his perma-scowl. I didn't even know what a pneuma was and I didn't press it. Instead, I set my hands in my lap and took several deep breaths.

Magic was real. I could handle this. I'd always suspected that something *more* existed—my garden was living proof—but I hadn't dared to dream *this* big. This was incredible. A wide grin spread across my face, before fading to a dubious frown. "How are you like vampires?" The biscuit sat in my stomach like a rock.

"Before we get to that, let me tell you the history of how we came to be here." Galen reached across the table and took my hand. "Up until two-hundred years ago, humans and faeries shared Erador. Fae are long-lived... nearly immortal, which means we reproduce at a much slower rate. Humans have always been the dominant species because of their ability to breed easily, along with their propensity for destruction and war.

"Our people prefer to live with the land. We feel a kinship with nature—a foreign concept to those who lack the ability to see its magic. For much of history, faeries avoided human society, choosing to live a nomadic lifestyle. Humans, however, were set on an insatiable path of *progress*. They built civilizations and then fought between themselves, devouring the natural world in the process. Faeries tried to adapt, but we were hunted... deemed monsters and demons. The Fae eventually found strength in numbers. We sailed across the sea from the Old World and discovered land that hadn't been tainted by humanity. We created a home that was ours—a haven for faeries. We protected it with spells and wards, keeping humans out."

"Wards?"

"Invisible walls of magic. With strong wards, a place can be hidden in plain sight," Rafael answered. "Even an entire city, when enough faeries are gathered together."

Galen eyed him and continued. "We named our Kingdom Aurelius, which translates to *golden* in the language of the Fae. It was a golden age for us, lasting thousands of years. Humans rarely stumbled into our sanctuary, and if they did, we made sure they never left. We were able to grow our numbers and thrive."

Aurelius... *my* Aurelius, was an ancient Fae civilization? I stopped breathing.

Galen gave me a grim expression before continuing. "We were cursed one-hundred years before we were exiled to this world. We still don't know how or why, but one cloudless evening, all faeries felt magic leave their bodies, like part of their soul had been ripped from them. Some of the elders instantly died, unable to live without magic. Some children became ill and perished, from a sudden lack of immunity. Later, we found out that humans began *producing* magic that same night—housing our stolen magic in their blood, like wine in a bottle. Most of them couldn't access it, their bodies incapable of channeling it.

"The Fae wouldn't have learned that magic had found a new host, if there hadn't been some that could wield it. Chaos broke out in human society; fires were accidentally started, people turned their loved ones into dust in the midst of an argument, some drowned as their lungs filled up with water. The magic rebelled. These stories trickled into Aurelius and some faeries left to look for answers—to find a way to break the curse. Naturally, they began to mingle with humans again.

"Desperate Fae ripped humans apart as they tried to take back what was theirs. It wasn't until they tasted human blood that they realized they *could* get their magic back. In doses. Temporarily."

"This is why we're compared to vampires," Louis chimed in. "But we're *nothing* like them. They're *soulless*—resurrected from the dead. They can't even—"

"A topic for another time, Louis," Rafael said, silencing his brother with a hard stare.

Galen cleared his throat. "Once humans realized we required their blood to use our powers—that Aurelius existed and housed an entire community of Fae—they began to strategize. Their goal was simple; eradicate faeries from the world, while we were at our most vulnerable. We fought back, so they exiled us."

Galen sighed, his eyes softening as they met mine. "We're still cursed, which means we must drink human blood to wield magic."

I pulled my clammy hands from his, shivering in the heat of the day. I was sitting with three faeries who *drank* blood?

Did they view me as a food source?

I blanched, resisting the urge to back my seat away from the table and run.

Actually, running was probably a good idea. I forcefully pushed my heavy chair back and stood. The brothers were watching, waiting to see what I did next.

I stood locked in place, paralyzed with panic. My heart was beating wildly, my stomach was in my throat, my eyes were fixed on Galen. Had he been thinking about my blood while he was kissing me last night? My stare sharpened as fear turned to anger.

Galen carefully stood, as if he might spook me if he moved too fast. "Marigold... please sit down. We're not going to hurt you."

"Why should I believe you? W-what do you want with me?" I asked, voice quivering.

Cautiously, he made his way towards me, walking around the table. "You should believe me, because I've gone out of my way to protect you and make you feel safe since we met. And I'll continue to do so. As for what we want... if you sit down, I'd be happy to tell you."

He was standing beside me when he'd finished speaking. His hand reached out, but I jolted back.

"Don't even *think* about touching me."

"I won't touch you. Now, sit."

I looked at the other brothers. Rafael had a smug little smirk on his face.

"Does my *fear* bring you joy, *sadist*?" I snarled.

His smile dropped as he stared at me through thick lashes. "Actually, I was enjoying the sight of Galen getting his ass handed to him. It doesn't happen nearly enough, in my opinion."

Galen was about to lunge, but I turned towards him next. "I'll sit. Just please... don't *growl* again. I'm still recovering from the last one."

Rafael and Louis both laughed, while Galen helped me into a seat. Veins bulged in his arms and neck as he silently seethed.

"So... I have magic in my blood?" I asked while gazing at the blue and purple lines that ran along my wrists.

"Yes, you're human, but you're likely also Fae," Galen replied. "In fact, I'm confident that you are. Some faeries *can* use magic without drinking blood, because they're also part-human. We refer to them as hybrids. They aren't common; faeries and humans don't usually interbreed."

I laughed. *cackled*. I was beginning to disassociate. "You can't be serious. I can't use magic. Sorry to disappoint you, but I'm just a simple, boring *human*. What did your mother call me... *a pet*?"

"My mother is a piece of work. And I'm perfectly serious. Last night... when we kissed... I could *feel* your power," he whispered.

A surge of heat rushed through me and I dropped my gaze. "Oh," I squeaked.

Louis laughed and opened his mouth to speak, but Galen shot him a look that shut him up.

With a thick voice, I asked, "Who cursed you? Why?"

Rafael answered as he stared out towards the mountains. "We don't know. The accepted theory is that a human got hold of a spell book—one that doesn't require magic to wield. Whether they meant to or not, they shifted the flow of magic. Energy can't be created—only transferred. Giving magic to humans *took* magic from faeries. There were attempts to break the curse—whispers of spells and prophecies. But none of that mattered once we became trapped here."

"A world walker tricked you." I looked to Galen. "You told me that yesterday."

He nodded. "Both humans and faeries wanted to find a solution to the blood shed between our people. Years of war had decimated all of us. Our father, Randall, was the newly crowned King of Aurelius. He was told that the curse was contained to Erador—that if we left, it would be lifted. A fresh start in a new world. Faeries gathered in Aurelius to prepare for the journey. We brought food, livestock—anything that would help us colonize a new world. Some humans chose to come as well. We'd been mingling for nearly a century by then. Some had bonded to faeries for various reasons, despite the war, while others wanted the opportunity to begin again in a new world."

"And some were forced against their will," Raf quipped.

Galen side-eyed him. "It was a time of many wrongs on both sides. Today, we pay humans for their blood. Relations between faeries and humans have evolved in Nymera, out of necessity."

Rafael snorted in response.

"As I was saying," Galen said with a sigh. "We migrated over by the thousands. As the last few faeries crossed through the portal, the world walker betrayed her own people. She sealed us in—closing the portal before anyone had time to react. Our curse had *not* been lifted. We had a world to call our own, but our source of magic had been cut off. We were handicapped—left only with the group of humans that crossed over with the faeries. With our magic so limited, we're a mockery of what Fae are meant to be."

If he was looking for sympathy, he was barking up the wrong tree. I liked my blood right where it was.

"Are you going to try and drink my blood?" I sneered at him.

Louis choked on his coffee, coughing as he recovered. He looked up at Galen to gage his reaction.

"No," Galen said defensively. "I wouldn't force myself on you. We're civilized about the exchange. Blood-lust does exist, but I'm more than capable of rising above it."

I met his fiery gaze and gave it right back.

Louis cut in. "It's important you understand that we don't *want* to drink blood. We've been forced to due to this twisted curse. Many Fae are vegetarians. We do our best to treat all living beings with respect and dignity."

"You shouldn't have to worry about anyone wanting your blood while you're living at the castle," Raf said to me while glaring at Galen. "It's well stocked."

"Exactly how much does one have to drink to restore their magic?"

"It depends on several factors," Galen replied. "Age of a faerie, how powerful they are, the quality of magic. Typically, we just need a... *sip*, now and then, to satiate us. The magic stays in our system until we wield it, and then we have to replenish it."

"H-how do you get it?" I choked out.

Galen smiled at me, flashing his fangs. "We have sharp teeth. We've also discovered a method to safely extract blood using needles and syringes, though its not nearly as fun."

I was going to be sick.

"Have some water, you're looking a bit... peaky," he chuckled, handing me a glass.

"You just told me you *sip* from humans. *Of course*, I look *peaky*," I snapped. "So... you don't murder people for their blood?"

"No... Why would we want to do that? We'd lose access to our source of magic," Galen said.

"And... does it taste awful?"

They all laughed this time, but Galen answered. "It doesn't taste like blood to us because of the magic. It tastes better than you can imagine." I wished I hadn't asked.

"And how many humans live in this world?"

Raf replied, "Tough to say, with how quickly the human population has been shrinking. They may soon become extinct in Nymera."

My eyes grew large.

"My brother is exaggerating, as usual. No one's going extinct. But we do need access to your world, *our home world*," Galen said. "Some Fae don't have a steady source anymore. Our people have been waiting a long, long time for a world walker. We want to go home."

"I see," I mumbled, staring down at my empty plate.

And there it was; the reason they hadn't harmed me. They wanted me to take them back to Erador. Well, they were about to be severely disappointed, because I had no clue how I'd arrived here.

They wanted to come to my world and drink the blood of my people, because the human population here was... *shrinking*.

Did they think I was an idiot? Even if I could world-walk—*which I couldn't*—I'd *never* let them into Erador. And Galen was wrong; I wasn't a faerie.

I was never going to get home... I was stuck in a world of blood-thirsty monsters. Cold dread creeped down my spine, giving me the chills. "I can't world-walk!" I cried in a burst of anger. "And I can't help you."

"It's a lot to process," Galen said evenly. "But for what it's worth, I think you can. First we'll help you learn to wield your magic, then we can worry about opening a portal. One step at a time."

Rafael stood quickly. "Now that we've gotten that over with, I'm heading to town." He shrugged on a black leather jacket.

"Beers or brothels this time, brother?" Louis asked, also standing.

"Both," Raf replied with a grin. I resisted the urge to lift my lip in disgust.

"Marigold, I believe we'll be seeing a lot more of each other. I look forward to it," Louis said with an exaggerated bow. Raf had already disappeared. I hadn't even seen him leave.

Galen turned to me. "We need to talk to my mother soon, but I'd like to show you around first. I want you to feel at home here."

"Like a fish feels at home on a hook?" I bit back. I couldn't tell if the hunger in his expression was for me or my blood. He could stay hungry. In fact, he could starve.

His mouth tugged into a cocky half-grin. "Does that mean you're hooked? If you want me to come to your bedroom tonight, all you have to do is ask."

I gasped in outrage. "Absolutely *not*. Last night, I was in a state of duress, which you took advantage of. It won't happen again."

He had the nerve to scoff. "You kissed me first, if I recall. And you're going to kiss me again," he challenged. "You won't last three days."

"Why? Do you plan on eating me before then?"

He laughed, rolling his eyes. I kept a healthy distance from him while we walked to Robert. He leaned down and whispered, "I plan on doing much more than that."

NINE

I returned to my room to freshen up. Too soon, Galen was leaning against my door frame in a dark green tunic and tight breeches that showed off his muscular legs. "Ready to go for a ride?"

I smiled up at him instinctively, like I'd been trained to do my entire life. *No. I was in a new world, and I was making new rules.* I let my face drop into a scowl. "It depends. Do I get my own horse this time?"

"Whatever you want, it's yours." He grinned.

I raised my brows. "In that case, I'd like to go home."

Our eyes locked and he approached, stopping just short of touching me. I backed up, hitting the bed. He brushed a lock of hair from my face and I flinched away from him.

He frowned. "Do you think I'm going to attack you?"

"I don't know what to think. We've just met."

"I promise, I won't bite you—unless you ask me to. You could be the savior we've been waiting for. I'm not going to hurt you. I realize it'll take some time for you to trust me..." His voice trailed off as his eyes shamelessly traveled down my body.

He was delusional. "It's almost impressive," I spat.

"What is?"

"*Your Prince-sized ego*. I didn't ask to be your savior—and I have no loyalty to your people." Morbid curiosity wormed its way into my brain. I chewed at my nails, huffed a sigh, then finally asked, "Why would I *ever* ask you to bite me?"

He gave a low chuckle. "Because, Marigold... it would feel good. *Very good*. In fact, some people beg for it." There was nothing subtle about his heavy-lidded gaze. It flipped my stomach inside-out. I ducked around him, putting more distance between us.

"And if I can't use magic—if I'm not your savior—then what? Your mother will throw me in the dungeon to become someone's next meal? I'm not so convinced *that* would feel good!"

How dare he presume that I'd put his people before mine. I thought arriving here might give me a break from responsibility, but instead I was supposed to be a hero for the Fae? My blood was *boiling* as I bared my teeth at him.

"I'd never let her throw you in a dungeon," he said earnestly. "And you *do* have magic. Like I said, all Fae have a particular scent, a specific taste, that's unique to them—whether magic flows in their blood or not. I can feel it beneath your skin, thrumming like an electric current. Humans may have magic in their veins, but they are *not* one of us. There's nothing *human* about the power that radiates from you."

His tone was seductive, but his message was clear; faeries were better than humans. He sounded like the aristocratic men of Aurelius who thought they were superior because of their blood—because of their money—because they were *men*.

"You're not subtle about your distaste for my kind," I growled, pointing a finger at his chest.

"I do *not* have a distaste for humans. In fact, quite the opposite. They taste lovely," he laughed.

The thin ice he'd been walking on *cracked*. I snarled and launched forward, attempting to smack him. Instead, I found myself gripped in a firm hold. "I do not *dislike* humans," he murmured into my ear. "They're not my enemy and neither are you. Some Fae *do* hate humans and think themselves better than them. I'm not one of them. However, you're *not* human and the sooner you accept it, the sooner you can stop fighting *this*."

I tried to jerk away from him, but he held me close. Heat radiated from him, causing my pulse to quicken, frustrating me even further. My body was *traitorous*. He was trying to prove some point. If he thought I'd submit to him, just because he was stronger, then I'd teach him that I had fangs too. I sunk my teeth into his forearm and he growled in surprise, letting go.

"Did you just bite me?" he asked in disbelief, staring at the crescent-shaped imprint on his arm. It hadn't even broken the skin.

"I wanted to see what the fuss was about," I panted. I tried to hold back a grin, before we both broke into laughter.

"You're a feral little thing," he said as his eyes flashed. "And if you think that biting me is going to deter me, then you've got a lot to learn about faeries."

I rolled my eyes. "As long as you understand where my loyalty lies."

He sighed. "You've had enough years as a human, it won't kill you to spend a little time discovering your faerie side." He moved to sit in one of two cushioned seats that faced the fireplace and I joined him.

"Arriving here was the first magical thing that's ever happened to me. Wouldn't I have *sensed* it before now? Yesterday I lived in a much simpler world. It's difficult for me to comprehend what magic is—what it feels like."

"It will come naturally to you. You just turned twenty-one, you're very young still, especially for a faerie that's part-human. You might be just starting to manifest your powers. It's no coincidence that you ended up in Nymera when you did."

"I'm a human that might be part-faerie," I reminded him. Humanity would always come first. *Human* is what I identified with, no matter what he *thought* I was.

"Whatever you are, I'm glad you're here. Try to let go of the things that are beyond your control." He stood up and offered his hand. "Now let's go for a ride."

Galen had a snowy white mare named Hibiscus waiting for me when we arrived at the stables. Galen's bay horse, Napoleon, was tacked up as well. We'd brought Robert along, leaving me to wonder why we needed a chaperone. Surely Galen could protect us if needed.

"We're going to Monrovia's city center," Galen said. "Our castle sits on the outskirts of town; our kind prefer not to live on top of each other. Faeries like to be surrounded by nature rather than buildings, although some do choose to live in the village. Monrovia is our capital and was the first town to be established when we arrived here. It's the largest in

Nymera, but might feel small compared to Aurelius. We've only been here two-hundred years, after all."

I nodded, feeling quiet and contemplative after everything I'd learned. If Galen wanted to be a tour guide and just talk at me, that was fine by me.

"Due to the magic shortage, I usually travel with at least one guard. Tensions are high amongst our people right now and I'm not risking your safety. Faeries become hot-tempered when they've been without magic for too long," Galen explained.

Magic shortage was a very diplomatic way to say that the human population was declining. I didn't like that he was sugar-coating the situation, especially when it concerned *my people*. Did he not think I was smart enough to read between the lines? I had yet to see another human since arriving, making me feel even more like an endangered species. We weren't even welcome in his home. Was I supposed to feel grateful that his mother had made an exception for me?

Everything I'd grown up believing was a lie. I'd spent my life blissfully ignorant and I didn't understand why—*how*? Faeries had been completely erased from Erador's history, as far as I knew. Humans could make magic, but couldn't access it. Faeries could wield magic, but couldn't produce it. *They drank from humans like... like vampires.* And vampires were *real*.

How was I supposed to process so much new information? I'd spun in too many circles and now everything felt fuzzy. If only I'd inherited Ophelia's even temper and sharp mind instead of my mother's sensitive nature. How was I going to navigate this dangerous world without getting myself killed?

It was difficult to talk on horseback, giving me the perfect excuse to observe the scenery, while Galen spoke. "The Kunzite Mountains surround us. Lavinia, our second largest city, sits in a valley tucked inside the middle of the range. Most of it has been built into the cliffside, connected by sky bridges. It's stunning—built with Kunzite stone, the color of lavender, and surrounded by waterfalls. It attracts artists, musicians, writers... you'd love it."

I gave a stiff smile as I peered at the monstrous lilac snow-capped mountains that loomed over us.

"Nymera is one large land mass full of different biomes and habitats. Monrovia is located in the tropical grasslands, surrounded by lush forests.

It's warm and humid most of the year, which makes it an ideal location for growing food and raising livestock. Plenty to hunt and forage for as well. Merivale Lake is behind us. It's so large that it looks like an ocean. Beyond that lies the actual sea."

Monrovia was sprawling—wild and untamed. Bright green grass blanketed rolling hills, while puffy clouds drifted across brilliant blue skies. Bowing jacaranda trees hung over the trail, exploding with purple blossoms. They shaded us from the beating sun, but the heat was still sweltering. My curly hair couldn't be contained—coils sprang to life as sweat formed at the nape of my neck.

We passed fields of crops. People hard at work stopped to wave at us. Their children came closer, playing alongside our horses. Some homes were made of stone, while others were built into hillsides and around trees, blending in with the scenery.

Butterflies flitted around us as I tried to study the elaborate patterns of their neon wings. Beetles that glittered like jewels buzzed by as well, leaving colorful trails of glowing dust in their wake. Ribbons of pink, blue, yellow, and green hovered in the sky before dissipating into the atmosphere.

Animals walked along the road as we passed; I didn't have the nerve to ask if they were faeries. Dogs, deer, foxes, and bobcats... black bears, porcupines, and even a zebra. I wasn't an artist, but felt compelled to start sketching, just so I could remember every detail.

When an elephant passed us, my mouth hung open as his large trunk reached out, almost close enough to touch. It was impossible not to grin like a child as I took it all in. I felt as if I was in a dream and might wake up to Thea's knocking at any moment.

My dream from last night... I'd almost forgotten it. The women in my family took our dreams seriously—even pragmatic Ophelia insisted that they were important. She claimed that the gods communicated to us through them, as did the dead.

My mother's face flashed into my mind and I closed my eyes, trying to recall the blurry memory. She and Ophelia had been in the throne room, discussing my departure from Aurelius... like it had been fated to happen. Mama said she'd watch over me. I rubbed goosebumps off my arms. I knew she was close; I could feel her in the gentle breeze that blew through my hair.

I couldn't stop wondering what Ophelia had wanted to tell me. I'd become a living example of what happens when a sheep wanders too far from the herd. *A wolf finds you.* I side-eyed Galen, looking regal and *gorgeous* as he sat on his horse. His bronze hair shimmered with a million shades of gold and red under the glowing sun. I kept catching him stare at me. Every single time, my stomach dipped.

We trotted through town until hooves met cobblestone, then dismounted and tied-off the horses. I gave Hibiscus a scratch on her pink nose, while I fed her an apple I'd taken from the stable. As we made our way into town on foot, I stayed close to Galen, letting him rest his hand on the small of my back.

Magenta flowers and dark green ivy crept along the white-stoned homes we passed. A thin, turquoise river snaked through the middle of town, dividing it in half. Cream-stoned bridges arched over the water, connecting the two halves. Oak trees with sprawling branches created a canopy over the roads.

The streets were filled with people going about their day. Galen was protective, keeping his arm around my waist as we weaved our way through the bustling crowds. Vendors sold unfamiliar produce, aromatic spices, textiles, trinkets, and jewelry. The smell of seasoned meat, sweet breads and baked goods wafted around us as we passed through an outdoor market.

Magic must've helped build all of this. It was the only explanation for so much progress in such a short time. The villagers appeared to be thriving in a world they weren't native to, yet Galen had said they were desperate to go back to Erador—to the Kingdom that I was to one day rule—that his father had once ruled. Humans had stolen their city when they'd left.

If Galen knew who I was, would he consider me his enemy? Even though I hadn't been the one to curse or exile them, I still felt the weight of what had happened. Would they blame me for the sins of my ancestors? I wasn't even related to the royal blood line, but if they considered themselves the true rulers of Aurelius, then I was a direct threat to them. In some ways, Galen and I were fated to be enemies.

I glanced up at him, observing his confident demeanor as his eyes darted around the streets, staying ahead of any potential danger.

Would they still want to leave Nymera if they weren't cursed? Did Ophelia know about their curse? Had she ever tried to break it? I held onto the necklace she'd given me yesterday and gathered strength from its warmth. It sometimes felt hot against my skin—other times, ice cold. The star gave off a faint glow when it heated. I assumed if it had any significance, she would've told me. Then again, she hadn't been as forthcoming with information as I'd once thought.

We walked from shop to shop, talking to the locals and sampling their wares. I ate a glazed cinnamon pastry in the shape of a six-pointed star. We sipped sparkling blood berry wine that tasted incredible, but looked gruesome after all I'd learned today.

The apothecary was my favorite stop. There were hundreds, no, *thousands* of glass vials filled with dried herbs and oils—many I'd never heard of. I carefully picked up each small bottle and inspected the contents, thinking of the impact new plants and medications could have on Aurelius.

"Is it very different than home?" Galen asked as we meandered to the seamstress to get my measurements.

"Aurelius is ancient... as you know. Buildings have been built on top of buildings. Change happens both quickly and slowly in a city that big. Monrovia feels fresh, energetic, lively..."

Galen grinned down at me. "I'm glad you like it here. I think faeries have been able to thrive in Nymera in a way that we couldn't in Erador—with the exception of the blood curse, of course. It took hiding ourselves in Aurelius, to know peace. If we could break the curse, then maybe we'd know it again."

"Were you born in Erador?"

Galen shook his head. "No, I'm not *that* old, though sometimes it feels like it. As heir to the throne, it's easy to forget that I'm my own person, with my own needs."

His gaze lingered and I cleared my throat, turning away as I said, "I'm impressed with the way your people have learned to coexist with nature. In Erador, we tend to demolish the natural world... or bend it to our will. We cut down forests to plant decorative gardens, dump sewage into the rivers, kill wildlife to make space for livestock. But here... I can hear the birds singing in the middle of the city. There are parks to rest in—your water is clear and clean. I wish humanity valued nature as much as your people seem to."

"Human or faerie... there are always those who'll choose personal gain over coexistence. Destruction *is* creation, depending on the mindset. We have a saying here: *A forest of trees can create a home, but too many homes will destroy a forest.* Greed leaves us all with nothing. Balance is key, but difficult to maintain. If you ever figure out how to stop corruption, let me know." He looked tired... *sad.* A glimpse of the man behind the Prince.

I felt an impulse to comfort him. If only he knew how much I could relate. "How do you think faeries would treat humans; hypothetically, if I was able to open a door to Erador?"

He came to a dead stop, surprising me as he pulled me to him in one smooth motion. His arms wrapped around me as our bodies molded together. He was too close; his seductive scent, his charming smile... those canines.

"If the leaders of our two worlds met, I believe we could come to an agreement that would satisfy all. It would just take a little... *balance,*" he said, before cradling my head and dipping me back. His nose brushed against mine before I shimmied out of his grasp and glared at him.

I wanted to believe him, but it had been the polished Prince who'd answered, not the one who had dreams of his own.

All I could envision was the worst-case scenario; magic-starved faeries pillaging human villages, leaving a trail of blood. Taking over economically, then politically. They were powerful enough to make every human in Erador a slave—curse or no curse. And like Galen had said, faeries were just as susceptible to greed as humans. A faerie set on destruction—they'd be capable of *unimaginable* devastation.

A vision from last night's dream appeared; Ophelia sobbing into her hands. She'd looked so vulnerable, so helpless. I never wanted her to feel that way again. I wouldn't let her down. I wouldn't let my world down.

"I think some would take what they wanted, rather than obey a treaty that was signed by a few world leaders."

"Then it seems that I'll have to convince you otherwise. We're not mindless, blood-thirsty beasts. Let me prove it to you." He took my hand in his and kissed it. I jerked it away, but the glint in his eyes told me he liked a challenge.

It was refreshing that he didn't seem to mind my opinions. In Aurelius, intelligence in women was not a virtue—neither was a loud mouth. Here, it seemed that women stood on equal ground. So far, from what I'd seen, they could dress how they wanted and say what they wanted. I'd even seen women dressed in armor, standing amongst male soldiers.

I observed the villagers, both in animal and Fae form, going about their everyday life. I'm sure some were good, some were bad, and most were simply trying to get by—just like humans. I didn't fault them for the curse or for what they were, but I couldn't help them—not in the way Galen wanted me to. Not when they'd acquired a taste for human blood.

After visiting the seamstress, we weaved our way through the streets, back towards our horses. A scuffle outside of a tavern caught my attention. Two large men were laughing as they pushed a woman back and forth—snapping their teeth at her. I watched in horror as one of them held a flame in front of her face and the other restrained her.

Before I knew what I was doing, I'd rushed over and kicked the faerie holding the woman in the shin. He yelped in surprise and let go. I sheltered her with my body and hissed at them like a cat protecting her kitten. I'm not sure who was more surprised: Me, the woman, or the men... perhaps Galen. He trotted over, Robert at his side.

"Who do you think ye are, girlie, starting a fight with a man twice your size? How'd you know I like them feisty?" A tall, thickly built, blonde male sneered down at me.

The other one turned towards Galen. "What is the meaning of this, Prince? Are you going to start getting between us and our sources?" He stood up straight, puffing up his chest, towering over all of us. He had to be at least seven feet tall. "Because if you are, then you're asking for war." His brown hair was sweaty and matted to his head. His eyes were wild, like he was hungry—like he wouldn't think twice before punching a Prince.

"Let's all take a moment to calm ourselves. I apologize for my friend's behavior—she doesn't know how to pick on someone her own size." Galen flashed me a look, daring me to contradict him.

I dared.

"You mean to *defend* these men? They were pushing a woman around in broad daylight? Imagine what they do behind closed doors!" I hadn't eased my grip on her. I quickly assessed her condition. She was about my height—shorter than the average faerie, with shiny black hair and skin the color of cinnamon. She seemed unharmed, staying silent while the men argued.

"Marigold..." Galen glowered. It sounded like a warning and a plea. *Don't make things worse.*

"It's our right to fight for our source. She's been hoarding a human. We were only encouraging her to share," the blonde one argued.

"He doesn't want you to drink from him. His blood is not mine to share. *And not yours to take*," the woman bit back with teeth of her own.

The brunette held up his fist, readying himself to fight. I tugged the woman along and ducked behind Robert and Galen. I knew how to start a fight, but hadn't a clue on how to end one.

It all happened at once. The brunette swung at Galen, the blonde at Robert. Galen crouched in time, but Robert didn't. A fist grazed the side of his face, knocking him off balance.

He recovered, but the blonde was ready. Sword out, he charged the guard. Robert stepped to the side and tripped the blonde, who fell hard. One beat later he was up, circling the guard, his eyes narrowed with malice.

Galen came at the brunette, fists bared, not bothering with his sword, ready to strike when the moment presented itself. The brunette pulled a dagger out from somewhere and came at Galen, lifting the knife high and aiming the strike in a downward motion towards his shoulder. Galen dodged and came around, punching him in the lower back. The brunette fell fast and hard—shaking the ground as his body made impact with the dirt.

As we turned to look at the fallen man groaning on the ground, the other one struck. He grabbed me by the hair, balling it up in his fist, while he pulled me towards him. Wherever his hand went, my useless body followed.

His cutlass was cold against my collar bone, sitting diagonally across my chest. It was so sharp that with each panicked breath, it sliced deeper. I could feel warm liquid pooling in the fabric of my gown. I tried not to panic, but the tangy smell of fresh blood—*my blood*—made me see stars.

"I can tell that you'd be a spit fire in bed. Do ye like it rough, girly? I bet you do," he whispered, pushing his hips against my backside. I jerked away from him, preferring the steel of the blade to his touch.

"Prince, give us Melisandre back and I'll give you your woman," he snarled through gritted teeth. He smelled like sweat and stale beer. I whimpered as he pulled my head down to his chest and sniffed at my hair. He groaned, making me dry heave in response.

The position change caused the sword to push against my breasts, slicing deep. I gasped in pain. "She has magic! I can smell it in her blood. Maybe I'll just take her instead," he said.

He had me in such a tight hold, I couldn't look around, but I could feel a blast of hot air as Galen's power surged and he shouted, "ENOUGH."

The blonde pulled me back in surprise and my head swung in a way that I got a full view of the Prince. He was standing above the brunette, with one hand aimed at him, the other at the blonde—at me. His hands were holding orbs of fire. His face was set in stone, zoned in on the kill.

He sent white-hot fire towards the brunette, showing no mercy as the man screamed in pain. Flames licked at the back of the man's neck. He tried to cover his head with his hands, producing an even higher octave of frantic cries. A truly terrible sound... to hear a grown man's agonized sobs.

Galen's flames sputtered out and smoke filled the air. The man's hair and skin were gone where fire had touched. All that remained were bloody blisters from only seconds of flame. He was shaking and retching. The smell of burnt flesh singed my nostrils. I bit my tongue to keep from vomiting on the spot.

The blonde seemed to consider his options before letting me go and sprinting away. As soon as I was free, I approached the shaking woman. "Are you okay?" I asked.

Her eyes were wide as she glanced at my chest and said, "Yes, thank you. I didn't mean to cause trouble. Are *you* okay?"

"I'm fine," I breathed.

"You're covered in blood," Galen gasped, running over and steadying me.

I peeked down. My top half was soaked in dark liquid. It looked shockingly bad, but I felt fine.

Melisandre approached me carefully. "I'm a healer, Miss. May I look you over?"

"It's nothing." I waved her off, but she ignored me, inspecting the cut under my collarbone.

"Theres a lot of blood, but your wound appears to be scabbed over..." She continued to investigate.

"Scabbed over? But how—" I touched my chest and felt no open wound—only a thin line of raised, rough skin. I released an astonished gasp.

Last night in the bath, I'd been perplexed when I found no swelling around my ankle from my fall—no scratches from the thorny brush I'd been running through, but I'd been too exhausted to give it much thought.

The slice from the sword had been much more substantial—and it had *just* happened. A wave of dizziness rolled through me, making me slow blink and stumble.

"Hold onto me for support. Robert, bring her some water," Galen barked.

"Are you a healer too, then?" she asked. Galen turned towards us with pricked ears.

"No, not that I know of," I said, shaking my head aggressively.

She looked towards the Prince. "Forgive me, Your Highness. They wanted my human. I wouldn't tell them where he was. I-I'm protective of him."

"I understand," Galen sighed. "It seems we had fortunate timing to show up when we did. I'm sorry you and your source are being harassed. A sign of the times, I'm afraid. I'll assign more guards to this section of the city."

He was winding down from his adrenaline rush—the crazed look in his eyes was starting to recede. "One more thing… Do I need to remind you of the law? Can I trust you aren't breaking it?" He gave her a stern look and she bowed, nodding adamantly. His shoulders relaxed as he accepted her answer.

A gurgled moan escaped the lifeless brunette and I studied him. His wounds were still fresh. Oozing pink blisters covered his body, while some parts had burned so deep, I could see exposed white tissue.

"Are you able to heal him?" I asked. He was going to be in excruciating pain when he woke.

"Yes, but I don't heal monsters—not when magic is in short supply. May his pain act as a reminder to stay away from me and mine." Her eyes blazed with loathing as she looked down at him, then softened when they fell back on me. "I'm Melisandre, Meli for short. I need to return home. But thank you, for everything. If you ever need me, I own Arrowroot Apothecary." She bowed deeply and hurried off.

Galen twisted towards me, glowering. I knew that look. Thea had given it to me many times. I was about to get a lecture. "Next time, talk to me before rushing in to save the day. You're too important to die over disagreements that don't concern you."

He reached out and brushed a thumb along my collar bone. It was slick with blood when he pulled away. He left me speechless, as he sucked the finger into his mouth, held my gaze, and tasted my blood. I covered my mouth in shock and jerked away from him in disgust.

"Keep your hands off of me," I growled. He backed up and put his hands in his pockets. His only reaction was a slight tick of the jaw. And then—so brief that I was sure I'd imagined it—a golden glow shimmered around him. I did a double-take, but whatever I'd seen didn't reappear.

He gave me a satisfied smile. "So you're a healer. A powerful one. Good thing, since it seems you're prone to injury."

I flushed in embarrassment. Contrary to what he probably thought of me, I didn't often find myself in dangerous situations that required *rescuing*. I could usually hold my own. If I'd been taught to fight like a man, perhaps I could've won at a fist fight too.

I glanced down at the burned faerie in front of me. Had I caused that? I felt responsible. But I didn't regret helping Melisandre. Women needed to look out for each other.

"Would you have intervened, had I not been here?" I asked, refusing to meet his gaze.

"I would've sent Robert over to assess the situation. While Melisandre didn't deserve to be harassed, those men were starving for magic. Would you fight for access to an Oasis if you were lost in the desert, dying of thirst? Not having magic makes one go mad." He continued to stare at me, seeming to actually want an answer.

"I-I'm not sure. I don't think I'd ever harm another being for my own benefit. But I've never been desperate enough to find out."

I felt my privilege in that moment. I didn't know what hunger felt like, let alone what it would be like to lose something essential to my being. I knew grief, but I didn't know that kind of loss. I played with the skirt of my dress, feeling like an impulsive, ill-mannered idiot.

"I understand the desire to help, but you must use more caution in this world. It's brand new to you. It's my fault for taking you off castle grounds so quickly." He walked ahead of me back to the horses.

Ugh, *disappointment*—even worse than anger.

When we returned to my room, Galen paused at the threshold of the door. "I'm giving you the rest of the day off. My mother can wait." Was this his idea of a peace offering? I gave a small smile at the news. He took that as an invitation to close the space between us and I scurried backwards.

"Don't come any closer. And stop trying to *seduce* me. It's wrong, now that I know you want my blood. *And* I'm your prisoner."

"You aren't my prisoner. You're our *guest*." He stood his ground.

"Is that so? Would you like to escort me back to the forest and help me go home?"

He sighed and took a step.

"Stop—stop right there. There's no future for us. You said it yourself. Faeries and humans don't belong together. I want *nothing* to do with you. I just want to go home."

His eyes narrowed. "You're *not* human. I'll give you your space, but you won't get rid of me that easily—and you're not going home yet. You need to learn about your Fae heritage... and why it's worth saving." He backed up before turning and leaving. The door locked behind him.

Prisoner.

My only visitors the rest of the day were servants dropping off food and emptying my chamber pot. A large black cat snuck in with them at some point, curling up on the foot of the bed. I was happy to have the friend, though its presence made me even more homesick.

"Hello, little darling," I cooed as it purred. "In Aurelius, we have castle cats who wander the hallways and catch pests," I said, scratching its back until it fell onto its side, stretching across my unmade bed. "Is that your job too?" It stared at me with large, slanted gold eyes.

"If faeries are so powerful, why do they need kitties to catch their mice? Have they not found a magical solution?" I scooped up the cat and plopped it in my lap, continuing to stroke it until it curled into a ball, still vibrating with contentment. "I suppose the rats here might actually be people... *spies* even." I gulped. "Which means you could be a spy too." I stared at the cat with a look of trepidation.

It peered up at me, holding my gaze, revealing nothing. I cautiously took it out of my lap, placing it back on the bed. It twitched its tail, still watching me.

"Are you a cat?" I asked. It blinked back. "Fine, keep your secrets."

For gods sakes, I was losing my mind. It was just a cat. I hoped. I'd stop talking out loud to it, just to be safe... but I'd let it stay.

And it did stay... quietly lying by my side, as I cried myself to sleep.

TEN

The Queen sent for me at sunrise. When the maids arrived, they fussed, making sure I looked presentable for Her Majesty. Did Galen know she'd summoned me? Had she learned the truth? I'd been counting on him being a buffer between us. My empty stomach roiled, making me regret not eating more last night.

Lusha dressed me in a navy gown with a high collar that covered most of my neck—a symbolic, if useless, layer of protection against the Queen. If she decided to drink my blood, there wouldn't be much I could do about it. Would I fight back or just let her have me?

I straightened my spine and decided I'd fight if it came down to it—maybe I'd get one good swing in before she killed me.

By the time I'd been escorted to her private library, I'd thoroughly terrified myself with thoughts of what she might do. Despite the dread she elicited in me, the library ambiance was bright and elegant. I had a hunch she hadn't designed this room. There was a warmth present, that so far I didn't find her capable of. It seemed like she'd be more at home in a dark cavern... or a spider's web.

Walnut bookcases lined the library on two sides. A floor-to-ceiling panoramic view of Merivale lake was the focal point of the room. Glittering aquamarine waters stretched beyond the horizon, farther than my eyes could see.

I took a seat in a worn leather chair that faced out towards the water. Turquoise waves sparkled in the distance. I watched boats sail by and wondered what it would be like to live the simple life of a fisherman. Were they staring at the castle from their boats, wondering what it would be like to live such a grand life?

"No matter where you go, there you'll be," my mother used to say to me. She'd always believed in destiny. We could try and divert course, but we'd eventually end up right where we were meant to be. With that logic, there was no point in wishing to be somebody else. We couldn't outrun destiny—we couldn't outrun ourselves. Still, it would've been nice to be *anyone* but me, at this particular moment.

I chewed on the thought, letting the view pull me into a state of temporary tranquility. My gaze fell to the black cat that had followed me here, like a tiny shadow. It lounged lazily on a cushioned seat by the bay windows, stretching before falling asleep in a ray of sunshine.

"Hello, Marigold," Sylvia said tartly, making me swivel my head in surprise. She came in unannounced, flanked by several guards and servants. The Queen wore a voluminous black dress that snaked along the polished wood floors as she made her way towards me. A severe crown sat on her head—its pointed palisades sharp as daggers.

The servants scurried in circles as they set trays of tea and biscuits on a small table. Two of them pulled a rust-colored velvet settee near the table and assisted the Queen in sitting down. She excused them once they'd poured tea, which I would *not* be touching, *thank you very much.*

And then we were alone.

"My son says that you're a world walker," the Queen said, not mincing her words. "From Erador."

I nodded in confirmation. I very much doubted that I'd brought myself here, but if it bought me time and kept her teeth out of me, I'd go along with it. I'd gotten here *somehow,* that much was true.

"And you expect me to believe that you traveled here while sleeping?"

Her cold, calculating eyes were so terrifying, it was difficult to form words. "Yes, Your Grace. I fell asleep in Aurelius, in a garden. And woke up here."

She let out a short laugh. "My sons might've fallen for your pitiful damsel act, but they're not the ones you have to convince—I am. And I think you're hiding something. Maybe you're a virgin sacrifice, pushed through the portal to appease our wrath. Or could you be a spy, sent by your realm?"

"What motive would Aurelius have to spy, Your Grace? We've lived without you for hundreds of years. The general public doesn't even know you exist." I smiled, steeling my spine.

Her eyes narrowed into slits. "You dare speak of the Ancient Kingdom to me? *I am* the rightful Queen of Aurelius and any human that resides there is an enemy to the Crown," she hissed, showing her fangs. "As for motives... perhaps the greedy little humans have bred too quickly and are seeking new land. Erador is probably overrun with rats by now. I know a few felines who'd happily fix your pest problem. All we need is a world walker to open a door for us. Know of anyone?"

She stared at me as she took a sip of tea, curving her long fingers around the teacup. Her red nails had been sharpened into points.

"If you think you can intimidate me into doing your bidding, you're wrong," I said with a glare and a death wish.

She was a hair-raising monster, worthy of a starring role in my nightmares, but I couldn't let her kowtow me. The wylks had taught me something; predators used fear to their advantage. They wanted their prey scared and on the run. *But what if instead, the rabbit stood up to the fox?*

In a heartbeat, Sylvia was at my side. One of her hands gripped me by my hair, savagely pulling my head back, while the other rested on my chest like a necklace. Her mouth hovered over my throat, taunting me. She was close enough that I could feel her breath through the thin webbing of lace that wrapped around my neck.

My blood went ice cold, while my pulse thumped violently. She slowly stood up, letting me go, then sauntered back to her seat. "Intimidation, sweet girl, is only the beginning," she crooned.

My hands went to my throat as I stared at her in shocked outrage. I was unscathed, but I'd received her message loud and clear; she was an apex predator, not to be trifled with.

"What I'm trying to understand is why your Kingdom sent *you*. Surely, there were more qualified candidates," she continued. "Can you even wield a weapon?"

My fists were balled so tight, fingernails were beginning to cut through skin. "I assure you, I wasn't *sent* here, Your Grace. And you're correct; I'm no warrior. I pose no threat."

She curved a brow. "Now that is simply not true. A woman's most dangerous weapon isn't made of *steel*. You managed to sink your claws into my son in one afternoon. He's weak—I didn't know *how* weak until I witnessed him panting after a human. *You* are a distraction. If you become a problem, I will find a solution. Do you understand?"

I nodded my head, avoiding her gaze, wanting to *roar* at her, wanting to scratch out her eyes.

"Consider yourself lucky; you're currently too important to dispose of. The power radiating from you is significant. Galen was right about that, at least." She took another sip of tea. Her lipstick looked like blood on the rim of her white teacup.

I nearly jumped out of my seat when a glowing cloud appeared above her, floating around her crowned head. I'd never seen anything like it, but it reminded me of the small flash of gold I'd seen above Galen after he'd tasted my blood. It was jungle green with a red, pulsing center—slithering around the Queen before vanishing. My hands gripped the cold, cracking leather of my seat.

"I've already sent soldiers to check the ruins where you were found—where our people originally entered Nymera. There's no open portal, and I've gathered that you can't wield magic. You'll need training if you are to take us back. You're useless to me until then. However, I intend to find out exactly what secrets are hidden in your blood. One way or another."

"Training, Your Grace?"

"You'll live in the castle with the rights of a guest. You'll master your magic and learn the customs of our people. Then, you'll open a door for us—back to our home world. And if you can't, if you *won't*... we'll kill you." With that, she clapped and a slew of servants ran over, removing dishes. I sat in stunned silence as they moved around me.

The tightness in my chest unfurled and I took a deep breath. I would live to see another day—only to die when I couldn't world walk. But after having her canines so close to my jugular, it felt like a win.

And I wasn't going to the dungeons. Had Galen convinced her that I'd be more amiable if I wasn't bitten, chained, and starved? Heat bloomed in my belly. He was the only one looking out for me. "Guards, take her back to her room. She'll dine with us tonight. Let Lusha know that the girl will need to look presentable by this evening. We have guests arriving today." She snapped her fingers and they hurried over, grabbing me roughly.

As I was dragged back to my room, home felt impossibly far. She'd called me a distraction. It had been meant as a warning, but she'd revealed a chink in her armor. She didn't want Galen growing attached to me, as if my influence might loosen the control she had on him.

He was my best chance at getting home. I just had to convince him to see things from my perspective. I bit my lip as I thought about the implications of getting closer to him. The idea was appealing, I'd admit.

I was a mere mortal moth, it would be easy enough to let the fire-wielding Prince draw me in. But was I really foolish enough to fly towards the flame?

I flitted around like a caged canary once I was back in my room. By the time Lusha arrived, I'd decided that I needed to find a library—one that wasn't in the Queen's private wing. Reading was the best way to focus my chaotic mind, and learning about this world would help me feel like I had a semblance of control.

"Lusha, is there a library in the castle that guests are allowed to access?" I asked as she readied my bath. Golden hour was upon us, drenching the white marble bathroom in warm sepia tones. My eyes grew wide when she used magic to fill the tub with steaming water, pausing to add rose oil, before continuing. Hot water poured from thin air like a faucet, inches from her outstretched hands, pooling in the copper basin.

"Yes. Several. I don't know if humans can use them though," she said apologetically.

I stepped into the flower-scented water, clenching my jaw as I adjusted to the heat. My heart sank at her words. "Why aren't humans allowed in the castle?"

Lusha began scrubbing my skin, answering in a hushed tone, "It started when King Randall died. The Queen decided that human interactions should be minimized. When faeries learned how to extract blood through hollow needles, the castle banned them completely."

"And how... how do you feel about that rule?" I asked hesitantly.

Lusha stayed quiet while she massaged shampoo into my hair and rinsed it. "You're a bold one, Miss," she eventually said. "You should be careful about who you talk to about human faerie politics. I'm a human sympathizer, but I'm from the southern part of the continent—from Elysia. Humans and faeries work side by side there. They provide us magic and in exchange we feed and house them. The system worked well for a long time, but now things are changing. My ma wrote me last week, telling me more humans have gone missing."

I stood and she wrapped a warm towel around me. I almost slipped on the wet floor, gasping, "What do you mean, *missing*?"

"Entire families are being kidnapped. Haven't you heard? My mom lost her best friend, Primrose—along with her whole family—to snatchers a few months ago. Now, Ma and Pa are struggling to find a source. I do what I can for them, but... it's not enough. Faeries have been banning together to guard the homes of humans day and night, but they continue to disappear. The snatchers are powerful—full of magic."

"But what about the Kingdom—surely they have a royal army that's helping?"

Lusha led me to the vanity and began brushing out my wet hair. "The Princes and their soldiers take turns patrolling different areas, but the snatchers always seem to be one step ahead of them. Towns are too spread out to protect everyone at once."

I looked off in the distance, deep in thought. I'd confront the Princes. There had to be more they could do—maybe something I could do.

I scoffed at the ridiculous notion. As if *I* could do anything to stop *faeries*. Thanks to my sheltered upbringing, I was nothing but a hinderance to myself and others. I'd proven that yesterday in the village when I'd tried to help and made a mess of things.

Lusha smiled as she caught my gaze in the mirror. "Don't worry, Miss. You're safe here. I hope your stay at the castle is a sign that humans will start gaining access again—that things are changing for the better." She paused, before whispering, "The Kingdom will have to do something to improve human relations soon. The riots have been getting bad in the rural villages where magic has become scarce. Word is, some families have gone weeks without blood. Magic grows the crops that feed all of Nymera. Some women are losing their pregnancies without steady access to it. The sick and injured depend on the magic from healers. Things are getting very bad, very quickly, I'm afraid."

Six gods. Galen hadn't told me how dire things truly were. It sounded as if they were at the brink of war and economic collapse.

I must've looked aghast, because Lusha put a hand on my shoulder. "I'm sorry. I assumed it was common knowledge by now, especially for humans. Where is it you come from? If these problems haven't found your home yet, maybe my family can relocate there."

Her words stabbed me in the chest. I wanted to tell her the truth, but I didn't want to get her hopes up. I wasn't a hero. "I'm sorry, but it's not safe there either," I murmured, averting my eyes.

"Ah, well. Let's be glad we're at the castle then, eh?"

As conversation lulled, my anxiety shifted to a more immediate concern—this evening. Would I be the main course... or the dessert? I studied my reflection, watching blood drain from my cheeks, as I recalled how close Sylvia's fangs had been to my neck. What fresh horrors would be waiting for me at dinner?

Lusha began applying my makeup and I made a concerted effort to relax as I watched her work. Worrying about tonight was useless. My stomach was still in knots, but color returned to my face as she put a balm on my lips, making them look like plump ripe berries. Next came my eyes; Kohl was added to make the lashes look darker and thicker. She finished with a shimmering powder over my face, chest, and arms.

"How would you like your hair done this evening, Miss?" Lusha plastered on a grin and I wanted to tell her that she didn't have to fake a smile around me. I'd had enough of those for one lifetime.

"Is it an option to wear it down?" I wasn't allowed to let it fall freely in Aurelius.

"Of course." She grinned. "At court, everyone is encouraged to flaunt their beauty. If you're still here for the Hyacinth festival, you'll see just how flamboyant faeries at Court can be."

I shook my head adamantly. "No, I prefer to avoid crowds... especially crowds that drink human blood."

She snorted. "Fair enough. I'll just tame your curls, then."

She went to work, adding a serum that smelled of almonds, before running her fingers through my hair. My eyes grew wide as perfect voluminous, shiny curls began to form. I startled in my seat when I realized she was using magic.

"Lusha, don't waste your magic on me! I don't have anything to repay you with." Heat rushed to my face as I realized how that had sounded. "I didn't mean to suggest—n-not that you'd even want my blood... I-I—"

"Don't worry." She laughed. "All employees are given a stipend of magic each week, to assist us with any duties we have around the castle. I'm a water wielder, but I can also manipulate matter—reshape it. Naturally, I'm quite gifted at styling hair."

That didn't seem right. Castle staff received magic for unessential tasks, while those in small towns struggled to grow food? It was wildly irresponsible. Did the Queen *want* her people to suffer? *To riot?*

Although... if I was being honest, Erador faced similar problems. Aristocrats wanted for nothing, at the expense of everyone else. Swap money with magic and our worlds weren't all that different.

Greed and power were insatiable beasts that fed like locusts. They were the root cause of evil... spreading through society like a plague. Even growing up in a pretty castle on a hill, I knew that. I'd dined with the monsters, watched my aunt appease them—feed them. And tonight, I would dine with new ones.

"Thank you for making me feel so beautiful tonight," I said, running my fingers through perfectly curled flaxen waves.

"We aren't done yet. Wait until you see the dresses that were delivered for you," Lusha squealed in excitement. Her exuberance was contagious. I decided I was done sulking for now. I'd resume tomorrow. She opened my wardrobe and pulled out several dresses, laying them out on my bed one by one. It was like feasting my eyes upon a treasure chest full of dazzling jewels—each gown more unique and vibrant than the last.

My gaze fell upon a slinky olive-green dress. It was different than anything I'd ever worn. Lusha helped me into it and I admired the details. The off-the-shoulder sleeves were made of a sheer fabric that draped delicately around my arms. Instead of a corset, the fabric molded to my body, feeling silky and cool against my skin. The sweetheart neckline plunged just enough to tease at cleavage. The moss colored skirt fell in soft layers, with deep slits that showed off my thighs as I walked. It was more revealing than even my undergarments back home. I gave Lusha a beaming smile.

Galen must've ordered these yesterday when my measurements were taken. How much had he paid to have these tailored and delivered in one day? My throat tightened. I'd never received a gift from a man. I'm sure it was nothing for a Prince with unlimited resources, but the gesture had still been kind.

I stood in front of a full-length mirror and gasped. Had Lusha manipulated more than my hair? I felt like one of the six gods. The gown hugged my body like a second skin. A new dress and a little makeup had transformed a girl into a woman. I felt attractive in a way that I wasn't used to. I felt *seductive*. Luscious locks of gold fell past my shoulders, making me look like my mother. I held back tears, feeling an immense sense of comfort in the idea that she was with me tonight.

"Don't cry, you'll ruin your makeup," Lusha hushed, drying my eyes with a handkerchief. Her kindness gave me the glimmer of hope that I'd needed. I took a deep breath and reminded myself that they *needed* me, therefore it wouldn't be beneficial to *eat* me.

ELEVEN

I arrived at the Great Hall before the Queen. She struck me as someone who rushed for no one. Taking in my surroundings, I decided whoever had designed this castle had impeccable taste. The room stretched on and on, continuing past the sizable Dining Room into a sprawling, domed Ball Room. The last rays of a rose-gold sunset gleamed against waxed marble floors.

Flowering vines crept along intricate, swirling copper frames that supported the high, arched ceilings. Curving panels of stained-glass windows made up most of the dome, depicting the changing moon cycle.

Vines met at a center point, dangling down around a glass chandelier. The elaborate fixture consisted of thousands of small glass spheres that cascaded like drops of rain. I inhaled sharply as I studied it. *Simply beautiful.* It certainly didn't scream *magic shortage.* How much human blood had it taken to build such a fantastical display?

My attention swung back to the table of faeries when I heard someone cough. The head of the table was empty, but all three sons dutifully sat around it. Three unfamiliar faces also stared back at me; an older couple with silver in their hair and a beautiful female who watched me through velvet lashes. I thought she looked about my age, but then remembered faeries were nearly immortal.

She had straight white-blonde hair that ran well past the curves of her petite breasts. Stunning almond shaped-eyes curved towards dainty, pointed ears. She was elegant—the epitome of ethereal beauty—and sitting right next to Galen, her focus turned to him. Side by side, they looked like a well-matched pair. A perfect balance of masculine and feminine;

both blessed with high cheekbones, strong jawlines, and refined, straight noses. Too beautiful to be human.

I stumbled when I saw a glow radiating from each of them. His was a deep golden red. Hers, a soft yellow and pink. At first I thought I'd been seeing things, but no; shimmering energy floated around faeries in various colors and shapes. I couldn't see the subtle glow straight-on, but I kept catching glimpses from my periphery. Each aura—or whatever it was—was unique, like a magical finger-print.

In Erador, auras were something oracles in traveling circuses claimed to see. I'd never been allowed to go to any of the shows that came through Aurelius, but I'd heard stories. I'd always just thought seers had a talent for telling people what they wanted to hear—a clever gift for reading body language. But now I was questioning everything I thought I knew.

There was an open seat between Rafael and the older gentleman, but I hesitated, unsure of proper protocol. Was I supposed to pull up a chair or wait to be seated?

Everyone turned to me at once and I resisted the urge to bolt. I froze in place as an inky *black* aura spilled from Rafael. My round eyes met his as tendrils of smoke stretched towards me, like two grasping hands... before blinking out of sight. His mighty power had seemed ready to swallow me whole for one terrifying moment. His jaw ticked as he turned away. Nobody else seemed to notice, their attention still on me.

Louis jumped up and helped me to my seat. "You look stunning, Marigold," he said with a warm smile. The glow that swirled around him was bright and playful—the same shade as his turquoise eyes.

I blushed at the compliment, smiling awkwardly before I sat down. "Thank you. I believe this dress suits me better than the one I arrived in." I flashed a look at Galen in silent thanks. His stare nearly scorched my soul with its voracity.

The silver-haired male looked me up and down. He had a scar that ran from his temple down to his jaw. What could leave a *faerie* with such a scar? I tried not to stare.

"Hello, Marigold, is it? Are you being courted by Rafael, then?" he asked, acknowledging our seating arrangement.

Rafael responded before I could. "Absolutely not." His sultry voice dripped like warm honey, but I could *feel* his revulsion—see it in his stiff posture. Apparently, the idea of courting me thoroughly disgusted him. Was there anyone he deemed worthy of his attention?

"I suppose *courting* isn't your style." The man gave him a knowing grin. I internally rolled my eyes. Men were *pigs*.

Studying Rafael, I noted a bruise blooming across his left cheekbone. He'd no doubt done something to deserve it. I was no seer, but I could see right through him.

He was a Prince, born too late to be King. Over time, he'd probably developed an ego complex from always being under Galen's shadow, turning to brothels and bar brawls to seek temporary relief from his shallow existence.

Many bored noblemen became rakes; they weren't unique, but of course thought they were. If he followed the typical pattern, he'd be a perpetual bachelor until he was ready to sire heirs. Only then would he choose a wife—one that would look the other way when he strayed. He was the kind of man that Ophelia warned me about—the kind my governess enjoyed.

"I haven't seen you before," the older man said. "We're longtime friends of the family. I'm Arnold. This is my wife, Dahlia... and my daughter, Isla."

"It's nice to meet you," I said softly.

"Ah! I better warn you now." He winked. "I'm essentially deaf in the right ear and the other one isn't much better—not even healers have been able to help. To be fair, I'm over five-hundred years old, so it was about time *something* broke down. If you want me to hear you, you'll have to speak up. I admit, I make a terrible dinner guest."

I groaned. Having to make conversation with Rafael for a whole meal might be the death of me. I eyed him warily, staying silent. How much blood did one have to consume to gain an aura so black?

Dahlia spoke next. "What's your relation to the family, Marigold?" She studied me with a pinched face. None of the Princes jumped in, leaving me to give a vague answer. "I am a... distant cousin—just visiting for a quick holiday."

"Oh lovely, where are you traveling from?" She could tell I was lying. I could see it in her tight-lipped expression.

This time Galen saved me. "She's from Lavinia. She's traveled here to be part of the Hyacinth Festival."

His eyes were dancing with amusement, but the joke was on him. There was no way I was going to a party full of blood-thirsty faeries—I'd rather join the wylks in the woods.

The conversation ended abruptly when the Queen arrived, as everyone stood and bowed. The skirts of her royal purple gown billowed in on an invisible wind. Tonight her aura was a ruby red storm cloud, marbled with green veins. It rolled overhead so aggressively, I half expected to hear the distant roar of thunder.

"Arnold, Dahlia, Isla—so lovely to see you. Galen and I are honored to host you over the next few months. I'm confident that your stay will end in a betrothal." She smiled widely, motioning to Isla and Galen.

Galen's eyes darted towards me and I looked away, feeling suddenly breathless. I hadn't eaten yet, but I was almost positive I was experiencing symptoms of food poisoning. There was a stabbing pain in my intestines... my chest felt heavy. I was burning up.

Why had he pursued me if he was already promised to another? He must've been hoping for one last fling before he married. Pigs. *All of them.* He could stay cursed; the soulless, blood sucking, *prick.* My dress that had been comfortable moments ago was now too tight, suffocating me.

I looked at his soon-to-be fiancé. Isla was tall, thin... flawless. If she was Galen's type, then he probably *had* seen me as a pet. I wanted to stand up and tell him that *he was the dog.* I'd just been a chew toy. One of many, apparently.

I let my petty emotions take over for the length of several deep breaths before I sat up straight and pretended Galen no longer existed. I had no claim to him... *I didn't even want him.* So what if I was feeling a little possessive? It was just a natural reaction to the stress I was under.

As food was served, conversation flowed around the table. Rafael said something under his breath and I had to lean in to hear him. "Don't be so *obvious.* You look like you want to jab poor Isla with your fork." His smooth chuckle made the nape of my neck prickle.

"I have no idea what you're talking about." I avoided eye contact, focusing on my first course of sliced pears and candied nuts over a bed of purple lettuce. The food in this world was to die for, *unlike* the company.

"You're a terrible liar. You won't survive long here if you don't learn to hide your emotions. Galen may have led you to believe we're a benign and merciful folk, but don't forget that we value power above all else, just like your humans." Rafael moved his chair closer to mine.

Scooting away from him, I attempted to converse with someone else. "Arnold, if you're over five-hundred years old, does that mean you were born in in Erador?" I spoke at full volume, hoping he'd hear me.

The conversations around the table abruptly stopped. A fork dropped and clinked against a plate. All eyes were on me.

Arnold responded, unfazed. "Oh yes, I was born in Aurelius. I'm one of the thousands who came here to start a new life. I wish we'd known how things would play out—I would've brought more blood with me." His callus laugh grated against my bones. "The day the curse took hold of us, my father dropped dead. It was a dark time, trying to find our missing magic. I watched humans march through our fallen wards, destroying what we'd built. I was there when humans savagely secured faeries in chains and burned us to ash. My first wife, my children... all *murdered*—like so many others. I tore apart the men who killed them and drank from their corpses, but it didn't bring back my family. Humans gave me this scar when I was chained and unable to heal." He motioned to the long, ugly line down the side of his face and I winced. "I don't mind it, actually. It serves as a reminder of who they really are."

I looked down at my food, trying to slow my thundering heart. The table stayed silent as he paused to take a sip of wine. "We need them—don't get me wrong—but I'll never forgive them after what I've lived through. There's a reason humans weren't blessed with our gifts; they're not *worthy*. Keep that in mind—next time you sink your teeth into one of them. Don't let them trick you into thinking they're like us." He'd seemed docile—*friendly*, even, moments ago. But he'd turned into a fuming beast before my eyes.

I checked that my hair was still covering my rounded ears.

Galen stepped in. "Arnold, I apologize on behalf of my... *cousin*. She's never met an elder and was unaware of the trauma they carry from their days in Erador."

"Quite alright. I want the future generation to know what we went through—the anger we *still* feel—so they'll never forget. We show humans too much mercy—more kindness than they deserve." He grinned at me, before continuing on his salad.

"Things are different now, Arnold," Louis said. "Most faeries believe in equal rights for humans. It would benefit the council to acknowledge this. If you haven't noticed, we're experiencing a magic shortage."

Sylvia hissed at her son, while Arnold pretended not to hear him. No one else spoke up. They ignored Louis as if he was a young radical, who didn't know his own mind. Tears hovered at my lashes, but I pushed the emotion away, along with my plate. I'd lost my appetite.

I stared at the ornate floral centerpiece, attempting to shrink into nothing, as the first course was removed, and the next plate arrived. This one came with a pairing of sparkling blood berry wine and I took a generous sip.

"I didn't expect you to prove my point so quickly," Rafael whispered.

"I don't belong here," I replied with a clipped tone.

"Neither do I."

"Of course you do. You're a Fae Prince, where else would you belong?" I asked, fiddling with the napkin in my lap.

I glanced his direction and found him intently staring back. It was the first time I dared to really look at him. His irises were a caramel-brown with flecks of gold in them. They glowed as if illuminated from within... a trick of the candlelight, most likely. Then I picked up the scent of his cologne. It was piny with notes of a crisp, drizzly morning. Goosebumps formed on my arms.

"Do you feel like you belong... where you're from?" he asked.

I cleared my throat, trying to find my way out of the misty grove I'd wandered into. *Gods*, that scent... I'd have to hold my breath to get through this dinner.

He'd asked me a question... I stared blankly at him.

"Are you alright?"

"Er... yes. What was your question again?"

He arched a brow. "I asked if you fit in back home."

Well that was a nosy question. I felt a flush crawling up my neck. "Uh... no. Not really. I suppose you're right. It doesn't take showing up in a different world to feel like an outsider."

"Do you get along with your family?" he asked, still studying me.

I treaded cautiously. Why did he even feel the need to converse with me? "I do. My mother died a decade ago. I live with my aunt. She's the only real family I have."

Lived. Past tense, because this was my home now... indefinitely. Until the Queen tired of me and drained me like a glass of wine.

"I'm sorry to hear that. The death of a parent... there's a void that never leaves you."

"Galen mentioned you lost your father... I'm sorry for your loss."

It took him a moment to respond. He focused on his drink as he swirled it. "Yes... he died twenty years ago. He wasn't perfect, but a much more competent ruler than *her*."

I choked on my wine. To say such a thing about his own mother, while she sat so close. His boldness made me smile. I covered my mouth with my napkin, stifling a laugh.

He had an expression on his face that I couldn't decipher, but it felt as if he was staring straight into my soul, rather than my eyes. And I didn't like it.

"How old are you and your brothers, if you don't mind me asking?" If he could be nosy, so could I.

"Galen is the oldest—he's one-hundred and fifty years old. I'm one-hundred and five. Louis is the youngest, he's only thirty-three. And you?"

I tried to mask my surprise. Both him and Galen had already lived longer lives than any human could hope to. "I'm twenty-one. You have a few years on me. It's strange—that you all look roughly the same age. When do you stop aging?"

"We seem to settle into our physical form around twenty-five. We age *very* slowly after that—you see that Arnold has greying hair..." He nodded his head towards the old man. "Fae can live over one-thousand years. He's considered middle-aged. He's only had one child in the last two-hundred years. We reproduce rarely, especially now."

"What must it feel like—to have so much life ahead of you? How would one fill their time?" I pondered out loud.

"Most faeries have a deep love for nature, art... reading. One would assume that wisdom would grow with age, but unfortunately that's not what I've found to be true. Many elders seem to insist on staying ignorant—stuck in another time. The same faeries that claim we're more evolved than humans, are the ones that prove that we're not. And of course it's always the small-minded thinkers that worm their way into power. The castle is full of them." He curled his lip, not hiding his disgust.

"You speak so highly of your family."

He gave a tight smile. "We can't choose our family. But I hope I can create my own someday. It's a nice thought, at least. Currently, I'm very far from that goal. And glad to be."

"Who knows, you could be a father already—with the way you boast of visiting brothels." I covered my mouth in shock.

Had I said that out loud?

His eyes darkened. "So you think you have me figured out, do you? I wonder how my brother—you know, the one you kissed yesterday—would feel about your interest in my sex life."

Rendered speechless, I turned away from him. And then I had nothing to do besides watch Isla flirt with Galen. Everything he said brought forth another giggle from her perfect mouth.

What could possibly be so funny?

Out of boredom, I decided to delicately breech another subject with Rafael as the third course came. "If humans aren't allowed in the castle, where does the royal family get their blood? Do you keep them with the livestock?"

I was pushing the limits of table conversation, but felt compelled to provoke him in the same reckless way a child might poke a sleeping cat.

"Brothels are one option," he said with a rogue smile.

"*Brothels*? The women working at brothels are *humans?*" I hissed in outrage.

"And Fae males and females. But yes, of course. What's better than blood and magic? *Sex*, blood, and magic." He said it sardonically, *trying* to get under my skin. My curiosity played right into his hand.

"Are they slaves? Are they bitten... during *sex*?" I whispered the last word.

"Slaves exist, but not legally. In most establishments the humans are treated fairly and paid well. There are limits to how many times they can be bitten in one day. It's quite an advantage for a sex worker to have magic flowing through their veins. They never want for customers." He gave a low laugh as he watched me squirm.

I resisted the urge to slap him in his obnoxiously handsome face. "You're a brute," I huffed.

"And my brother's not?"

I eyed Galen who was still talking to Isla and huffed again. "He at least pretends to be a gentleman."

He gave a crooked smile. "Is that your type, then? Charm over substance?"

I gave him an incredulous look. "At the moment, my type is *anyone* but you."

He laughed, shaking the hair from his eyes, like a shaggy *dog*. I became very focused on the peas on my plate and avoided his gaze until he took the hint and fell into conversation with Louis.

He had no decency. How dare he pick on his brother—who'd been there for me, when no one else had. And *six gods*... the way he smelled. I felt flustered. *Annoyed.* He was obviously full of dark magic and I was an easy target—a sitting duck.

Had he been casting a spell on me while I answered his intrusive questions? I wouldn't put it past him. I made a mental note to be more careful around him from now on.

Through the rest of dinner, I listened to idle chatter, hoping to learn more about the Fae. I was disheartened to find a lack of substance that echoed of dinners back home. Easily a thousand years between them, yet discussing the same empty topics. Mostly gossip.

Perhaps they were holding back on my account, but I suspected a simpler explanation; humans and faeries were all the same deep down. And then there was me. Born to be an outcast. An orphan. Alone.

This realization caused a feeling of profound sadness that left me in a fog through the remaining courses. I didn't look at Galen again, but I could feel his stare burning into me.

The last course was not a dessert, but a beverage. A golden goblet, holding a thick red liquid, was placed in front of each person. I didn't have to guess what it was. The metallic smell hit me and it took all my willpower not to gag.

"My favorite course!" Arnold looked positively gleeful as he sniffed at his cup and took a generous sip. He smiled at the Queen with teeth coated in blood.

I was nauseous—paralyzed—unable to wake myself from this nightmare. I didn't dare look up to see if the brothers were drinking theirs. With the shortage, I assumed not a drop was to be wasted. Rafael subtly poured my cup into his. I looked at him in surprise and he shrugged.

When we were finally excused, I raced for my room, while Robert followed. I'd avoided Sylvia. I'd successfully ignored Galen as well. And yet, my gut twisted every time he crossed my mind, which was *too often*. Would Isla be the one he pinned against a door tonight?

Back in my bedroom, I curled up in a sunken chair, wallowing as I digested the food and conversation from dinner. I'd survived my first meal with the entire family. Arnold had revealed himself to be a monster, taking pride in his hatred for humans—wearing it like a badge of honor.

Their curse was gruesome. They sipped on human blood like a *digestif*. I felt suddenly cold, despite the roaring fire that crackled in front of me. Arnold's family had been murdered by my kind, if what he said was true, but the anger he clung to was potent and dangerous. He wanted blood, for reasons beyond magic. He wanted *revenge*.

A jarring knock ripped me from my thoughts. I almost got up to open it, before I remembered I was locked in.

"It's Louis," I heard through the door. I invited him in, not bothering to move from my seat. "Sorry to disturb you, I—"

"You didn't bring wine?" I interrupted, gesturing for him to stop right where he was.

He laughed and disappeared, returning several minutes later with a bottle and two glasses. I thanked him with a wide grin. "Have they been keeping you locked in here?" he asked in a way that suggested he cared about my welfare.

"Yes and no. I had a meeting with your mother this morning. She's *lovely*."

He grimaced. "I apologize on her behalf. She doesn't have many redeemable qualities, I'm afraid. Be thankful she's not *your* mother."

I gave him an apologetic look before turning back towards the hearth. "Come sit down. And bring the wine."

"You're lucky I'm used to being bossed around." He gave me a lop-sided smile before plopping down beside me. "I'm sorry I didn't check on you sooner. I thought Galen was taking care of you, but when I saw that Isla had arrived, I realized he's probably been busy entertaining her. Are you doing alright?"

I wanted to let out a ferocious growl like the one I'd heard Galen use the other day, but instead I said, "I'm alive. I'm not in a dungeon. No one has taken a bite out of me. I suppose, all things considered, I should be grateful."

"You don't have to be *grateful* for any part of your situation. I'm sorry you've become part of something bigger than any of us. She won't let you go... now that she knows what you are."

"Why did Galen tell her? Did any of you consider helping me get back to my world before handing me over to her?" I turned to him, daggers in my eyes. All of the wine tonight had made me bold.

"You mean too much to this world. I know you have no loyalty to us, but you're our only hope. We've been waiting for a world walker—praying to the gods for centuries. And now, here you are, when we need you the most. There are children, innocents, an entire civilization... that will be doomed if you don't give us access to our home world. Does that not help you see our position?"

He had valid points, but how could I face my people if I made that choice without their approval? What kind of future Queen did that make me? I refused to release an entire world of wolves onto my flock. Erador had innocents too. They deserved to be protected from the hatred I'd witnessed tonight.

"I understand," I replied. "But I need to know more about the Fae. I find no redeeming qualities in your mother... your *Queen*. Does she represent the views of your people?"

"Gods, no. She serves those with an equally warped perspective and neglects the rest. I speak of my *own mother* this way. She holds the power, but she does *not* represent me or my people. Most faeries born here are sympathetic to humans—are friends with them. Please, at least get to know us. I came here to let you know that I've been assigned to train you. I'm going to teach you how to use your magic."

That surprised me enough that I finished my wine and poured another glass. "What if I can't wield magic? Will you tell your mother and let her have her way with me?"

Louis took a sip from his goblet, set it down, and then looked at me with complete sincerity. "You can trust me. I believe that you're the savior we've been waiting for. But if you aren't, my brothers and I will protect you from her."

There was that word again. *Savior*. It made me want to unleash my anger, my loneliness, my fears onto this world, just so I could prove that I was no one's hero. Instead I said, "Fine. I'll work with you. But please, don't let me down." My voice cracked as I tried to hold back the storm of tears that threatened to fall.

I felt his hand on my shoulder. "I won't. It'll get easier with time and training. I'll help you find your magic, then you'll see how wonderful it is to be Fae." His eyes gleamed with mischief as he headed for the door. "Rest well, friend. You'll need it for tomorrow."

TWELVE

I changed out of my gown with some difficulty. Lusha didn't hover as Thea did. I brushed my teeth and then crawled into bed. As I was dimming the oil lamp, I heard a knock on my door that pierced through the quiet night. My heart pounded back in response. *Who was here at this hour?*

"Yes?" I called, hoping there would be no answer. A beat later, the door began to unlock, then open. I jumped behind the bed with no other option for defense.

I cautiously peered over the mattress and saw a flash of fiery hair appear in the doorway, before Galen ducked into my room.

"Hello," he purred. His eyes smoldered as he took me in. "I'm not disappointed to find you in your nightgown, but that green dress... *Wow,* were you trying to torture me?"

"What are you doing here?" I scolded him, covering myself with a blanket. I didn't know where to look, where to put my hands.

"It's alright, I don't need a thank you for the dresses. Seeing you wear one of them was reward enough. You looked so lovely tonight."

"Galen," I sighed. "Thank you for the dresses, but *what* are you doing here?"

"I had to see you and explain. About tonight... about Isla."

His typically suave demeanor was less polished tonight. I wasn't the only one who had overindulged. His lips were stained red with blood berry wine—at least I hoped it was wine.

"Isla is a beautiful girl. And my mother would be thrilled if I chose her as a bride..."

He paused long enough that I replied, "That's nice," with a twinge of pettiness.

"There's *nothing* nice about it. I don't want Isla. I want *you*." I remained silent as he approached. "I've been having dreams of you," he murmured. Too close, he was too close.

"In fact, I woke up this morning in a cold sweat. I spent all day with Isla and you never left my mind. You must think me mental; three days you've been here. This is out of character for me, but of course, you don't know me well enough to know that. I haven't been able to function since I saw you stumbling through the woods in that horrid dress."

He ran his hand through his glossy hair until it stood on end, making it look like he'd been struck by lightning. As he moved, his warm scent wafted around me. "We have a lot to learn about each other. I don't know who you are in your world, whether you're a Princess or a peasant, but I don't care."

He reminded me of a lynx as he stood there, within arms reach... perfectly still. His eyes were dilated with predatory intent, as if he might spring forward at any moment.

It felt as if the air had been sucked from the room as I tried to form a coherent response. "If we're telling truths, I was... jealous tonight. But that doesn't change anything. I don't belong here. I want to go home. You and I—a faerie and a human—it would *never* work, even if I find myself attracted to you. And what about Isla? It sounds as if you're already engaged to be married. Is that enough reasons for you?"

"She is *not* my betrothed. My mother is responsible for bringing Isla here—not me. Are you promised to anyone in Aurelius? Is that what makes you want to rush back to your world?" He glanced at my hands still gripping the blanket. He was looking for a ring. Did he really think I would've kissed him if I was engaged to someone?

"There was someone who I cared about, but he and I weren't meant to be. I don't want to be promised to anyone, anywhere."

"You don't have to promise me forever. You don't have to promise me anything. Just give me tonight. Are you going to make me get down on my knees and *beg*?" He approached carefully, taking my hand and kissing it.

He was persistent, I'd give him that. And *damn it*, he was beautiful. Those sparkling green eyes, that golden skin, his perfectly sculpted cheekbones. I let out a shaky sigh.

There was an undeniable chemistry that drew me to him—a wild freedom that I wanted to chase. I was in a foreign world with a different set of rules. My chastity meant nothing here. The idea of giving into temptation—*gods*, it would feel like taking off a corset after *years* of not being able to breathe. It was reckless... and yet, no one was here to stop me.

It may have been the wine, or the thrill of rebellion, but I let the heady feeling take control. All the years of doing what I was supposed to, saying no when I wanted to say yes, denying myself simple pleasures for the sake of duty—it all melted away as I stared at the auburn-haired Prince before me.

I closed the space between us and kissed him with everything I had. As our lips met, I could feel a smile spread across his cheeks. He tasted of smoke and wine—of danger. I pulled him closer. This was a mistake and I didn't care.

I dropped the blanket and then we were body against body. His hands roamed down my back and over my curves; I could feel everything through my thin gown.

His tongue found mine and I opened for him, until we were tangled together. I pulled at his hair, while he lifted my chemise higher and higher, then his hand was on my bare thigh. It sent a current of scalding, hot energy through me.

His kisses weren't sweet like Deric's. They were deep and searching... reaching every part of my nervous system.

My breath caught when he began exploring places that had never been touched. I gasped, wrapping a leg around him to balance myself, as he continued to tease me, traveling up... up...

This was moving too fast. I should push him off. I should demand he leave at once. He moved even higher... and then he stopped.

I was shivering.

Why had he stopped? I needed *more*. I let out a whimper.

Galen's eyes were simmering embers. "Tell me what you want," he whispered.

I couldn't breathe. I could barely speak. "More."

"More what?" He smiled.

"Please... Touch me."

"So polite," he said, nipping at my bottom lip. He pushed my underwear aside and I tensed. "You're shaking. Are you nervous? Am I the first one to touch you like this?"

I nodded helplessly as his fingers roamed between my legs, causing a throbbing ache deep inside of me. They moved slowly, as if trying to memorize each valley and peak. I took shallow, quick breaths, feeling light-headed.

"Fuck... how lucky am I?" he breathed, gently spreading me open, rubbing the moisture that had formed. Warmth pooled at my core. I laid my head against his shoulder, wanting to sink my teeth into it.

"You're so wet. I want you just as badly." He guided my hand to the hardness that pressed against his buttoned pants. I moved tentatively, tracing the shape of him.

He encouraged me to continue roaming, while his breath hitched with every stroke of my hand. But I felt clumsy and unsure compared to him. He knew *exactly* what he was doing. The room started to spin.

He nibbled my ear and licked down my neck, moving from one sensitive spot to the next, until I felt loose and tight, hot and cold. I was in purgatory, teetering between heaven and hell. It was excruciating... needing more than he was giving me. But I didn't know what *more* entailed.

Galen stepped away, removing his top layers, and breaking the spell. *This was moving too fast.*

"I'm not ready to..."

He closed the distance between us and kissed away my worries. "We're not going to have sex tonight. I just want to touch you. Let me pleasure you."

I nodded, dizzy from a potent mixture of excitement, nerves, and alcohol in my bloodstream.

His upper body was sun-kissed, covered in a thin layer of golden hair. Tight muscles ran down his abdomen. He looked built to fight, to hunt... to seduce women. I'd never been presented with anything so tempting and so terrifying.

He gently guided me to the bed, laying beside me. "I'll take the lead. If at any time you don't feel comfortable, just tell me to stop."

I needed to tell him *no*. Instead, I wrapped my fingers around the back of his head and pressed my body against his, trembling with anticipation.

We didn't rush as we laid there kissing, touching... My body temperature slowly rose until I was burning with fever.

Cupping my breasts, he rubbed lazy circles around hardened nipples, then licked and sucked through the fabric of my gown, until the peaks were unbearably sensitive—until I was moaning and arching into his touch. He moved lower down my stomach, trailing kisses along the way, while he lifted my chemise.

"Sit up," he commanded, sliding the gown up and off. My underwear was next. With one flick of his wrist, I was naked.

I should've felt shy, but instead I felt *free* and uninhibited. Was this what it felt like to be Fae? Was my faerie blood the reason I was so willing to betray my good sense and bask in this moment?

Galen prowled over me like a mountain lion, pinning me beneath him, caging me in. My legs were splayed on either side of him as he bent down to lick along the hollow dips of my hips, my belly, up to my breasts, suckling a nipple into his mouth. Then he kissed me with an intensity that left me panting.

"Your magic sings to me, Marigold. Can you feel it?" Pressure was building beneath my skin, like a volcano aching to erupt. I was molten lava. My blood felt effervescent, as if my veins were filled with sparkling wine.

With one hand still fondling my breast, he brought his other hand lower, tracing it down my abdomen... beneath my navel. He paused for a moment, making eye contact with me... before sliding a finger inside of me. I bucked in surprise. He watched with a grin as I came apart at the seams.

"Relax for me, Marigold." He ran two fingers down my middle and over the bud of my sex in a rhythmic pattern. My breathing grew fast and shallow. I was clawing at him now.

"Galen... please. It's... too much," I said each word between gasps.

"Do you want me to stop?"

"*Gods, no.* Do... not... stop." I lifted my hips, trying to outrun the feeling chasing me. I was writhing, arching, aching, as his fingers continued to play me like a piano.

"Hold still. Let it come to you." He ran his tongue along my neck, before returning to my lips, teasing me as I tried to kiss him back. I tilted my head until my neck was completely exposed, trusting him not to bite me. I was a fool for trusting a blood thirsty *stranger*. But in this moment, I didn't care. All I wanted was him.

He circled around a bundle of nerves and then pushed one finger... two fingers, inside of me, pumping in and out. Slow and deep. He curled his fingers, hitting a spot that made me cry out, as he swirled round and around.

I moved with his rhythm, hungry for friction. I was a wave crashing against the shore... over and over. I left my body as I reached the pinnacle of an ancient song strumming in my core. My muscles spasmed and clenched as I gripped his shoulders. He supported me until my legs stopped shaking. And then I melted into the bed, covered in a sheen of sweat, as I came back into myself.

He eased his fingers out of me and settled his hips on top of mine, pressing his full weight into me. I could feel him throbbing against my thigh. He stared down at me for a moment, wonder on his face, before he rolled to his side and propped his head against his hand.

"Satisfied?" He couldn't contain his smirk.

"You..." I breathed. "Are exceptionally gifted at *that*." I gave him a delirious smile. He bit my bottom lip and tugged in answer, sending another wave of pleasure through my core.

"Do you need me to help you relieve your... I've never... touched a man that way," I said awkwardly.

"We'll do it all soon enough, if I have any say. Tonight, this is enough. You're perfect." Galen nuzzled into me and threw a leg over one of mine, locking me in place.

After a few minutes of warm, content silence, I asked sleepily, "Should you leave now? We don't want to be caught."

"Do you want me to leave?" Before I even had a chance to respond, he was on me again; kissing my throat, making me see stars, until my nails were digging into his back in blissful agony.

"Is it alright if you stay? We won't get in trouble?" I choked out the question as his tongue ran along sensitive skin. The Queen's cold eyes flashed into my mind and I shivered. Or perhaps it was his mouth giving me the chills.

"We won't get in trouble. It isn't considered taboo to share a bed with someone here. Sometimes multiple someones. We don't adhere to the same rigid rules as your humans. My mother might not like it, if she thinks you're pulling me away from her choice of bride, but perhaps she should get used to the idea of us."

My mind was still stuck on the multiple someones. "You mean sex with more than one person... at the same time?" I must have misunderstood him.

"Yes. You *are* innocent, aren't you?"

I cringed, my cheeks growing hot. "You come from a sheltered upbringing. Will you tell me more about your life back home?" he asked, pulling away to study me. I didn't feel ready for him to know who I was.

"Maybe later." I smiled, tugging him on top of me. His gleaming white teeth beamed down at me in the soft orange glow of the fading oil lamp. We didn't talk for the rest of the night.

The next morning, Galen was out of my bed before dawn. I instantly missed his warmth. I watched him dress and tried to contain my awe at the back muscles that rippled as he bent down to retrieve his clothes.

"I have to get ready for a meeting with the Elders. You'll find that I have a relentless schedule. What I would give to stay here and eat you for breakfast—maybe lunch too." He bent down to kiss me goodbye on the forehead. "I'll see you at dinner. Don't be surprised to see Isla. Her family will be living here until the festival. I'll talk to her soon—let her down gently."

"No... don't!" I cried out with a little too much urgency. "Don't change your plans for me. Last night was a mistake... The wine went to my head. I need to focus on returning to Erador. I can't afford to be distracted."

I couldn't allow myself to care for him, was the truth I left out. I needed Galen's friendship more than whatever *this* was. If I lost him, I'd have no one. Not to mention Sylvia's *wrath*.

There were a million reasons why this would never work. Last night shouldn't have happened. I'd once again been reckless and selfish—caught in a perfect storm of alcohol, hormones, and pent up... *something*.

But when his eyes narrowed, it felt as if I'd been punched in the gut. I'd hurt him and he wasn't hiding it. "If that's what you'd prefer. Then, of course. I'd hate to be a distraction."

He turned and left without another word, severing our connection with the slam of a door. I laid in bed awhile longer, thinking of our incredible evening together... and how easily I'd ruined things. I'd pushed him away, just like Deric.

I'd never witnessed a courtship founded on feelings—on love. I couldn't remember much about my parents' relationship. There was a fog that existed over my early years. Ophelia had told me it was due to witnessing such a traumatic event. I remembered almost nothing of my father. He'd left no impact on me, other than feelings of abandonment. I knew deep in my bones that he and my mother hadn't been a love match.

Just like the women that came before me, I wasn't destined for love. Thinking I had choice would only complicate things, if I managed to get back to Erador. I'd channel all of these feelings into serving the Crown... even if I didn't want it. Romance only existed in books anyways. And love with a faerie Prince... it was so unfathomable, it was laughable.

He didn't want a mortal human. He'd grow bored of me once the novelty wore off, then disappointment and pain would be all that was left. I'd made the right decision.

I didn't have much time to ponder my feelings. Lusha came in with a tailor and they began getting me ready for my first day of training. I couldn't believe what I was seeing as they fitted me for tunics, shirts, leggings, and even leather armor. *Why did I need armor?*

"Who sanctioned this? Surely not the Queen," I said while the tailor circled me, measuring and pinning.

Lusha giggled before saying, "Prince Louis and Rafael both insisted it was necessary for your training. You don't like pants, Miss?"

"I don't dislike them, I've just never worn them," I said defensively. Lusha raised her brows in confusion, as if she thought I'd lived under a rock before coming here. *Not under a rock; just from a different rock entirely.*

"Lusha, I need to tell you something—*privately.*"

She nodded before asking the tailor to leave us for a moment. "What is it, Miss?" Her blue eyes were so sincere, it was easy to open up to her.

"You may want to sit down," I said, pointing to one of the cushioned chairs in front of the hearth. She hesitated for a moment before complying.

"Lusha, I'm not from Nymera." Her eyes grew large, but she didn't interrupt me. "I lived in Erador until a few days ago. I somehow crossed a bridge to this world while I was sleeping. The Princes found me in the forest... and I believe you know the rest."

Lusha's face contorted from surprise to professional neutrality. "Please don't tell anyone," I pleaded. "I don't know *how* to world walk—I don't know that I'm capable of *any* magic. I don't want to become a false prophet for your people. I just want to get home."

Lusha gave a firm nod before standing and brushing her skirts. "Well, that explains a few things," she said slowly. "It seems almost too good to be true. We've waited so long for a way back to Erador. Your secret is safe with me. I'll do what I can to help you adjust to your new life here. And I might have the occasional burning question or two." She gave a shy smile and I felt a wave of relief roll through me.

"Of course. I'm happy to answer questions. After all, it's the home world of your people too."

"So you don't wear pants in Erador?" We laughed together before inviting the tailor back in.

Thirteen

I met Louis on the terrace overlooking the gardens. He was wearing a sky blue shirt that complimented his copper hair. Over it he wore a brown leather vest that laced up the middle. He also wore bracers, brown breeches, and a sword at his hip. It seemed a little overkill for our first lesson. He led me to a private space, a short walk away, while I stayed tucked behind him, feeling self-conscious in leggings and a tunic.

White Corinthian pillars lined the small circular area that appeared to be designated for sparring. Crows sat atop the pillars, cawing and flapping their wings at us. They were heckling me—waiting for me to embarrass myself. I scowled at them.

Springy, soft grass blanketed the ground. Haystacks draped in a tough canvas material looked designed for target practice. A rack of wooden swords and other weapons I'd never seen before sat outside the circle, waiting to be wielded. I shuffled my feet nervously, feeling exposed without heavy skirts to hide beneath.

"Is your clothing uncomfortable? You keep tugging at your pants," Louis asked with a playful grin.

"This is my first time *wearing* this type of clothing, thank you very much. You may keep your observations to yourself." I crossed my arms and glared at him, daring him to say another word.

"Now, how would you learn anything if I did that?" Louis circled me with an eagle-eyed keenness. I stiffened as he moved my feet wider, tucked my shoulders back, and told me to engage my core. A mask of anger was better than how I really felt—like an absolute fraud.

"Have you ever used a weapon before? Have you ever been taught to defend yourself? Any experience hunting?" Louis asked.

No, no, and no...

"Unfortunately, where I'm from, women of my position aren't allowed to participate in such things. We're taught the life-saving skills of cross-stitching and pianoforte." I couldn't hide my bitterness. If Ophelia *had* somehow known I was going to come here, she'd left me ill-equipped.

"So we're starting from scratch. Well, the good news is, we have a blank canvas to work with." He gave me a kind smile. I already felt defeated. "Don't look so blue. We'll ease you into everything. There are certain exercises you can practice to quiet your mind and still your body. They're necessary for controlling your magic. We'll start there. Then, we're going to work on some basic movements that'll help you find balance and build strength. Next, I'll teach you how to defend yourself. You'll learn to wield magic as you grow stronger, both mentally and physically."

"Will you teach me to attack too?" Defense was great, but I wanted to be self-reliant. I didn't want to depend on anyone in this world—or Erador, for that matter. If I ever got back.

"Yes, but that's not a priority at the moment. We don't know what kind of magic you wield yet, although Galen mentioned something about healing powers? Some magic takes as much effort as breathing. Other types take practice and precision. Your healing seems to happen passively, but there's likely more to it. I'm not a healer, so we'll have to find someone who is—someone who can mentor you."

Melisandre. I'd ask Galen if I could arrange a meeting with her. "I've been healing quickly since arriving here, but I haven't *felt* any type of magic when my body has mended itself."

I tried to remember the last time I was truly injured or sick. It had been a long while. I'd gotten Scarlet Fever as a child. Perhaps I'd been healing fast for years now, but with my sheltered lifestyle, hadn't noticed. That felt too pathetic to admit out loud.

"I think you'll be surprised at how easily it will come to you. You've been living with humans your whole life. You're just beginning to learn what it means to be an immortal. Your magic will emerge as you grow stronger."

"Y-you think I'm immortal?" I stuttered.

He mentioned it so breezily, like it wasn't yet another soul-shattering piece of information. I thought of Ophelia, my only living family member, aside from my estranged father. She couldn't be immortal—she had silver in her hair. But I *had* always thought she was too perfect to be human... *Aku's Hell*, was she hundreds of years old like Arnold? I braced myself on my knees as stars danced across my vision, earning a quirked brow from the Prince.

"Technically, Fae aren't immortal," Louis quipped. "We're just very long-lived. Magic slows the aging process. Not only do you produce magic, but now that we know you're a healer, we know you can access your magic... so congratulations, you're not cursed."

"And that's because I'm, supposedly, both human *and* faerie?"

"Precisely. I know of one other person like you—a hybrid."

"You do? Who?"

"You don't discuss this with anyone else. Understood?" Louis rarely looked serious, but he did right now.

"Who would I tell?"

"True. And, well... it's a poorly kept secret. Since he isn't limited by the curse, he's much more powerful than the rest of us—just like you might be." He was drawing it out.

"*Who*, Louis?"

"My brother, Rafael. It's a sensitive subject... we have a lot of family drama. You see, Rafael is a bastard—" He paused when he saw my face.

"He most certainly is!" I declared, crossing my arms. The crows started cawing, echoing his laugh.

"Hah! To be sure, but I meant Sylvia isn't his mother. Our father had a human consort. She became pregnant, and humans and faeries *don't* breed—it's strictly forbidden. But our father didn't make her abort the baby as would be customary. Instead, he took in the child and raised him—as a recognized Prince, nonetheless. Our mother was furious. Or so I've been told—I wasn't born yet. But honestly, when is she not angry? The other day she—"

"Louis, focus!" I grinned, shaking my head.

His freckled cheeks reddened. "Sorry. Where was I... Oh yes—those close to the family knew he wasn't hers, which mortified her. She was—*is*—horrible to him. But back to the point—he's half-human, half-faerie. The combination seems to break the curse."

Rafael said he went to brothels for sex and magic... Or maybe he'd said that's where other faeries went. But he'd taken my goblet of blood. Did he drink it just so I wouldn't have to? That didn't track—he was too much of an asshole to do something so selfless.

"If human faerie pairings can break the curse through their hybrid offspring, why would that be discouraged?" My mind was spinning. Was my mother a faerie? My father? I couldn't recall obvious features. Were they *both* half?

"You have too much faith in us. Faeries and humans are ancient enemies. We've figured out how to co-exist with this curse, but some elders still believe themselves above humans. Others believe that breeding with humans will dilute a faerie's power. My mother and her advisors... they benefit from that kind of intolerance. Magic is a commodity here—one that they control. Hybrids who don't depend on blood threaten the system they've built."

"So they encourage divisiveness," I scoffed.

"Unfortunately, it goes beyond that. There are some crimes that are considered unforgivable—breeding with humans is now one of them. When our father reigned, it was already frowned upon, but after he passed, it became a criminal offense. If faerie-human relations result in a child, the couple is expected to stand trial. And they're almost always sentenced to death—their children as well. Father would've never stood for it. He valued every life, even after his parents and brother were murdered by humans."

I covered my mouth as bile threatened to rise. In this world, people like me were killed for simply existing. As *children*. Entire families eliminated. Evil didn't even begin to describe Sylvia and her advisors.

I wrapped my arms around myself, while my heart sat in my throat. "So Raf and I are the only two hybrids you know of?"

"Yes, and I'm sure Sylvia thought about trying to kill Raf after our father died, but he's too strong—he's the most powerful shadow wielder in Nymera. My mother is cruel, but she's calculating. She's not going to start a fight that she won't win."

"And Raf's mother?" I asked, already knowing the answer.

"Killed. Not long after he was born. Even our father couldn't protect her," he said, looking at the ground. My heart sank.

"Sylvia murdered her?" My voice caught as I tried to get the words out.

"I don't know. No one in our family will talk about it. But that's what I've always assumed."

Tears formed in the corners of my eyes. Raf lost his mother without ever getting to know her. No wonder he seemed to hate everyone around him. He'd been forced to live amongst those who wished him dead—who'd killed his mother. The *fury* he must feel. It was a feat that he could even sit at the same table as the Queen.

"We do our best to have a justice system—to abide by a set of laws. My brothers and I are responsible for overseeing the training of the Royal Fae Army. Rafael and I are expected to travel to villages across Nymera to maintain peace and order, with specialized teams. We monitor how magic is being used—how shortages are affecting the citizens. We've taken vows to protect faeries *and* humans. I've never come across a hybrid child, but if I did, I'd look the other way."

Louis's voice dropped to a whisper. "As for you... I don't think the Elders have found out what you are yet, but even when they do, they won't kill you. To them, a world walker is much more valuable than a dead hybrid. A world walker creates infinite possibilities. They're at least predictable in their motives; gaining and keeping power is what drives them."

The faeries could've broken this curse long ago, if they'd been allowed to mate with humans. Intolerance shaped this society, and now it was buckling in on itself—because of a self-perpetuating *sickness*—because of a hateful policy that helped no one, except for the Queen and her council.

Louis called on his water magic, swirling it around us until we were encased in a thin bubble. "This is a shield. Once you learn to wield magic, you'll want to use one whenever you're discussing a sensitive topic. There are spies everywhere. Usually the smallest creatures make the best spies. *Always* be on your guard."

His eyes darted towards the birds that sat on the columns, then scanned the rest of our surroundings before asking, "Are we on the same team?"

I tilted my head, meeting his hard gaze. "What do you mean?"

"Are we in agreement that my mother is unfit to rule? That she needs to be stopped?"

My mouth fell open. "Yes... if you're asking if I'm on your side or Sylvia's, then the answer is *yours*. Respectfully, Louis, your mother is a lunatic."

"That's why I'm so funny—all the trauma." He grinned, before his face grew dour. "The Elders are a group of six faeries that were all born on Erador. Faeries continue to grow in strength as they age, so they're all extremely powerful. They've acted as the council for the royal family since before the crossing. They're particularly involved with criminal justice and human-faerie relations. They haven't been chosen by the people, but instead arrived on this world with power and have continued to keep it. My mother is fully aligned with their mission to keep Fae lines pure. My grandmother is one of the six, and she taught my mother to look down on... well, most people, but especially humans. Their prejudice has gone unchecked since my father died. And now their leadership threatens us all. Raf and I want to see their reign end."

I stared at him, pleasantly surprised. I hadn't expected *treason* from Louis. And against his own mother. "And how do you plan to do that?"

"We'll need your help. And you'll need to learn how to use your magic. Quickly. There is more, but we aren't in an ideal setting to discuss details. Rafael will find you when the time is right and tell you the rest."

I lit up with hope at his words. Princes with power and persuasion, who also dreamed of a better world; I suddenly felt less alone.

"I'll help you." I paused, furrowing my brow. "What of your *other* brother? Is he not to be trusted? If you overthrow your mother, will he become King?"

Louis swallowed, throat bobbing, as he stared at the ground. "Galen is in a difficult position. He's been groomed to be King, which means he's often stuck in the middle of political arguments between the family. He actively works with the Elders, as heir to the throne, but he has no voice at the table. Our mother tests his loyalty—expects him to prove himself to the Crown. I wouldn't wish to trade places with him."

My mouth went dry and my chest suddenly felt tight. Louis noticed my expression and said, "It gets worse, unfortunately. Arnold is one of the six Elders. The entire council is encouraging a marriage between Galen and Isla to keep the royal family linked to the council. It's too risky to tell him anything. Who knows what he might confide to her—and in turn, what she'd tell her father."

My heart skipped a beat when he mentioned Isla. I'd encouraged Galen to pursue her. The sweltering sun beared down on me as I chewed my nails, wracked with guilt. "So if you wage war against the Elders and your mother... what will he do?"

Louis sighed. "Only Galen can decide that, when the time comes."

I felt sick to my stomach. But what was to be done? I couldn't let my feelings for him distract me from getting home—and I *really* didn't want to end up in the middle of their family feud. Louis had confirmed what I already knew; I couldn't get involved with Galen. And I had to get *stronger*. This world was getting more dangerous by the second.

I cleared the lump in my throat and said, "Please... tell me how I can access this magic that apparently runs through my veins. I'm sick of feeling useless."

Louis's frown curved into an impish grin. "Happily. Did you bring your blood sacrifice? It's required the first time you wield. A rabbit or kitten will do."

I gawked at him, speechless.

He cackled, leaning over and slapping his knees. "I'm kidding. I just needed a laugh after all that heavy talk. You should've seen your face."

I glared at him before punching him in the arm. "Not funny."

"I beg to differ," he laughed, then took a deep breath. "Magic is as ancient as the universe—at least, that's what faeries think. We believe magic created our worlds. It also created six gods to rule the worlds. Gods created us and through them, through the universe, we've been gifted with the ability to wield magic."

I had a difficult time believing in the gods, but I also would've never believed in magic. My mind was more open than it had ever been. Anything was possible.

"There's a cost to spending energy. If you run ten miles, your body will need water, food, and rest to recuperate. It's no different with magic. Fae bodies are powerful conduits, capable of channeling a large amount of energy. If you use more magic than your body can handle, you'll burn out and die. Luckily, we're well designed. Our bodies are quick to build muscle—to recover from physical activity. And we're difficult to kill.

"We also have more evolved senses than humans. You might not think so in your current state, but it sounds like you haven't had many opportunities to test your skills. Perhaps that was on purpose... maybe someone didn't want you to know what you are. You must train your body to hone your senses. Fitness and endurance are the most important parts of training. The stronger you are, the more magic you can safely wield."

Had Ophelia purposefully kept me in the dark? For so many years I hadn't known why I'd been so sheltered—more so than most women in Aurelius, which was saying something. In turn, I'd pushed against the restraints however I could. Had she been trying to prevent me from learning that I was different? If so, it hadn't worked. I'd always felt like a misfit. And the loneliness I'd felt from being isolated and overprotected had been excruciating.

Louis continued. "There are six types of elemental magic. Earth, Wind, Water, Ice, Fire, and Shadow. Each element was created by a god. The god who protects and guides me is Sivo, ruler of water. He has gifted a sliver of his power to me and all other water wielders. I'll channel his magic until I turn to dust and my power cycles back to him."

"I know of the gods," I said, happy to finally know something. "Most of my people have lost faith in them though. You have proof that they exist?"

"Proof of the gods?" Louis raised his brows at me. "You need more proof than *magic*?"

"I-I... don't see why they'd bless faeries with so many more gifts than their human counterparts—if we both originate from the same place. It doesn't seem right."

"Ah," Louis said softly. "Well, faeries would consider a human's ability to breed easily and often a gift that we don't possess. Who's to say we have more gifts? We're the ones who've been exiled and cursed, after all."

I didn't bother arguing about it, so Louis went on. "Most faeries can channel an element—some can wield multiple. Fire, ice, and shadow are more... *volatile* than other types of magic. They can overtake an undisciplined wielder. Magic can kill its master if not properly harnessed." He emphasized the point with a stern expression.

"And then of course, there's our shifting abilities. All faeries have an animal form—a *pneuma*. It manifests when it decides to. I cannot shift yet, but my brothers can."

"*Pneuma...*" I repeated, letting the foreign word roll of my tongue.

"Yes, it translates to *spirit animal* in the language of the Fae."

"Will you tell me what your brothers are?" I asked, trying to feign only mild interest.

I imagined they were both sharp-toothed predators. I thought of the deliberate way Galen stalked me before he'd seduced me last night. My skin prickled as the flash backs threatened to make me flush.

"No. They'll show you if and when they want to. What if you were to shift and become a butterfly? You'd be an easy target and viewed as inferior to many. Some faeries will proudly display their animal form, while others will never reveal it. Pneumas can become status symbols—another way to divide our already fragile social system. It also takes considerable magic to shift back and forth. What was once as natural as breathing is considered a luxury for many now."

"When do Fae typically learn how to shift?"

Louis flashed me a look I couldn't quite read. "Most can shift after puberty—around eighteen years old. I'm not sure what the gods have in store for me, but they seem to be insisting on my patience."

"You believe the gods decide what your animal form is?"

"I do. Our powers aren't always passed through lineage. It's much too random. I can wield water. Galen, fire. Raf, shadow and earth. My mother also has earth magic, but as you now know, Raf isn't related to her. Animal forms are even more unique. It's rare for family members to take the same form."

I yawned, the lack of sleep beginning to catch up to me. Louis shot me an expression of mock-outrage. I grinned back and said, "Are you ever going to *show* me what you're capable of? Or are we going to discuss the theory of magic for the rest of the lesson?"

Louis narrowed his eyes at me before stepping back and aiming his palms towards the sky. His shield dissolved into mist. Water droplets began forming, hovering above his cupped hands. Soon he was rotating a ball of water the size of a dinner plate—moving it up and down with an invisible force. He formed the ball into a life-sized dolphin, making it race circles around us. Suddenly it was an eagle, soaring above us, before turning into a *puddle* and dumping on my head.

"You-You're going to pay for that!" I sputtered, my soaking hair hanging over my eyes. I was drenched. Louis laughed as the surrounding birds crowed along with him.

"Will I? Why don't you try getting me back... with *magic*." I wanted to wipe that smug smile off his face more than anything.

I tried to reach inside and search for any type of feeling or source I could pull from. It was impossible—I felt ridiculous. I held my hands up in a threatening posture, before dropping them to my sides. The frustration that followed caught me by surprise as tears threatened to fall. I would *not* cry at my first training session.

I would not.

"Hey, it's alright. I haven't even told you what to do yet—what to feel for. I just thought your anger might bring something to the surface. Don't worry, you're just too sweet for retaliation. It isn't a character flaw."

Sweet? My blood froze over at the idea that I was sweet. Women were little more than chattel in Aurelius. Men wanted us docile. We weren't allowed to show any personality *besides* sweet. It made me furious.

My rage awoke something in my veins. I felt a wave of dizziness before a pins and needles sensation covered my hands. I leaned into the discomfort and frost began to form on my fingers. I gasped in surprise and the ice vanished, like it had been a mirage.

"Did you— Did you see that?!" I'd found *magic* inside of me. The rush was exhilarating. Glowing pride washed over me.

"Ice wielder." Louis smiled. "Now, can you please stop insisting you're not Fae?" I tried to bring back the magic, but it was elusive, like trying to force a sneeze.

"Ugh. Why is it so difficult?" I kicked a rock and sent it sailing towards a column. Apparently, I had a faerie temper to go with the magic.

"You're not ready to use serious magic. It's impressive that you were able to access anything on your first day of training. You need to be cautious when experimenting with it until you're stronger. Don't practice without me until I say so. Understood?"

I was dying to see the ice again—to master it—to feel less vulnerable in this foreign land, but I agreed and meant it. "You said faeries are difficult to kill. What does that mean exactly?" I flexed my hands open and shut, straining to bring magic to my fingertips.

"Yes. While most of us don't heal as quickly as a healer would, we do heal from most injuries as long as we have magic in our blood. If we don't have magic, we're just as helpless as humans."

Helpless as humans. Humans weren't helpless. We were clever, adaptable... capable. I felt a flicker of frost coat my fingers again.

"If we're decapitated, we're dead. Unless there happens to be a healer nearby who can put us back together."

"You mean to tell me, if someone *cut off your head*, and I learned to use my healing powers... I could make you whole again? That is the most *absurd* thing I've heard so far." Even as I tried to accept that I was one of them, my humanity shuddered. No wonder humans had wanted faeries out of Erador.

"Correct. We can regrow most of our organs as well, although it hurts like a bastard. The easiest way to kill us is to go for the heart. Fire can burn a heart to ash, shadow can turn a heart to dust, and ice can freeze a heart until it shatters. It's the one thing we can't regrow—well, that and our heads—but if the brain or heart are simply injured, we can heal them."

He was so nonplussed about this. Meanwhile, I felt warning bells going off, telling me this world and its inhabitants were dangerous—telling me to *run*.

Finally, it was time for the physical side of training. Louis proceeded to kick my ass for the next hour. He made me run laps, lift weights, exercise different muscle groups, and practice my balance as he came at me from different offensive angles.

He taught me how to get out of several different holds using my size to my advantage and how to throw him off balance so I could escape his grasp. He showed me how to break a nose with a headbutt to the face and how to strike with a dagger in a downward thrust. There was also a spin maneuver that ended with a knee to the groin. There were a few noblemen in Aurelius I would've like to use that particular move on.

By the time we were finished, my mind, body, and spirit were mush. I was so sore and overwhelmed by all the new information that I requested dinner in my room that evening. Galen did not visit me.

FOURTEEN

My days began to fall into a familiar pattern of training, reading, and dinner with the Ruhn family. Galen had been giving me the cold shoulder ever since the night we'd spent together. It left me confused and pathetically pining for him. When had I become someone who *pined* for a man?

Every evening, Isla sat next to him, laughing at everything he said, while I gritted my teeth until it was time to be excused. He usually looked a bit hollow and distant, barely looking my way.

Rafael rarely joined us for dinner, but when he did, his behavior towards me was aloof at best. He didn't *seem* like a revolutionary. Yes, he had motive, but according to Louis, Raf basically lived at the local brothel. That didn't sound like someone who had the motivation to rise up against his Kingdom. Still, I waited for him to pull me aside.

When Galen assigned Robert to be my personal guard, I began to have more freedom around the castle; though, he was such painfully *dull* company, I sometimes wondered if Galen was trying to punish me. The guard still refused to answer any of my questions with more than a few mumbled words, but at least I was able to walk the gardens and use the library. Despite being a grubby human, I'd been granted access to all of the public libraries in the castle, but it was the *Grand Library* that I always found myself in.

The first time I'd entered through its gilded double doors, I'd been wonderstruck. Adorned in pastel tones, it glittered like a sunrise. It looked more like a temple than a library, which made perfect sense to me—there was nothing more sacred than a room full of books.

Massive arched windows illuminated the space in bright natural light, making the white marble floors shimmer. Lavender pillars, made of Kunzite, lined the wide aisle that stretched down the center of the room. The purple stone was translucent, refracting light like crystal when the sun touched it.

Diamond chandeliers, cloaked in baby pink cherry blossoms, floated above polished tables that sat near the entrance. The flowers created a sweet nutty scent that hung in the air and settled into the pages of the books—thousands upon thousands of books—sitting on Mahogany bookshelves in neat rows. The shelves extended to the back of the room, towards two sets of gilded spiral staircases that led to a second-story balcony, overlooking the rest of the space.

Murals, featuring all six gods and their stewards, covered the vaulted ceilings. They stared down at me, idling away on their thrones of painted clouds. I rolled my eyes at the beautiful, omniscient beings who probably looked at us as if we were ants.

Today I sat at one of the library's tables, fidgeting. A pile of books on elemental magic sat beside me, while Robert stood nearby, arms crossed. I was propped on my elbows, flipping through a book on medicinal magic, when the beam of light spilling across my page, suddenly disappeared.

I turned towards the window for an explanation, expecting to see rain clouds. Instead, I saw a dark haze floating above me. My heart stopped as I watched a form materialize. *Rafael*. He... he'd just appeared beside me, out of thin air. I swallowed hard as I took in his black leather armor and his stone-faced expression.

Was I hallucinating or had he just arrived in the form of a black cloud?

I didn't want to give him the satisfaction of appearing awe-struck, so I lifted my chin and squared my shoulders as I acknowledged him. "What do you want?"

He arched a brow, giving away nothing. "I'm heading to the village. Want to come?"

My mouth bobbed open before snapping shut. I was finally going to get some answers, if he didn't eat me first—he was staring at me as if he might.

I studied his broody pout before deciding I'd take my chances. If I died, at least it wouldn't be from boredom. Glancing over at Robert, I emphatically said, "Yes, please." Raf gestured for me to follow him, but

I sat unmoving. "I'd like to visit an acquaintance at the apothecary while we're there."

I scowled at him, just waiting for him to say something that was going to set me off. *If he refused me, I swear I'd—*

"Sure, that's fine." Raf shrugged, crossing his arms and rocking back on his heels. I snapped my mouth shut again. He was being suspiciously nice. The silence of the library pressed into us as we glared at each other.

He turned to my bodyguard. "Robert, your services aren't needed. Go find someone else to follow around. I'll take good care of her." Robert grumbled under his breath before stomping off.

The same white mare was saddled up for me when we arrived at the stables. "Hello, beautiful girl," I cooed to Hibiscus.

"You seem to be a natural with animals," Rafael observed. "That one doesn't like me very much." He gave a wide berth around her as he got on his elegant, black steed.

"It would seem that she has an excellent sense of character, then." I praised her with a rub down her neck as she nickered at me.

"Why do you hate me?"

I turned to him, startled. I thought it was a mutual feeling. I couldn't exactly say, *"Your aura is as black as a starless night."* Even now, I could see shadows wafting off him. It was off-putting.

"You weren't very friendly when I arrived," I said dryly. "In fact, you seemed to relish in my discomfort. But you did take that goblet of blood from me—that was a kind gesture. For that reason alone, I wouldn't say I *hate* you." I mounted my horse before easing her into a trot.

"I'm a bastard," he muttered under his breath, riding beside me. "I haven't received much kindness in my life and... I suppose it's made me guarded... around people I don't know."

I tried to hide my shock at his candidness. I hadn't thought him capable of conversation beyond cynicism. "Louis told me about your childhood—that you and I are... *similar*. Perhaps we should call a truce."

"Consider my white flag waved," he said with a hint of a smile.

"I just need to know one thing..." I said, hesitating. This was probably a bad idea. But I couldn't trust him until I knew.

He pursed his lips, squinting at me through his lashes. "Shoot."

I took a deep breath. "Have you ever used your magic on me?"

His brows shot up. "Magic? Can you be more specific?"

"You know... like *dark* magic. To make me feel *strange*... around you." I was whispering for some reason. I didn't know how to explain the effect he'd had on me during that first dinner, but it had rattled me. Beyond his cologne's ability to give me vertigo, I felt an unsettling pull towards him, as if he was a carnivorous plant and I was a fly.

"Strange?" he asked with a half-grin. It looked as if he was trying to stifle a laugh.

I narrowed my eyes at him. "Never mind." If he was going to mock me, then it had been a mistake to ask.

"Wait—no. I didn't mean to upset you. I've never used magic on you, I promise. I'll be the first to admit that I'm an ass, but I would never *manipulate* you with magic—or without magic, for that matter."

He met my gaze with a straight face. No sardonic grin. No snarky attitude. I believed him. I must've been displacing my feelings for Galen onto him that night. But that cologne of his... How could I ask him what kind of scent he wore without sounding like a lecher? I wanted to douse myself in it. It smelled like *home*. It made me feel nostalgic for a place I'd never been. That made no sense, but neither did anything else in this world.

"White flag waved." I grinned, before urging my horse into a gallop and racing ahead.

We ran for miles. It was refreshing to share company with another, without the need for words. As our horses began to tire, we slowed back down to a walk, almost to the city.

"You ride well. In a dress, nonetheless. You must ride often back home?"

My heart ached for my horse, though I knew she was being well taken care of by Deric. I ached for his sweet smile too.

"As often as I can," I replied.

An odd feeling tugged at me—a gut impulse telling me to confide in him. And since we'd called a truce, I was going to choose to believe it was intuition... and not his magic. "Since I know one of your secrets, it seems only fair that you know one of mine. Can I trust you?"

He gave a wry grin. "Secrets are my specialty. I'm a shadow wielder, after all." Dark ribbons of smoke began to waft around him and his horse. I watched them swirl in a hypnotizing pattern.

Shadow wielder... I was an *idiot*. It wasn't his soul that was black, but his *magic*. I'd been seeing shadows, not an aura. Did he not have one? I didn't even know what the glow around faeries meant—what it even was. I'd been too afraid to ask and sound insane.

Any remaining tightness in my chest relaxed as I took a deep breath. "I'm niece to Queen Ophelia of Aurelius. I grew up like you, in a castle full of strangers. My father abandoned me when my mother died, so my aunt raised me. You aren't the only one who has a difficult time opening up to people."

Our gazes met and I felt like I was free falling. It was rare to be this vulnerable. His honey-brown eyes had softened. He was looking at me as if... *as if he cared*. But that couldn't be true.

"I won't tell anyone," Raf promised. "I'd suggest you do the same. Sylvia would be threatened by what you just told me—and likely use it against you. She believes that *she* is the rightful Queen of Aurelius."

I nodded. I wished I could tell Galen who I was, but it was too risky. If Sylvia found out... I didn't want to think about what she'd do to Ophelia if given the chance.

"So... you don't need blood, but you drink it. Why?" I asked.

My sudden topic change confused the Dark Prince. He stared blankly at me, before exhaling a laugh and shaking his head. "I do *not* drink blood. If you're referring to the goblet at dinner, it was just a simple magic trick. I turned the blood to dust. I'm gifted at making things disappear. I can turn myself into shadow, if I so desire. It's convenient in a pinch."

I'd read about each of the elements in one of the books I'd borrowed from the library, but I still had a lot to learn. I knew that shadow wielders made excellent spies. They also had the most versatility in their magic—they could turn into mist, cover themselves in darkness, or solidify their shadows and use them as a weapon.

The man before me was absolutely lethal, but I'd known that since I'd first laid eyes on him. And here I was... *alone with him*. "Louis tells me you're the most powerful faerie in Nymera," I remarked casually.

"I was—until you came along, world walker."

Without warning, black mist exploded from Raf, settling over me like a thick blanket. I shifted in the saddle, preparing to run as the smoke twisted and stretched. It was reshaping itself into a semi-opaque bubble, with us at the center of it. A shield, I realized—so we could talk privately.

Raf's eyes darkened as they met mine. "My father used to say that the most powerful faeries were chosen for a higher purpose—that it's our duty to protect the vulnerable."

I scoffed. "A nice sentiment, but there seem to be plenty of powerful faeries that disagree with it."

"Yes. But their magic is stolen from human blood. *Ours* beats within us. Whether you believe it or not, *you're* very powerful. You owe us nothing, but—"

"But... you need my help overthrowing your evil stepmother and her council?"

Raf huffed a laugh. "Yes. I'll cut to the chase. We need your help. You're the best chance we have."

"Then your chances aren't great," I sighed. "Tell me what it is that you want, then I'll decide if I can help. I do *want* to help, for what that's worth."

"It's worth *everything*," he said with complete sincerity. "Louis and I have been spying on the Elders since my father died, but it was a brothel worker that proved to be the most proficient spy, she—"

I interjected haughtily. "Why am I not surprised that you've found a way to utilize *prostitutes* in your attempt to overthrow the Kingdom?" I'd only meant to tease, but it had come out sounding judgmental.

His eyes sparked with heat. "Here I am, trying to save the world... and you cut me down before I've even begun. If I didn't know better, I'd say you were jealous of my friends at the Siren Inn."

I scowled. "They can have you. You're just like every other strutting peacock I've ever met. All cock and tail feathers—zero substance. That is to say... you're *not* my type—which I believe I've already told you."

Raf's gaze darkened. "All cock, am I? I suppose you're not the first to tell me that."

"*Of course* that's what you took from that. Point proven." I rolled my eyes.

"You proved nothing, except that you think about my... *assets* in your spare time. So tell me, freckles... Why can't I spend *my* spare time at a brothel? Does the Princess think herself above the common folk? Some women have to *work* to survive, you know."

He thought I was a spoiled brat. *Let him think what he wanted.* When I learned how to throw a punch, he was going to be my first target.

"It's not the *workers* I find vile," I said frostily.

Raf gave a low laugh and rolled his shoulders once... twice... like I'd gotten under his skin. *Good.*

"As I was saying..." He glared. "I was tipped off by one of the workers at the Siren Inn. She learned from a reputable source that the Elders are behind the systematic kidnappings that have been happening across our lands. Hundreds of humans have gone missing over the last year. It has caused widespread panic, resulting in an increase in violence... murder. While the Elders have made it abundantly clear that they don't respect human life, it's still a new low for them—taking magic from their own people. The faeries *need* humans. The shortage is causing hysteria—famine in some areas, infertility, feuds between families..."

"Why would they try to create civil unrest? How would that benefit them?" I asked.

"Power and control, I assume. It's easier to control people who are scared."

The missing humans that Lusha had mentioned... the Elders were responsible? The *Kingdom* was responsible? The irritation I'd been feeling for Raf disappeared as overwhelming *fury* took hold.

My lip curled as I said, "Sylvia has to go."

"That she does. As do her henchmen."

"Do you think the people they kidnapped are still alive somewhere?"

"We're hopeful that they're being held captive. Most likely, they're being bled and kept for the Kingdom's personal magic supply. We've been searching all over the continent for them, but so far we've had no luck."

"But how can I help?"

"We need you to open a portal to Erador, when you're ready... and let a select few of us through. If the Elders manage to hoard all of the magic, then faeries will be completely at their mercy. We have to break the blood curse—it's the only way we can take back power."

My heart skipped. They had too much faith in me. I could barely wield magic. I'd just let them down. "I-I don't know that I'll ever be capable of opening a portal..." I choked out. "What if I can't?"

"You won't know until you try. You aren't in this alone. You have me... and Louis."

My stomach twisted. I *was* alone. I had been for a long while. "We have to find and rescue the abducted humans, then take them back with us. I won't leave them to be drained and discarded."

Raf's smile grew so large, I could see both of his dimples beneath dark stubble. "Of course. We need to bring you back to the spot where you arrived. Sooner rather than later. We need answers. *You* need answers."

I couldn't allow myself to think about everything that was at stake. Raf was right; I had to *try*.

"What of Galen?" I asked. He deserved an opportunity to prove himself—to come with us and help break the curse.

A shadow crossed over Rafael's face. "Galen is too unpredictable to count on. He's the Elder's puppet. They've been training him for too long. He's, more or less, one of them at this point."

My body temperature dropped as ice flowed into my fingertips. *Anger.* Anger was what most effectively channeled my magic. They were going to *leave* their brother behind, because he was a *liability*? Without even giving him a chance?

"You would leave him here... to defend his people against the Elders—by himself? You'd betray your own blood?" I didn't hold back my disdain.

If they wouldn't tell Galen, then *I would*. He deserved the opportunity to pick a side before things got too ugly. I wouldn't let them abandon their brother—*their future King*—like my father had abandoned me.

The rage he'd provoked had me squeezing Hibiscus's sides too tightly. Her trot transitioned into a gentle canter as she responded to my cues, surging ahead of Raf.

An onyx cloud momentarily blacked out the sun. Apparently, I'd hit a nerve. He caught up to me easily, as if my horse had willingly slowed at his command. "I've known him for one-hundred years. Don't pretend to understand the *complexities* of my brother. He's proven himself unworthy time and time again. He's the Elder's executioner... did you know that?"

I sneered while Raf continued his rant. "He turns human sympathizers to *ashes*. He's a royal hit man. Don't be so quick to assume that he'd be on our side if he knew what the Elders were up to—maybe he already knows. Are you willing to put every human here at risk for *him*?"

"So who takes the throne? You?" I eyed him with every ounce of loathing I could muster. He was going to let Galen fall on his sword for the Crown and then take it from him?

His gaze burned into me. "I don't want it. You're getting ahead of yourself. First, we need to break the curse, then we can worry about Galen."

"Don't you think it's worth trying to get him on your side now, if that's how you feel?"

"No. He's a control freak. He'll either turn against us and get us killed, or get in the way and get us killed."

Raf's stubbornness was what was going to get him killed. He was blinded by his rivalry with his brother. Galen had goodness in him. I'd seen it—I'd felt it. They'd be stronger together.

"*Fine.* For now, I won't say anything to him. But this isn't over," I hissed. We rode in silence the rest of the way, the air between us, once again, thick with hostility.

FIFTEEN

The Arrowroot Apothecary was tucked between a bakery and a book shop. The stone building was covered in lush layers of pink bougainvillea flowers that climbed all the way to the tiled roof. The shop door was painted a deep shade of plum and covered in tiny, silver, hand-painted stars. I recognized this door... I'd been here with Galen.

Bells on the handle jingled as Raf held the heavy wooden door open for me. Melisandre was busy behind the counter, grinding something into powder with a mortar and pestle. She looked up as we approached, greeting us with a warm smile.

A sparkling, purple aura floated above her like a halo. Her mauve robes were nearly the same shade, bringing out the warm undertones in her skin. She wore a jeweled headpiece that delicately dangled across her forehead and a stack of thin, gold bracelets on each wrist. Dark curls framed her round cheeks, bouncing as she trotted over to us. She leaned in for a hug, smelling of cardamom and vanilla.

I peered around the space. It was bohemian yet organized... bursting with collections of wondrous oddities. Most of the items for sale sat in glass bottles, jars, and clay pots. There were rows and rows of tinctures, elixirs, balms, and potions scattered throughout the store, sitting on various shelves and tables.

Dried herbs hung from the ceiling beams, creating a fresh, spicy aroma. I could pick out the stronger fragrances like peppermint, lavender, and ginger. Mushrooms, flower bulbs and spices sat in various baskets, along with animal parts and bones. Crystals and polished gems glittered behind display cases. It was the kind of space I could've happily spent an entire day in. I wanted to learn what every single item was and how it was used.

"I'm glad you finally found your way to me." Meli's large hazel eyes twinkled as she grinned at me. Something about her graceful, warm energy reminded me of Cara.

"I meant to come sooner. Is this a good time?" I asked.

She nodded in answer, then turned to Raf. "She'll be safe with me, Prince. Come back for her once we've had time to have a cup of tea and a proper chat."

I glared at him, hoping he'd leave us be. Begrudgingly, I accepted that we had to work together... despite how infuriating he was, but right now I was ready for him to go be a thorn in someone else's side. Rafael mumbled something about an errand and then vanished into smoke.

I grinned at his departure and turned towards Meli, who was pouring tea. This was the first time I'd been left on my own since arriving—and I didn't think Meli would stop me if I wanted to leave. I stilled as freedom whispered in my ear, beckoning me to make a run for it. Was it worth it? Louis and Raf needed my help... and I needed theirs.

I bit my lip, feeling anxious about the decision that had suddenly been thrust upon me. Was it foolish to not try and escape?

"Are you alright, Lady? You don't have to drink the tea if you don't like it. I won't take it personally," Meli said with knitted brows.

I took a generous sip, burning my tongue on the hot liquid. I had no idea how to get back to the garden. Even if I did find it... then what? Unless the Queen was lying, the portal was closed. It would be useless to run, I decided, with a sigh.

"I apologize. I have a lot on my mind, but I don't mean to waste your time. Thank you for the tea—it's delicious." I took another sip to emphasize the point. "I came here to ask about your healing power. How it works—how you mastered it."

"Have you decided to accept that you're a healer, then?" She asked with a smirk. I looked down sheepishly as she took my tea and set it on the small table that sat between us. Next, she cupped my hands in hers.

"Healing follows its own rules. I began to heal quickly from wounds around the age of sixteen, when my bleeding began. There aren't many like us. I sought out another in a nearby village to learn more. She had the ability to mend others with her hands and taught me the art. It took years to master, but now when I touch someone, like this..." She motioned to my hands in hers. "I can feel their pain. I can locate the source and tell whether it's physical or mental. I've found that one is not any more real than the other. Once I pinpoint the pain, I move my hands to the spot where it resides—" She set her hands on my head. "—And absorb it. My magic seeks out what needs to be mended and makes quick work of taking away pain."

"I feel that you're hurting up here," she said, tapping my skull. "Sometimes we lack the ability to mend our own mental wounds. May I?"

I nodded tentatively. She placed her hands around my head and took one, two, three deep breaths. I watched her eyes crinkle in concentration. A small gasp left her as my shoulders sagged, and I suddenly felt less burdened.

She had taken something from me that I hadn't realized I'd been holding onto—a deep well of sadness and fear—not only from my mother's death, but my father's rejection. Grief for my old life and guilt about Deric, about enjoying parts of this new life.

I could *breathe*, as if a boulder had been lifted from my chest. I dove towards her, wrapping my arms around her in gratitude, not caring if it was the proper thing to do.

"This feeling of relief—it won't stay with you. Your problems will come back and you'll still have to comb through those emotions and work out the knots. But I hope I helped you realize what you can hold onto, and what you can let go of. Sometimes we hold on to pain because it's the only thing we think we have left of someone, but that's simply not the case. Our loved ones live on through us."

The truth of her words hurt. I wore my mother's death around me like a shawl, afraid to forget her. "I'd love to come back and practice with you—when you have time, of course. I'd be happy to pay you for your trouble."

A bold statement for someone with no money. My cheeks burned with embarrassment as I waited for her answer.

"No need, I'd be happy to help. I could use some female company. I spend almost all of my time with a human man." Her eyes looked like crescent moons when she laughed.

"And I, Fae males. Please... some female company would be lovely." I'd found a kindred spirit across galaxies—that in itself felt like fate.

"You have a human... partner?" I wasn't sure if that was the right word choice.

"He's my source. I protect him, house him, feed him... and in turn, he provides me with magic. He's a skilled botanist as well. He grows many of the medicinal plants I need to make my potions. My magic can handle most injuries and illnesses, but sometimes medicine is a cheaper, equally effective alternative. I'm one healer in a village of thousands. I simply cannot fix everyone. Poor Odin would have no blood left if I did." She laughed, somehow able to make light of the curse.

"What's it like for Odin... as a human?"

Melisandre's friendly demeanor vanished. She looked at me suspiciously, straightening her spine.

I fumbled to explain myself. "I ask because I'm not from this world. I recently arrived from Erador. I'm a hybrid, though I thought I was only human until recently..."

Meli stared at me like I'd grown another head. "Y-you just arrived from *Erador*? But how? No wonder you're under the Kingdom's protection—this is incredible news! Are you going back? Are you taking others with you?" She nearly bowled me over with her enthusiasm.

"I'm not sure how I arrived here. I was sleeping in my world and woke up here. I might be a world walker, but don't know how to use my powers if I am. I'm hoping to go back... eventually. I'm currently under the Queen's watchful eye, learning how to wield my powers. Nobody knows about magic where I'm from. Faeries have somehow been erased from history."

"*Erased from history*? In two-hundred years? That seems nearly impossible without the aid of strong magic. You must have a powerful mind manipulator in your world to have accomplished that—or perhaps the gods have decided to get involved. But... why would they want to hide our existence?" Meli looked hurt—offended.

I took her hand in mine. "This is sensitive information, Meli. Please, don't tell anyone. I won't pretend that I plan to open a bridge to Erador for all. My people wouldn't be safe. In time, I hope to have more answers for you."

"I understand. And to answer *your* question... about Odin—it's been getting increasingly dangerous for us. You saw the men harassing me the other day. That's far too common for any faeries that reside with humans these days. There's a tension growing. The magic shortage—the fear of what will happen if humans die out—it's caused panic. Odin and I have talked about leaving, but the rural areas are hurting even more than the larger villages. Nowhere feels safe anymore." Meli looked at me with an intensity that bordered on desperation.

I wondered... did she care for Odin as more than her source? I didn't ask, knowing it would put her safety in jeopardy to even suggest such a thing.

"I've got just one more question." I hesitated, but she gave me an encouraging smile. "I've been seeing glowing colors around people... auras, I believe. It's a new development... I'm not sure what it means." I trailed off as I looked down at my feet, afraid I might just be losing my mind.

Meli's smile widened. "You aren't crazy." She looked past me with an unfocused gaze and I knew what she was doing—reading *my* aura. "You say aura? We say *Uhra*... like Ooh-Rah. It means *soul* in the language of the Fae. Most cannot see them. But healers, oracles, necromancers—anyone who is clairvoyant can see uhras. Typically, I just catch a glimpse of someone's soul; but with trust and connection, sometimes I see more."

"Can you see mine?" I asked, feeling self-conscious.

"Yes... it's gold and blindingly bright. You stand out—you need to be careful with who you trust. There's a lot of energy buzzing around you. It's bound to attract attention, especially from those who seek power. I'm sure the Queen keeps uhra readers near her— something to be mindful of."

"What do you mean *readers*?"

"Some faeries spend a lifetime trying to interpret uhra shapes and colors. Some make a career of it. A red soul shows dominance... passion. Blue... empathy, tranquility. Yellow... optimism and warmth. Green... independence and ingenuity. Personally, I don't believe in over-simplifying something as complex as a soul. Uhras can shift and change throughout one's life or even with our moods. They can mask themselves if a soul is conflicted enough—show a false color, for example. Trust your gut when it comes to reading them. That's my advice."

Meli had no idea how much she'd already done for me. She was a beacon, guiding me through the fog I'd been stuck in since arriving. I'd never be able to repay her for her kindness.

"What does it mean if someone has no uhra at all?" I asked.

She raised her brows. "That they're dead. Everyone has a soul."

Right on cue, Raf appeared. I'd been so absorbed in our conversation, I hadn't heard him come in. He was leaning against the counter—a bemused smile playing on his lips as he looked at us. His wavy, dark hair spilled over his brow and I watched him push it back, only for it to immediately spring forward. He was always shaking that same lock of hair out of his eyes. It was irksome... just like everything else about him.

"Are you ready, Goldie?"

I snapped to attention. *Goldie?* That's what my mother had called me once upon a time. I hadn't heard that nickname in a decade. I said goodbye to Meli and fell in step with Raf as we walked back to our horses.

"What was your errand, *Raffie?*" I couldn't resist smiling. The nickname sounded as ridiculous as I thought it would.

"Call me that again and I'll turn you into dust." He doubled down on his surliness and for some reason I found it hilarious.

Maybe it was the gift of a light heart that Meli had just bestowed on me, but I couldn't stop laughing. He was so distracted watching me, he tripped, making me laugh harder. I was hysterical, bending over and clutching my stomach.

"Stop it. People are watching," Raf said under his breath, scowling at me. The surrounding villagers were indeed staring as they quickened their pace to pass us.

He let out a snort, covering his mouth, before another laugh bubbled out of him. And then we were wheezing, keeled over, with tears in our eyes. There was no explanation for the fit of madness, other than we both seemed to be in desperate need of a good laugh.

Finally... Goldie and Raffie had come to a truce.

Later that evening, I sat around a table with the royal family and their guests. Rafael and Louis were both absent. The seating chart had shifted to Arnold and Galen closest to the Queen, which meant I had to sit next to Isla. I knew I shouldn't have had any issue with her—I'd *encouraged* Galen to pursue her, after all—but having to converse with her was a different story. I kept to myself and prayed she'd do the same.

"So Marigold, do you have your dance picked out for the Hyacinth Festival yet?" Isla smiled at me innocently.

I choked on a piece of bread. *Dance?*

"Oh, I won't be dancing," I said politely, before taking a generous sip of wine.

"Don't be *silly*. Everyone that's part of the ceremony has to dance. Are you going to partner with Louis or Rafael?"

I cringed, unsure of how to respond.

Galen cut in. "She'll be dancing with me." He looked like he'd surprised even himself. The slight slur in his voice let me know he'd been drinking.

"With *you*? But I thought—" She turned, looking back and forth between us.

"What's this about?" snapped the Queen. "Galen, you'll be dancing with Isla, of course. Have you lost your mind?"

Galen glared at her, his green eyes locked in a silent battle with her icy blues. "No, Mother. I can think of no higher honor than dancing with the first *world walker* we've had in two-hundred years. In fact, it's cause for celebration." Galen stood, ushering the footmen over. "A round of champagne, please."

They scurried over with a chilled bottle, fresh from the ice chest. "To Marigold. To Erador. To Nymera. May we unite the worlds!" He threw back a glass and poured another, then sat back in his seat dramatically, appearing quite pleased with himself. Everyone at the table was so stunned, it took a moment for someone to break the silence.

Arnold sputtered, "A-a world walker? Your *cousin* is from *Erador*? Why am I just finding this out? How?"

He turned to the Queen, standing and leaning his hands on the dinner table in barely contained ire. "Your Grace, you've been hosting a world walker for *weeks* and haven't told me—the council?" He pounded his fists on the table and the guards ran over to Sylvia's side, weapons raised. He lifted his hands up in apology. "I meant no harm. I just didn't think I'd ever see the day. When will she open up the portal? Are we going to address the public? We need to convene and tell the others!" His head was about to spin off his body.

"*SILENCE!*" yelled Sylvia. He sat back down and crossed his arms.

"Marigold is a *hybrid*. Raised as a human. She does not yet have access to her powers. She managed to arrive here while she was sleeping—or so she says. We've been hosting her while she learns how to access her magic... so she can open a doorway. I was planning to wait until the festival to announce her to you all." The Queen flashed a murderous glare at Galen. I felt my blood drop to a frigid temperature as tensions around the table escalated.

Arnold turned to me. "The gods gifted a *mongrel* with world walking gifts? What kind of blasphemy is this?" He looked so irate that I stood and backed out of my seat, grabbing a butter knife. The way he said mongrel made my gut twist.

"And you *believe* her? That she can't open up a portal after she's already done it? Have you even interrogated her? Perhaps she needs proper persuasion. Hand her over, I'll get her to open a bridge out of this world by tomorrow morning." He bared his teeth at me and my hands iced over in response. Dahlia was hanging on his arm, trying to pull him back to his seat.

"Enough!" Sylvia commanded. "Guards, please take Arnold back to his rooms until he's calmed down. Take the women back to their prospective rooms as well. Galen, you're staying with me." He defiantly glowered at her. I felt like a carcass being fought over by a pack of rabid wylks.

I glanced back at Galen as I was escorted out. He stared back with raw, unfiltered agony in his eyes. His amber uhra was dim, with a flickering dark blue flame at its center.

I recognized his pain, because the same sunken feeling lived in me. Hopelessness, loneliness... self-loathing... it should've been impossible for so much to be conveyed in one look, and yet I'd felt all of it—as if I'd been looking into a shattered mirror.

His outburst had been a cry for help. He needed someone who cared. But it couldn't be me. I turned away and didn't look back.

I was fast asleep when I heard a quiet rapping on the door. I was rubbing my eyes, when the door unlocked and Galen strode in. I sat up, only able to see the outline of his body in the darkened room.

"Galen?" I asked groggily.

"I'm sorry for waking you. I wanted to make sure that you're okay." He sat on the side of the bed. I moved over, making room for him. He smelled like a whiskey barrel.

"I apologize for tonight," he said raggedly. "I didn't mean to start a fight with my mother in the middle of dinner—nor did I mean to embarrass Isla... or put you in danger. I just... *snapped*. First, she tells me who to marry, then they made me—" He took a deep breath, followed by a long exhale. "I'm a mess, Marigold. I don't deserve your forgiveness. I-I'm worthless," he said, his voice cracking. It was difficult to believe that this was the same male who'd come to my room weeks ago, drenched in confidence.

"Hey... It's alright. I'm okay," I assured him, rubbing his back. "I was surprised Arnold didn't already know. Why was your mother keeping it a secret? The Elders wouldn't harm a world walker, would they?" They'd been waiting two-hundred years for someone to rescue them. I couldn't imagine they'd jeopardize that, even if I *was* a mongrel. The word scuttled around in my stomach, making me want to hurl up my dinner.

"No, they need you. I think my mother was keeping it a secret for her own purposes. Everything is a game to her. They run my life. I can't escape them. The other week they made me—" He looked down at his hands, unable to get the words out. I took them and held them firmly.

"I killed someone," he murmured, his voice barely audible. "A faerie... He was caught harboring a pregnant human. They captured him, but she escaped. The Elders claimed the baby was his. They'd been holding him—torturing him—to get to her. But he wouldn't reveal where she was. They brought me in to burn him slowly... to make him talk." He squeezed my hand until it throbbed.

"They didn't need *my* flames. They have their own ways of getting information. But he wasn't the only one they were trying to break. They want my unwavering loyalty. It's not the first time I've been forced to hurt people for them. He was barely hanging on. I couldn't do it—it was clear he'd been suffering for a while. So I turned his heart to ash... in seconds. I told them it was an accident. But they knew I was lying. They'll make me pay for what I did."

Rafael had been right. The Elders were using Galen to torture people. He'd *killed* someone, someone who'd died protecting the woman—the *human*—he loved. But what Galen had done had also been a kindness; he'd ended the man's pain.

My insides twisted with disgust, anger, devastation... but it was empathy that overtook me—rooted itself deep into my gut. I cared for this man. And I was worried for him—worried he'd lose himself if he continued to wander through darkness. He needed a guiding light. And I was a healer. Maybe none of this was a coincidence.

He was broken before me—splayed open and bleeding his soul onto my sheets. I pulled his head down to my lap and brushed his hair with my fingers as he cried. It was a level of closeness I'd never experienced with a man before. My heart swelled.

"They've made you hurt others?" I tried to comfort him with my touch, even as I internally screamed.

"Yes... Since my father died, they've been seeking out improper pairings and any hybrid offspring. I've tortured for them... killed for them. In the name of the law. I-I don't agree with their views. Please don't think less of me. I already hate myself."

My heart cracked open. I didn't think less of him. Maybe I should've after what he'd just admitted... but I also understood that his hands were tied. "What you've done doesn't define you, Galen. You ended his suffering. What you did was *brave*. What can we do to stop this from happening again?"

"They're too strong to be stopped. And I've been conditioned for violence since I was a boy—long before they made me hurt anyone. As a child, my own mother whipped me to build character. She thought I lacked the ruthless edge that is needed in leadership. I'm afraid by the time I become King, I'll have no goodness left." My heart sank at his confession. He'd been raised with brutality instead of affection. Had he ever known love?

"Great leaders don't resort to *fear* to control others. What she views as weakness, I see as strength. The fire inside you can burn the world down or... it can burn *for* the world. It's your choice. Not hers. She has it all wrong," I said.

We sat in silence and I bit back what I wanted to say next... until I couldn't keep it in. "What if you escaped back to Erador with me?" My chest pounded as I awaited his answer.

He glanced up at me with shining eyes. "I couldn't leave my people behind. It would be a coward's choice."

"Not if we broke the curse. You could be a hero to your people."

"No. It's too late for me to be a hero."

We didn't talk after that. Instead, I continued to stroke my fingers through his hair, shedding silent tears for the faerie who'd died protecting his family. And for Galen... who was destroying himself for his Crown.

"I didn't want to hurt any of them," he whispered into the night.

"I know."

SIXTEEN

I felt numb as I headed to training the next morning. When I saw Louis, I didn't bother to greet him with a smile.

"Good to see you too," he said, throwing a wave of water at me. I instinctively lifted my hands to block it, not even realizing that I'd produced a shield of wind until Louis whooped in excitement.

"You just produced your first shield! And with a new element!" He came in for a hug, but pulled back when he noticed my lack of enthusiasm. "Are you okay? What's wrong?" He studied my face as I squinted at him with swollen, bloodshot eyes.

"Galen... H-he confessed that the Elders have been making him hurt people. They've been searching for *improper pairings* and hybrids. He *killed* someone. I don't know how to make it stop—what to do." Louis patted my back as I soaked his shirt with tears.

"Fuck... How have they managed to hide something like this from Rafael and I?" He swore, clenching his fists. "The Elders, my mother, they're soulless—they've lost their damn minds. Killing faeries because of who they choose to love? Hunting hybrids? I can't even imagine what they're doing to humans if they're treating faeries this way." He spit on the ground as his cheeks turned blood berry red.

He shot a stream of water at a nearby column until the force of the flood uprooted it and knocked it over. I joined him, sending ice crystals towards the column, coating it in a heavy frost. I kept going until thick cracks began to form in the marble—until tiny fissures exploded into a million shards. Channeling emotion into magic... it was cathartic, but I could feel the danger in its embrace—lulling me in, demanding I give more and more of myself.

Louis coached me as I alternated between wind and ice, aiming at his shield of water. Wind seemed to channel from a place of sadness, eager to join with ice. Sadness and anger were an undeniably compatible pair. Misery loved company, after all. I'd spent too much of my youth defeating one, only to battle the other. And now they were taunting me—swirling around in an icy gust, as I struggled to find control.

Next, I practiced shielding, which required more mental discipline than I currently had. Louis sent a stream of water at me, while I tried and failed to block him. Too soon, I was soaked and frustrated. I hadn't managed even one shield, besides the one I hadn't meant to make. I scowled at the youngest Ruhn brother, wanting to give up.

Louis patted my wet head. "Look at the bright side, someday you'll be able to use wind magic to dry yourself off. Wind wielders can even learn to *fly*. If I could choose another element to wield, it would be wind. It can be an invisible weapon, your greatest defense, or even a pair of wings." He was trying to cheer me up. And it *was* exciting to think about what I might be capable of one day. But today, I just wanted to go back to bed.

By the end of the lesson, I was lost in my thoughts—standing alone in the middle of a frozen tundra where no one could reach me. A dull edged knife seemed to be imbedded in my chest, slicing deeper whenever I thought of Galen. He'd infiltrated my mind to the point of *obsession*. I couldn't concentrate. Despite the energy I'd expended, I had no appetite.

I hoped he was alright. After one-hundred and fifty years with Sylvia as his mother, how could he be? The terrors he must've experienced as a boy—at the hand of his own mother. It made me realize that there were worse things than losing a parent; at least I knew what unconditional love felt like. My mother's death had shaped me, but it was her love that had truly defined me. How had Sylvia shaped her son? Had her lack of love defined him?

I needed to see him. What was he doing right now? Working, I supposed. Always doing what he was told. As Robert and I walked back to the castle, I could no longer resist. I had to at least ask. "Will you take me to Prince Galen? *Please*."

I knew I was going down a path of no return, but perhaps I'd been wrong to push him away. He needed someone. And the truth was, I couldn't fight this any longer. I was lonely. I needed someone too. I needed *him*.

Robert answered, "Anytime you request to see him, I've been instructed to bring you to him straight away—on Prince Galen's orders. Follow me."

He led me to the back of the castle. My pulse raced as he unlocked a door on the outside of the building and it swung open into complete darkness. My vision slowly adjusted and I saw a set of spiral stairs descending into the inky depths. I followed close behind him as we climbed lower and lower, until there was no natural light left. I knew what horrors lived at the deepest levels of castles. He was leading me to the dungeons.

Dusty sconces lined the walls, cradling frail, flickering candlelight. Shapes formed in the shadows, making me see things that weren't there. The air was musty, growing cool and damp as the temperature dipped. And still we went lower. Claustrophobia gripped me, squeezing my chest until I was gasping for air. I concentrated on one foot in front of the other, counting the beats of my drumming heart.

What was Galen doing down here?

I was clinging to Robert by the time we arrived at an iron door. I braced myself as he unlocked it, ushering me into a jarringly bright room. Fires lined the walls, burning along the stone floors. I could only assume earth magic had created this gigantic lair. It was odd to see such an expansive space underground.

No prisoners in sight; only Galen, shirtless and glistening, as he dueled with another male. There were no weapons, just fists wrapped in protective layers of fabric. They moved like two primitive dancers: Swerving, side-stepping, ducking, and swinging. They were moving faster than I'd ever seen men move. But I supposed they weren't men... they were faeries.

My stomach lurched as Galen turned towards me and froze. I watched in horror as he was struck in the stomach, causing him to fall backwards and skid across the floor.

He glared at his sparring mate as he stood up and brushed himself off. "Leave us, Frederick." The man disappeared in a flash of black smoke. A shadow wielder. Louis had told me they were exceedingly rare; it couldn't have been easy for Galen to find him.

"Hi... sorry for startling you." I motioned to a violet bruise forming under his ribs, feeling suddenly shy. I hadn't meant to interrupt his training session. He stalked towards me with nothing but a pair of black pants on. The light of the fire played on his olive skin, highlighting every hard line. My mouth went dry.

Crossing his muscular arms, he towered over me. I mirrored his stance, not knowing what to do with my hands. They wanted to reach out and touch his sweat-sheened chest.

"Hello, Marigold. You didn't startle me. I picked up your scent as you were coming down the stairs. In fact, that *scent* of yours has been driving me crazy, leaving a trail wherever you go. If you want to sneak up on me, you'll have to learn how to shield. You should also be honing your senses—you wouldn't want a predator catching you unaware again."

I gave a nervous laugh. "I doubt I'll run into another pack of wylks anytime soon."

"I wasn't talking about the wylks." He gave me a beguiling expression that caused my heart to beat so erratically, I was sure he could hear it.

I cleared my throat, trying to regain composure. "You forget, I'm part-human. My senses will never be as sharp as yours."

"I *never* forget what you are."

My stomach dipped as our eyes met. "Does it disappoint you—that I'm human?"

"No," he said, circling me like a shark. "But it would be easier to court *you* instead of Isla, if you weren't. And you'd be less distracting." He came into my personal space. The sweat-laced scent of cloves hit me in a crashing wave. Leaning down, he softly kissed my neck. The tickle of breath was a phantom breeze, sending chills down my spine. He lingered, before pulling away with a heavy sigh.

"You're *wet*." He smirked.

"Excuse me?"

"Your hair, your clothes. Is it raining? Did you fall into the lake?" He held a lock of damp hair between his fingers.

"Training. Louis. Water." I'd forgotten that my hair and clothing were still not dry. The more I wielded my ice magic, the less I noticed temperature changes in my own body. I was shivering, but not from the cold.

"So what brings you down to my lair?" Galen asked, sliding his hands into his pockets.

"Well... you've been ignoring me for weeks. Then last night, you announced that you wanted to dance with me instead of Isla—at some festival I don't belong at. You also revealed to Arnold that I'm a world walker, before showing up in my room..." I didn't finish my thought. I didn't want to bring up what he'd told me last night. "I-I don't understand what you want—what game you're playing."

I tracked him as he prowled behind me, until I could feel his heat at my backside. He traced his hands along my shoulders and down my arms, before resting them on my hips. His confident swagger never failed to disorient me, even after I'd seen all of it drained last night. I now knew it was a shield to deflect from the pain he kept hidden.

"No games. I wasn't ignoring you. I was protecting you... *from me.* You should know to stay away after last night." He spoke into my ear, making the hairs on the back of my neck prickle with pleasure. "I find myself struggling with what I want and what I should do. *What I want* is to take you right here. *Gods*, what I want is to undress you so... very... slowly."

His hands wandered from my hips to my stomach, then up. They brushed along the sides of my breasts, making my breath hitch. "I want to claim you—bury myself inside of you, until you are begging for me to bite you—"

"And what *should* you do?" I asked, panting. I was going to combust if he took his fantasy any further.

"I should leave you be. I should court Isla. I should be the Prince I've been groomed to be for the last one hundred and fifty years."

It felt like he'd just poured a bucket of ice on me. "Don't become what they want you to be, please." I turned around so I could look at him. "I have my own Kingdom I'm obligated to. It would get complicated... if we were to get involved."

Duty always got in the way of desire.

"That's right. You *did* ask me to return you to Aurelius Castle the first day we met. Marigold, are you a *Princess*?"

The last bit of heat died in me—at the word Princess. I stepped away from him, giving us several feet of space. "No, not exactly. It would be easier if you didn't ask questions that might affect my safety."

"I understand. I wouldn't trust me either."

"It isn't personal." There was so much more I wanted to say... but I couldn't. "So are you going to keep ignoring me? Because I don't need you to protect me. I see you, Galen... past the charm, past your title. I see all of you."

"Marigold, I—" He froze, flustered, and began again. "How would you like me to approach our relationship?"

"I'd like to try and be friends. I'm..." I paused, finding the words difficult to say out loud. "I'm lonely. You were the first person I connected with here. And I think you could use a friend too. Can we not enjoy each other's company *without* sex?"

He gave a sinful smirk. "We can try." I tried to contain my laugh.

"Why do you train down here?" I asked, looking at the space comprised entirely of stone.

"My magic can get dangerous out in the open. Wind... trees... people. Down here, I'm safe to play with fire whenever I'd like." Flames hovered over both of his hands. He turned away from me and sent large tangerine streams soaring away from us. My face felt the impact of the heat, even as it was directed away.

He formed a large circle of fire around us that rolled along the floor like molten waves. I lifted my hands and a snowy blizzard swirled around us, instantly cooling the hot air. Where ice met flame, the air sizzled and hissed, creating steam.

We turned to face each other. I fought the magnetic pull that whispered, "*Touch him. Kiss him.*" Flame danced in the reflection of his eyes. What would happen, if we chose to stop fighting this tension?

Galen's fire stopped abruptly and my ice followed. We moved apart, breathing in the warm fog we'd created. "Let's get you back to your room, love. You're too damn tempting... and I only have so much self-restraint. If you're smart, you'll stay away."

I nodded, but he knew as well as I, that neither of us would listen to his words of wisdom. We were on a path of inevitable collision. My only chance of escaping unscathed was to get home before he made me his. Immortal enemy or not, I wanted him. *Badly.*

SEVENTEEN

I missed the rain. The weather here was always pleasantly balmy and it didn't fit my state of mind. I'd been in Nymera for over a month now. My magic was getting stronger every day and I was beginning to get through my workouts without every muscle screaming at me. I was getting faster too, even able to knock Louis on *his* ass sometimes.

I should've been happier at my progress; instead, I moped around like a love-struck teenager. I'd never been in love and doubted it felt as awful as this, but *something* was wrong with me. I feverishly devoured books, searching for the cure to my self-imposed ailment.

This was more than loneliness. I was used to being alone—*enjoyed* being alone—so why did I suddenly crave Galen's attention more than food, water, and air? My skin felt as if it might crawl away from me, abandoning my pathetic skeleton, if it didn't get what it desired soon. His touch was the answer. He was the illness and the remedy.

It wasn't until I discovered the romance section in the library that I found relief. I lost myself in love stories—the kind I'd always avoided—because I'd thought that if I didn't believe in love, then it couldn't afflict me. Except it had. Or something like it had.

I couldn't stop dreaming of his body over mine, couldn't stop fantasizing about him biting me. The shame of it left me feeling agitated. The lack of discipline I had over myself was... unsettling. Louis reiterated over and over how important it was to maintain control. He warned of burnouts and worse if I didn't master my emotions. And yet, even while meditating, a flame flickered inside me, demanding I surrender to its warm embrace.

It was easiest to forget about Galen when I was with Meli. She was a nice break from the castle in general. Today, we'd left her shop to go work in the gardens where her and Odin grew their medicinal plants.

After spending the morning weeding and pruning, we sat under the shade of a jacaranda tree, quenching our thirst with tea and biscuits.

So far, I hadn't made much progress when it came to healing others, but I was getting better at sensing pain.

The first step to mending others was learning to read energy. It felt similar to meditating—something I now did daily, thanks to Louis. When I meditated, I scanned any sensation within myself, breathing out the feelings that weighed me down.

Today I practiced reading Meli's energy instead of mine, combing through her mind and body until I found a tangled nest of pain.

Meli had told me the blocks in her energy were what I was to seek out—those were the fears, anxieties, and traumatic events that lived in everyone. Physical pain was more acute while mental pain throbbed.

I gasped when I was hit with an overwhelming wave of anxiety—a tight knot in her chest that radiated down to her abdomen. It was fierce and primal, hissing at me like it hadn't wanted to be found. What was she hiding? I pulled back into myself and gathered the courage to ask what was wrong.

"Meli, I don't want to violate your privacy. I appreciate that you're allowing me to practice on you, however, I must ask... are you okay? Is there anything I can do to help?" I was concerned. This was my fourth lesson with her, and each week I could feel the pain growing stronger.

She pulled out of my grasp, and for a moment, I thought she was going to tell me to leave. But then she let out a heavy sigh and began to speak. "I'm in terrible danger—as is Odin. He's more than my source; he... *he is the love of my life.* He has been for years now and we've been able to keep it a secret. We're very careful—hardly ever seen together in public. But I-I recently found out that I'm pregnant. And... our rulers don't approve of hybrids. They'll kill me if they find out. They'll murder my child and take Odin. I have herbs that would end the pregnancy, but I can't bring myself to do it. I've already grown attached. I want this baby, but I'm so scared."

I moved closer to comfort her while she cried into her hands. Once she'd stifled her sobs, we sat in silence, listening to the whistling wind rustle the leaves. Purple blossoms fell from the trees, fluttering around us as I combed my fingers through her dark curls. I wouldn't let anything happen to her or her baby.

"How far along are you?" I asked. "Are Fae pregnancies the same length as human ones?"

Meli nodded. "Roughly. Human gestation is around forty weeks. A faerie's is about a month longer. You must think me foolish to end up in this situation, but I'm two-hundred years old and this is my first pregnancy. I didn't think I *could* get pregnant. Faeries struggle with infertility, especially with the curse. We must maintain magic in our blood the entire pregnancy or we are susceptible to miscarriage. It's a true miracle that I'm pregnant, and yet we haven't been able to celebrate. I believe the baby was conceived about twelve weeks ago, which means I'll start showing in the next few months." A new round of tears fell and I held her until they dried again.

"I'll help you. I'll figure out how to get you to Erador, I promise. I'm going to learn to world walk—for you, I'll try. It's just that... it's such rare magic, I'm not sure where to begin." I'd looked in every library in the castle, scouring countless books, but hadn't found anything helpful yet.

She trembled as her shoulders sagged. "You'd do that for me? I-I can't thank you enough for even considering it. I'm eternally in your debt." She got down on her knees and kissed my hands.

I laughed uncomfortably. "Meli, get up. I'm your friend. *Of course,* I'm going to help."

"You're more than my friend. You have many gifts and your magic is strong... special. You've been chosen by the gods."

"Chosen for what? I did nothing to earn this power that everyone thinks I have—I certainly haven't done anything to deserve being favored by the gods."

"Don't say such things. We don't know how or why our gifts are assigned to us, but I can ensure you that they aren't a coincidence. You were sent to unite our people—to save us."

I didn't want to hear this. It was hard enough to accept that I was part Fae... that maybe I was capable of world walking. But a savior? No. Saviors didn't have panic attacks and hide in their rooms, fantasizing about princes, while actively avoiding them. They weren't afraid to try and fail, to love and lose.

I'd ended up in this world because I was a coward who'd run away from her problems. I was the *opposite* of a hero.

Meli jumped up like she'd been stung by a wasp. "The Oracle! You need to go to the Oracle!" she declared with enthusiasm. "She'll be able to help you access your powers. Her magic is as rare as yours. Her and her twin—who stayed on Erador—are powerful witches. They can see the past and the future... they receive prophecies from the gods." Suddenly her excitement drained from her and she paled.

"But perhaps it's not worth it. She will demand a steep price for her help... And she lives deep in the mountains."

We sighed simultaneously and then the sound of a gate opening and closing caught our attention. Meli smiled widely at a man with alabaster skin and pale blonde hair that fell around his shoulders. Odin, I assumed. He was holding a basket and looked like he'd arrived to harvest herbs.

He sauntered towards us, staring at me apprehensively with round, storm-grey eyes. We exchanged pleasantries and then I couldn't help but exclaim, "You're the first human I've met since arriving here!" I stood to shake his hand and he backed up a few feet, looking at Meli uncertainly.

"Odin, this is Marigold, my friend from Erador." I'd given her permission to tell him about me, and I was glad she had, because his face eased into a relaxed smile.

"I should've known. It's nice to meet you. Meli is always in her best moods after a visit from you." He shook my hand and set down his basket before settling down beside us in the grass.

He had a calm, quiet energy that complimented Meli's gregarious nature. I searched for his aura, curious if I could read a human's soul, since I couldn't see mine or Raf's.

I saw a faint flash of sage green edged with silver. His uhra was soft and unmistakably kind.

Odin tilted his head as he asked, "I'm the first you've met since you arrived? There are no humans at the castle?"

"None. I've only seen the family drink blood from a cup." It was difficult to imagine Meli biting Odin. I couldn't see any marks on him... perhaps she healed him afterwards.

"Ah, I see. Easier for them to treat us like livestock if they don't have to interact with us. I just heard news of another attack. This time two humans were found drained on the side of the road near the mountain pass. It seems faeries will be their own demise, as well as ours." Odin sighed. Meli sat stunned, clutching her belly.

"Why are faeries *draining* humans? Don't they value the preservation of magic above all else?" I asked, clenching my fists until my nails bit into skin.

"I wish I had an answer... Such attacks were rare until recently." We all sat in silence, letting the sorrow of the situation sink into our souls. I didn't tell them that the Kingdom was likely behind it.

Meli looked towards Odin. "Marigold has offered to help us get off this world, when she is ready to open a door to Erador."

His eyes lit up at her words. "You'd do that for us?" He moved closer to Meli and hugged her, resting his forehead against hers.

"I'll try... that's all I can promise." They weren't the only ones who needed a world walker's help. I was terrified of proving myself useless, of letting everyone down, but I could no longer afford to let fear guide me. I had to start believing in myself.

With a shaky exhale, I said, "I'd also like to extend the invite to anyone you two deem worthy of going to Erador—faeries that treat humans as equals—humans that may need our help. Invite those you trust, then we can formulate a plan when the time comes."

I watched them find any excuse to touch each other while we talked. They held hands, teased each other, snuck kisses... It was almost nauseating—how in love they were—mostly because of the jealousy that roiled in my gut. How did they make a relationship between faerie and human look so *effortless*?

"Does it hurt... when she bites you?" I asked, trying to appear nonchalant—as if the idea of drinking blood didn't repulse me. They both looked at each other, before erupting with laughter.

"Quite the opposite," Odin said. "I understand why you'd be disturbed by the idea, but the magic makes it pleasant for us. Some even find it addicting. But, Meli doesn't have to bite me anymore." He turned to her. "You haven't told her?"

Meli flashed me a wry smile. "We performed the blood-bond a few months ago, which makes us a mated pair. Once a couple is bonded, they share abilities and magic. Odin now has the power to heal, while I have my own supply of magic."

"The blood-bond?" I'd never heard of it.

"Yes," Meli said. "All faeries have the option to bind themselves to a partner for eternity. We didn't know if it would work between a human and a faerie, but it did. And now I don't *have* to drink from him. With these uncertain times, we decided it was worth the risk, in case one of us is killed."

"It's illegal to make the blood-bond with a human?" I asked, not surprised, but still outraged.

"It's a sacred right, gifted by the gods themselves. Some faeries see it as blasphemous to give humans our gifts. But I don't see it that way," Meli said defiantly. "We're all children of the same world. I think they *want* us to share our gifts. Perhaps, they regret not giving humans the ability to use magic and the blood-bond is a way to mend their mistakes."

I studied them. They were *good* people. I caught a glint of their uhras swirling together, like paint blending together on a palette. It was obvious that they were made for each other. And yet, couples were being torn apart and murdered, for simply following their hearts. Only monsters who gained power through hate and fear, would *criminalize* love.

"I was told that humans didn't possess the right physical traits to wield magic" I said, turning to Odin. "Did the bond change you physically?"

"Nothing noticeable. Perhaps internally something shifted. After we became blood-bonded, my senses grew keener and my blood sang with the magic that had always been there, but I hadn't been able to access. I feel more... *alive* now, more connected to the world." He gave a smile to his mate before nuzzling his nose against hers. "I'm just so grateful that I get to share my life with her."

They were proof that romantic love was *real*. The way they looked at each other made me yearn for something similar. "How does one perform the blood-bond?"

They exchanged a look. Meli answered, "We both drank from each other while we... consummated the bond. Two souls nearly become one, once bonded. I can feel him, whether he's near or far. I can sense his moods, his desires. We can even speak mind to mind. It's a closeness that makes us feel like half of our soul is missing when we're apart."

"But one can live without the other, if... one dies?" It was an intrusive question. I regretted asking it when their faces fell.

"It would be excruciating, and the loss would linger forever, but one doesn't immediately die if their mate does—though many lose the will to live if a bond breaks," Meli said softly.

I stared at the ground, unable to meet her eyes. I wouldn't let that happen to them. I'd find a way to deliver them to safety, no matter the cost.

EIGHTEEN

I found Rafael and Louis at breakfast the following day. It was rare for them to be in Monrovia at the same time, since they took turns patrolling nearby towns. Lately they'd been visiting villages still reeling from recent attacks; monitoring human Fae relations, searching for evidence, and taking stock of the magic supply in each city. They had their own agenda as well. Secretly, they were searching abandoned buildings, trying to find the missing humans, and learning anything they could about the Elders.

I pulled up a seat, peering around to make sure no servants were close enough to listen. As I threw an ice shield around us, I received a look of glowing pride from Louis.

"I was in the village yesterday visiting Meli," I whispered. "She's been getting harassed due to the blood shortage. I want to take her to Erador with us. It's time we discuss how I'm going to learn to world walk... I'm ready to go to the garden and see if I can open a portal. I'm ready for answers."

We'd been waiting until I had more control over my magic, waiting until they gathered more evidence. I was sick of waiting. Louis and Rafael formed shields of water and shadow over us, while I let mine sputter out, grabbing toast and fruit.

"World walking will demand a lot of energy. If you try to open a doorway and aren't ready, it may consume you," Louis said before shoving a bite of omelet into his mouth.

"I'm ready to *try*. The longer we wait, the more time *they* have to amass power," I replied.

Raf ran his hands through his hair before shaking it out. One stubborn lock fell back over his eyes and I had to hide my smile. He met my gaze as he said, "You're right. But there's something else we need to tell you."

Louis blurted out, "Healers have been going missing."

Rafael scowled at him. "Don't say it like that. You're going to scare her." He turned towards me. "Several have disappeared from surrounding towns, while others voluntarily left their homes with vague excuses and quick departures. We haven't been able to find out where they're going, but we can only assume they're all in the same place."

Meli. My stomach fell to my feet.

"You think they're with the missing humans?" I set down my half-eaten toast, losing my appetite.

"We don't know. It's been difficult to gather evidence. The Elders have so many spies and a seemingly unlimited amount of blood for bribery. It doesn't help that we keep hitting dead ends," Louis grumbled, tearing off a piece of croissant.

"Well, do *you* have spies? You're only two males—you can't possibly solve this by yourselves," I said.

"Of course I have spies," Rafael bit back. "But I'd like one more. Would you mind if I ask Meli some questions? In return, I'll make sure her and Odin are protected."

"I think she'd be happy to help, but only in ways that don't put her in danger. She's not in a position to do anything risky," I said firmly.

"Nothing dangerous. I promise. We just need all the eyes and ears we can get."

A weight lifted from me, knowing that Meli and Odin would now be getting real protection. It was the kindest thing Raf had ever done for me—well, not *for me*, of course. All the same, it eased my mind to know they'd have more security.

"It sounds like the perfect time to go to the portal. We're at a dead end and need answers—hopefully visiting will give us some," I reasoned.

Rafael turned to Louis. "If she's ready, we should go. We need to be a step ahead of them. At any moment they may force her to open a doorway for them, by any means necessary. If they make it to Erador, they'll be unstoppable. We can't let that happen."

His eyes blazed with fervor; I'd never seen him look so... *passionate.*

My stomach dipped. I was finally willing to admit that I might've been wrong about him. I'd reduced him to a spoiled rake when we'd first met and it hadn't been an accurate assessment. In fact, I didn't even know if he *was* a rake. I'd never seen him with a woman... not that a Prince was likely to parade around with prostitutes—especially one as private as him. Regardless, I'd decided that what he did in his personal time was *his* business.

His cruel quips, his secretive nature, his aloofness; maybe those were traits he'd needed in order to survive. Sylvia never would've let him live this long if she'd seen fire behind his eyes. Any hint of ambition towards the Crown would've caused an internal war between the family. But it seemed like war was coming, regardless. Perhaps it had always been inevitable.

I studied him as he said, "We don't have time to waste. Sylvia and her advisors are asking for a fight—challenging anyone with a shred of moral fiber to rise up and demand justice. But first, we need to even the odds. We've got to find the humans, break the curse, and rally faeries to our side. It's the only way we can win against them."

"I agree, but if we're caught—if something happens to Marigold, then all is lost," Louis replied in a low voice. "We must appear obedient. Going to the garden is a risk. If we're caught, my mother might imprison Marigold... or turn her over to them."

If anyone would've walked onto the terrace at that moment, they'd assume we were all fighting over the last slice of coffee cake. Our heads were bent over the table and we had vengeance in our eyes. But then I heard Isla's trill of laughter as she and Galen entered through the terrace doors and I was jolted back to reality.

"I'm a shadow wielder. I won't get caught," Rafael growled. "And neither will she if we go under the cover of darkness. Marigold and I are going—*tonight*."

Sneaking through the woods with a shadow wielder, in the middle of the night, was not my idea of a good time—but for Meli, I'd do it.

Before Galen made it to the table, Rafael was gone. *Those gods damned shadows.* Any warmth I'd been feeling towards him was replaced with annoyance at his abrupt departure.

At least I had Louis. My head swiveled around as I realized... he'd left me too. I curled my frosted fists. I was going to freeze their balls off for leaving me as the third wheel.

I was stuck with Galen and Isla. My heart dropped into my stomach as I took in Isla's porcelain doll face. It took considerable effort not to flare my nostrils like a bull seeing red as Galen helped her into her seat.

"Good morning, Marigold. What a beautiful day it is. Don't you look pretty as a portrait," she beamed. She was radiant in an indigo dress with matching violets in her hair.

I would've liked to believe the compliment, but her smile never quite reached her baby-blue eyes when she looked at me. I was wearing a yellow dress that accentuated my curves and flowed into a loose skirt. I *did* feel beautiful—until she sat down.

She reminded me of the elegant, two-faced aristocratic women I encountered so frequently at court in Aurelius. They were demure, sweet, *breezy...* until you felt a dagger in your back. Pretty little *assassins*. And was I any better? Smiling back at her as I fantasized about ripping out her throat?

"Good morning. I trust you both slept well," I said with too much sugar as I sipped my bitter coffee.

Isla looked at Galen with a knowing grin. I was going to be sick. Had they been sleeping together? My bed had grown cold over the last month and I'd taken to thinking of Galen when I couldn't sleep. It led to the filthiest dreams I'd ever had. I blamed the romance novels.

A flush crawled up my neck as I tried to push away the images that were now at the forefront of my mind. Thoughts of him swiping everything off this table, picking me up, and spreading me out... then ripping my dress off with those strong, capable hands.

I could feel his eyes on me, assessing what my rosy cheeks meant. I met his gaze and held it. A fire smoldered in his eyes, making me bite my cheek to keep from smiling.

He cleared his throat. "How have your meetings with Melisandre been going?" At least he was steering the conversation away from anything that made Isla giggle.

"Good. But I haven't been able to heal anyone other than myself yet."

"With your aptitude, I'm sure you'll be healing me from my battle wounds in no time." He smiled and I watched his canines push into that delicious bottom lip of his.

"You're a healer?" Isla stepped in, resting her hand possessively on his bicep. I deflated with a long shaky sigh.

"A healer in training... I still have a lot to learn." I needed to get out of here. *Now*. It was a unique kind of torture, sitting with the man I wanted... and the woman he was promised to.

"Excuse me, but I have somewhere to be." I got up, screeching my chair across the floor as I bolted. Robert trailed behind me, while I nearly slammed the door in his face in my haste to escape.

It was the weekend. I didn't have training and Galen knew it. The sad little human had nowhere to be.

But then I remembered the plan—*tonight*. Tonight, I would find out if I could open a door between worlds. I regained my focus. I *did* have somewhere to be.

Raf decided to make an appearance while I was eating dinner in my room. I'd been enjoying a candle-lit meal with myself before he ruined the ambiance.

He didn't even bother to use the door, opting to go through the *wall* in his shadow form. I had a book in my nose and looked up to find him standing in front of me—staring in his dark and mysterious way.

His black shirt accentuated his toned body, clinging to his muscles. I could tell that I was feeling *especially* lonely, because my heart skipped a beat when his glowing eyes locked with mine. A reaction to him scaring me senseless, no doubt.

"How *dare* you come into my room unannounced!" I slammed my book shut and stood, thanking the gods I was fully dressed and presentable.

"I didn't want anyone to see me using the door. I *assumed* you'd be waiting for me to come by and tell you the plan. Or did you think you were just going to jump out the window at midnight and hope I caught you?"

Was he trying to irritate me or did it just come naturally to him?

I noticed him staring at my chest—at the pronounced rise and fall of my breasts as my heart rate returned to normal. "Eyes up here," I hissed.

His gaze flicked up to my face and he smirked. "Your necklace is glowing."

I shoved it under my bodice, huffing. "Regardless of your excuses, a gentleman would never come into my room *uninvited*."

I became flustered as he stepped closer to me, within range for that misty forest scent to waft its way towards me. It assaulted my senses, disorienting me even further.

"Does it make you nervous to be alone with me? I can hear your heart racing. I suppose a *gentleman* wouldn't point such things out... but I never claimed to be one." He smiled at me in his wolfish way.

I rolled my eyes at him. "You startled me. Don't let it go to your head. Are you going to just stand there and *preen*? Or are you going to tell me the plan?"

Ignoring my question, he turned his attention to the book I'd been reading. He picked it up from the table with a tendril of shadow. I was mortified as I watched it float over to his waiting hands—at the realization that he was about to find out that I read romance.

"A Night to Remember," he read aloud, before opening to the middle of the book. *"He looked deep into her eyes before whispering, 'I am going to give you the ride of your life.'"* Raf gave me a wide grin—the largest one I'd ever seen from him. Two dimples and a full set of pearly white teeth... that were about to be smashed in.

"Give me that!" I yelled, diving for it and snatching it back.

"Don't be embarrassed! We all need to find ways to... release our stress." He couldn't resist loosing a laugh and I felt the crests of my cheeks bloom with embarrassment.

"If you're quite done *humiliating* me, perhaps you can tell me the plan and then *see yourself out*."

"Of course, *Princess*," he said with an exaggerated bow. "Tonight, at midnight, you'll look out your window and find me below. It'll be dark, so if you can't see me, trust that I will be there." He emphasized this point with raised brows, making sure I understood.

"Yes, yes. You're all shadow and smoke. If I can't see you, I'll still believe that you're there." I glared at him, as I tried to control my temper that he knew just how to stoke.

"You'll wear this." He threw me a black cloak. "And you'll throw *this* out your window." He stepped back and grew three black vines that were long enough to reach from my window to the ground.

Watching him grow *something* from *nothing* was so remarkable that I just stared in awe as seed transformed to plant. His shadows weaved the vines together into a tight, thick braided rope.

He proceeded to tie knots down the vine, creating grip along the entire length of it. "Don't forget to secure it to something before you throw it out the window."

I gave him the largest eye roll I could muster. "I understand the concept of a rope ladder. Thank you for your wisdom, Prince of Pricks." I smiled at my joke and he had the good sense to laugh along.

"Do you feel comfortable climbing down a rope?" he asked with genuine concern, dropping his self-possession momentarily.

"Yes, I'm not a *complete* saint. I used to climb out of my own bedroom window, once upon a time."

"Did you? The Princess was a little renegade, all along. *I'm shocked.*" His smile beckoned for me to smack him in the arm, so I did. It was hard and unforgiving and I was sure I'd caused more pain towards myself than him.

"I'm not a Princess." I stuck out my tongue at him before he promptly disappeared into smoke and shadow.

Nineteen

I had a difficult time settling down after Rafael left, feeling anxious about the night ahead. I watched the clock and paced until both the hour and minute-hand pointed up.

Peering out the window, I saw nothing but endless darkness below. I pulled out the rope from under my bed and secured it to the window frame. Finally, it was time to put on my cloak, lace up my boots, and begin my descent. I had just enough space to squeeze through the iron bars that were meant to keep me contained.

It was exhilarating until I reached the half-way point. How was I supposed to get back *into* my room? I wasn't sure I had the strength to climb back up, but that was a problem for later. As I touched grass, I found a black horse waiting for me... but no Prince.

It was too dark to tell if it was Raf's horse, Zagreus. Had something happened to him? Before I could panic, the horse bowed before me, beckoning me to get on its back.

I was going to *kill* Raf.

Could anything be straight forward with him? I didn't waste another breath contemplating, as I hoisted myself onto the simple black saddle. There were no reins or halter, but I held on where I could and hoped it knew where it was going.

The horse shook its head and I tensed. That head toss was eerily familiar.

No.

No... It couldn't be.

Was *this* Rafael? Was I seriously straddling Galen's brother right now? He *had* promised me he'd be here. Feeling like an idiot, I let out an exasperated sigh and hissed, "Raf? Is that you... in your shifting form?"

The horse's ears tilted back and he nodded his head in an exaggerated display. I laughed, deciding this was officially the *weirdest* night of my life. I wasn't even going to ask how he'd gotten the saddle on—though he certainly deserved to be heckled after teasing me about my book.

We were nearly invisible as we made our way through the castle gardens and past the first perimeter. I let out a long breath when we reached open grasslands. It felt inappropriate to kick his ribs, so instead I leaned over his neck and whispered, "How fast can you run?"

He took off quicker than a bat on a midnight wind as he headed for the tree line. I could barely see anything and was forced to trust that he'd get us there safely. Once we were in the forest, I leaned down low to avoid branches, laying almost flat against his withers as his mane whipped me in my face.

I was flying—*we* were flying. It was the closest I'd ever felt to my magic. It was dancing along my skin, coursing through my pounding heart, tingling in my fingers that were wrapped tightly around his course black hair.

The only indication that we'd entered deep forest was the loss of a starry sky that had provided little light, but much comfort. The moon was a sliver amongst the black night, which made it the perfect evening to sneak out.

A journey that had taken hours on my first day here felt like minutes with Raf's agile, swift movements. He weaved through the trees effortlessly, which I couldn't see, but could *feel* as his muscles gathered in unison, pivoting back and forth.

Soon he began to slow down and as he did, I felt the pull of the garden. It had always called to me, so I wasn't surprised to be guided towards the night-kissed ancient walls tonight.

"Stop here," I whispered, hopping down and scratching his cheek, like I would've my own horse. He leaned into the touch and I nuzzled my cheek against his.

There was a barrier between us that had been removed with him in his equine form. I didn't question it as we approached the ivy-covered stone.

Something grabbed me and I almost screamed. Raf covered my mouth with a rough hand. "It's just me. And no, before you ask—I'm not naked. I was wearing clothes when I shifted and I'm wearing them now."

"But what about the saddle?" I goaded, giggling. He pinched my arm and I smacked him away.

I found the gate and pushed open the door. It took my eyes a moment to adjust to the starlit garden. The tree branches that canopied the forest stopped at the stone walls, seeming to hit an invisible barrier.

I peered up to see a mosaic of stars. They were so numerous that Rafael's face was cast in silver light. We both looked at each other in complete wonderment, humbled by our insignificance and struck by the serenity of the scene above us.

The jasmine that grew along the walls filled the air with a sweet scent. Night noises created music; crickets, a breeze through the leaves, Raf's steady breathing... I was absolutely *certain* this is what my afterlife would look like. I couldn't have dreamed up a more peaceful scene. No words were needed as I took Rafael's hand and led him to the wall I'd fallen asleep against over a month ago.

There was a part of me that wanted to howl at the moon, that wanted to say to Raf, *"Run away with me. Let's leave it all behind and never look back."*

When his eyes met mine, I knew he was thinking the same thing. He rubbed my hand in encouragement as we stared at the wall. I took a deep breath, took a step forward, and touched it.

Nothing. No electric charge. No magical current.

I looked over at him, doubting myself, and he encouraged me to try again. "Command your magic. Ground yourself, like you're meditating. See if you can identify the part of you that answers to this place."

I sat on a patch of grass, leaning against the wall. Raf sat next to me, still holding my hand. I closed my eyes and spiraled deep into myself. I began at my feet and worked my way up as I searched for answers.

Where are you? Help me. Please. Tell me what to do—how to reach you.

I scanned past my stomach and then stopped at my chest, feeling a slight tug.

I'm here. I'm real. I'm part of you—but you're not ready. You need to get stronger. You need to find answers. Don't forsake me. You're on the right path.

I was so startled to feel my magic *speak* to me, that my focus lapsed and the connection disintegrated into glittering dust. "M-my magic—I know it sounds mad, but it *spoke* to me. It told me that I need to find answers—that *I am* a world walker... but that I'm not ready."

Heat flooded my chest as I let it sink in. For the first time since arriving, I didn't feel like a fraud. I wasn't just a lost, lonely girl who'd stumbled into this world, but a *world walker* who was destined to come here. None of this was a coincidence. This was my purpose.

"There is a reason we call this forest the *Whispering Woods.* It's full of surprises. I'm glad we came tonight. I think you needed to know that this is real. That you are *extraordinary...*"

Raf stared at me with moonstruck reverence, the stars reflecting in his irises. I gazed back, lost in the galaxies that were his eyes. He inched closer as he brushed my wind-blown hair away from my face. A calloused thumb slowly trailed down my temple, over my cheek, to my lips. I stood frozen as he traced over them with infinite patience.

TWENTY

I breathed in tight, nervous gasps as he moved even closer... close enough for his scent to pull me in. The smell of leather and soap, of cedar and rain—it all combined to make my head spin. I sighed as the warmth of his body enveloped me. I felt so small in his arms... so safe.

He dipped his head, closing the last bit of distance between us. It was enough to make me startle and dart away.

He shook his head, like he was coming out of a fog and said, "I'm sorry. I lost my mind for a moment. The stars, the midnight adventure..." He ran his fingers through his wavy mane and sighed. "It won't happen again. It has been too long since I've been with a woman. *Clearly.*"

Part of me had *wanted* to kiss him and find out what those flawless lips would feel like—what that smart-ass mouth would taste like. But Galen was his *brother*. I refused to be part of a love triangle—or whatever it was between Galen and I. And it wouldn't be wise to add an avalanche to their already rocky relationship. But he could've left out the part where he'd told me that he was feeling particularly desperate.

"Raf, this might've been the best night of my life. You, the stars, the magic in the air. Don't be sorry. But I care for Galen... I'm not *with* him, but all the same. I can't—I won't go down that road with you."

"I understand. Like I said, it won't happen again." Rafael turned back into his horse form without another word.

He dropped me off where he'd picked me up, the vine still hanging from my softly lit window. I stared up with dread, but a new wave of confidence washed over me. I was a world walker—I had a purpose. I gripped the rope, readying myself to say goodbye.

Wordlessly, he shifted back into himself and placed two fingers over my lips, as if to silence me. He gathered me in for a hug and then... I was nothing but mist, flying towards my window at an alarming speed. I would've screamed, but it happened too fast. *Seconds.* And then we were standing in my room.

"You could've warned me!" I sent a string of curse words at him as I looked at my hands to make sure I was whole again.

"And miss seeing the surprise on your face?"

I was relieved that we were back to our normal banter, even if he took cruel delight in teasing me. "We didn't do this on the way down because...?"

"I knew it wouldn't have been a *Night to Remember* if you didn't get to climb out your window." His smooth laugh reverberated through me as he looked deep into my eyes.

His expression grew serious. I was still gripping him. Silence stretched on.

I began to pull away, but he held me firmly, not letting me go. "So little Renegade, tell me the truth. How'd I do? Was it the ride of your life?" Before I could answer, he'd disappeared... and so had my book. But his laugh echoed on.

I couldn't sleep. Too much adrenaline coursed through my veins. The image of a black stallion soaring through a sea of stars kept flashing into my mind every time I began to drift off. As the first soft wisps of morning entered my room, I heard a knock.

"Come in," I yawned, before sitting up in panic and turning to the window. *The rope.*

It was gone. Relief flooded through me. Raf must've somehow removed it while I'd been tossing and turning in bed. I chose not to think about the details of how he'd accomplished such a feat without me noticing.

Galen burst through the door. He looked livid. His wild eyes scanned the room. "Where were you last night?" he demanded. Flame flickered from his fingers and my heart slammed against my chest in response.

"What do you mean?" I asked breathlessly.

"*What do I mean?* You're going to *lie* to me? Do I mean so little to you?" He paced back and forth in agitation.

"If I'm lying to you, you should know it's for a good reason."

Who was he to demand answers from me? He didn't own me.

"I came to see you last night—shortly after midnight. I was worried when you weren't here. I was afraid my mother had taken you. But then I saw a rope at your window... a *black* rope. There's only one person I know that could've produced that; someone who wields both shadow and earth magic." He stopped walking in circles and approached me. His flames had been put away, but the scowl on his face remained.

"Are you sleeping with Rafael?" he asked bluntly. He was leaning over me, our noses nearly touching. I could feel heat radiating off of him. He... he was *jealous.*

"No!" I said defensively. His hands gripped my thighs possessively.

"I'm not," I insisted. "But it wouldn't be your business if I was. Are *you* sleeping with Isla?" My glacial tone matched the frost coating my fingers.

How dare he with his double-standards.

I'd thrown him off with my question. He stammered, "I-I've slept in her bed. Nothing more. I want *you*, Marigold. If I bedded her, the entire time I'd be picturing *you*, damn it!" He stood and went back to pacing.

"Are you going to tell me what you were doing with Rafael in the middle of the night? Climbing out of windows, nonetheless? Was he helping you escape? If so, why are you here? Were you just going to leave without saying goodbye?" He looked out of his mind; waving his hands in the air, then shoving them in the pockets of his tan breeches.

I'd never seen a man so... emotional over me. It melted another layer of ice around my heart. He cared. And as if to confirm his feelings, a splash of color hovered around him; an angry red, with a vibrant blue center. More blue than I'd ever seen. He'd evolved into something new since I met him.

"I'll tell you. If you *promise* not to tell the Queen. If you tell her, it could ruin everything. Do you understand, Galen? Can you put me before your Crown for this secret? Or would you rather not know?"

He considered for a moment. "I won't tell her."

I hesitated before deciding to trust him. "Rafael helped me go to the ruins in the forest... not to escape, but to see if I could find any answers about my magic... to see if I could open a doorway." I looked down at my hands... hands that had held Raf's so comfortably—hands that wanted to ease Galen's temper by grabbing him by the face and kissing him. Hot shame burned in my belly.

"And... what did you discover?"

"The magic exists in me, but I can't access it yet. I need help. I need answers from someone or something. I've looked in the library—there's nothing. I don't want to be in a position where your mother asks me to wield my powers and I'm not ready. She may kill me on the spot." That wasn't *exactly* my motivation, but I couldn't trust him with the complete truth.

"I'll help you. I've wanted to help. But I didn't want to push you." He came back over and sat beside me. He took my hand and played with my fingers, avoiding my gaze. "I'm not my mother," he whispered.

"I know you aren't, but every time I tell you something that she can't know, I put you in a precarious situation. I don't want to make things harder on you than they already are." We locked eyes and I could see that he'd forgiven me. And I'd forgiven him.

I wanted him to kiss me, but instead he dropped my hand. "You didn't do anything wrong. I just wish you could trust me." Galen stood and exited the room without another word. The crackling fire snuffed out with his departure and I felt instantly cold. Down to the bone.

TWENTY-ONE

The next morning, Louis was vibrating with anticipation as I approached the training ring. Before we spoke, he created a fountain of water around us, making sure our conversation stayed private. "How'd it go?" He looked relieved to see me in one piece.

"I wasn't able to open a portal or walk to any worlds... but I could feel the magic calling to me. We're on the right path, Louis." I was in a content mood today. Despite the conflicting emotions that Galen had elicited this morning, I felt like I'd made real progress. I was hopeful that I'd eventually go *home*.

"That's excellent news! Did you come across any trouble?"

I grimaced. "Galen came by my room while I was gone. And again this morning. I had to explain where I went. I didn't tell him the real reason I was there, but he knows I went... and that I wasn't successful opening a portal. He promised not to tell your mother."

Louis's eyes widened before he composed himself. "It's alright. It's clear to anyone paying attention that he's infatuated with you. I don't think he'd do anything that would put you in harm's way. He could use a good influence." He grinned, playfully bumping me.

Louis found the tension between Galen and I much more amusing than I did. It felt more like soul-eating agony to me. "I'm glad you can find humor in the situation," I said, hitting him with wind magic that lifted him up several feet in the air, before dropping him on the ground.

"Ouch. That's going to bruise!" He laughed in his happy-go-lucky way that was currently pissing me off.

"Sorry. I'd heal you, but I haven't learned how yet." I smiled sweetly. "I've heard mention of an Oracle—someone who might be able to help us."

Louis's face fell and he let out a long breath. "Yes... There's a witch that lives in the mountains—she should be a last resort. Her knowledge comes at a steep price."

"What kind of price? I assume you don't mean money."

"It depends on what you have to give. She can sense what our fears are—what we value the most. She feeds off hopes, dreams... and other things."

He looked a bit green and I didn't want to ask. Unfortunately, I needed to know. "She's a true witch? Is she Fae? Human? We don't have any other options, Louis. We don't have time to waste."

"Witches are their own entity. There are only a few scattered amongst our worlds. They rarely breed, but are truly immortal, with an infinite lifespan. Their magic wasn't affected by the curse and they don't wield it in the same way we do, but that's not to say they don't enjoy blood. They aren't above eating... *anything,* and can channel magic from blood, emotions, bargains... their magic can trap *souls,* Marigold.

"And on top of that, they're spider shifters—all of them. Not small spiders, but larger than you and I. Some Fae journey to the Oracle to gain insight and never return. Others give something vital of themselves and are never the same."

I'd never seen Louis look so nervous, but I was desperate to help Meli and find answers. He scanned my face, set in a determined scowl, then looked at the sky like he was cursing the gods. "Have I told you that I *hate* spiders?"

I grinned, raising a brow. "A Fae male, capable of creating a raging river, afraid of spiders?"

He glared at me. "We'll need Raf's help. And Galen's. We'll need to get approval from my mother, she won't let you just wander off castle grounds without good reason."

I frowned. Spiders didn't scare me, but she did. "How do we go about asking something like that?" I gnawed at my lower lip as I began to fret.

"I'll talk to my brothers, we'll come up with a plan." He seemed more confident as the idea sunk in. It gave me a small boost of hope, but my stomach was still in knots, thinking of all the things that could go wrong.

"I'll be leaving for a few days next week. Rafael will take over your training while I'm gone. You're ready to start advancing in your magic and you need a sparring partner. Ice and shadow play well together—better than ice and water. Plus, you need to learn how to shift into your animal form. And... I can't help you with that until I manage to find my own."

I didn't want to train with Rafael. Whenever I was around him, I felt like a walking contradiction; hot and cold, tight and loose. I wanted his friendship, yet was ready to throttle him at a moment's notice. He'd be relentless and unforgiving. He wouldn't have Louis's patience... which was probably the point. I couldn't expect other magic wielders to play nice. *Especially* if I was ever to face a real opponent. Like Sylvia.

"What about Galen? Ice and fire... that sounds ideal." I smiled hopefully before Louis shot me down.

"He has no time in his schedule to train you. He's in meetings all day, if not doing the Queen's dirty work."

And flirting with Isla. I sighed. He squeezed my shoulder in a comforting gesture. "Don't look so worried. Raf doesn't bite. *Remember?*"

I trained extra hard with him during the remainder of our lesson. I created shields of wind and sustained them as long as possible. I summoned an ice storm that swirled around us and left us shivering despite the muggy weather. I may have been advancing when it came to magic, but it seemed all other progress would be halted until we went to the Oracle.

The thought of having to wait dampened my mood. Louis encouraged me to have some fun, but it felt wrong to lose focus now. I was desperately holding on to the idea of returning home soon. But he was probably right—a little fun would be good for me.

There was just one tiny problem. The only person I wanted to have *fun* with was busy courting another woman.

A week later, I asked Louis if he would escort me to the library to pick out a few books. We'd just finished our last training session together and he'd be heading south to Elysia in a few days. Robert was off duty, which meant Louis was begrudgingly acting as my chaperone.

Following me around like I was a criminal made him uncomfortable. I also suspected he would've already been at a tavern, looking for a woman to keep him company, if I hadn't been standing in his way. I'd have two days off before training with Rafael began and I needed some fresh reading material, so Louis would just have to be patient.

I felt severely underdressed in a dirty grey tunic and leggings as we entered the Grand Library. I peered at the mural-covered ceiling, the endless rows of polished bookshelves, and then at a large, statuesque figure sitting at a mahogany table.

I froze when I realized it was Galen. He was hunched over reading, while a black cat laid next to him, batting its tail back and forth. It basked in a ray of sunshine that spilled across the dark red wood. It was *my* cat—the one that had followed me around when I'd first arrived. When it had stopped visiting, I'd been worried, but apparently it had just grown bored of my company.

Cats. They were too fickle; I'd always been more of a dog person, anyways.

When Louis saw an opportunity to ditch me, he took it. "Galen can act as your chaperone. I've got places to be." Louis shoved me towards his brother and darted away. *Traitor.*

My heart began to pound when I made eye contact with Galen. I wanted to hide behind a pillar, dive behind a bookcase. Instead I danced in place as he prowled over to me.

"I've been doing some research for you, world walker. I haven't found much yet, but I'll keep searching until I do." There was an undeniable hunger behind his eyes. I met his gaze in silent challenge. I wanted him too. And I was finally ready to let him see how much.

"Thank you, I appreciate it. I need all the help I can get," I replied, rubbing goosebumps from my arms.

"Can I help you find something?" He gave a sultry smile as his gaze wandered over me.

"Books on healing magic. Or really anything that will keep me from dying of boredom this weekend."

"A wielder of two elements, a healer, *and* a world walker. How does it feel to be chosen by the gods?" He looked up towards the mural on the ceiling, then winked. "They say ice and fire wielders are extra compatible, you know..."

"Who are *they*?" I asked, biting my lip.

"Fine, you caught me. It's just me that says that." He was shameless, and I was smitten. Even his terrible jokes caused a stupid grin to spread across my face. I didn't recognize myself around him.

I wasn't sure what had changed, but his guard was down today. He hadn't flirted with me like this in weeks... I *hated* that I loved it so much. All logic, all sense of pride, *vanished* when he looked my way.

Our conversation ran dry. I was paralyzed; the tension between us had pinned me in place. I felt like a preserved butterfly that had been stabbed and mounted on the wall.

I pictured him leading me back behind a stack of books, pushing me against one of the shelves. I could almost feel his lips against my skin as they traveled down my neck and continued...

down...

down...

"There you are!" Isla announced herself, coming from behind a pillar, book in hand. She looked stunning in a flowing white dress that made her look even more *Faerie Princess* than usual.

"I found what I was looking for. Are you ready to leave?" She stopped short when she saw me. "Oh, I apologize. I didn't see you there." She looked down at me... at my dirty clothes and frizzy hair. I shriveled beneath her hard stare. "What have you been rolling in?" Her nostrils flared as she stifled a laugh.

"I just finished training with Louis." I lifted my chin high, trying to will the rising heat in my cheeks to stop.

"Training for what? It looks like you've just mucked out the entire stable."

I glared at her, daring her to say another word. I was tempted to threaten to send her to another world—one where there was no oxygen. "It doesn't concern you," I said, turning away from her. "Galen, am I free to look for books or do I need an escort?"

His eyes were sparkling with mischief. *Of course he was enjoying this.* "Go ahead, I'll wait for you right here."

I left without another glance towards either of them, walking as fast as my sore legs would carry me.

I could hear Isla speaking to Galen as I moved away from them. "Why do you have to wait for *her*? I thought we were going to take a walk around the gardens." Isla's shrill voice echoed through the silent library and this time it was me holding back a giggle.

I selected a few books, then meandered, taking my time returning to the Prince and his future bride. I browsed the romance section, but the novel I wanted wasn't there. Raf still had my book and had been conveniently absent as of late. He'd taken it right when the enemies were about to become lovers, and I'd never forgive him for it.

When I found Galen, Isla was gone. "Where did she go?" I asked, trying to sound nonchalant.

"I told her I'd see her at dinner—that you were a *complete menace* and needed to be watched like a hawk." He came closer, tugging on my loose braid. My stomach fluttered in response.

"How is training going?" he asked, taking my books from me and flipping through them. I tried to focus on his question instead of his beautiful bone structure, but my brain felt full of cotton when he was near.

"Well enough. I'm getting faster, but so is Louis. Eventually, I'll be less out of shape. And he'll have it coming..." I trailed off as he began to inch closer.

"I've seen you naked. I wouldn't describe you as out of shape. In fact, I'd be very sad to see any of your curves go." I suddenly felt uncomfortably hot. *Flirt.*

"Someone may hear you!" I whispered.

He looked around the empty library. "I'll take my chances." He set my reading material down on the table and took my hand as he led me towards the rows of books.

"Where are we going?" I asked as my heart began to race.

He remained silent until he pulled me behind a tall shelf. "How anyone can look *so good* covered in sweat and filth is beyond me," he murmured. He leaned down and kissed me, stealing the very breath from my lungs. Before I had a chance to gasp for air, his hand was up my shirt. My heart exploded as his fingers grazed delicate skin.

"Galen... th-this is a public place. We might be caught. Plus... I thought we'd decided that this is a bad idea." My voice, my entire body, was quivering.

He paused, while his hand rested under my shirt. He cupped my breast, gently rubbing circles around my peaked nipple as he stared into my eyes. He gave me another deep kiss, leaving me panting before he answered.

"I was in a dark place. I didn't want to bring you into that. But that hasn't stopped me from wanting you. I'm beginning to think I *need* you like a long winter needs the first bloom of spring."

A lump formed in my throat. I couldn't breathe. "What about Isla?"

He frowned down at me. "I've told you, she's my mother's choice. You *know* who my choice is."

"Have they made you... hurt anyone else?" I couldn't look at him, but I had to know.

He lifted my chin up, forcing me to make eye contact. "No, but I fear the day they do. Being Prince is just an illusion of power. I'm a pawn to them and I don't know how to leave the game. I don't deserve someone as wholesome as you. I'm hesitant to corrupt you. But sometimes, when I'm feeling selfish, I fantasize about what we could be doing together... if you were mine."

Every word he spoke melted the permafrost around my soul. "Don't talk like you aren't worthy of happiness."

"I'll never be worthy of *you*. But I'm beginning to wonder if you're my only chance at happiness." He caressed my cheek and I leaned into it. He was always so *warm*. We stared at each other, knowing we were teetering on the edge of something.

TWENTY-TWO

He smashed his lips against mine, pressing me up against the bookshelf. Several books pushed through to the other side, falling on the floor.

Clunk.

Clunk.

Clunk.

The sound reverberated through the library. We were unfazed as he hoisted me up, aligning our hips. I wrapped my legs around him and we rocked together; pulling hair, biting, *clawing*, as we desperately tried to close any space between us. Our teeth clashed as his tongue flicked to the roof of my mouth and I licked along one of his canines. *I needed to be closer.*

A metallic tang coated my tongue. *Blood*. I'd nicked myself on his fang. "I-I'm sorry..." I blurted out, my chest heaving as I caught my breath.

His eyes were large and wild. "Don't be sorry. You taste... *fuck*, you taste phenomenal. Potent, *powerful*... like you're the gods damn sun that I'm lucky enough to orbit around." He huffed, kissing the shell of my ear, breathing me in, as he moved to my neck. Licking, sucking, nibbling. I knew what he wanted.

It should've terrified me, but instead it sent lava down my spine. His desire was my desire, traveling down my core and heating my blood.

I didn't know exactly when the idea of his bite had become enticing. At some point, dirty dreams had turned to curiosity... and now curiosity was throbbing throughout my body, begging him to claim me.

I cried out as he raked his teeth along delicate skin. He'd successfully worked me into a crazed state... I was boneless in his arms. I'd submitted.

I *needed* him. I rubbed myself against the hard bulge in his pants, wanting *more*.

A preternatural stillness washed over him and I froze. I wanted it. Could he feel how badly I wanted it? Would he just bite down or would he ask? My blood felt thick as it sloshed through my pumping heart. It was fluttering in rapid, frenzied beats as his tongue trailed down to the crook of my neck.

Then he was gone. In one breath, he'd been thrown across the library by a shadowy force. I heard his body *smash* against the stone wall as the bookshelves around me shuttered. He fell to the ground in a crumpled heap. A black fog poured in and then I was blind.

I stumbled towards him in the dark, not taking time to process *who* attacked or if I was also in danger, before I was at his side. I could barely see through the opaque mist. I stroked his cheek to rouse him as I frantically called, "Galen, can you hear me?" but he remained unmoving.

The smoke cleared and I smelled blood. I scanned the rest of his body. His arm must've hit first, because it looked broken in several places. Bone was protruding from his forearm, while a wound on his head gushed. The coppery scent surrounded me. It smelled like *him*—smoky, spicy, warm. *Galen*. I stroked the hair out of his eyes as I hovered over his lifeless form.

"Did he bite you?" I heard Rafael's silky voice echo against the library walls. My head whipped around. He was wearing his signature black, looking dark and menacing as shadows slithered behind him. His golden eyes glittered as he studied me.

I stood up and *hissed*. Ice coated my fingers as I curled them at my sides. "Did you do this? Why!?"

I lunged, throwing the full force of my body at him and punching him in the chest. I was tempted to turn him into a *fucking icicle*—he'd thaw eventually. I hadn't seen him since our midnight ride and *this* is how he decided to make an appearance? I was wild with wrath, nearly frothing at the mouth.

He held me easily as I struggled and clawed at him like a hellcat.

"Did he hurt you?" Raf asked, more sternly this time. He pushed my hair away from my face, touching around my neck and chest, presumably searching for a bite wound.

"No!" I yelled, shoving him away. "And if I *had* let him bite me, it would be none of your business. Help him!" I was sobbing—out of my mind at Galen's limp body.

"He'll be fine. He's Fae. That's just a scratch for us," he said evenly, while sliding his hands into his pockets with zero remorse.

"You're a monster. If you aren't going to help, then leave us." I raised my hands and whipped a wave of icy wind towards him.

He easily dodged it and looked down at me with a twisted grin. "Impressive." And then he was gone, leaving smoke in his wake. I was seething with icy *fury*... I'd get my revenge, but first I needed to help Galen.

A healer's blood would fix him. Meli had told me as much for this very reason. She said there might come a time where I was desperate to help, but didn't yet have control over my magic. She'd also warned that I should be cautious with who I choose to give my blood to. But in this moment, there was no one I'd rather use my gift on.

I reached for his belt, for the scabbard, and unsheathed a gold and emerald dagger. I cut into my palm until blood began to pool at the seam. I didn't feel the pain as it sliced. My adrenaline was high, giving me focus and clarity. I opened his mouth and let my blood trickle onto his lips. My hand began mending itself immediately and I had to cut myself one more time to ensure I'd given him enough. Sitting back, I watched, holding his hand.

Galen's eyelids began to twitch, then open. He looked up at me in a daze. "What happened?" he groaned, attempting to sit up as he took in the scene, the blood, and then his arm.

"Rafael. He threw you across the room. You hit your head... and broke your arm."

"That *bastard*. You healed me? How?" He looked down at his arm with knitted brows, then licked his lips. I watched his pupils dilate as he realized what I'd done. Nearly all the green in his irises was gone as he said, "Y-you gave me your blood." It wasn't a question.

Before he was even fully healed, he was on top of me with the sharp stare of a predator, making my heart leap into my throat. "I can still taste you on my tongue. You're going to drive me mad... I need you. Now. *Please*... Can I bite you? I promise, I won't hurt you."

I couldn't say no. After what had just happened, I didn't want to. Seeing him unconscious had shattered me. I didn't want to hold back—I was *done* holding back.

"Yes," I said, my voice thick with emotion.

Before I had a chance to reconsider, his canines were scraping along the flickering pulse above my collar bone. For one fleeting moment, a wave of heart-stopping pain pierced through me as he bit down. I inhaled sharply, ready to shove him off—but before I could, a wave of sensation washed over me, making me shudder. There was a sweetness to the sting.

He released a low groan, while the soft pressure of his lips sent a cascading waterfall of pleasure down my spine. And then my soul was on fire with red-hot desire.

The magic that tethered us together felt primitive in its pull—ancient in its hypnotic power. He could have all of me. I was his; he could drain me if that's what he wanted. As long as this feeling didn't stop.

I was throbbing, aching, burning—absolutely obliterated by this tidal wave of lust. Somewhere in the back of my mind, I knew that it was a dangerous level of pleasure. This feeling was too powerful—this Golden Prince, too perfect.

He drew back, looking as unhinged as I felt. "Are you okay?" Galen asked shakily, wiping tears from my eyes with his thumb. My emotions were so heightened. Seeing him broken on the floor, then experiencing euphoria minutes later... It was as if I was having an out of body experience.

I was floating, detached from reality, as I peered down on the scene below. Galen's mussed bronze hair and his grey velvet tunic, coated in dark crimson stains. Me, splayed on the ground, staring up at the ceiling, holding a hand over the swollen bite. Us, lying together on the marble floor, in a pool of Galen's blood. It would take a crew to clean this up.

His lips were the cleanest part of him. The copper smell of his blood was overpowering, making me feel queasy. My neck throbbed where he'd bitten me, but it didn't hurt. I silently hoped my healing magic would work quickly. As much as I'd secretly wanted it, I didn't want it on display.

I eventually found my voice and replied, "It felt like my heart was going to burst out of my chest, from how much you made me feel—how much you *make* me feel." A small truth.

He looked drowsy as he kissed my cheek. "I feel the same. I've bitten humans, but never a faerie. Never *you*. That was... other worldly."

"*Literally*," I giggled. His strong arms wrapped around me and I didn't want him to let go.

Galen and I spent the remainder of the day in my room, making up for lost time: Talking, sleeping, cuddling, and kissing. He'd been gentle with me since the library, refraining from anything too physical, as if having me close was pleasure enough. The Queen expected us at dinner, but he boldly declared that she could be disappointed and instead ordered food to the room.

Lusha drew me a bath, turning pale when she saw the state we were in. He excused her until morning, asking for her discretion. She nodded ferociously, before turning crimson and fleeing the scene.

I should've resisted any scenario that suggested we were involved, but it felt so nice to be taken care of. He bathed and massaged me with sweet-smelling oils, dabbing at the small hurt on my neck, coveting every inch of me. It made me feel loved like a child. We drank wine in front of the fireplace, then fell asleep in each other's arms.

The next morning, Galen woke me up at sunrise, pressing into my backside. I couldn't hold in my grin, as I realized he was real, and this wasn't a dream. I felt a hot puff of breath behind my ear, then his splayed hand on my stomach, as he began to explore me.

I gasped as his fingers made their way down my navel. "I'm ticklish," I hissed, arching away from him.

A low growl left his throat as he yanked me back, lifting one of my legs, and opening me wide. "That's because you're a delicate flower. I wonder... is your nectar as sweet as your blood?" he asked before dipping his fingers between my thighs and spreading my petals.

He traced slow, deliberate circles around *that* spot—the one that made me jolt and shake every time his fingers brushed against it. As I began to whimper and clutch the bedding, he pushed a finger inside of me, keeping just enough friction on that little bud to drive me crazy. We moved together as I trembled beneath the touch of his hand.

I was still experiencing shockwaves when Galen flipped me around, face to face, and guided me to his erection. Trailing curious fingers along his length, I experimented with what he responded to. I wrapped my hand around, gliding it over velvety steel.

He took slippery nectar from between my legs, rubbing it up and down his shaft, while he watched me with heavy-lidded eyes. I copied his movements, feeling curious and eager to please—studying him as he twitched and groaned. It was surprisingly rewarding—to be the one controlling his pleasure. When he reached his release, he spilled onto my stomach, shuddering.

He noted my look of surprise and said, "If we have sex and I release in you, it could produce a baby. I'm on a tonic that would prevent such a thing. Has anyone ever explained this to you?"

"I'm well read," I said with false bravado. Adeline had explained the basics. It didn't stop me from feeling completely over my head.

"Humans have such a short lifespan, yet they spend a third of it staying chaste." He said with an edge of condescension. I buried my face, but he pulled my hands away. "No, don't feel ashamed... sex is natural—as natural as eating, drinking... as natural as *magic*, to a Fae. It's your *customs* that are backwards, not you."

He was wise not to laugh or even smirk as he made sure I knew the ins and outs of procreation. After our conversation, I could feel hard evidence of just how much he'd liked our talk. "Has corrupting me turned you on?" I asked mockingly.

His entire face lit up. "You have no idea. I'm dying to taste you. Do you trust me?" I nodded slowly, heart racing, as he climbed over me.

"Do you taste sweet like honey? Or something fruitier? Melon, perhaps?" he asked with a husky tone that vibrated against my skin, as he moved lower and lower. He made his way down until his head was between my thighs. He spread me open, meeting my apprehensive gaze. The sight was both erotic and anxiety-inducing. I protested, trying to sit up, when I realized what he was about to do.

"Lay back, love. I don't want to hear the words '*no*' or '*stop*.' You are mine until I say so. Understood?" My heart tumbled over itself as I felt his breath at my sex. This was... so intimate. A flush crept across my skin.

The way his fiery green eyes stayed locked on me, while his lips grazed sensitive skin, caused me to wiggle and writhe under the scrutiny of his piercing gaze. He slid me forward, forcing me fully on my back, then settled in with a possessive growl. His tongue boldly ran along my center, causing me to release a startled groan. Soft, warm kisses turned into swirling tight circles as he expertly flicked his tongue over and over. I arched up, twisting and kicking, needing relief from his relentless pursuit to devour me.

"Lay still for me," Galen commanded. I did my best, but... *six gods*, he was asking for the impossible. I was drenched and he still wasn't done with me. I squirmed in anguish, cursing *Cyro*, and whoever else was responsible for gifting him so thoroughly.

I'd caught fire, though his flames were nowhere in sight. He moved his tongue in and out, up and around, gripping my thighs with bruising force. "Galen..." I breathed, fisting his hair.

Then his fingers were working me, while his mouth continued its conquest, wringing every ounce of sensation from me. I panted, legs quaking, as I reached the top of the mountain. Frost bit at my fingers while I bucked, thrusting my head back as I rode wave after wave.

"Galen..." I moaned. He made no motion to move from his position, perched between my legs. "Galen... it's too sensitive. *Please*. Stop," I said desperately.

"Not yet," he huffed between greedy mouthfuls and dove deeper. He couldn't mean to make me shatter again. I'd die from it.

The pleasure had turned to something else. He held me down with a flat-palmed hand over my stomach. Just as I thought the sensation would kill me, I came a third time. Frost spread over my body... over the bed. Galen looked up at me, licking his lips. "You taste like sunshine, ice wielder. Explain *that* to me."

We laid tangled in a heap as we drifted down from the clouds. He nuzzled into the crook of my neck and promptly began to snore.

I stayed awake, mind racing, as morning light filled the room. Could I truly let myself fall for this male? Was there a universe where our lives—our people—could co-exist? I had my doubts, but for the first time, I was willing to set them aside and find out where this could lead.

I'd let him bite me and it had felt better than I wanted to admit. I prodded the puncture wounds to find that they'd scabbed over but hadn't completely healed. In contrast, my wound from the village brawl had disappeared in hours. I pondered why a bite would heal slower than a cut. My stomach sank and I took a deep breath, shutting down the shame that was creeping its way in.

I was trying not to let negative feelings worm their way into my head, but I could already hear my guilty conscious asking, *what would Ophelia think?*

Annoyed, I countered the intrusive thought. *Ophelia hadn't even told me about faeries or magic—she might very well be Fae. It was her fault for letting me walk blindly into this world.*

I snuggled into Galen, until the voices faded. Over the last decade, I'd let my fear of abandonment keep me from living life to the fullest. I'd let it fester into insecurity and self-doubt. Somewhere along the way, I'd grown ice around my heart. It was time to admit that my loneliness was partially self-induced. I'd pushed people away, declined invites, and judged others without truly knowing them; until I'd found myself jaded and alone.

Galen had walked right past my boundaries—more accurately, he'd set them on fire. And now he was sleeping soundly on my chest. I watched gold lashes flutter as he dreamed, feeling the full weight of his presence upon my heart.

He terrified me as much as he elated me. Sometimes he was over-ly confident, sometimes his moods were unpredictable, and I did worry about his relationship with his mother. But he'd saved me, in more ways than one. He was exactly what I needed at this moment: Safety, warmth, *passion*. We were both a little broken, but together we were whole.

TWENTY-THREE

I woke to the sound of Lusha gasping and slamming the door. "Sorry, Miss Marigold!" I cracked an eye open. I'd fallen back asleep—it was well into mid-morning now. Galen was passed out on his back, his mouth gaped open. I laughed softly and it was enough to wake him.

"Hi." I smiled, kissing his shoulder.

"Hi," he said with a reciprocal peck, sitting up. His stomach muscles expanded as he stretched. Feeling bold, I stared at every beautiful inch of him.

"Galen, if it's not too personal, would you tell me what your *pneuma* form is?" I rolled over until I was laying on my belly, my chin resting on my folded arms. He rubbed the sleep out of his eyes and scratched his head until his hair stood straight up.

As I watched him stretch again with feline grace, I blurted out, "I know what you are—I'd bet my life on it."

"You shouldn't make bets with your life, love. Especially in a land of cursed faeries that would happily take you up on it." He stood up and faced me. My mouth went dry as I took in his muscular, lean body.

In a matter of one... two... three seconds... a gigantic, golden lion appeared in my bedroom. His fur was the same fiery color as his hair; auburn with flecks of gold that weaved through a brilliant, thick mane. His head was the size of my torso. He was so big, he filled up nearly all the floor space in my room, leaving me sitting on my bed, unsure if I should be afraid of making any sudden movements.

Many things in this new world had surprised me, but nothing had prepared me for the awe-inspiring sight of Galen's lion form. I wanted to reach out and touch his velvety face, bury my cheeks in his luxurious fur; but instead I watched him in silence... waiting for his next move.

Galen approached me slowly and it took all of my bravery to keep from backing away as he laid his massive head on my lap and *purred*. I cautiously stroked between his eyes, up into his silky mane, scratching behind his ears. His purr increased in volume and I grinned down at him, giving him a kiss on the nose.

"Thank you," I whispered, my voice thick with emotion. "You are glorious, in both forms. And I want you to know that I'm done fighting this. I'm ready to be yours, for you to be mine... if you still want me." He blinked up at me with emerald eyes that held the reflection of his soul, even in his feline form.

"Losing my mother... I think it stunted my ability to dream. It was a loss that consumed my adolescence, but I think I'm finally ready to let myself live again. I still have doubts... I might never be able to let them all go. And I think you may understand that, in your position. Sometimes duty takes precedent over what we want—over who we wish we were. But right now, I sit here before you, telling you that I care... and I don't want you to disappear again."

Galen transformed back into his Fae form and appeared on his knees before me. "I'm not going anywhere. Although, I feel at a slight disadvantage kneeling before you in the nude." We laughed together at the situation—at the fate that brought us together.

"Somehow, you look at me like I'm not a liability, even after seeing me broken—knowing what I've done. It makes me want to be better. It makes me feel *invincible*. I'll try to not be a disappointment to you," he said as he sprinkled kisses on my hand, up my arm, and along my neck. "Let's keep this a secret for now—until we have more leverage with my mother and the Elders. Once you can world walk, they'll approve of our relationship. The last thing I want is for them to target you because of me."

He tapped his fingers against my thigh as he waited for my answer. To his relief, I gave no protest. The less Sylvia knew about us, the better. I hadn't forgotten her warning to stay away from her son.

"You have my heart... and my protection. You have since the day I met you," Galen whispered, resting his chin on my head and holding me tightly. Warmth bloomed in my chest and it felt like hope. Perhaps with all three Princes on my side, I had a fighting chance at making it out of this world alive.

Later that morning, we sat at a small table in my room, eating a light breakfast of biscuits and raspberry jam, while sipping on tea. It was a peaceful moment and I wanted to savor it. I wanted to experience more of *this* with him.

"Could we spend the day together and pretend that you're not Prince Galen and I'm not from another world... just for today?"

"I'd like nothing better. I had a few things I was supposed to do today, but I'm happy to put them off in exchange for the chance to charm your pants off." He leaned over to kiss my cheek while I chewed a piece of biscuit.

"But I'm not wearing pants," I replied with a hard swallow. My periwinkle dress was the color of today's blue skies. It left little to the imagination with a deep neckline that plunged down, showing off freckled, tanned skin.

"Even better," he said, grinning like a wolf.

"Would you like to go to the lake today? We could go swimming. The water is pleasantly cool in the heat of the day, although you probably don't mind the heat with ice in your veins. I, on the other hand, am always hot. I should've been born in the arctic."

"Well, now you have your own personal cooling system," I laughed, waving my fingers at him and blowing an icy breeze.

"I knew there was a reason I couldn't stay away." He nipped at my finger, pulling my hand to his and licking sticky jam off my palm. My stomach dipped in anticipation of what today would bring.

"I don't have anything to wear. I'll have to ask Lusha if I can borrow a swimsuit." It was difficult for me to picture faeries wearing the full body costumes women had to wear in Aurelius when they wanted to go in the water.

"Why would you wear a *suit* to swim? Nature intended for us to swim in the nude."

I blinked at him. "I suppose that works too..." I was so very far from home.

We made it down the gravel path, to the private beach that the castle butted up against. There was no one else in sight; not even Robert had followed us down the winding trail. I was surprised to find sand, just like beaches on the ocean. It had been ages since I'd seen the sea, but I still held nostalgia for its salty, pungent smell.

The lake air was sweet in comparison. A floral aroma drifted in with the warm breeze. And then there was the intoxicating scent of the Prince who walked beside me. I took a deep breath.

Dense forest sat on either side of the castle's private beach, sheltering exotic birds that chirped and trilled. They were so colorful that I could spot them from a distance. Vibrant blues, neon green, and one large red bird with extravagant tail feathers. The sand glittered in different shades of pale pink, contrasting against the cerulean water. The waves were gentle, fading in and back out with a soft *hush*, like a mother soothing her infant. It made me think of *her*.

Was she protecting me from afar? Keeping me out of the Queen's schemes? Sylvia had been quiet for too long. I let the gentle wind and the hum of the ocean melt my worries away... until all that was left was Galen. His uhra *shimmered* a bright gold in the sunshine, like a pearlescent seashell. It overpowered his typical red and blue, which were barely visible. An after-effect from my magic, I assumed. Was that what *my* soul looked like? I'd tried to find mine in the mirror, but for some reason, it evaded me.

We set down our basket of picnic items and laid out a blanket. Were we to strip down in front of each other in broad daylight? I could hear Thea tutting at me from here.

"Would you like to swim?" Galen asked, taking my hand and walking to the water's edge. I dipped a toe in and found it delightfully warm.

"Perhaps a drink first?" I suggested. Liquid courage felt necessary. Why did this feel so *awkward*? There was a new layer of vulnerability—of expectation between us. Something held me back from fully relishing the moment, but I couldn't figure out what it was.

He poured us each a glass of sparkling wine and came over to sit behind me on our blanket. Wrapping his brawny body around mine, he worked the knots from my shoulders, easing my anxiety. I leaned back into him, savoring his warmth.

"I don't know that I've ever had a date like this," he admitted.

"What is courtship typically like in Nymera?"

"I wouldn't really know. I've never gotten to experience a *typical* life. Most of my time with women has involved more sex than conversation. And I had no interest in bringing Isla here... I've never wanted anything serious until now," he confessed.

My stomach twisted at his words and I took a swig of champagne. "Can I ask you about something? It might be a sensitive topic..."

"Of course. I'll tell you anything—everything," he replied, nuzzling into my hair. Such feline mannerisms he had.

"Why did Rafael attack you yesterday?" I couldn't see his face, but felt his body stiffen.

"The most *obvious* reason is that he was jealous of what he saw; me... on you."

Jealous? That was ridiculous; though I refrained from scoffing out loud. Raf had tried to kiss me last week, but it was because we were caught up in the moment, not because he *wanted* me. He'd said as much.

"If you say so. But you seem to mutually resent each other. Does it go deeper than sibling rivalry?" I fidgeted with my necklace, currently hot between my fingers.

"Rafael is... disrespectful to everything I stand for. Everything I am, as heir to the throne. He shirks his responsibility to the Crown at every opportunity and then seems to resent me for not doing the same. I can't run away from duty as easily as he can."

It was an honest answer, if not one-sided. Raf couldn't fully understand the pressure that came with being the heir, but he had his own reasons for not respecting the system. The Elders and Sylvia had tried to end his life before he'd even entered the world. And Galen was complicit—working with them to eliminate hybrids. It was difficult to acknowledge that truth. I stayed silent in contemplation.

"Can I confess something to you?" Galen's smooth voice pulled me back to the present.

"Anything." I silently cringed. *Please don't let it be more murder.*

"Since I tasted your blood, I've felt... *high*. On you. Blood has never felt like this in my system before. Usually it's just magic. With you, it's *euphoric*. Maybe it's because your magic is strong." He paused, kissing the shell of my ear. "But I think it's because of how much I care about you."

I turned around, needing to see him. "My blood makes you feel drugged?" I blurted out indelicately.

"Not drugged... just *happy*. Content. A rare feeling for me." I decided it was easiest to take it as a compliment.

"Honestly, I *hate* how good it felt. Being bitten—it shouldn't feel... *like that*. It seems like *another* advantage faeries have over humans. It isn't right. And yet, I can't stop thinking about it," I admitted self-consciously. Mortification burned its way through me.

Galen reassured me with a kiss. "Don't be embarrassed. Even before the curse, faeries bit each other on occasion. There's a reason our canines are extra sharp." He rubbed his tongue along a tooth to emphasize. My heart rate doubled with the gesture. I was dangerously close to knocking him over and having my way with him.

"The blood-bond?" I breathed.

"Yes. You've heard of it? The closest equivalent for humans would be marriage, but it's *more* than that. It's sacred to us—the highest declaration of love. Not everyone chooses to bond. It's a serious commitment for beings as long-lived as us. But that's the primitive reason behind why it's so... *rewarding*. It's supposed to be."

His words doused my shame, like cold water washing over hissing hot stones. As guilt dissipated, I acknowledged that joy and self-loathing couldn't co-exist.

My virtue didn't define me; it held no real value, at least not to me. If I wanted to give Galen my blood, if I wanted to give him my body, I should be allowed to make those choices without feeling dirty about it.

Aurelian society had no voice here, which gave me the opportunity to find my own. Women were considered equals in Nymera, even if humans weren't. It was a reminder that social constructs were subjective—and another way to control people. I was going to follow my own moral compass from now on.

Galen slowly stood, finishing his drink. "Would you like to get naked with me?" he asked with a wry grin.

We undressed each other slowly, nerves settling, as fizzy bubbles made their way into my bloodstream. I felt pleasantly buzzed and the effects of the sun added another layer of haziness.

Once we were undressed, he stepped back and admired me, looking exceedingly confident in just his skin. I let my eyes glide over him as if he was a polished bronze statue on exhibit.

"You're breathtaking," Galen said, approaching me. "It's been the sweetest torture... coveting you from afar. And now, you're finally *mine*." He scooped me up, taking me into the water. Before we'd even fully submerged, he was making me squeal as he tickled his way around sensitive spots.

We kissed in the wave break like lovestruck mermaids, splashing around as if we were always this carefree. When he dunked me, I froze the water around him in retaliation, leaving him immobile until he melted his way out, while I laughed maniacally.

Once he was free, I tried to appease him by clinging to him like a barnacle. I trailed kisses along his neck, but he had the nerve to be distracted. "What's wrong?" I asked, noting his faraway gaze.

"I've never been able to wield fire underwater before," Galen said, perplexed. "And my flames—they were *blue*. Your magic is so strong that I can transcend the usual limits of my abilities." A deep V formed on his forehead, making my stomach drop.

"What does it mean?"

"I don't know—that your blood is rare... special. *You* are special."

"I don't want to be special," I declared impulsively.

He chuckled. "I don't think you have a choice, love. There are worse things to be. I'll protect you—I'll carry you around in my pocket if necessary, like a little good luck charm."

I laughed, while I internally panicked. Blood that enhanced power would paint an even larger target on my back. *If Sylvia knew...* I let out a shaky breath. "Please don't tell your mother."

His eyes softened. "You can trust me. Keeping you safe is my number one priority, now that you're mine. Everything else is just noise." I swallowed hard as my heart exploded.

Gods, I didn't want to mess this up. The way he made me feel... It was terrifying—electrifying. And I had no idea what I was doing. I rested my head on his shoulder while we bobbed in the waves.

We both turned when we spotted someone heading our way—a messenger marching down the steep hill. We dashed to grab our towels and were waiting on the shore when he arrived. The man looked as stiff as his freshly starched uniform as he read from an unrolled piece of parchment.

"Dear Prince Galen,
Her Majesty formally invites you to attend dinner this evening. If you and your pet decide not to make an appearance, the Queen will assume that you're both eager to spend the rest of your liaison in the dungeons.
Sincerely,
Your Queen"

Signed *Your Queen*, not *Mother*. The messenger read the letter verbatim, balking at the end. I curled my lip, holding back a snarl... I wanted to kill her for the way she treated her son. But to my surprise, Galen was *laughing*. "The woman has a flare for the dramatic, I'll give her that." I didn't find it quite as funny.

So much for keeping our relationship a secret.

TWENTY-FOUR

After we'd both freshened up, Galen came to my room, sun-kissed from our day at the beach. He dazzled in a suit that matched the color of his eyes, while I wore a champagne gown that hugged my curves, spilling around my feet like liquid gold. If he was the sun, then I was a garden that bloomed beneath his glow. *Together*, we were a force of nature.

Galen immediately closed the space between us, kissing my collar bone as he slipped off the thin strap holding my dress up. "I'm not going to make it through dinner," he purred, running his hands down the exposed skin of my back.

I stepped back so I could give him my best attempt at bedroom eyes. My voice shook slightly as I asked, "Will you make love to me tonight?"

After spending such a perfect day with him, I'd decided I was ready. I wanted him to be my first, even if our two worlds ultimately tore us apart.

"Are you sure?" he asked, delicately kissing me where he'd bitten me yesterday, making me forget how to speak. I wobbled, grabbing onto him to steady myself. "Come sit down." He led me to the bed. "No expectations. I'll spend the night and we'll just see where the evening leads." His words sent a warm caress down my spine.

"I like the sound of that." I smiled, leaning my head on his shoulder, before releasing a heavy sigh and scowling. "So... dinner is going to be interesting. Any chance your mother will let me keep my head?"

Galen chuckled, cupping my cheeks as he kissed my nose. "I'll make sure she doesn't touch a single hair."

I smiled weakly. "Will you be alright if Rafael is there? After yesterday..."

A low sound rumbled from his throat—the guttural growl of a lion. "I doubt he'll show his face so soon, but if he does, I'll do my best to play nice. I've had my fill of entertaining the guests with my family drama."

"Will Arnold be there?"

"Arnold is in time-out for the foreseeable future, if I have any say," he said with a flash of temper.

"And Isla?" I couldn't look him in the eyes.

"I'll talk to her. But tonight, she doesn't know about us. And it's important I keep up impressions—for now. I made a mistake the other week, announcing I'd dance with you at the festival. I was just so sick of being told what to do, who to love..." He gazed into my eyes and I broke the contact. I wasn't ready for words of love. "They'll lose their minds if I fight them on this. I don't want the Elders to punish you for my actions." He grabbed my chin, forcing me to look at him. "Do you trust that she means nothing to me?"

I nodded, feeling deflated after being so high in the clouds moments ago. "You're okay... lying to her?"

"I don't want to *lie* to her, but it's preferable to Arnold's wrath. Once you can access your gift, you'll be untouchable. We just have to wait until then." I knew what he said was meant to comfort me, but instead it reminded me of all the reasons we'd avoided getting involved in the first place.

I'd been trying to ignore the fact that Galen and I currently had drastically different opinions when it came to opening a portal. He expected me to create a permanent doorway between the worlds, while I planned to *leave him* and take his brothers, along with the humans that supplied his world with magic.

Eventually, the plan would include him. *It had to.* Otherwise, we'd be on opposite sides of a war. The mere thought of it made me nauseous. It wasn't his fault he'd been left in the dark. Soon, when the time was right, I'd tell him the truth. Until then, guilt would burn a hole through my gut.

I cleared my throat. "Speaking of my *gift*... there is something I've been wanting to talk to you about. I want to visit the Oracle in the mountains. I believe she might be the missing piece to the puzzle."

Galen rubbed his temples and gave an exasperated sigh. "*The Oracle?* Marigold, she's mad. She might claim your first born for all we know.

It's not worth the risk. We can keep researching. Maybe the Elders know something. They did cross over from Erador, after all."

Claws that I didn't know I had, dug in. "Your people are *desperate*, Galen. I've heard stories of farmers that aren't able to feed their village, mothers that aren't able to carry their children to term. Every minute wasted is more blood on our hands." The words tasted like ash in my mouth, knowing that I couldn't help most of them until we broke the curse.

"You don't think I know that? I spend most of my waking hours dedicated to serving them, however I can, at any cost."

I'd offended him. It would've been wise to back down, but instead all of my pent-up rage began spilling out. "And what of the humans being kidnapped? How are you *serving* them? And where exactly does the royal family get their blood? Since humans aren't even allowed in your home." As the words tumbled out of me, it became clear to both of us that I'd been saving the hard-hitting questions for a rainy day. It was a cloudless evening, but the storm had arrived.

He straightened his back and gave me a hard stare. "Most of the royal supply that we drink day-to-day is stored in cellars beneath the castle. We trade with humans all over the continent in exchange for blood. It's like any other kind of trade, just much more valuable than food, wine, or spices. It's *magic*—humans have *our* magic. The majority of them live comfortable lives selling something to us that once was ours. Do you think we keep them in the dungeons and drain them at our leisure? That I have something to do with the humans being kidnapped? Do you think so little of me?" Flames flickered behind narrowed eyes.

I backed away from him as my magic surged in response, even as I stamped it down. He was *not* my enemy. *What was I doing?*

I let out a deep breath and gentled my tone. "If that's true, then why isn't the royal family also experiencing a shortage?"

His eyes softened when he heard my shaking voice and noticed my frost-covered hands. "Do you think my mother would ever allow the Kingdom to become vulnerable? Magic is everything to Fae, and power is everything to her. Naturally, she's hoarded enough blood to never worry about running out."

I nodded, not meeting his eyes. "What would you say if I told you the Elders were behind the kidnappings?" I whispered.

Galen went owl-eyed before all the blood drained from his face. He reached me in two strides and gripped me by the shoulders. "Don't ever repeat those words. What you just suggested, it's treason—towards my mother, towards the Elders, towards me."

My mouth bobbed open and then closed. Heat traveled up my neck before burning into my cheeks. Tears began to gather in the corners of my eyes. I knew he was loyal to the Crown, but *blindly* loyal? When people like me were disappearing?

He wasn't the man I thought he was. "I... I think you should go," I choked out.

His hand caressed my face. "Look at me," he said. I shook my head. "Look at me, *damn it*," he said more assertively. I flashed him a hard stare.

"There are things about the Elders that you don't know. They're too strong to be challenged. Otherwise, I would've fought them long ago. Rising up against them... against my mother—it would only lead to death. And I've been dead for so long in here—" He put a fist over his heart, "—that I thought eventually I'd just go out in a blaze of fire when I couldn't take it anymore. But you... you've given me purpose. You're my hope. You get us to Erador and it throws a wrench in their plans, especially if we can break the curse."

I blinked in disbelief. He wasn't mindlessly obedient—he wasn't on their side. It's exactly what I needed to hear. My heart felt like it had just doubled in size to accommodate the emotions bursting inside me, knocking over any remaining barriers between us. "What makes them so strong?" I asked.

"I... I can't say. You'll just have to trust me," he said with a haunted expression. "Just please, don't do anything stupid... or brave. Don't make them your enemy."

I wrapped my arms around him and rested my head over his heart. He and his brothers needed to talk. Lion-hearted Galen was *scared* of the Elders. *What did Rafael and Louis not know?* I had to get Meli out of this world. Quickly.

"We *need* to go to the Oracle. It's our best chance of getting to Erador. Has anyone asked her outright how to break the curse?" My voice sounded muffled as I talked into his broad chest.

"Yes, but her knowledge is limited to the world she's on."

I chewed at my cheek, feeling disappointed.

He cleared his throat and said, "Long ago, when our people still lived in Erador, my Uncle Aides received a prophecy—a riddle, really—instructions on how to break the curse. It proved unfruitful, but we still have it written down somewhere—in my mother's library, I believe. I can try to retrieve it."

I looked up at him with astonishment. *Why hadn't he mentioned this earlier?*

My question must've been written on my face, because he continued, "We've all been stuck here for so long that we'd lost hope of ever breaking the curse. We grew complacent, but you're quickly changing everything. Not just for me, but for my people."

And what about *my* people? No. I had to stop blaming him for things out of his control. He was on my side. It wasn't his fault that their curse *demanded* human blood—that his mother and her council were sick in the head. I let my frustration melt away and gave him a tight hug, clinging to the fabric of his shirt.

He leaned down, fisting my loose waves as he cradled my head, before kissing me with a ferocity that left me reeling. I was breathless when he pulled away and murmured, "I'll set up a meeting between you, the Elders, and my mother—even though I hate it, even though I don't want them near you. We'll need their permission to seek out the Witch of the Woods."

I nodded my agreement and thanked him with a smile. "It'll be alright. I have a fire wielder to protect me."

His eyes flashed as he said, "Your fire wielder might *catch fire* if this dinner lasts too long. I hope you know that I'll be having completely indecent thoughts the entire time."

I gave him a playful grin, nipped at his earlobe, and whispered, "I suppose it would be cruel to mention that I'm not wearing any underwear..."

His eyeballs nearly popped out of their sockets as I pushed him out the door before he could investigate the situation any further.

TWENTY-FIVE

The evening was bound to be awkward. This was the path we'd chosen and I couldn't avoid the repercussions of my actions, even if I wanted to. For the sake of appearances, Galen showed up to dinner first. I took a few deep breaths before the guards ushered me in. Queen Sylvia sat at the head of the table as usual. Louis, Galen, Isla, and Dahlia were also in attendance. I sighed with relief; at least some of the dinner guests had decided to opt out tonight. I sat by Louis, across from Isla.

"What a pleasure for you *both* to join us. You preferred not to have your midnight rendezvous in the dungeons tonight?" Sylvia's menacing glare was fixed on Galen; she didn't even bother looking at me. I watched Isla's face fall and felt a pang of guilt.

"If I must remind you, Mother, I'm sitting by Isla this evening. Please treat her with the respect she deserves."

I hadn't expected him to sound so convincing; this was going to be difficult to sit through. The first course appeared and I began sipping on a cold soup of leeks and potato. I avoided the gaze of, well... *everyone*. I glanced at Louis, who seemed to be thoroughly enjoying himself. Dahlia, on the other hand, looked as tightly wound as her braided coiffure.

"Are we back to courting Isla then? After your display the other week of *insisting* you'd be dancing with Marigold at the Hyacinth Festival, I assumed you'd lost interest in poor Isla. Men are such fickle beasts." She gave a bored smile directed at the other women at the table.

"You act as if sex and courtship are mutually exclusive. Would you like me to share your long list of consorts with the table? Or perhaps, we can find someone to court you," Galen said with a cool calm. The Queen gave him a look that would've turned lesser men to stone.

Louis apparently had a death wish, because he chimed in next. "I must've missed something... Galen, you're courting Isla, but sleeping with Marigold? A bold choice, brother. I shall love to see how this plays out for you." I was tempted to aim frost where it would hurt him most, but the chances of hitting the Queen instead were too high.

"Is it not my right, as future King, to enjoy myself before I marry? Do we not eat several courses this very evening for the sake of variety?" My blush reached my ears and I didn't dare look at Isla. This was going worse than I could've imagined. I would've gladly accepted conversation of the weather, of court gossip—any meaningless drivel would've been better than this. I *was* the court gossip. I was going to die from humiliation.

"I, for one, don't care." Isla shocked me back to life with her words. Shooting a smug smirk my way, she continued, "She may have him for a few weeks, but I'll have him for eternity. We all have our fun with humans—they have their perks, after all—but we know better than to fall in love with them." An icy breeze blew my hair away from my face as I fought to control my anger.

To imply that I was just his *source...* Frost crept up my wrists like vines along a tree branch. I shoved my hands into my lap to hide it, but the ice continued to spread up my arms. The air grew cold around us as I fought the impulse to claim what was *mine*.

Isla blew out a foggy swirl of breath and flashed me a look of satisfaction; she'd successfully gotten under my skin. Louis kicked me under the table, sending a clear message: *Keep it together*. And then I remembered what was at stake and began to breathe again.

Galen sent a supercilious smile to Isla that I'd never seen him use. "Thank you, Isla, for being the only rational one at this table." I wanted his mask to fall, just for a moment, to let me know that this was killing him too. I could read nothing from his—*my*—golden uhra. "I'm glad we've all come to an understanding," Sylvia said.

The rest of the meal was silent. Or perhaps, I just chose not to listen.

Back in my room, I sat in front of the hearth, waiting for Galen. He was walking Isla to her quarters and taking too long. Was she trying to seduce him? This was messier than I could've imagined. I heard a click of the door and then saw Galen smiling down at me. I ran to him and he enveloped me in a big hug.

"That was terrible," I confessed. He had a bottle of wine and poured me a glass, settling beside me in front of the fire.

He groaned. "It was. She tried to get me to stay the night. I explained to her that while she was the accepted choice of the council, you are *my* choice. And until the engagement is official, I'll be spending my time with you." He slung back his wine, draining the glass, then poured more.

The thought of them locked in an intimate embrace—Isla trying to pull him into her room... I looked down to find my cup covered in frost and took a generous sip. We both looked at each other and finished our drinks.

"How did she take it? She's okay... *sharing* you?" I tried to sound nonplussed, even as my insides roiled.

In Erador, marriages of convenience were common amongst royalty, which meant so were affairs. They were private though... to admit to one would be to fall from grace. If anyone was the mistress in this situation, it was me, and I *hated* what it implied about me, about us. Our relationship was only a small seedling, struggling to take root, and it felt as if it was already getting stomped on.

"She accepted it. She's not pleased, but she won't make a fuss. She wants the Crown, not me." He set down his glass and stood. He prowled over to me and put an arm on each side of my chair, caging me in.

He leaned down for a kiss, but I pulled away to ask, "So the plan is to tell her the courtship is off, once I've learned how to world walk? And *then* you think the council will accept us?" Even more reason to leave for the Oracle right away. I didn't want to be the *other* woman. To be with Galen, I'd have to swallow my pride—something I didn't think I'd ever willingly do for a man.

"Yes. I think when they have a world walker available to them for the first time in two-hundred years, they'll be glad to make you our future *Queen*."

I didn't want to be their Queen, but he kissed me again and I let my thoughts fade. He lifted me up from the chair and carried me to the bed, trailing kisses along my collar bone, seducing me slowly. Each sweet brush of his lips stoked the embers that were burning in my core.

"What exactly is the Hyacinth Festival?" I asked, my voice catching as his mouth roamed.

"It's a dance. Similar to your Debut, I'd imagine."

I sat up, pushing him off. "It's a *courtship* ball? Why would I be invited? I'm not Fae royalty." My chest tightened. A dance was bad enough; a dance with blood-drinking faeries, *worse*; but a dance where I had to watch Galen court another woman all night? I was definitely not going.

He sighed. "You're our guest. We're trying to acclimate you to this world—to our people. You're someone who is very important to me... to the Fae. Gifts like yours don't just show up at random. They're bestowed by the gods. And if I have it my way, you *will* be royalty... soon enough." He went back to kissing me, then his fingers were at the nape of my neck, undoing the buttons of my dress.

I was starting to spin, like I'd had one too many glasses of wine. I had to tell him who I was before this went any further. I already was promised to a throne. I couldn't be his future *Queen*. "Galen, I... I have a *very* big fear of parties—of crowds." I felt his lips brushing along my spine and I shivered. *Gods*, it was hard to concentrate with his hands on me...

My voice came out an octave higher as I said, "It hasn't come up because, well... it hasn't had to. I can't tell you what a relief it's been to get a break from the constant social events... They were never ending in Aurelius."

He stopped undressing me when he heard the panic that laced my voice. "You lived in a castle full of court gatherings... and you have a fear of crowds? How did this come about? How did you function?"

I had to tell him. If we were going to give this a real shot, then our relationship needed to begin with a foundation of honesty. *Would he see me as his enemy once he knew who I was?* I could be making a catastrophic mistake. Rafael had warned me not to tell anyone, but Raf was also an *ass*, who'd attacked his own brother.

"When I was ten, my family and I were at the castle visiting my aunt, Queen Ophelia, for the annual ball." I paused to search his gaze, which stayed patiently locked on me. "I saw my mother collapse in the middle of the crowd. She was poisoned... Sh-she died in minutes." I felt so vulnerable telling him, that hot tears sprung up.

"My father left that evening and I never saw him again. The Queen took me under her wing from that day forward. I still panic when I'm in a crowd. I get light-headed, overwhelmed... sometimes I faint. I haven't danced at a ball. Ever. In fact, the reason I ended up here was because I ran away from my Debut. Like a coward. I'd planned to just get some air, but then I... ended up here."

I was trusting him with the sharpest shards of my soul—shame that whispered over and over that it had somehow been *my fault*. Why else would my father have left?

Galen pulled me onto his lap and cradled me for the second time in two days. "Your ancestors took over Aurelius after my family left," he said slowly. He looked pensive as he processed what I was telling him.

Ophelia had married into the royal family, but it felt pointless to tell him that. I was still the heir to the Aurelian throne. *And so was he...* if he chose to see it that way.

He took his time responding. Eventually, he said, "Thank you for telling me who you are. I don't blame *you* for what happened—you aren't the reason we lost our Kingdom." He held my gaze. "And I'm sorry that you had to witness your mother's death. As a child, nonetheless. And what your father did... he betrayed you when you needed him most. Did your aunt treat you well?"

I nodded. The weight on my chest began to lift. I let out a long breath that I hadn't even realized I'd been holding. "Yes. She raised me like her own. She never had children. And..." I paused, building up courage. "I'm the heiress to the Aurelian throne... against all odds."

His brows raised as he rubbed his stubbled chin thoughtfully, before giving me a glowing grin. "I knew you were special, but this is... beyond my wildest dreams. It's *destiny*, my love. We were meant to be," he rejoiced, kissing my worries away. His mouth made an unhurried descent down my throat... and then across the swells of my breasts.

I'd thrown so much at him today; between my confessions, accusations, and difficult truths, he'd stood strong. It seemed *nothing* would scare him away.

I traced his jawline with my hand, entranced by his masculine beauty... dipping my gaze to meet sparkling eyes. I held his face, pressing my lips against his. He was *mine*. And now he *truly* knew who I was. It made me feel so close to him. But I wanted to be *closer*.

Licking down his neck, I wrapped my arms around his strong shoulders and straddled him. I wanted to free fall into the deep end of whatever this was between us. With unbridled fervor, I gave him all my hope, all my fear. Each kiss melted into the next.

His fingers finished what they'd started, loosening buttons until my dress fell away and pooled around us. In one smooth motion, he leaned me back and slid me to the edge of the bed.

He kneeled on the floor and began pulling the remainder of my dress off. His eyes turned molten when he saw that I was, indeed, not wearing any undergarments. His night beard tickled me as he kissed my thighs, making me wriggle away.

He peered at me, eyes shining, before lowering his head. The first swipe of his tongue sent fire to my loins. His fingers slipped inside me, while he continued to tease me with his mouth; nibbling, sucking, tasting, savoring.

Soon I was pleading his name, demanding he take me. *All of me.* He rose up until he was bracing himself over my trembling body, kissing me until we were both shaking with anticipation.

"It might hurt, since it's your first time. I'll give you time to adjust... I'll be gentle." I could feel his sizable length, thick and hard as he rubbed himself down my center. I opened my legs wider in an attempt to accommodate him. He was soft as silk, hard as steel, throbbing as he ran himself along my aching core.

He'd told me what to expect, but I still didn't see how he was going to fit. But the need to be closer surpassed all my fears. "I'm ready," I said with thick emotion, lifting my hips to meet his.

"If I get carried away, tell me if you want me to stop... and I will," he said roughly, his hair falling into his eyes. Eternally composed Galen was coming apart at the seams—trembling as he stared down at me in awe.

We didn't break eye contact as he guided himself in with a slow, heavy slide. A pinch of discomfort followed as I was coaxed open, stretching beyond my capacity. There was more pain than I'd expected. I bit back a whimper, gripping the sheets, but I didn't protest as he moved deeper.

He paused when my inner walls squeezed around him, resisting his advance. "Breathe..." he whispered. He slowed his progression, but didn't stop. "You feel better than I could've imagined," he murmured into my ear. "You're wrapped so tightly around my cock. *Gods*... Marigold. I can barely—"

He grunted as he carefully pulled out... and then back in, letting out a shaky breath. I could feel him growing even harder—stretching me wider, deeper. Stomach muscles cramped as waves of pleasure lapped over me, even as the sensation of being ripped open continued. I didn't know how much more I could take.

Galen reached down and expertly rubbed the bundle of nerves between my legs, giving me time to adjust. That's all it took to remember the ecstasy that came with his touch.

The discomfort began to fade... and a delicious need surged within me. He groaned as I relaxed, allowing him to plunge deeper, deeper... sinking into me until our bodies were flush.

We stared at each other in wonder. Physically, we were as close as two people could get, but it was so much more than that. His golden uhra shimmered around us. And in this moment, we were one. He began to move over me, and then we were rocking together.

He was an attentive lover, noticing what I responded to. Soon I was lost to his touch, his toe-curling kisses, his rhythm. He hovered with feline grace as he began to thrust faster. I moved with him, moaning like a feral animal. This felt so good, so right. I wrapped my legs around him, panting as we built up to the crescendo. Could I die from bliss? If so... *what a way to die.*

Frost-tipped fingers burned into flesh as I gripped his shoulder blades, begging for relief. He was driving deep into me now. I gave him all of me as I tilted back my head and cried out his name.

I was building up, up, up... until I exploded into a million pieces. Ice coated the walls of the room as wave after wave crashed over me. Galen roared as he pulled himself out of me and released onto the sheets.

He fell beside me and we sagged into the bed. Once our heart rates returned to normal, he asked, "How was it? Are you alright?"

I couldn't believe *that* was what I'd been missing out on. I felt empty now, without him inside of me. How did people function in society when they could be doing *that* instead? "We are never leaving this bed again," I said with a grin, rolling on top of him.

"As you wish," he said, suckling a peaked nipple into his mouth, while I sat astride him. He was already growing hard beneath me.

"You can... be ready again so fast?" I blinked in surprise.

He laughed. "Not always. But with you, right now, it would be impossible *not* to be ready. You have no idea how many times I've thought about this moment—all the places I've wanted to make love to you, all the ways I plan to take you."

Places? Ways? Apparently I still had a lot to learn.

Fast as lightning, he flipped me. I was on my stomach and he was behind me, rubbing against my backside, spreading my cheeks with the head of his erection. "The question is, love, are *you* ready for *me*?" The dominance in his voice caused a spike of adrenaline to run through me. The insatiable ache between my legs pulsed in answer.

"Yes..." I said, biting my lip as he massaged slick folds.

"I'm going to take you like this. It will be easier for me to touch you... while I fuck you from behind." He pulled a pillow from the top of the bed and tucked it under my hips. He bent my knees and opened my legs, making me jolt up when he buried his face into my sex.

Tsking, he gently guided me back down until my cheek was pressed into the mattress. Gripping my wrists with one hand, he pinned them behind my back, while his other hand explored me.

I let him take complete control, arching as he whispered, "Good girl."

I bit my pillow to keep from screaming as he toyed with me, curling his fingers impossibly deep, keeping me teetering on the edge. "Please, Galen," I begged.

In silent answer, he sat up behind me, pushing into my swollen entrance. Deeper... deeper. I moaned as he filled me completely. I was sore, but I was too dizzy with lust to care.

"If only you could see yourself, bent over... with me inside you," he purred. He released my hands and I went pliant, melting into the bed as I fisted the sheets.

He began moving in controlled, languid circles. I stopped breathing as he gradually picked up the pace, gripping my bottom and pounding into me with painfully slow precision. His other hand was tucked between my thighs, playing with me, making me twitch, but holding back.

More, I wanted more. "Deeper..." I moaned.

He let out a low chuckle, lifting my hips up, opening me up to a new angle of pleasure. "My greedy girl…" he huffed. "I'm greedy too, when it comes to you." He pulled out before sliding back in with a low thrust.

"I don't want to share you," he growled, with another thrust. He paused and I trembled around him, desperate for release. "Tell me you're mine."

He pulled my hips back, plunging in at the same time. I let out a muffled whimper into the bedding.

"I'm yours," I gasped. I was so close, so desperate for him to finish what he'd started.

"One more time."

"I'm yours," I said again, louder.

"Should I let you cum now, sweetheart?"

"Yes…" I moaned.

His fingers wandered between my thighs as he slammed into me over and over. We were frantic, spiraling towards the finish line, lost in the pleasure. The primal sounds of our bodies clapping together, of our labored breathing, sent me soaring off the ledge. I convulsed as stars exploded behind my eyes. He swore and pulled out of me, crashing to the bed.

We laid there catching our breath, feeling raw inside and out. "Thank you," he whispered, before wrapping his warm body around mine. "For the first time in a long time, I know what happiness feels like. And I'm not ever letting you go."

TWENTY-SIX

The morning sky was a blushing pastel painting as I laid in Galen's arms, soaking in the scene. Peony pink clouds watched from the heavens, while we luxuriated in our lavender haze.

A few strokes of his hand and I was ready for him. We found our pleasure quickly—anxious to claim each other before the day was upon us and real life resumed. We'd spent almost all of yesterday in bed, but today we couldn't escape the realities of life.

"I'll never tire of this. Of you." Galen's smile was radiant, reaching all the way to his eyes as they crinkled with joy. It made my heart skip, to let these feelings settle, to let him in. It was so new, so special. As the fear of intimacy retreated, a new one took its place. The fear of losing *this*—this little ember that I wanted to cocoon and protect from any outsiders who might put it out. I crawled on top of him as he attempted to peel away, refusing to let him leave.

"You little monkey. Don't make this more difficult than it already is." He pulled me closer, before rolling, until he had me pinned under him. "I'll... come... find... you... when... I'm... free," he said between kisses that started at my forehead and ended at my belly button.

I groaned as he stood up and began searching for his clothes. A shirt there, pants here, underwear tangled in the sheets. Once he was dressed, he came back over for one more kiss. "Have a good day, love. I'll be thinking of you, until I see you again."

The door clicked shut and I bit back a grin. I pulled the comforter up to my chin and cozied into the heat he'd left behind, before it disappeared as swiftly as he did.

I fell back asleep until Lusha woke me with a knock and a tray of tea and toast. It was like she could read my mind; breakfast in bed and a slow start to the morning was exactly what I wanted. I sat up, staring at the unnecessary fire Galen had lit before he left. I knew why he'd started it—it was a reminder of the fire that had burned between us all weekend. I cooled the room with a steady breeze of ice magic until I had to wrap the covers around me.

In one weekend, everything had changed. Galen had claimed me; body and soul. Nothing about our relationship was going to be simple, but there was a warmth in my chest that flickered for him—that yearned for him even though he'd just left.

Were there things to work through? Yes... he was the Elder's puppet and the son of a wretched woman—and that came with some horrendous truths. But he'd opened up to me, and I him. There was a new level of trust between us. Together, we'd find a path forward.

Deep in thought, I was startled by Rafael, who appeared at my bedside. He was overdressed in leather fighting gear, looking absolutely *shameless* as his eyes drank in the sight of me in bed... in a nightgown.

"It's your first day of training. Time to get dressed," he said like a drill sergeant.

I bared my teeth at him. "How *dare* you come into my room uninvited *again*. How dare you approach me after what you did to Galen. I should stab a dagger through your heart and leave you to bleed out," I hissed, wringing the sheets that shielded me, pretending they were his neck.

"You could try." He smiled, baiting me. I lunged for him and he deflected me easily, laughing as I fell to the ground. "I just saw him downstairs. He looked fine. In fact, he was *glowing* with health." He rolled his shoulders back and stretched his neck from side to side.

"Get. Out." I sent wind towards him, but he blocked it with minimal effort.

"Fine. I'll go. Meet me at the stables in an hour—preferably in a better mood." I flipped him off before he and his shadows disappeared.

I stood at the entrance to the large barn door leading into the stables as Rafael approached me. "We're riding to a spot farther away to avoid any spying eyes. What I teach you stays between us. Anything discussed at our lessons is considered confidential. Understood?"

I nodded. I didn't owe him any loyalty beyond common courtesy, but I would keep his secrets. They seemed to be all he had.

Hibiscus and Zagreus were saddled and waiting for us. "Why don't I just saddle you up?" I snickered, surprised I was capable of joking with him after what he'd done, even if it was at his expense.

"You're hilarious," he said with a deadpan expression. "That was a onetime offer; sorry to disappoint." There was a hint of humor in his black-rimmed eyes. His lashes were so voluminous, they looked lined with kohl. Beauty had been wasted on him.

We both mounted our horses and stood in silence, staring at each other. "After you," I said impatiently.

"Oh yes, in Aurelius, it's males first, isn't it?" he purred, before taking off in a gallop.

I raced to keep up; Hibiscus seemed to love the sensation of flying as much as I did, stretching her neck as she thundered down the open field. I leaned forward, scratching where fur met mane, as I distributed my weight evenly so she could run without hinderance. We were neck and neck with Raf and Zag in no time.

He glanced at me with unmistakable surprise on his face, before he whispered something into Zag's ear and shot ahead. I thought about using my wind magic to slow them down, but decided I didn't want to startle the horses. Instead, I settled into the ride. The cold air caused magic to buzz beneath my skin. Tears streamed from my eyes in exhilaration. I needed more of *this*.

We slowed as we came upon a towering tree line and I followed Raf down a barely visible trail. Spanish moss hung from arching oak trees that swooped and curved into a wide canopy, covering us completely. We walked for a while before we entered a clearing.

The meadow was covered in tall grass and an array of wildflowers. A sparkling pond shimmered in the distance, surrounded by magnolia trees with fat, white blossoms. Raf jumped off Zagreus and smacked his rump, signaling to him that he was free. I followed his lead as I watched the horses make their way over to the water.

"What a beautiful grove. Do you usually get it to yourself?" I spun slowly as I admired it. Orange flowers swayed in the breeze, releasing a sweet, spicy scent. It was so private... so lush.

Raf's face held a content, thoughtful expression, making me wonder if this was his happy place. "Nobody knows about it except for me... and now you. I created it awhile back. I needed a place I could train in private. I don't like the family to know my business."

I inhaled sharply, peering at him in disbelief. "You *created* it? How? With your earth magic? I thought everything you grew was black."

One man... had made all of this?

"I can blend my shadows and earth magic together if I want to, but I'm perfectly capable of growing plants without help from shadow magic."

"*The power to create... and destroy,*" he'd once said when describing his magic.

"You've left me speechless..."

"I didn't think that was possible," he mused.

A frown returned to my face. "You should learn to take a compliment," I snapped back.

We watched the horses wade through the water as they cooled down. Curiosity eased my temper... I'd been wondering about something. "This might be a silly question, but can you communicate with horses?" Shape shifting magic hadn't been explained to me beyond the basics, but he had a unique relationship with Zag. They seemed to understand each other.

"It's perfectly fine to ask questions—you're new to this. As all of us were, at one point," he said with a warm smile that contradicted his otherwise cool demeanor. "While I'm in my shifted form, I can speak mind-to-mind with other shifters, as well as other animals that have an interest in talking to me. When I'm in my Fae form, horses seem to understand most of what I say. But they don't talk back."

"So... why doesn't Hibiscus like you?"

He gave a wry grin. "You'll see soon enough."

"And you'll help me find my animal form?"

"I'll try. It'll take time. Your magic will decide when you're ready. I found it helpful to spend time with the creatures I'm naturally drawn to when I was searching for mine. I studied their physical forms; how fetlock meets hoof, for example. And their behavior—what motivates them."

We watched the horses romp, kicking up dust, while I listened to him. "Some people don't get the opportunity to interact with their *pneuma*, their spirit animal. It can take them longer to learn how to shift. Louis, for example, has probably never come across the animal he'll shift into. The magic will eventually help him on his path... Connecting with your spirit animal is about trusting your instincts and thinking like a beast. I understand that might be a big ask, for a delicate Princess, such as yourself."

I was in no mood to banter with him, but I couldn't resist saying, "I bet that part comes naturally to you. *Pig*."

His eyes sharpened, lingering on me before returning to the horses. "During our time together, we'll practice more advanced magic. We won't sit back while the Elders and Sylvia decide how to use you. You and I—we're stronger than all of them combined. We make our own magic; they have to *steal* theirs. When we find the missing humans and take them back to Erador, we'll take their magic with us. It'll be a crippling blow to the Kingdom."

I met his smoldering gaze. He'd been planning their downfall for a while—long before I'd arrived. My stomach turned, thinking of what Galen had said about the Elders. I hated that I'd found myself in the middle of their brotherly feud, but if they wouldn't talk to each other, then I'd have to be their mediator.

"Galen told me that the Elders are more dangerous than we realize; he implied that they have tricks up their sleeve that we don't know about."

Raf's lip curled before it dropped into a neutral frown—because a *frown* was the natural state of his face.

"Has anyone ever told you that you have *resting prick face*?" I smiled at him sweetly.

"Excuse me?"

"You should try smiling more. It's better for your wrinkles. You're over a century old now, yeah? You might want to start thinking about a skin care routine that doesn't involve scowling all the time."

He crossed his arms, giving me a ghost of a smile. "Thanks for the advice... as for the Elders, all we can do is try and work around them. And continue to spy on them, though it's almost pointless without access into any of their homes or studies. If only their wards weren't so strong—strong enough that not even I can break them. So yes—I'm aware how powerful they are."

I rocked back on my heels and said, "Just wanted you to have all the information..."

Even though you don't deserve it.

"Thank you—truly. Like I said, you and I are stronger together. And despite what you think, I was just trying to protect you the other day..." He trailed off, avoiding my gaze.

"Do you always break arms and ask questions later, when you're trying to protect someone?" Now I was the one crossing my arms.

He sighed. "No, it's just... Galen and I have history. Anyways, I'm sorry. I'm not sorry for what I did to him, but I'm sorry for upsetting you."

I pursed my lips, unsure of how to respond. "Thanks for the apology."

He gave a curt nod. "Let's get started. I'm going to shift... and I want you to pay attention to how your magic responds." He stood back and took off his jacket, throwing it to the ground. My eyes grew wide in silent question.

Not missing a beat, he answered, "The magic allows us to keep our clothes when we change shape—it hides them in some separate dimension, until we shift back." His mouth curved into a cocky smile. "I was just getting hot... but I can continue stripping, if you'd like." I glared back, unamused.

"I don't understand how it works, but that's magic for you. It requires a leap of faith." With that, he shifted, never breaking eye contact.

I watched as hands turned to hooves and his body contorted into the shape of a dark horse. It was so fast that I couldn't get a grasp of *how* things shifted... just that they had.

"You changed too fast. I could barely process it," I complained, before falling silent as I admired his equine form. It was my first time seeing it in the daylight. His obsidian black fur seemed to swallow the sun's light. But from the corner of my eye, I could see a rainbow of colors in his coat, like a black bird that only looked black at first glance. Our eyes weren't complex enough to see the range of colors that birds could see—I'd read that somewhere. I wondered what he looked like to a bird.

Rafael tossed back his head before running towards the other horses, bucking and charging, until they all ran a lap around me. I laughed in delight. Magic was *wonderful*—the best thing that had ever happened to me. He trotted over to me; his long, wavy mane hung over his brows, just like it did in his faerie form.

Perhaps I was a horse too... I'd always been drawn to them. My stomach flipped as he walked over and blew hot air in my face. "Thanks for that," I grimaced, wiping my cheeks with the back of my hand.

Inches from me, he shifted back. We stood nose to nose. Pin-pricks of sensation tingled along my arms, along my legs. My magic was trying to rise to the surface, but I panicked and squashed it down, stepping away from him. He stared at me as if he could see right through me. It made me uneasy. And he was far too close.

"You know... I'm surprised your pneuma is a horse. Your temperament has always suggested something... *moodier*. Something more dangerous." I shivered at the power that rolled off him in dark, rippling waves.

He paused, and just for a moment, his mask dropped. I'd stunned him with my observation. "What is it?" I asked, my voice catching in my throat.

"I want to share something with you. But I know you hate me. Would it be foolish of me to trust you?"

TWENTY-SEVEN

The air between us felt charged as I replied, "I-I don't hate you." He stared at me until I continued, "You can trust me."

My feelings for him were... complex, but I didn't *hate* him. In fact, if anything, I saw too much of myself in him. We were both stubborn loners, who were more sensitive than we cared to admit. I was still angry with him, but it was becoming clear that it would be best if I stayed out of the feud between him and Galen.

Raf's eyes darkened before he seemingly accepted my answer by backing up... and backing up, putting substantial space between us. And then he shifted.

Grey shadows exploded into a huge cloud of smoke. I was no longer staring at a man, but an *enormous* black dragon. Scales the size of my fists coated his entire body, looking more like volcanic rock than skin. He had a long, black snout that blew steam in my direction in hot puffs. I could feel heat pouring off him from where I stood. Large golden-brown eyes stared down at me, eyes that I'd recognize anywhere.

Along his head were rows of spiked horns that protruded from his skull and wrapped down his back towards wings that were fanned out for my benefit—wings that were so massive, they shielded me from the sun. As rays of light filtered through the membranous skin, I could see a rainbow of colors in them, as if he was coated in a layer of oil.

I was unabashedly goggling, but felt incapable of tearing my gaze from the most majestic creature I'd ever seen. Curved spikes continued down his tail. They looked sharp enough to prick a finger on. Beyond the horns, he had long, curling talons and equally fierce teeth. A shadow wielder who was also a dragon... I swallowed hard. I wasn't sure if even Aku, god of shadow, ruler of hell, would be a match against this male.

I approached slowly, trying to remember that it was just Raf. I eventually got close enough to touch his nose. His scales were cool, despite the heat that radiated off him. He opened his mouth to reveal white teeth that were bigger than my head.

I backed up quickly, tripping over my feet. Before I hit the ground, he'd caught me in his Fae form. I was shaking, sweating... my heart was galloping. He was *glorious.* "How?" was all I could get out.

"I'm a Pooka; a mythological creature that usually takes the form of a black horse, but I have the ability to shift into whatever I want." A wide grin spread across his face, softening his hard features. He seemed to stop breathing as he waited for my response.

"A Pooka..." My mind quickly cataloged all that I knew of the creature that had been nothing more than legend to me until now. "A steward of the gods... Aku's steed... known for picking up unsuspecting strangers and taking them on midnight adventures." I laughed. I should've known. "You're magnificent, Raf. Are there others like you?"

"I'm not sure... I've never met another. I've told very few about what I am. I don't trust the family with this information. Sylvia would start using me for her own benefit... or be so threatened that she'd slit my throat in my sleep. It's much better for her to think of me as useless. Galen can't know either."

I felt a twinge of annoyance, realizing he'd just put me in the situation of having to lie to Galen. But I understood why he didn't want them to know. I buried the feelings. "Thank you for showing me. I can't wait to see what other forms you've been working on."

He stepped back and shifted again—this time into a large black pegasus, almost identical to his pooka form, but with *wings.* I let out a slow exhale... Glossy, black wings flapped up and down, creating a breeze. My hair flew wildly around me as I studied him. They were perfectly sculpted and covered in countless silky feathers.

"Will you take me up?" I asked, holding my breath.

He shifted back and shook his head. "Maybe someday. Not today. We've got work to do." A surly expression returned to his face as he began to circle me. "I showed you mine, now it's time for you to show me yours..." He crossed his muscular arms and gave me an insidious smile.

"I can't," I said defensively. "I don't know how."

"Don't worry about your pneuma. Let's work your magic. Ice and wind... the possibilities are endless." I kept my eyes glued on him as he assessed me, like he was searching for a crack in my porcelain mask. "I wonder if the Princess can build herself an ice castle?"

"A... a castle?" I sputtered.

"It doesn't have to be flashy... or even large. I want you to make bricks of ice and then use wind to move them into place— a test of your endurance and fine motor skills. It takes practice to be precise. Precision is important when it matters the most. Precision will save your life."

This sounded like it was going to hurt. I'd produced ice easily enough the last month with Louis, but it had been unrefined. Broad strokes were fine for shields, for blowing hail around, but forming bricks and moving them? It would require finesse.

I was determined not to embarrass myself in front of Raf, so I took a deep breath and focused. I felt his eyes on me as I used both hands to form a cube, growing it slowly... until it was the size of a brick.

A trickle of sweat cascaded down my temple. It took so much concentration. The easiest way to access my ice magic was to think of things that made my blood run cold: Injustices, greed, Sylvia, her council—and the way I'd been treated my whole life in Aurelius, like I was made of glass, simply because I was a *woman*.

I was surprised how easily I brought forth the bitter feelings—I'd felt nothing but a warm golden glow when Galen had left my bedroom this morning, but now I was *furious*.

"Very good, now your wind," Raf instructed. "I want you to alternate between the two, so that you aren't moving too fast, so you know when you're approaching burn out. The signs aren't subtle. You'll have labored breathing... your body temperature will begin to fluctuate. In your case, you'll probably begin to have chills. *Stay in control*. Stop when you hit your limit. With practice, we can build up your endurance."

I smiled at that, half listening as I moved my brick to the location that I'd chosen. Ice, wind... ice, wind. Back and forth I built my fortress. Brick by brick, everything else faded away.

I began to feel a sharp pang in my lungs when I was on the third tier of my structure. I ignored it. I was used to shoving down uncomfortable feelings. I had so much to prove. There was no choice other than to keep pushing. I couldn't let myself down. I couldn't let *everyone else* down.

Brick by brick.

The ice in my veins felt lethal. I wanted to be lethal... I wouldn't let the Elders win. They were hurting innocent people. They wouldn't stop until we were all dead. After meeting Arnold and feeling his infinite rage, I knew it in my bones. They were going to destroy everything, everyone—with their greed, their hate.

Hazy images of the father who abandoned me appeared in my head. They were blurry... but I could still feel the desolation, the pain of losing two parents in one day. It didn't matter how much time had passed, how many tears had been shed. Shards of ice remained imbedded in my soul. I thought of my mother who should've been here to tell me what I was—*who* I was. I was making two bricks at a time now. Salty sweat trickled down my temple and into my eyes. I would never overcome the anger that shielded me from my grief, therefore I would *never* stop building this castle.

I could hear Rafael in the back of my mind, shouting at me to stop. I ignored him. He didn't know my limits. *Only I knew my limits.*

On and on I went, fighting through dizziness... then nausea. The ice crystals in my veins felt as if they were infiltrating my organs, my heart. By the time I tried to reel back my magic, it had taken control. My hands shook as I attempted to lower them. Panic set in as my bones grew stiff and my skin turned blue. I couldn't stop the avalanche inside of me.

A helpless feeling took over as I realized that I was going to freeze to death. Raf was in front of me, shoving my arms down as he continued to yell. I couldn't hear what he was saying, but the fear in his eyes communicated enough... I'd taken it too far. And then everything faded to black.

TWENTY-EIGHT

The sun was an obnoxiously bright orb, blinding me as I oriented myself.

Where was I?

I tried to sit up, then promptly toppled back down. My legs were useless—all of my limbs were. There was a ringing in my ears as I heard my name over and over again. I closed my eyes.

"Marigold... Marigold... Come back to me. It's Raf—keep breathing. Stay awake." I was in his arms. He looked so worried, but all I felt was... confusion. Why was he being so *loud*?

I was so tired. If I could just sleep for awhile... then maybe...

"Marigold!" he was shouting again.

"What?" I grumbled. *Let me rest*. He lifted us off the ground and we began moving. I sank into him, not caring where we were going.

I heard my mother's voice. "*Goldie, wake up. Fight the sleep. You burned out. You need to stay awake.*"

It felt so real that I attempted to raise my head. "Mama?" I called out weakly. Another hallucination. A deep cold was creeping over me, gnawing at my bones, setting my flesh on fire. I clenched my jaw, trying to keep my teeth from chattering as I thrashed back and forth.

"It's just me... it's Rafael. I need to warm you up—*quickly*. Stay with me."

"If you continue to shout, I'm following the light," I groaned, before my eyes rolled to the back of my head.

A cool mist kissed my skin, making me wonder if Aku had arrived to take me away. Death's strong grip burned hot against my frigid skin as he held me firmly and led me to eternal darkness.

My vision was fuzzy, but I was able to pick up shadow and light. I was curled up in someone's lap... covered in a heavy layer of blankets. There was a fire crackling nearby. *Galen.* My lids fluttered. I licked my dry lips, trying to form his name, but instead found myself being pulled back into an endless sea. I thrashed, desperate to resurface, before sinking into darkness.

Cold air hit my face as I trudged through a damp, soggy forest. The smell of wet leaves, evergreens, and morning fog greeted me like an old friend.

This place was eerily familiar. In fact... I took in my surroundings with a grin. I knew exactly where I was. These were the woods that surrounded my first home. I greedily gulped down the fresh air, looking up towards ominous rain clouds.

Dew clung to my lashes, my hair. I pulled a hood over my head, trying to fight the chill seeping into my bones. A branch snapped and I turned, following the sound. Wylks? My heart jumped to my throat.

A giggle echoed behind me. My mother's laugh. A flash of golden curls disappeared behind a wide tree trunk. I didn't waste a second before I was sprinting after her. Dirt went flying as my boots kicked up mud. "Mama!" I called.

Only silence answered. "Mama?" I said again, uncertainly. Nothing. My gut wrenched as I realized I'd lost her. She'd been right there and I'd lost her.

I turned back towards the path, halting when she suddenly materialized in front of me. The color was drained from her face—her were eyes wide and filled with terror. "Run," she said, grabbing my wrist roughly. She was frantic.

"What?"

"RUN!" she cried.

My eyes shot open as my heart slammed against my rib cage. It had only been a dream. Things were sharp once more. I was staring at an unfamiliar maroon paisley wallpaper. Layers of gauzy, black fabric covered shuttered windows. There was a sweet smell in the air; perfume and... opium? I'd only had laudanum once—years ago when I was sick with scarlet fever. The thick, saccharine scent was difficult to forget.

"Goldie, can you hear me?" Raf. *Not Galen.* His voice was thick with emotion.

"Y-yes. Where are we?" I tried to sit up, to get out of his arms, but he didn't give an inch.

"We were training. You built a whole damn castle out of ice. I tried telling you to stop, but you were... *unyielding.* I eventually took your hands and *forced* you to stop. And then you collapsed."

He hadn't answered my question. A dark brown tendril fell over his forehead as he stared at me. I gazed back. The Prince of Shadows, too beautiful to be real. Straight, prominent brows, deep-set eyes, a jaw chiseled from sandalwood... *and those lips.*

Full lips. It was disgusting, how delectable they looked. *Grotesquely* kissable. I wanted to brush my thumb along the center crease of his bottom lip—a spot he frequently bit when he was trying to smother a smile. But as I tried to lift my hand, I whimpered in pain and was ripped away from my fever dream.

I was out of my mind—completely befuddled. I closed my eyes and took a shaky breath. I didn't want Raf. I was with his *brother.* Feeling humiliated, I croaked, "I'm fine. I'm just feeling a little weak and... discombobulated."

"Discombobulated?" he huffed, shaking his head. "I'll take that over *dead.* You terrified me. Was that your way of trying to get even with me?"

"No, of course not. I just—" I glanced down at the wool blanket I was wrapped in, noticing the scratchy texture against my bare skin. Wait a minute, was I... was I *naked* under these blankets?

"Did you undress me?" I asked slowly, dumbly. Raf shifted and I felt his hard abdominal muscles press against me. It sent a wave of warmth down my spine as I realized... *Was he naked too?*

I gasped, trying to scramble away from him to no avail. It was like trying to run straight after being spun in circles. My mind was dull, while my body felt woozy... clumsy. I flopped in his lap, creating friction, making things so much worse, as the crest of my cheeks burned.

I stared at the dusting of dark, curly hair on his chest, beyond mortified, as I fought a terrible impulse to run my fingers through it.

What was wrong with me? What would Galen think if he saw us like this? My heart drummed wildly as I waited for an explanation, shooting an accusatory glare at Raf.

"You were hypothermic. Skin to skin is the fastest way to warm someone. Don't worry, I didn't see anything—I was too busy trying to save your life," he said irritably. He didn't even look apologetic.

I envisioned him tearing away my frost-coated clothing and felt hot blood surge down my limbs. What was the *opposite* of hypothermic? Because I was pretty sure I was now in the process of overheating.

"I almost burnt out?" I asked, gripping his biceps determinedly as I steadied myself, trying to push out of his arms. He didn't bother assisting as I rocked awkwardly, attempting to propel myself as far away from him as possible.

"You *did* burn out. You're lucky to be alive. I didn't know I was dealing with someone as stubborn and stupid as me. Luckily, you're a healer and your body fought back. Not everyone would've survived the stunt you pulled."

I almost bit out a snide remark, but instead I sank back into him, defeated and exhausted. "I got swept up in the magic. It channeled my feelings into something tangible. I have so much more *anger* inside of me than I realized... It was such a rush. I-I couldn't stop."

He sighed. "It has happened to all of us. Magic can possess us if we aren't careful. I'm sorry it happened during our first lesson together, but it *was* an important lesson to learn. You can't let your emotions fuel your magic. It's why Louis has you meditating and strength training. You *must* be stronger, in body *and* mind. Each element heightens different emotions—feeds off them.

"My shadows try to convince me that I need no one. They'd pull me into the darkness forever if I let them. And if earth magic had its way, it would root its way into my body and absorb the life right from me. It's the cost of magic. You can't ever become complacent."

"I'm sorry for losing control—for scaring you."

He brought his hand towards my hair as if to stroke it, hesitated, then placed it back down. "I hope you'll consider still training with me. I promise to take better care of you next time."

I responded by launching out of his arms and tumbling onto the carpeted floor. I felt more liquid than solid, but managed to pull myself into a sitting position next to him. We sat side by side, facing the fireplace on a thick, patterned rug. I stared at it as I pulled the blankets tightly around myself, avoiding eye contact.

Raf stood up, tossing a blanket around his bare shoulders as he clinked around his small kitchen. After some time, he handed me a steaming cup of tea, sweetened with a generous dollop of honey. Averting my eyes, I stared at my drink as if my life depended on it. I blew on it, letting the scalding liquid slide down my cracked throat, trying desperately to think of anything besides the imposing half-naked male sitting beside me.

After a few sips, I responded, "I want to keep training with you." I paused, finding the next words difficult. "But you should know, Galen and I are spending time together... and he treats me well. So you don't need to protect me from him. We *all* need to work together if we're to take down the Elders."

"Understood," he said gruffly. "I'll try to stay out of the way. Maybe find a place more private than the library next time." His thorny tone pricked me, drawing blood, like the black rose he'd given me not long ago.

"He can't know about *this.*" I waved my hands to emphasize the unfamiliar room we were in—the lack of clothing.

"If he treats you so well, then why do you feel the need to hide *this* from him?"

I narrowed my eyes. "Because you attacked him *days* ago and everyone has their limits." We stared each other down in an apparent battle of wills. "Where are we, *Rafael*?"

He cringed before saying, "We're at the Siren Inn... A brothel."

I stood up in horror, trying to steady myself. "How *dare* you bring me here!"

If Ophelia found out about this—*the scandal it would cause*. I took a deep breath... I was in Nymera. Things were different here.

He jumped up to support me, his hands on my waist. "Let me explain, I have an apartment here—"

I cut him off. "You're such a frequent customer that you have *your own apartment!*" I blanched. Pig. Rakish *pig*.

He chuckled, rubbing the nape of his neck. "I don't sleep with the women here—they're like family to me. Do you really think I need to *pay* for sex?" He gave me a dubious look that caused my pulse to race. "I live here because the women who work here were friends with my mother. The humans that knew her are gone, but the Fae workers remain. They took me in so often in my youth, I eventually leased a room. It's a retreat from the castle. The workers pass useful information to me... whispers they hear from their clients. Like I told you before, one of them tipped me off about the Elders—a personal guard got too drunk with one of them and divulged information."

"The intimacy of pillow talk extends to *prostitutes?*"

"Of course. They're not that different than you and I; they were just born into different circumstances. Most of the people working here are intelligent, kind, and willing to risk their lives to fight for what's right. I owe them *my* life more than once over. Clashes with the Queen, with Galen—I'd be dead if I hadn't had a place to escape to."

"I see." I chewed my lip.

He'd needed a hideout from Galen? How far back did their rivalry go? "How is your mother connected to the brothel?" I asked.

"She was born here—her beauty was legendary. So much so that my father decided to house her in the castle, as one of his personal consorts. He treated her well, protected her... until she died." He glanced down at the cup of tea in his hand. I moved closer, resting a hand on his back. We were both parentless.

"I was only two," he continued. "I don't have any memories of her, but I can still feel the love she imprinted on me... if that makes sense. It has guided me in the darkest of times." We stood together, thinking about those we'd lost. And those who'd be next, if we didn't act soon.

"Let's get you back to the castle." Raf dropped my hand. And with that simple gesture, we built our walls back up, brick by brick.

We crossed the drawbridge as the orange glow of dusk dusted the mountain peaks. Galen was waiting for us, clearly worried and agitated. I watched the two men size each other up as we approached. If they had antlers, they would've been locked in a display of strength. I was transferred from Raf to Galen, like a paper-covered parcel.

Were all Fae men this tiresome or was it just these two? Rafael disappeared into smoke and Galen led me up to my room.

"You look terrible. What happened during training?" He eyed me warily. "I've been waiting hours for the guards to alert me upon your arrival. I was beginning to think he kidnapped you." His voice was dripping with disdain for his brother. And I couldn't blame him.

"I burnt out. I let my emotions get the best of me... It wasn't his fault." I let him support me as we walked up the stairs. Everything hurt.

"It was *absolutely* his fault. I don't like this arrangement. I'm going to find time to train you myself," he said vehemently. His uhra flashed bright red, letting me know just how mad he was.

"You don't need to do that—you have enough to worry about. He isn't so bad. I wish you would try to get along."

He dropped his supportive arm around my waste and grabbed me roughly. "He *attacked* me. Whose side are you on?" He held my arm, twisting, until I yelped in surprise and he loosened his grip.

"My loyalty lies with you, of course, but Louis and Raf are on *my* side. They're teaching me to protect myself. Meanwhile, you're working with the Elders. Maybe I should ask you whose side *you* are on." I regretted the words as soon as they were out.

We arrived to my room and Galen silently unlocked the door before gesturing, "After you." I hesitated, afraid of the heat I could feel emanating from him. His flames were barely contained. I took a deep breath and walked through the threshold. He slammed the door behind us and I flinched.

Pushing me against the door, his fiery eyes danced over me, lingering on the fluttering pulse at the hollow of my neck. This is where he'd first kissed me. His heat seared into me as he pressed his body into mine—until

I could feel every part of him through the layers that separated us, until we were molded together. He kissed me deeply... possessively, marking his territory with scalding assertiveness.

He looked down at the tunic I was wearing, grabbed the collar, and *ripped* it... like it was made of tissue. And then he was ravaging me, cupping my exposed breasts, needing me as desperately as I needed him. He nipped at my neck, my collarbone, my breasts.

Mine, his eyes said, pinning me in place. "I'm on your side... And I will *kill* anyone that lays a finger on you. I'll disintegrate *anyone* who threatens you. It's in my nature to defend what's mine, *it's in my blood*. Asking me to sit back while *he* puts you in danger is like asking a lion not to hunt. I'll claim you over and over until you believe me when I say that *I love you*, Marigold."

I didn't know how to respond to his declaration, so I kissed him with everything I had, then used my wind to push him onto the bed, earning a look of smoldering approval. I hadn't heard those words from many people and I could only imagine he hadn't heard them often either. I certainly hadn't expected him to say them so fast.

"I love you," he whispered against my skin as he undressed me.

"I love you," he growled into my ear as he kissed his way down my throat.

"I love you," he purred between my legs as he made me climax.

And I couldn't say it back, even though I felt it. My heart was *racing* for him. My thighs were shaking for him. My fingers gripped his hair as I pulled him on top of me.

I love you, he said with his eyes as we swayed together. And my heart felt as full as the moon above.

TWENTY-NINE

D ays ticked by as I trained with Raf and spent each evening with
Galen. I'd been wielding my magic effortlessly since the burnout.
It seemed I'd mastered a new level of control after losing it so thoroughly—though I wouldn't forget how close it had come to killing me. It wasn't
a lesson I wanted to learn again.

Galen hated that I was spending so much time with Raf, but with
Louis still gone, he reluctantly allowed it. He didn't have a choice; he was
too busy to monitor me. I rarely saw him in the hours between sunrise and
sunset, but he was always waiting when Rafael dropped me off at the castle
gates.

It usually went something like this: Galen's eyes would simmer and
Raf would flash his teeth with a warning growl. I'd stumble over to Galen,
exhausted from training, and he'd protectively put his arm around me,
while they continued to glare at each other. Then Rafael would disappear
in a cloud of smoke and Galen would usually mutter something like,
"*bastard*," under his breath.

The tension between them was palpable. It seemed inevitable that
moon and sun would eventually collide—and I hoped I wasn't anywhere
near when it happened. Or maybe I hoped I was close enough that I could
stop it. I didn't want to see either of them hurt.

Galen arranged a meeting with the Queen and her council as
promised, and too soon, the day was upon us. I'd been dreading this
moment, but there was a bright side—it was a step forward; a step towards
going home.

As long as they didn't deny my request to go to the Oracle.

Raf and I had decided that when we went to the witch, he'd be asking about the kidnappings as well, since every path he took kept leading to dead ends. Meli had confirmed that healers were missing from nearby towns, but she didn't know where they'd gone. Meanwhile, people were continuing to get abducted. Mostly humans, but also healers.

Desperate times called for desperate measures and going to the Oracle was *absolutely* an act of desperation. I'd seen enough worry in the Princes' eyes when we talked about her to know that no one in their right mind willingly went to the witch.

Galen and I were taking a carriage to a manor owned by the royal family, currently unoccupied. It was a discreet location, far from civilization, used for interrogation and intimidation, according to Galen. A place where people went in, but didn't come out.

I could tell he was nervous, continuously tapping his foot and weaving fire between his fingers, which in turn made *me* nervous. It didn't help that Arnold was sharing a carriage with us, while Sylvia rode by herself. I had no doubt that her voluminous skirts filled an entire vehicle, along with her massive sense of entitlement.

Galen sat beside me, keeping his hands to himself. Isla's father glared at him, while I tried my best to avoid eye contact and conversation, staring out the window instead. We rode past grasslands buzzing with life. Sleek antelope and shaggy buffalo grazed as glittering mountains loomed overhead. We'd be going into those mountains soon enough, if this meeting went as planned.

Galen and Rafael had both told me to play nice, to tell the Elders what they wanted to hear... as if I had another choice. We arrived too soon and Galen helped me out of the carriage. He leaned close and whispered, "My hands were tied. Whatever they say, I'm on your side." I looked up at him, puzzled. *What had he done?* My heart dropped into my stomach.

The manor was ornate, bordering on gaudy. Tropical plants, marble statues, and black and white checkered tile greeted us in the entryway. We made our way to a large obsidian table that filled the entire dining room. It instantly made me feel uneasy, as if the stone itself had dark memories stored inside of it—warning me, *bad things happened here*. The curtains were closed, making me feel claustrophobic.

My chest began to hammer. I thought of Meli and Odin, as I was shoved into a seat, and steeled my spine. I wouldn't let them end up here.

The Elders sat on one side, while Sylvia commanded the head of the table. Galen was at the other end. I sat alone. I'd never felt more like a prisoner.

I plotted an escape route. If things went south, I'd need to get behind Galen, who sat closest to the exit. The guards that lined the room would catch me before I'd get far—unless I turned them into ice sculptures and created an indoor hurricane. I wasn't defenseless. I'd even snuck a dagger in on a garter belt, thanks to Raf. The cold steel against my thigh was a constant reminder that this damsel could and *would* fight back.

"Welcome, world walker and Princess of Aurelius." A bronze-haired man, whom I assumed was Radley—the head of the Elders—flashed his bright, white teeth at me. *Princess?* Galen had told them that I was to inherit the Aurelian throne? My chest splintered and I fumbled, caught off guard. I quickly recovered and bowed my head in greeting, avoiding Galen's gaze.

Rafael had warned me about Radley. He loved to hear himself talk. Some found him charismatic, but his charm was reserved for those he found worthy. He had a fiery temper to match the flames he wielded. Arnold and Radley fought over leadership of the group, but Harkin was the real one to fear, according to Raf.

She was volatile and quick to use her earth and ice magic. While the other Elders preferred to distance themselves from humans, opting for blood in a cup, Harkin liked to play with her food. She apparently brought two *leashed* humans with her, wherever she went, sipping from them at her leisure. She claimed they weren't slaves, but instead, faithful servants. I was relieved she hadn't brought them today.

I glanced up at the group to see if I could identify her. Instead, I was hit with a crashing wave of uhras that twisted with dark, oily power. Each soul was the same deep shade of red; a burgundy so dark, it was nearly black. A massive storm cloud flickered, hovering over them all, as if their souls had been stitched together into one mighty monster. I was a minnow staring into the gaping jaws of a shark.

A high-pitched screaming rang in my ears. And then silence. They were staring. I blinked away the horror and steadied my quaking voice. "Th-thank you. My time here has been an eye-opening experience... to say the least." I gave a polite smile; the kind women were expected to hand out like candy in Aurelius. Inside, I was trembling.

"Galen tells us you're... *remarkable*. And now we finally know who took over the Ancient Kingdom when faeries were exiled. *Your ancestors!* We've been so curious, the last two centuries. It seems we should've given the human rulers more credit—convincing a world walker to turn her back on her own kind. Very impressive, indeed. Did she spread her legs for the mortal King, I wonder? He must've had a cock made of pure gold to sway such a powerful faerie. And it seems *that* very power trickled down to *you*. I've been asking myself, have the Six Gods forsaken us? Why else would they bless a *mongrel* with such gifts?"

No one had ever talked to me with such blatant disrespect. I froze in shock as Arnold replied, "Bite your blasphemous tongue, Radley." A cruel smile played on his lips. "The gods have sent Marigold to us. Now that she is ours, her power belongs to *us*. She holds value as a hostage, as well. What lengths do you think her Queen would go to, to get her back?"

My nails dug into my palms, anger replacing fear. Galen had caused this. I looked over at him to find his eyes wild with outrage, with panic. What did he think would happen? That they'd hear the word *Princess* and decide I should be his *bride*? The feeling of betrayal sat like a rock in my stomach. A flush was spreading over my neck, up towards my rounded ears, while my fingers turned to ice.

Several of the others hissed and laughed. Three men and three women sat before me. Arnold, Radley, and a man so blonde, his hair almost appeared white. He looked to be the oldest of them all. His face had a waxy quality to it, like he was past his expiration date.

The women were even more intimidating. A black-haired faerie, with skin the color of bone, looked like she was in her animal form already. *Spider,* I wanted to hiss. Sylvia's mother, no doubt. There was also a silver-haired female with ebony skin, and a tall female with a copper mane of hair and eyes that blazed with fury. I guessed *she* was Harkin.

Intimidation and vicious words; that was all they had. *They needed me.* "You blame me for the mistakes of my ancestors?" I asked. "Surely, you have more intelligence... more grace than that. My Queen doesn't respond well to bribery or threats. And neither do I." They thought I was a direct descendent of the throne... Their ire was misplaced. *I was going to kill Galen.*

"Ah, we may be *graceful,* but you won't find our kind as *forgiving* as humans. We live too long to forget past grievances; instead, we let them

fester. While your people have forgotten who we are after a few genera-
tions, we've remembered *everything*. We have no forgiveness left in our
blood—blood that calls for the magic that was *stolen* from us." Harkin
purred her words, staring *through* me as she spoke with a smug smile
on her face.

Galen cleared his throat and stood. "She's not your hostage. She
is an honored guest, under my protection. I'll not sit by idly while you
fling insults at her. Perhaps, it's not too late to find your manners and
introduce yourselves."

Silence answered him. "No? Then I shall do it for you." He
continued, "Marigold, you've been introduced to Radley and Arnold.
The gentleman to their left is Samael. The ladies... My grandmother,
Anica, followed by Harkin, and Greta."

The redhead *was* Harkin. She hid behind no mask as the rest did.
They at least appeared civilized. She looked half-wild, ready to shift
into a she-wolf and tear me apart.

"Pleasure to meet you," I said with a scowl.

"Marigold is mastering her magic with impressive speed. However, world walking is a different beast and she needs our help. How
well were you acquainted with the last world walker? Did you see her
open a doorway?" Galen's jaw was ticked, his body tight, as he tried
to facilitate the meeting, directing his question towards no one in
particular. His mother sat back, coiled and ready to strike.

"You truly believe her lies? That she doesn't know *how*? You're as
foolish as your father." Harkin gave an insidious laugh and turned to
me. "Remind me, how did you arrive in Nymera?"

Galen's flames exploded. "Disrespect the late King again and I'll
rip your black heart from your chest and burn it to ash."

Sylvia raised a brow, but it was Radley who stepped in. He lifted his hands towards Galen in a gesture of peace, before snarling at
Harkin. "Speaking ill of the dead?" He clicked his tongue at her. "Do
we need to muzzle you... again?"

Harkin shot him a glare, shook her head, and then all eyes fell
on me. "Well, girl, answer the question," Radley pressed. I felt their
unified hatred bore into me.

I answered slowly, trying to hide how rattled I felt. "I fell asleep in Erador and woke up here. I traveled while sleeping." My hands fidgeted in my lap, aching to throw up a shield and protect myself.

"The Mongrel Prince took her to the portal without my consent, but she failed to open a doorway," Sylvia explained. "She would've tried to escape by now... if she was able to."

My eyes shot to her. And then to Galen. *He'd told her that I went to the garden with Raf.* It felt as if the dagger tucked against my thigh had somehow found itself impaled in my gut. He'd chosen his *mother* over *me*. I tried to still the power surging through me. I needed to stay in control. My breath was frosty as I inhaled in and out.

He had used my secrets for his own gain. After he'd *promised*.

In and out.

He'd told me I could trust him.

Sadness and rage were begging to be released in the form of a blizzard. I could barely focus with the roaring in my ears—the fire and ice in my blood.

"It's a difficult story to swallow... you must understand," Anica said, tapping her red fingernails along the marble table. "As for the walker... We don't know much about the woman who led us here. She had golden hair... quite similar to yours. We never saw her wield magic. The portal was waiting for us, then promptly shut when the last of us were through. King Randall made the mistake of trusting her, but my daughter will not repeat his mistakes."

Was I somehow related to the last walker? Why had Ophelia kept me in the dark? I wanted to scream.

"Anything else you can recall?" I asked, acid pooling on the tip of my tongue. I was shivering, while my icy breath spilled across the table like smoke. Galen's eyes were on me, begging me to keep it together.

Anica looked down her nose at me as she replied, "No. We barely interacted with her. She made a proposition to King Randall to send us to a new world, with the promise that it would lift our curse. His entire family had just been slaughtered by humans. He was in hiding—we all were. We had few options; she used our desperation to her advantage."

Arnold cut in—red-faced, eyes bulging. "The bitch knowingly sealed us out of our home world, never bothering to break the curse."

"A treasonous *whore*," spat Greta.

Their wrath pelted me from all directions, suffocating me, burying me. And like a branch, bearing too much weight...

I snapped.

Arctic wind whipped around me as my voice rang out clear and strong. "ENOUGH." I stood up, effectively silencing them all. "I'm sorry about what happened to your people, long before I was alive. However, your obvious disdain towards my kind poses a conflict of interest. Are you capable of working *with* humans? Or is spilling blood across Erador your only objective? *Protect* the remaining humans. *Find* the abducted people. *Stop* killing hybrids, if you want my cooperation. You do yourself a disservice, not allowing humans and faeries to interbreed. Aren't Rafael and I proof enough, that hybrids don't weaken magic, but make it stronger?"

It was asinine to speak so boldly, to order them about, like I was their Queen. They were well past reason and had shown themselves to be incapable of empathy, and yet I couldn't allow them to say what they had, unchallenged. To do what they were doing, unchecked. I braced myself for an explosion.

Several of them stood up in anger. Harkin readied her hands for an attack. Radley released flames along the length of the table, creating a barrier. "You seem to be under the impression that you hold sway here," he said with detached amusement, as if I were a zebra that had just challenged a pride of lions. "Let me set you straight; we might *need* a world walker, but we don't need her with all of her limbs... In fact, we could inflict quite a bit of damage to a healer. Some of us might even enjoy it."

Galen's fire roared, as he faced Radley. They both had flame the same fiery shade as their hair. "I gave my mother information in *exchange* for her word that Marigold remains unharmed. You don't want to push me any farther than you already have, unless you'd like to start a war. Or have you forgotten who commands the Royal Fae Army?" he seethed, baring his fangs, while they stared each other down.

Sylvia's voice echoed through the hall as she spoke with absolute authority. "Sit down, both of you. *NOW!*" She threw out vines that forced the men back into their seats. "Galen, you do *not* control the soldiers; I do. They bow to me—*they bleed for me.* You and your brothers oversee the army under *my* supervision. A monkey could do your job.

"As for the rest of you... have you forgotten who *you* bow down to? Do you need a reminder with a show of *strength*? Shall I have my guards remove *your* limbs for threatening my world walker?"

She looked disgusted with everyone in the room, turning on me next. "As for you, *Princess,* you're in no position to make ultimatums. If you mouth off again, I'll chain you and leave you to rot in a cell. I don't care if you're temporarily sleeping with my idiot son—no one is above *my* law."

I stayed silent, lowering my head. This hadn't been the time or place to challenge them. But I didn't regret standing up for myself, for my people. My heart thumped erratically as the full weight of my predicament hit me. Sleeping in a feather bed, with the heir to the throne beside me, had given me a false sense of security.

"I apologize, Your Grace," I said softly. "I requested this meeting for a specific purpose—to seek permission to visit the Oracle. I believe she'll tell me how to open a doorway to Erador." I shrank within myself to get the words out. Raf wouldn't have pandered to these people... but I didn't have his strength.

Radley and Galen's flames had been put away. Everyone was sitting down. The Elders continued to glare at me with centuries worth of malice.

"You may visit the Oracle. We'll send guards to ensure that you stick to the mission." Sylvia turned to the Elders. "Does anyone have reason to deny this request?"

Everyone shook their heads. "We defer to your wisdom, Your Highness. However, if she returns and has made no progress, we'll be requesting permission to take her, to see if *our* methods prove effective. You've seen her insolence. We can't risk her escaping," Arnold replied.

Galen's flames sent heat across the table as he let his temper slip again. "By royal decree, you will *not* touch her."

Sylvia sighed. "Galen, put your matchsticks away. Arnold, I've heard your concerns. We'll give Marigold until the Hyacinth Festival to open a portal for us. If she hasn't, I'll leave her in your care. I believe *that* will be motivation enough. This meeting is dismissed." She clapped and everyone stood.

Fear latched onto me and *shook* any remaining fortitude from my soul. The festival was less than two months from now. *It wasn't enough time.* I stumbled as guards hauled me out of my seat and marched me back to the carriage.

Arnold stayed back with the Elders. Only Galen appeared at the carriage door. A flash of trepidation crossed his face, followed by a carefully blank expression. "They haven't won, love. We have time. I won't let them hurt you."

The *nerve* he had. *This was his doing.*

I was so broken that I didn't stop him when he sat beside me and pulled me onto his lap. He kissed my forehead as he tried to comfort me. One last surge of anger rose up and I jerked away from him, sitting as far from him as possible. And then I let myself fall apart.

"Y-you told your mother that I tried to open the portal. You told *them* that I'm the heir to the Aurelian throne," I rasped as tears threatened to choke me. I held onto my necklace, twirling it in my fingers. It was as cold as the ice in my chest.

"Only to protect you…" His voice was laced with sorrow. "My mother has been threatening to send you to the dungeons since she found out about us. I offered her information in exchange for your safety. She does nothing out of the kindness of her heart. I did what I had to do. I couldn't see you shackled and broken. I couldn't let her crush your spirit." Silver tears lined his lashes as he looked at me.

"Did you tell her about my blood? How it affects your power?"

He shook his head. "No, I promise."

I nodded limply. He'd violated my trust. Even if it had been for my benefit; he'd lied. At the very least, he shouldn't have let me walk into the meeting unaware. I felt like a fool. He knew how *evil* they were, how eager they were to hurt people like me. And now I was their political enemy as well. Today had been a stark reminder that I was falling in love with my enemy's son. There would be no easy path forward.

"You betrayed me, regardless of your reasons. Will you continue to choose your mother over me?"

His tone grew frantic as he replied, "Of course not. I choose you, *always*. But she's the only protection we have from the Elders right now. I'm doing what I can to appease her, so that I can keep you safe. I won't let them have you. I'll fight her on this. I'll fight the whole fucking world if I have to." He tried to smooth my hair and I shied from his touch.

His face fell and he stared out the window. "I've told you, since the beginning… you're too good for me," he whispered. "Maybe I'm more like my mother than I'd like to admit. I lied—you're right. But my choices were limited. She's not one to respond to declarations of love. I had to give her something she wanted, and then I was afraid to tell you—of losing you.

"Before you arrived... I couldn't face myself, so I found ways to escape: Alcohol, blood, sex... whatever numbed me into oblivion. I have an endless rage inside of me. My childhood, the things I've been forced to do, memories that haunt me... I've accumulated over one-hundred years of night terrors. When I let that anger consume me, it's as if I'm standing on the edge of a cliff. And if I let myself fall, then I'll become *her*. I'll become my mother, instead of my father.

"When you came along, I was ready to let darkness take me. I'd given up on myself. And then I was blinded by your light. You're *sunshine*, Marigold. It's as if you fell from the sky to remind me there is still gentleness in the world." Galen met my gaze. His thumb brushed along the crests of my wet cheeks as he whispered, "I love you. I want to be better for you. You're my guiding light, my beacon. Without you, I'm hopeless."

Tears blurred my vision. It physically hurt to know just how much pain he'd been in. How tortured his soul was.

But how he viewed me... it didn't feel sustainable, it made my stomach ache. He had me on a pedestal, but *I wasn't a savior.* Not his, not his world's. I was just a girl who was very, very lost. He'd reduced my heart to ash with his actions. And yet, it was still beating... *for him.*

I should've shoved him out of the moving vehicle for what he did, but as I gazed at his distraught face, I yearned to take his pain away. I yearned for him to *devour* me. I'd never been more convinced that my animal form was something that a lion would *eat.*

Could two broken people form one whole one, or were we just fooling ourselves? Could trust grow back over time? Or was it like a faerie heart—forever broken once shattered?

"It'll take time to forgive you," I said softly.

"Take all the time you need, love." Galen gathered me into his arms. I let him shower me with kisses. They felt like drops of summer rain against my frigid skin.

I didn't want to think about the Elders—what they'd do to me if given the chance. I didn't want to think about the Oracle and her *price.* I didn't want to think about the people who would die if I failed.

After a long silence I said, "You won't become your mother. You get to choose who you are, Galen." I let those words sink in before I continued,

"I won't be a bird that you bat about with your paws. No more lies. We're partners. *Equals*. If you betray me again, you *will* lose me."

His uhra appeared as he smiled down at me. A blend of blue and red, both fighting for dominance. I knew where a red uhra would lead. I shuttered as I remembered the rotting souls of the Elders. I couldn't let that be his fate. He needed me. And I needed him too.

"I'll never do anything to jeopardize this again. You hold my imperfect heart in your hands, do with it what you will." He leaned his forehead against mine.

Today had been too much. Conflicting emotions battered me from all directions. Fear, guilt, anger, *shame*. So much shame. I'd cowered before the enemy today. I needed to find myself. But first I needed to lose myself... in him.

"Bite me," I whispered. *Take me to oblivion*.

Galen's face lit up in delighted astonishment. "Dear gods, I found myself a unicorn. There's no one else like you."

He kissed his way down my throat, whispering sweet nothings along the way. And then his canines were sinking into the delicate curve of my neck. We moaned in unison as he took me to a faraway land, where nothing hurt and no one could come between us.

THIRTY

I met with Meli a few days after the meeting. Robert had taken me on horseback and was now waiting outside of her apothecary while we convened inside. As I read Meli's energy, I could feel her overwhelming anxiety; it tasted sour in my mouth. Her morning sickness made my own stomach queasy. But it wasn't all bad... there was a kernel of hope. A tiny life force. No pain lived within this small miracle, only a warm glow.

"She feels strong and healthy." I grinned, looking into Meli's bright hazel eyes.

"She?" A smirk appeared on her face.

"Yes... Just a guess, of course." I instantly regretted speaking so boldly, but Meli encouraged me.

"I think it's a she as well," she said, rubbing her belly that was just beginning to swell.

"I've never felt closer to my magic than I have while growing her. I can already feel flickers of her spirit inside of me, like a little ember. I can feel *her* magic inside of me. Odin and I have broken the blood curse for our child. She'll never have to know what it feels like to be without magic."

The light in her eyes gave me hope. Meli put her hands on mine. "You've had an emotional week. Anything you'd like to talk about?" She did a healing adjustment that left me feeling better than I had in days.

"I... I think I'm falling in love with Prince Galen, Meli. I feel like I'm losing control... as if I'm walking along a tight rope. All it would take is one strong gust to send me sailing to my death. The Elders will imprison me soon, if I don't open a portal for them. I'm desperate to help the humans here, but I don't know how. I feel so lost."

I pulled my hand from hers. "No more healing, now that you're caring for another. Save all your energy for her."

"You sound like Odin. I refuse to stop. I'd rather slow down in other ways. Helping people is what keeps me sane. If I stayed at home resting, I'd be sick with worry all the time." She gave me a knowing smile. "And losing control is *part* of falling in love. Being vulnerable is never easy. And I understand the precarious path that you walk because I walk it too. We're all living in uncertain times. You must have faith in yourself, in the universe. You won't let us down. I can feel your heart, see your soul. Your spirit is strong—*brave*. I believe in you."

I wasn't a patient person. *I wanted to act.* I was desperate to do *more*. I didn't want one more person to go missing because I hadn't saved them in time. Waiting was the hardest part. Every moment of ecstasy with Galen reminded me that I was letting myself get distracted from my larger purpose. It was eating away at my morale. I was ready to face the Oracle, even if she killed me, at least I would've done *something* worthy of Meli's admiration.

"Thank you, Meli. I'm grateful for you. Do you feel safe? I'm worried about you, with healers disappearing, on top of everything else..."

"We're safe, I promise. Rafael's friends have been staying close. And they've been helping us spread word to those we trust, human and Fae families that aren't safe here. People will begin gathering in Monrovia over the next month. We'll be ready to leave when you are."

I raised a brow at Meli. "Rafael has friends?" He maintained an air of mystery, even though I saw him nearly every day.

She laughed. "Leon and Kaya. They both work for him and don't seem to be affiliated with the Royal Fae Army." She shrugged. "Not my business, but they're nice."

I pondered that. He'd never mentioned them to me, but not all of his secrets were for me to know. "I'm leaving for the Oracle with the Princes tomorrow. Hide yourselves until we return, *please*," I urged.

"We'll be ready," Meli said, resting a hand on her stomach. "And Marigold... All it takes is the right wave to bring renewed hope to the tide pools. You're the wave we've been waiting for. With your presence alone, you've changed everything. Don't forget the impact you've had on all of us."

Galen appeared in my room, looking princely in his grey velvet uniform, leather armor, and sheathed sword. It was the morning of our departure and I had clothing strewn around my floor and bed, thanks to a mad dash of last-minute packing. We'd stayed up too late, enjoying each other's company. I needed a strong tea. Several of them

He took in the scene with an arched brow. "Has Lusha packed what you'll need? We'll travel light so we can move quickly through the mountains. You'll bring only what your horse can carry."

"Yes, I'm ready. *Relax*, Galen." He was bossy when he was stressed. I walked over to him, giving him a hug, before he leaned down and kissed the top of my head.

Lusha had packed my leather gear, tunics, pants, socks, a heavy coat, and a simple cotton dress. I was wearing a pair of boots that laced past my ankles. Practical attire for the adventure ahead. She had braided my hair into a coronet, so that I wouldn't have to worry about it while we were traveling.

"Very good. Let's head down. My brothers are waiting," Galen grumbled.

Louis had just returned home last night and looked as if he'd barely slept. He had on a wrinkled tunic and purple bags under his heavy-lidded eyes, but still managed to greet me with a warm smile in the courtyard. "I've missed you," I said, pulling him in for a tight hug.

"Training with Raf that rough, huh?" He laughed as Rafael scowled at us.

He was especially stone-faced today, wearing a black ensemble that fit him like a glove. Sitting astride Zagreus, he looked like a brooding dark knight.

"He's been quite helpful and surprisingly competent; however, he is much moodier than you. Like a surly pirate," I teased, but Raf refused to meet my gaze.

Instead, he cleared his throat and addressed the group. "The trail to the Oracle is steep and unforgiving. It'll get colder and more dangerous the higher we climb. We may run into faeries who are more animal than man. Some prefer their animal form, some don't have enough magic to shift back. They'll be hungry for blood, perhaps more." Raf turned to me, sharpening his gaze. "You are to listen to us at all times. If we tell you to run, you run. Hide, you hide. Don't attempt to fight unless you're cornered—you aren't ready. And frankly, I'm sick of having to save your ass." Shadows spilled around him as I resisted the urge to make a face at him. *Bossy when stressed* was apparently a family trait.

"She's not yours to command," Galen growled at Rafael, holding the reins of my horse as I mounted Hibiscus. He took my hand and gave it a prolonged kiss. I sighed, trying not to roll my eyes at his alpha male bravado.

Louis got on his dapple grey horse, appearing stiff and resigned as he let out a loud sigh. All three princes were in a mood today—a reminder of the dangers ahead. And... I suspected they weren't looking forward to spending so much *quality time* together. Brotherly jaunts through the forest were rare for these three. I'd unwittingly crashed a family reunion the day they found me in the woods.

Galen's dark blue uhra floated next to Louis and his turquoise cloud, while Raf still appeared... *soulless*. He clearly wasn't dead, and I no longer thought he was going to possess me with dark magic, but it was mysterious, much like the rest of him.

A flash of blonde hair appeared in my periphery and I turned to see Isla approaching, shining like dew in the soft morning light. Galen looked taken aback, before quickly recovering. He dropped my hand and walked over to her. "I wanted to bring you something to keep you safe," she said, presenting him with a bracelet. "It's white heather... for luck. I made it myself."

They smiled at each other as she tied it around his wrist. And then she reached up and kissed him on the cheek. "Be careful. I'll miss you," she crooned—loud enough for all of us to hear.

My wrath was fast and furious. Icy wind began to gust around me, spooking the horses, who nervously danced in place. I was going to freeze the teeth out of her head. But before I could, Raf blocked me and murmured, "Pull yourself together, Goldie. It's just a bracelet." His jaw was clenched tight and Zag seemed to mirror him, bobbing his head up and down in agitation.

The wind instantly stopped, like I'd been slapped back into my senses. I felt hot with shame. If anyone deserved my anger, it was Galen. *He* was the one courting two women. I'd been foolish to assume she was out of the picture. He had to keep courting her for appearances. Logically, I knew this, but it didn't stop the sting of jealousy. I didn't typically have to see them together.

Galen looked between her and I before saying, "Thank you," to Isla. I commanded Hibiscus to move and gave Galen a frosty glare as I passed.

We began our journey with a group of six. Galen rode ahead with Robert. Instead of acting apologetic, he seemed to be angry with *me*. Fine, if that's how he was going to be, then I'd just ignore him. I trailed behind with Raf and Louis. Sylvia's assigned guard, Alaric, brought up the rear.

The first day was uneventful, trekking through the thick jungle as birds sang overhead. We journeyed through the day, stopping every few hours to relieve ourselves and eat. I spotted the red bird I'd seen at the beach—just a glimpse, and it was gone.

Louis and I caught up, filling me in on his adventures and discussing what I'd learned with Raf. He'd been in Elysia with a team of Royal soldiers, while his most trusted men had been on a secret mission, discreetly following traffic to the Elders' various homes, searching for a blood trail back to their sources. Unfortunately, it had only led to more dead ends.

"Any progress in finding your pneuma?" Louis asked.

"Not really. When Rafael shifts, my magic wakes up, but only for a moment... then it falls back asleep. What about you?"

"I've decided mine lives in water. It would make sense with my elemental gift—and I have an affinity for swimming. If I had more time, I could spend some of it in the lake and try to coax it out of hiding." He sighed. I imagined it was difficult to be the youngest, with two powerful older brothers to compete with.

"Yes, when we get back from the Oracle, perhaps we can have a day at the beach." I smiled. It would be a *very* different experience than my beach date with Galen. I blushed thinking about it. I could see his bronze hair bobbing ahead on his bay stallion and felt my gut twist.

Between the meeting and the exchange with Isla this morning, I was feeling anxious about our relationship. I'd bit all my nails down to the quick. Our chemistry was undeniable, but my trust in him had been whittled down to saw dust. I wanted him to apologize and had decided I was going to ice him out until he did. Surprisingly, he wasn't responding well to the cold shoulder, and now I felt even worse.

I shook away the confusion that fogged my mind and focused on the mission ahead. "Who's going to ask about the abducted humans? You or Raf?" I whispered, peering back at Alaric, who was beginning to catch up to us. He couldn't have looked less interested in our conversation. His eyes were alert, darting back and forth, keeping an eye out for any potential threats.

"We just decided this morning. He didn't want me to bear the weight of the cost, but I convinced him. He and Galen get plenty of opportunities to prove themselves... I haven't had many. This is probably not the best place to discuss the matter..." I agreed and we dropped the subject.

Raf rode ahead of us, avoiding everyone. I wondered if his shadows were closing in on him, as he said they sometimes did, convincing him that he needed no one. I contemplated whether I should do anything to help him. *No.* We'd been spending enough time together as it was—and I didn't need another reason to fight with Galen.

We eventually arrived at our stop for the night, aptly named The Foothill Inn. It was located at the base of the mountains and would be the last civilized stop before we moved into harsher terrain. It would be another two-day journey to reach the witch, depending on the weather.

It was a warm and breezy evening as we dismounted and handed the horses over to the inn's designated grooms. Rain and mud—potentially snow—would slow us down once we began ascending the mountains, according to Louis. We were now in early summer, which came with frequent thunderstorms. Looking up at the blue skies, it was difficult to imagine the weather turning on us.

Galen went to reserve our rooms, while the rest of the group and I found a large table in the tavern. My body ached from sitting on a horse all day. I was thankful for my magic, already hard at work repairing sore muscles. I was optimistic that I'd feel fine by the time I tucked into bed tonight.

Peering around the inn, I grinned to myself. It looked like something out of one of my romance novels—quaint, if not the cleanest establishment. Well-built tables and booths lined the walls. A small stage sat at the back of the tavern. Tonight, there was a band of three on stage, playing lively music that a few brave souls were dancing to. The room was crowded with faeries that weren't nearly as presentable as the villagers of Monrovia.

Many looked like they'd been traveling for quite some time. By the smell of this place, baths were a luxury in the mountains.

It was a rowdy atmosphere. Faeries mingled, spilling beer on each other, as they leaned in for conversation. The bar itself was a masterpiece. Walnut wood was intricately carved and painted with trees, mountains, flora, and fauna, depicting a story of some kind. A large spider had been whittled into the wood as well... an odious reminder of where we were heading.

A pitcher of beer, steaming cups of beef and barley stew, and a loaf of cracked rye bread arrived at our table and we dug in. We all ate in silence, too hungry to break for conversation.

Galen appeared and sat beside me before speaking to the table. "There were three available rooms. We'll be pairing up for sleep. You can fight over sleeping arrangements amongst yourselves. I'll be rooming with Marigold." His smug expression made me want to wallop him. He owed me an apology and he was *still* wearing her bracelet.

"You can sleep on the floor," I said icily. That took the smirk off his face. I watched his brothers fight over who was getting the bed. An image of the giant males sharing a small bed made me giggle out loud, earning a sharp glance from Raf.

I took a sip of beer, glaring back at him, wanting to drown out my annoyance at both him and Galen. Louis was the only one who'd bothered to acknowledge me today.

It was my first time tasting beer, and the sweet malty flavors danced on my tongue. "This is delicious!" I announced, gulping the drink down quickly. I reached for the clay pitcher to pour myself more, but Galen placed his hand over mine in protest.

"Pace yourself—you don't want a hangover. You'll need your wits about you tomorrow in the forest."

Who did he think he was?

I pushed past his hand and poured a tall glass of the amber liquid, chugging it to spite him. "I don't get hangovers, I have healing magic," I boldly declared. The men exchanged looks and it reminded me of my first day in Nymera, when they hadn't known what to make of me.

"I rarely see the three of you together. You should really try to get along. You're brothers in a world of enemies." I took another generous swallow and hiccuped.

"And who exactly are our enemies?" Galen asked.

"You're *Princes*. Royal families attract enemies. Take my mother, for example, she was killed just for being related to my Queen. We never know when loss will strike. Life is too short for you to *bicker*," I said with exasperation, shooting a hard glare at Galen, then Rafael.

"We are Fae Princes. Life is not too short for us. And luckily, we don't die easily, otherwise we would've killed each other by now," Raf said with an edge to his voice.

Galen snorted in response. "Yes, brother. You *did* attack me rather unfairly the other week. You struck me while I was at a disadvantage..." His eyes simmered like hot coals as they fell on me.

Heat rose to my face. The day he'd first tasted my blood. My thighs began to throb at the intimate memory. Pleasure pooled in my core at the very thought of his bite.

"You deserved it," Raf snarled. "In fact, if the tavern wasn't so crowded, I'd throw you against another wall—break the other arm."

Oh no. I had started this. I put my beer down. Perhaps, I should've stuck to one.

The roar of a lion silenced the bar. Galen was standing, leaning over the table, zoned in on Rafael. "You would find it more difficult this time." Fire played on his fingers, causing the wooden table beneath his hand to smoke, while taut tendons and veins emerged along his neck.

Raf was equally ready to snap as shadows twisted and darted around him. His eyes were glowing with challenge, as if he was just waiting for a reason to end this, once and for all.

One of the barkeeps ran over sputtering, "E-excuse me, Your Highness. N-no magic inside the tavern."

Galen rushed him, and for a moment, I thought he was going to turn on the man. I jumped forward, stifling his fire with ice as I put my hands over his.

His flames winced out without hurting me. His eyes grew wide, like I'd surprised him with my boldness, like he wanted to swipe the beers off the table and take me right there. Instead, he addressed the group, avoiding Raf's gaze. "Let's all get some rest. Tomorrow will be a long day." He took my hand, shoved past the crowd, and led me up to our room.

THIRTY-ONE

My heart was pounding as the door of the tiny inn room clicked closed. I was still angry, but *gods* I wanted him. I backed against the wooden door, trying to find my fortitude. Galen snapped his fingers, sending flames to the untouched logs in the hearth. The familiar crackle of a blazing fire began immediately. Smoke filled my nostrils, acting as an aphrodisiac as it blended with his scent. My pulse quickened and the butterflies in my stomach went rogue, darting around as if they'd caught fire as well.

He held so much power in those fingers of his. My gaze traveled over his capable hands, up his toned biceps... to the exposed skin above the collar of his tunic. I wanted to press a kiss against the soft hollow of his throat, to taste the salt of his skin on my tongue. He stalked forward... slowly, deliberately. I knew where this would lead if I didn't stop it.

"Galen. We need to talk about Isla."

He stopped short of touching me, tilting his head. "Marigold, it was just a bracelet. She means nothing to me, and I didn't appreciate you making a scene."

He took a step closer, testing my boundaries. One more and his hands were on my arms, rubbing the chill from them as my magic responded to his touch.

"A scene? *She* is the one who gave you a gift in front of me. Clearly, it was to provoke me. Does she love you?" My heart pounded, afraid to hear his answer.

"I can't control how she feels about me... and I doubt she loves me. She loves my power, my title. I don't care one way or the other. *You* are the one I want."

He leaned down, waiting for me to tell him no, but I didn't. His lips brushed along my neck, stopping right where my pulse fluttered, and I gave a pathetic whimper. I arched my back in response, like a cat rubbing against its master.

"Have you slept with her?" I panted as I broke away from him, jolting us back to reality.

"Of course not. You keep me plenty satisfied."

I silently stared at him, trying to decide if I believed him. His emerald eyes narrowed. "Are you looking for reasons to push us apart?" He gripped my throat with one hand, his fingers curled loosely around my windpipe. Adrenaline shot down my spine. This large male was undeniably dangerous, an apex predator—a literal *lion*. And his focus was locked on me.

"Take it off," I hissed, pointing to the bracelet. We glared at each other until he pulled it off with a slight tug and threw it in the fire. He slowly released me, still holding my gaze.

"You need to learn to respect me," he said in a rough voice. "It seems you've left me with only one option. *Punishment*. In the form of unrelenting, torturous pleasure."

Yes.

I yielded, letting him pull me into his arms. Our tongues clashed together like violent waves in a tumultuous, stormy sea. He broke away with a growl and knelt down until he was on his knees. He began unbuttoning my pants, pulling them down forcefully, while his unblinking eyes drank me in.

Mesmerized, I watched him peel my underwear off, ripping them away like cobwebs. I stopped breathing when I felt hot breath at the apex of my thighs—then his tongue as it parted my wet curls. The first stroke set me aflame as he lapped at me like an unstoppable wild fire. His touch was searing, making me writhe in delicious agony.

Soon we were rocking against the door as he *feasted* on me. What was it with us and doors? One of my legs hung over his shoulder, while the other shook so hard, it had been rendered useless. He supported me as he spread me open, licking me, devouring me... as if he'd spent an eternity starving himself for this moment.

Two fingers moved inside me, while his tongue continued to explore me with steady, mind-numbing pressure. Every time I came close to release, he pulled away, purposefully tormenting me.

I was going to evaporate into steam.

"You don't get to cum until I say so," he huffed.

"Please..."

This time, he didn't pull away when I began to climb. And climb. I looked down at his bronze head between my thighs and lost my gods damned mind. Muscles clenched as he sent me orbiting around the sun.

I went slack against the door and Galen gathered me into his arms. He deposited me on the bed with a gentle *thud*. We stripped frantically, needing to be skin to skin. He laid me on the shabby comforter of the creaking bed and climbed on top of me.

"I'm going to drink from you while I fuck you." His devilish smile made my stomach dip.

It wasn't exactly a question, but I nodded in consent.

He slid in, hard and deep, not giving me anytime to adjust—making me take all of him. I sucked in a breath as my body was forced to accommodate him. The line of pain and pleasure blurred until I forgot my name. I moved my hips to meet his, until his body was flush with mine. As he plunged in and out, my breathing became short and frenzied.

A hand came up and brushed the hair out of my face, caressing me. I opened my eyes and met his starry-eyed gaze. Cupping his cheek, I acknowledged the magnitude of this, *of us*.

I'd lived a grey existence, but now every moment was exploding with color. I was living in the here and now because of *him*. I'd been numb for so long and now I was feeling every emotion at once. It was an overwhelming experience—relentless in its pursuit to humble me and splay me open as I let my weaknesses show. Neither of us knew what we were doing, but that hadn't stopped us from *trying*.

Releasing a moan of ecstasy, I exhaled the feelings that were too much to fully process. Every moment with him was a blind leap of faith.

I watched, enthralled, as he moved over me with tireless thrusts. His stomach muscles stretched and tightened as we rocked together. I wanted him to go faster. *Harder*. Growing impatient, I tried to set the pace. Delirious with need, I dug my nails into his back and bit at his shoulder.

"Easy, love. I want to savor you," he whispered, quieting me with a kiss.

I went supine, letting him take full control as tears pricked the corners of my eyes. I was overwhelmed with realization of how much I cared. I'd been driven mad with jealousy over almost nothing.

He lingered at my neck, scraping his canines along the sensitive skin. Wherever his tongue went, goosebumps followed, spreading like flame over kindling. I was gasping for air, feeling more desperate by the second.

"Are you ready?" His smooth voice was the most seductive sound I'd ever heard.

"Yes..." I panted.

His muscles hardened beneath my touch as he leaned over me. He brushed velvet lips along my throat with open-mouthed kisses and paused. I held my breath as he sunk his teeth into the pulsing flesh at the side of my neck. I cried out at the rush of pleasure. It intensified with each beat of my heart—spreading to my limbs, my fingers, my toes. His thrusts were slow and luxurious as he unhurriedly took and took... and took.

I was going to combust.

The combination of his canines inside me, while *he* was inside me... I was in an opium-laced fever dream. The magic that flowed between us erased all pain, all doubt. All I knew was *him*. Euphoria swallowed me whole—a tsunami devouring everything in its path.

I became dizzy as he began to slam into me, no longer holding anything back. I wasn't sure if I was speaking coherently, as I repeated his name over and over. My heart fluttered as he pulled back and peered down at me with blood-rimmed lips. His eyes darkened as he watched me buck and twist beneath him. We climaxed together and magic exploded around us. The fire in the hearth lit up the room in a raging blaze, before everything went dark.

I lifted my sleepy head off of Galen's chest, smelling the distinct acrid scent of something burning. I sat up, glancing at the fireplace, disoriented. *Had I blacked out?* Everything felt fuzzy. A small fire burned; nothing out of the ordinary. Then I found the source—charred handprints had been branded into the bedding, on either side of me. Frost covered the dark marks, spreading across the bedspread and onto the walls.

"Are you alright?" Galen asked, stroking my cheek with a gentle touch.

"I think so. I'm... just... dizzy."

Galen sat up. "Do you need water? Did I take too much blood?"

I took a few deep breaths. I felt fine now. By the time I'd nodded, he'd left the bed and was back with a glass of water. He brushed my hair back as he held a glass up to my mouth.

"That was..." He grinned.

"There are no words," I agreed with a matching grin. "Actually, there are..." I paused, building up courage. "I love you."

His radiant smile nearly made my heart crack in half. I'd never said those three words to any man. I blinked back tears and he kissed me, clutching my cheeks in his palms.

Before I could overanalyze or panic, he responded, "I love you too. In one-hundred and fifty years, I've never felt anything like this. I want to consume every inch of you. I want to live inside of you. I want to make love to you until our souls are one." And then he claimed me until morning.

THIRTY-TWO

I didn't know we'd gotten *any* sleep, but we must've, because I startled when I woke in an unfamiliar room. The gentle breathing beside me anchored me back to space and time. I'd barely registered the dingy room last night. I'd seen nothing but my fiery-haired Prince.

I looked to the peeling green argyle wallpaper and then to the window that sat above the bed. Dawn was upon us and the soft light from the eastern sunrise trickled through sheer curtains. As flashbacks of last night played in my head, I began to take stock of where I still felt sore. I touched my neck and felt raised puncture marks. The bite was still tender. I felt like a bruised apple that had fallen from a tree.

An image from last night—Galen's silhouette against the amber glow of the fire—came back to me, making my stomach tighten. I snuggled into him before the reality of the day was upon us. He stirred at my touch and I watched him take in his surroundings. And then his gaze fell on me.

"Hi," he said with a sweet smile I'd only seen him use with me.

"Hi." I kissed him back, wanting to melt into him and stay there forever. I'd probably have a stupid grin plastered on my face for the rest of the day.

I got up and dressed myself, before undoing my braids, making the decision to wear my hair down. I didn't want the others to see Galen's bite mark—to treat me differently.

Galen was glowing a brilliant shade of gold this morning. His uhra was so bright, it never completely faded from view, like a shimmering second skin. It wasn't the first time I thought he'd looked like the sun god, Cyro.

My magic seemed to have filled his cup and then some. He wouldn't need to drink from the bottles of blood that he and the other cursed faeries had packed. Something about that simple fact filled me with pride. It felt good to provide a precious resource to a Prince who seemingly already had everything. I smiled at my reflection in the mirror, admiring my free flowing tresses. Things were looking up.

As we rode out and up the steep mountain pass, Raf spooked me when he silently appeared beside me. "Hey, I'm sorry about last night. Galen always knows how to provoke me." He brought Zag closer to Hibiscus and they said hello with a quick sniff before ignoring each other.

I held my breath as his all-too-familiar scent drifted my way. "I think we can agree that you mutually provoke each other. And I'm sick of being in the middle. The last thing we need is to start a forest fire." I shot him a sharp stare. "It would serve you both well to *try harder*."

He'd been aloof with me yesterday and then had nearly caused a fight in the tavern. I could only imagine what he'd do if he saw the bite on my neck. I subtly smoothed my hair around my shoulders.

He scoffed. "There'd be no forest fire. I'd cover his world in darkness before he lit a match."

Males. *Faerie males.* I rolled my eyes and asked Hibiscus to pick up the pace with a kick of my heels. She seemed eager to leave the dragon shifter in the dust. *That's why she doesn't like him,* I realized, loosing a laugh. I didn't blame her. His dragon form *was* terrifying.

I rode up to Louis and let his calming turquoise energy wash over me. I'd take any energy I could get. I was bleary-eyed with fatigue, but had no regrets about how I'd spent last night. "How long will we ride today?" I asked with a yawn.

"Until the conditions make it too rough to travel. If you look up at those clouds—" He pointed to a dark blue haze rolling towards us. "There is a storm forming off the lake. It'll be overhead by the day's end. Now is the time for us to make haste. We need to find a safe place to camp before the storm arrives—preferably a cave where we can stay dry." Did Louis have a special ability to sense rain because of his connection to water?

I was about to ask him, when an arrow flew past his head, missing him by inches. I looked behind me to see if it had struck Raf or Alaric, who were picking up the rear. They were unscathed and running towards us as Rafael shouted, "RUN!"

Then Galen was galloping towards us, yelling, "They've blocked the path! We need to fight!" The group raced ahead, while Louis hoisted me off Hibiscus and ran me to the cover of the trees. Hibiscus followed us as far as she could through the thick vegetation, whinnying as she fell behind.

"Stay down. If a stranger approaches you, use your wind to knock them back. Freeze them solid once they are on the ground. Fight to kill. Use your dagger as a last resort." Louis left me and ran ahead to join the other men.

I felt more vulnerable here than I would've had I gone and fought with them. I was a sitting duck. I tried to see what was happening through the dense forest. I could smell magic as shadow, fire, and water clashed nearby. The charged atmosphere was reminiscent to the heavy energy in the air before a thunderstorm. The attackers were likely thirsty faeries hunting for magic. *Blood Robbers,* Galen had called them.

I heard the sound of crunching footsteps behind me and whirled to face the threat. Stunned, I took in the faerie before me—the brunette male who'd harassed Meli—the one Galen had burnt to the bone. He looked fully recovered now, sneering as he approached with unmistakable vengeance in his eyes.

I took a step backwards as panic set in. I wanted to run rather than fight, but the brush and uneven terrain made any attempt to flee difficult, if not impossible.

"Leave me alone. Was Prince Galen's message not clear enough last time we met?" I growled at him, surprised by the ferocity in my voice.

"If you knew how *thirsty* I was, you'd understand why I don't give a *fuck* what the Prince thinks. I'll have my own fire once I take your magic—then he can be the one that burns." He was maneuvering closer to me as he talked, while I was working up the courage to send him flying.

He lunged and I struck with wind. I watched him soar into a solid pine tree ten feet away. He hit so loudly that I heard something inside of him *snap*. I'd never hurt anyone like that before. And then I was being dragged by my long hair that I'd stupidly left down, worrying more about a bruise than my safety. The blonde male—the one who'd restrained me in the exact same way in Monrovia—held me tightly against his chest that reeked of uncleanliness.

I gagged as he pulled me close and said, "You won't get away so easily this time. Your Prince is busy."

I screamed before he struck my head so hard that I saw stars. There was a blinding flash of white behind my eyes as I flailed to defend myself. By the time I was seeing straight, he'd shoved a dirty cloth in my mouth and was binding my hands behind my back. I tried to remember Louis's lessons... Rafael's words, but the ringing in my ears made my recall fuzzy.

I knocked back into him, shoving him as hard as I could, attempting to throw off his balance. It worked for a moment—he loosened his grip on my hair, allowing me to turn around and knee him between the legs. He roared in anger while I ran as fast as I could.

There was rope around my hands, but it wasn't tight. I could shimmy my wrists free when my head stopped spinning. I looked back to see if he was following me. I didn't see him. The brunette was gone too. Panic shot through me as my magic readied itself.

The blonde popped out in front of me. "You'll pay for that, you bitch!" he yelled, coming at me with fangs bared, ready to bite me wherever he could. The brunette tackled me from behind as I managed to get a hand free. I shot ice at the blonde as I hit the ground hard. I heard him scream and fall, but I was still fighting the brunette, kicking him as I tried to grab the dagger from my thigh.

He was on top of me, trying to pin my hands down. "How do ye like it, girly? From the front or back?" His fingers were fumbling under my dress, working to pry open my legs. He laughed as I resisted. I thrashed and fought with everything I had as I felt his hot, sour breath against my throat.

I screamed, waiting for his fangs to connect with flesh. Instead, he was thrown off me with shadows that lashed around his neck and choked him like a noose. I heard the blonde screaming as black vines tightened around his neck next. Then, they were both struggling from two nooses, suspended in the air. Raf left them hanging as he helped me up, turning me around to assess the damage. I pulled away before he could find the marks on my neck.

"Did they hurt you?" His typical stoicism was gone as he frantically asked over and over, "Are you okay? Did they bite you?"

I was in a daze, watching the two men fight for breath. Their faces turned red, then purple. "I-I'm fine. Just a bit disoriented. I was struck in the head." I felt the side of my skull where a large lump was forming.

Raf's response to my answer was brutal and swift, blasting them with a stream of shadow so violent, they disintegrated before my eyes. In seconds, they were nothing more than black confetti, raining down on us. The wind blew our direction, and I felt it settle over my hair, my face.

I hunched over and vomited as my stomach involuntarily clenched in response. Raf was at my side immediately, but I jerked away from him when he made a move to pull back my hair.

I was trembling from shock by the time the other men arrived. Galen's eyes were wild as he ran over to me. "What happened?" he demanded, frisking me for injuries. His gaze swept over the puncture marks as he examined me. I pushed away from him, needing space and a break from being manhandled.

"The two men from the village—the ones who were harassing Melisandre—they attacked me. I tried to fend them off with magic, but they were so fast... so much stronger than me." My pulse ramped up, while my vision blurred, darkening around the edges. The brothers surrounded me, telling me to slow my breathing, to sit down, but before I could heed their advice, I fainted.

"Goldie, I'm so proud of you. You fought fiercely." I woke up to my mother's voice, still fresh in my head. I gripped my necklace, glowing with heat, while I took in my surroundings. I blinked up at Galen as I realized his arms were wrapped tightly around me. He pulled my head into his chest, smothering me and kissing my temple.

"I'm never letting you out of my sight again," he said as I peeled out of his arms.

"I'm fine. Let's get on the road," I muttered.

"You're riding with me," Galen said possessively. The other men began to disperse as he helped me onto Napoleon and tied our horses together. I put up no fight as he climbed behind me and tucked me against him, like I was a frail baby bird who'd fallen from the nest. It wasn't far off from how I felt. I'd been disillusioned enough to believe I was a fledgling, growing flight feathers, nearly ready to soar... but instead, I'd nearly been killed by two starving faeries. Any confidence I'd built since arriving in Nymera had disintegrated with the males who'd nearly killed me.

"What happened? How many were there?" I asked, feeling grateful for the eternal fire that burned inside of Galen as I leaned into the safety of his arms.

"There was a group of four waiting to ambush anyone walking the path. They're all dead now—true deaths. Desperate faeries who turned to crime, unfortunately."

I stayed silent as I let myself ponder what could've happened if Rafael hadn't come when he did. Training was going well; I'd been advancing quickly, but when the time had come to fight, I froze. I forgot to use my shields. It had happened so fast. And those men had been ready to take more than my magic.

"They deserved to die for what they did to you," Galen continued. "But it's always a shame... to lose a faerie. They're under my rule, under my protection. Every time someone lashes out because they need magic, it's a reminder that the Kingdom—*that I*—let them down."

He tugged me closer, laying his large hand flat over my belly. "When you open a portal for us, you'll stop their suffering. They won't have to turn to crime. It'll be a new era of peace."

I bit my tongue, letting his words hang in the air. Was I misunderstanding him? Heat rose to my cheeks as I said, "You still expect me to open a portal for your entire Kingdom, even knowing what you know about the Elders? You think releasing one world onto another will bring *peace*?"

"There will be an adjustment period, of course," he said with an edge to his voice. "But yes, I think it's the only way forward. We can try to break the curse when we get to Erador, but first and foremost, my people need magic. They need *their* home world."

My stomach sank. We really didn't see eye to eye on this. Was he blinded by love for his people or did he simply not care about *mine*?

"It's *blood* they need. I don't want your mother and her council anywhere near the people of Erador."

Galen's body tightened around me as his tone turned combative. "We don't have a choice."

I peered around, making sure the rest of the group was still ahead of us and out of ear shot. "What if we just took a small party through to break the curse? *Without their permission*," I whispered.

"Love..." he sighed. "I'd never risk your safety in that way. If they found out what you were suggesting—" He paused. "You were sent here to save us—to right the last walker's wrongs. I know you'll do the right thing—your bleeding heart is one of the things I love about you, after all."

My entire body stiffened. *I was trying to do the right thing. How could he not see that?* Hot blood sloshed between my ears as I shrank within myself. My pulse was loud and angry.

lub-dub.

lub-dub.

lub-dub.

There was a gnarled knot in the center of our relationship. If we couldn't untangle it, then it would destroy us—put us on opposite sides of a war that was starting to seem inevitable. We couldn't continue to argue about this right now, not in a forest full of kindling. This was a conversation I couldn't afford to screw up; I *had* to make him see my side. *There was no other choice.*

I swallowed it all; the frustration that roiled inside me, the nauseating fear of what this meant for our relationship, the hollow sadness of feeling misunderstood. It stung as much as it ached. I loved him. I didn't want to lose him, but I wouldn't bow to his Queen. I wouldn't bow to *him*.

"Marigold, are you alright?" Galen asked, squeezing my knee.

"Yes, sorry," I rasped. "You're right. Of course." My mind continued to wander until the gentle rocking, combined with Galen's sturdy presence, lulled me to sleep.

I awoke to rain pelting my face while a fierce wind whipped around us. Galen still had a firm grip on me, keeping me secured in the saddle. When I began to stir, he murmured, "Excellent timing. The others found a cave up ahead—we'll be dry soon."

A glow illuminated the entrance to a cave off the main road and we steered towards it. Finally, this terrible day was coming to an end. The men helped pull my stiff, shivering body off Napoleon and took me straight to the fire.

Once everyone was in dry clothes, we sat in front of the blazing fire, eating dried meat, bread and fruit. Raf offered a flask of faerie whiskey to whoever was brave enough to try it. I sniffed at it and took a small sip. It burned down my throat and warmed the parts of me that the fire hadn't been able to reach. Galen grabbed it next and finished it off in one long gulp.

Rafael gave him a dirty look.

"I'm going to try and get some sleep," I announced, moving to curl up on one of the furs that had been laid out. A moment later, Galen had joined me in his lion form. He was splendidly cozy, especially once my face was buried in his soft mane. I could feel eyes on us, but I shut them out and wrapped my fingers around his fur as I fell asleep.

The next day of travel was smoother than the last, but the temperatures had dropped substantially. Coniferous trees covered in pale lichen surrounded us as we scaled the mountain, trudging through mud and slushy snow. We were all wearing fur-lined coats that were warm and dry thanks to Galen's fire that had blazed all night.

Rafael rode up beside me. "How are you feeling after yesterday?" he asked.

I'm sure the bags under my eyes were answer enough. I'd tossed and turned last night, thinking of his shadows. How they'd incinerated skin, muscle, and bone in seconds. He was capable of that kind of magic, and yet he let the Elders and Sylvia talk down to him. How many times had he fantasized about turning them all into dust, I wondered.

"Honestly?" I sighed. "I'm feeling like a failure. I should've been able to defend myself." I paused. "Also, remind me not to get on your bad side."

He snorted, giving me a hard stare, before the lines in his face softened. "I lost my temper. I should've waited until you were out of sight."

The look he gave me caused my chest to tighten and my skin to tingle. It was apologetic, but laced with something heavier.

"Thank you for saving me," I murmured. "I'd be having a terrible day right now, if you hadn't acted when you did. Perhaps I wouldn't even be here." My voice caught in my throat. I thought back to the day I arrived in Nymera. Black smoke had surrounded me and then all six wylks were dead. It had been Raf who saved me then, too.

"Galen isn't the only one who cares about your welfare." The depth of his words—the *way* he said it—made my stomach twist. I couldn't handle his kindness. It was easier to be friends with him when he teased me or pissed me off. Silence stretched on long enough that it turned awkward.

He cleared his throat. "Have you felt any closer to your shifting form with all this time spent outdoors?"

My magic danced beneath my skin in response, but I still didn't know how to *embrace* that feeling and shift. I looked down at my hands, just in case they decided to turn into hooves or claws.

"I feel..." I paused. "Like I'm on the edge of the cliff, but I don't know how to jump." I hoped he understood.

"Need a push?" His dimples flashed.

"Perhaps you just need to take me for that ride. Maybe I need to spend some time in the air."

He rolled his eyes. "A little more groveling and I'll think about it." A half-smile, designed to devastate, lit up his face before he nudged Zag forward without a goodbye.

We stopped to rest for the night, planning to make it to the Oracle by mid-morning tomorrow. The men exchanged stories of the Witch of the Woods, as they liked to call her, seeming to enjoy taunting me. "My cousin's friend went to the Oracle asking for a love potion, to win over the woman he desired. She gave him the potion... before turning him into a toad," said Robert. The most I'd ever heard him say.

Alaric spoke next. "That's not how it works. She tells you what the price will be *before* you pay it. My friend's brother went to her, wanting to know how to get rich. She said she'd tell him how in exchange for cursing him with a loveless life. He took the deal—he was in debt from gambling and was out of options. He's the richest man in his village now, but has no one to share it with. It's made him bitter and cruel. She feeds off those emotions for years to come. She doesn't let anyone leave without a price that will cost them greatly."

"She's not dealing with just *anyone*," Louis said. "Marigold is a world walker; she's both human and faerie... Her presence alone will be a gift to the witch. Plus, it would benefit her to help, if she ever wants to see her sister in Erador again." Louis was trying to make me feel better.

"To offend the world walker is to offend the gods," Raf said with mischief in his eyes. I glared at him.

"She's been leeching from others long enough. If she gives us trouble, we'll fight back," Galen said. I *really* didn't want to tangle with a giant spider; but I supposed if I had to, having three magical Princes, eager to help, was as lucky as I could hope to get.

"Can we please stop talking about her? It's making me rethink this decision." I rubbed goosebumps off my arms.

"Yes, but one more thing. Please think long and hard before you accept whatever deal she offers you. If it's something that is going to endanger your life, it's not worth it. We can find another way to unlock your magic." Raf's eyes were drilling into me as he spoke.

"Surprisingly, I agree with him," Galen chimed in.

"So do I," Louis added.

"You guys nag me more than my old lady's maid," I laughed. I thought of the count down the Elders had given me, of the humans that needed my help. There was little I wouldn't agree to at this point, but the Princes didn't need to know that.

THIRTY-THREE

L eaves whipped at my face as I ran through a misty forest—chasing my mother, yet again. She continued to evade me and I didn't know why. The mother I knew would never hide from her daughter. "Slow down," I called, panting.

"I can't," she said determinedly.

"Why?"

"Because he'll catch us."

"Who? Who will catch us?" I asked in frustration.

But she was already gone.

I woke up sweating, wrapped in Galen's lion form. I scratched his head absent-mindedly and locked eyes with Raf who was sitting on his makeshift bed a few feet away. I cleared my throat and stood up to stretch. I'd barely slept last night, thinking about the looming visit with the Oracle. When I did dream, it was the same recurring one that had been haunting me for weeks... My mother and I in the woods. Sometimes she was care-free, sometimes she was scared. But it was always the same... I never caught her.

I'd also dreamed of spiders crawling down my throat... my nostrils. I woke up gasping for air several times. Maybe that's why Raf was staring—I'd probably made it difficult for everyone to sleep.

What was my mother trying to tell me? And why wouldn't she just get on with it, instead of sending me cryptic dream messages?

As we climbed the last few miles of mountain before reaching the witch's cave, we were blessed with blue skies and singing birds. They were the only signs of life as the trees grew sparse and the air became thin. The habitat was rockier now, with large purple boulders casting spider-shaped shadows at first glance. Louis shot an unfortunate deer with a stream of water as we neared our destination, sensing a false threat. The laughter it brought forth helped cut the tension that was looming over us all.

The rocky trail ended at a cave large enough to be a castle. The witch's lair was a wonder to behold. It was completely formed out of lavender stone that shimmered under the direct light of the beaming sun. The Oracle's home had one main entrance and several smaller openings, where I imagined we were being watched from. The overall shape was that of a skull with multiple eyes and a large gaping mouth. It was a humble home for an immortal soul, even if it was made completely out of Kunzite.

Two male faeries approached as we hovered near the entrance. We'd made a plan: If anything started to go south, the guards and Louis would run out with me, while Galen and Raf faced the witch. I gripped Galen's arm as they drew near.

I could tell they were Fae, because of their pointed ears and snarling fangs, but they mostly just looked like the living dead. They were haggard, with tattered clothing, emaciated bodies, and unkempt beards. Their eyes were completely black, with no whites to be seen. I wondered if they'd once lived normal lives, before they'd made the mistake of coming here. I swallowed hard, glad I hadn't eaten much for breakfast.

"Lady Ellesmere of Aurelius, Princes of Nymera, you may follow us. You can leave your dogs outside," one of them said.

I exchanged glances with the brothers. "The guards come with us," I said firmly. My words were received with vacant stares.

"She will not see you unless the guards are left outside," the other one repeated. Their faces had been drained of emotion, like they were nothing more than vessels delivering the Oracle's message.

"That's fine," Galen replied. "They can watch the horses." He turned towards Robert and Alaric. "If anyone comes near the horses, tear their throats out."

I blinked at his language. I'd assumed the Oracle's men were just being rude, calling them dogs, but maybe they were canid shifters. Robert had never revealed his pneuma to me, and I'd never asked.

"Follow us." The two men turned around and walked slowly towards the cave. As we entered, it felt like being willingly swallowed by an ancient monster. I moved closer to Galen and he draped a protective arm over my shoulder.

The cave was littered with trinkets. I found the dolls and small wooden horses, abandoned on the floor, the most disturbing. Rusty weapons were scattered next to bone-dry skeletons. Gold coins and jewelry sat in overflowing trunks and bags on the floor. Spider silk covered everything. I couldn't tell if the riches surrounding us were a trap to lure people in or unwanted offerings.

The tunnel forked into several directions and I tried to take note of each way we turned. I started to frost the walls, willing the ice to stay as we moved deeper underground. Galen used his flames to light our way when it became too dark to see. Webs grew thicker, walkways narrower, forcing us to walk in a straight line, with Raf in the front. Her two guards stopped so suddenly, I nearly plowed into Louis.

One of them hissed, "She's coming... You may ask one question each. The penalty for breaking a bargain with her is *death*. She can smell trickery and deceit. Do not bother with games..." They faded into the dark, while the rest of us huddled together around a flame Galen had summoned. And then we waited.

A small woman emerged from the shadows and Galen clutched me tighter. My pulse flickered like a wind-blown candle as I took her in. I'd expected her to look eternally young as a true immortal, but instead she was old, frail, and withered. She was hunched over awkwardly, as if it had been a long while since she'd been in faerie form. Her white hair was long and matted together, her teeth stained brown. A simple white cotton dress hung from liver-spotted, pruny flesh.

So this spider liked to play games. Did she really expect us to believe she was less of a threat in the form of an old lady? Unfortunately for her, Raf had done his research, and he'd already warned us that she could take any shape that she wanted. Regardless of her form, I could *feel* her power buzzing around us.

If she was a parasite, able to siphon magic from anyone unfortunate enough to need her services, then she'd consumed her fair share. The energy surrounding us was suffocating, as if we were standing in a crowded room with limited oxygen. I clutched my stomach, trying not to vomit. This had been a terrible mistake.

"Hello, Marigold," the witch said with round, curious eyes. Her voice had a whimsical quality to it that somehow made her even more unsettling. "I've been waiting for you... holding onto your prophecy for such a long, long time. Your web was spun in the stars before you were even born. You can imagine my excitement when I learned that you were finally on your way to see me."

She had a prophecy about me. *Me?*

I broke out in a cold sweat as she continued, "Such a *sweet* soul you have." She stared past me, as if she was studying it, then turned to Galen. "I bet she tastes divine."

He wrapped his arms around me. There was no glow that emanated from her, but her eyes... they burned silver, with the light from a thousand souls. Ice crystals formed in my blood as I wondered how many people she'd devoured in her immortal life—if their uhras were somehow trapped inside of her.

"A world walker and three Princes. My my my... what a special occasion this is. This calls for tea. Shall I send for some?"

No one responded right away, so I answered, "Thank you for the offer, but as you probably know, we're in a hurry. If you'd be so kind as to answer our questions, we'll be on our way."

She frowned, letting me know I'd offended her, before a tight smile returned to her face. "Ah yes, you *are* part-human, after all. Humans are always in such a hurry. If we must be all business, so be it. Ask your question, lovely child."

I turned to the Princes and they gave me encouraging glances. I cleared my throat and asked, "How do I manifest my world walking gift so that I can return to Erador?" I braced myself for the cost as I squeezed Galen's hand.

"A rare gift... to traverse across galaxies. I am powerful, but even I cannot perform such strong magic. The cost for this answer is simple, and I believe you'll find it quite fair. Come back and visit me when you've found your pneuma. You must arrive—*and stay*—in your animal form for the duration of your visit. You'll have one week to pay the cost, once you've discovered what you are."

My eyes darted to the brothers. Raf's face was set in stone, Louis was looking at his hands, while Galen sneered at her. They said nothing to discourage me, but I had a hunch we were all thinking the same thing—*trap*.

Spiders weaved webs for one purpose: To catch their prey. But if she wanted me dead, why didn't she just kill me now? There was a missing piece to this puzzle, something I didn't understand. I had no choice but to go in blindly and hope the gods were on my side. They'd taken me this far.

"You'll let me leave... after I visit you?" I asked, thinking of the husks of men I'd seen earlier. A fate worse than death.

"You've already asked your question." Her rotted teeth flashed into a grin. I cringed, praying my animal form was something formidable—something that could hold its own against a witch.

"It's a deal," I said through gritted teeth. As I spoke the words, it felt as if manacles had clamped around my wrists. I looked down and saw nothing, but their presence continued to linger.

The witch's smile widened as she set her silver eyes on me. "The answer to your question is simple. You may open and close portals between worlds, in your pneuma form *only*. That has always been the way with walkers. You'll be stronger in your animal form—able to channel more magic. You'll know what to do, if you get the opportunity to return to your garden."

It was *so* simple. Had I spent more time training with Raf and less time on this journey, I may have already discovered it on my own. The wrath of *Beira* burned inside of me, as I realized this had all been a waste of time—that I'd willingly tangled myself in her web. *For nothing.* Icy wind began to swirl around us as I tried to control my frustration. Galen put his hands over mine, releasing a spurt of flame to snap me out of my rage-fueled spiral.

The Oracle released a giggle. "The lady is upset with my answer? Perhaps she'll be happier with my next gift. I shall tell you a prophecy that I've been holding for three hundred years. I'll be relieved to no longer hold onto this debt." She looked up at the sky and began to levitate. Silver light exploded from her, illuminating the violet walls of the cave.

The Princes jumped in front of me, as Galen shoved me back. Rays of light beamed from her eye sockets. She cackled like a mad hyena and then spoke in a glorious, layered voice that didn't belong to her, nearly singing the words.

Fae and Man will burn and die,
Two Chosen heirs can stop the fight.
She was promised by the gods
Her heart of gold can change the odds.
When two heirs share blood and throne,
Only then will peace be known.
A bridge may join two worlds as one
Or death and blood may overrun.
The fates will watch how this plays out,
A lock and key, on them we count.

The Oracle collapsed as her light dimmed, howling with wicked laughter, while I resisted the urge to flee. Slowly standing back up, like a corpse from a grave, the witch turned to the others. "Any other questions? Louis, I believe you have something you'd like to ask me."

This was my cue... I turned to Galen and whispered, "I'm feeling faint. I need to leave... *now.* Could you walk me out? Rafael can stay with Louis." My stomach dipped as he took my hand. I felt like a hypocrite lying to him.

His eyes were wide and worried. "Of course. Brothers, I need to escort Marigold out of the caves. We'll meet you outside."

We hurried out before the witch could stop us. My feet shuffled heavily as we left Raf and Louis behind in the dark depths of her lair. Every part of me resisted as we made our way back to safety without them.

Fresh air had never felt so precious in my lungs when we emerged from the cave and found the guards unscathed, waiting with our horses. I wanted to kiss the ground with relief, but then remembered I was shackled to this place and began to shiver with shock. How was I going to find the courage to go back in there?

"How are you feeling?" Galen asked with an enigmatic grin.

I eyed him suspiciously. "Much better. What is it?" It seemed premature to celebrate—when his brothers were still in there with that *thing*.

"The prophecy. Marigold, did you understand what it meant? Our Kingdoms are *supposed* to unite, through blood and marriage... through the *chosen heirs*. That's *you* and *me*. Together we'll create a legacy of peace. It's more good news than I could've imagined." He was holding me by the shoulders—kissing me, right in front of the guards. I blinked in disbelief. I hadn't had time to absorb the prophecy. I'd been more focused on getting out of there alive.

I threw a shield of wind around us before responding, "You... you think it's about *us*? Blood and throne? What does the *blood* mean?" I touched my neck, the bruise still tender.

"The blood-bond, of course. We'll join in all the ways two beings can join. We'll rule *two worlds* together. Your heart of gold with my political prowess—we'll be unstoppable. Our destiny, delivered by the gods themselves." He looked so overjoyed that I couldn't help but smile back.

In a hushed tone, I replied, "But our Queens aren't dead—they won't be for some time. What are we to do in the *present* to keep peace?"

This complicated everything. I wouldn't let the Elders into Erador just because of a prophecy told to me by a mad witch.

Was I defying the gods if I didn't want to be blood-bonded and married to Galen? I cared for him, but this was all happening so fast—too fast. I sat on the ground, head in my hands, not caring what the men thought. I needed oxygen. Overcome with the spins, I closed my eyes.

Galen squatted down beside me. "*Breathe*, love. There was a reason you were pulled to Nymera—that we've been attracted to each other since the moment we met. We're meant to be mates. Don't you see? Our relationship has been blessed by the stars. We can enjoy each other freely—the Elders can't touch you, unless they want to defy the gods themselves. We can announce the engagement at the Hyacinth Festival."

He was proceeding without any caution and I wanted to scream at him to shut up and let me think. Instead I stared at the ground. I needed to talk to Rafael and Louis. Would their interpretation of the prophecy be the same as Galen's? Perhaps we could sway him to our side, maybe he'd help us usurp his mother. *But what if he couldn't be swayed?*

I pressed the heels of my hand into my eyes, rocking back and forth as I tried not to have a full-blown panic attack. The most pressing matter had nothing to do with the prophecy; I had to discover my *pneuma* and fulfill my bargain with the witch without getting killed.

My head was swimming, but my heart was still in the cave with Galen's brothers. I hoped Raf would be able to help Louis through whatever he faced. I pictured him carrying out Louis in a toad form and grew clammy.

"Are you disappointed... that fate has put us on the same path?" Galen asked with knitted brows.

I returned his gaze. "No... No!" I said in an unnaturally high voice, as I let him help me to my feet. "I'm worried about finding my shifting form... of returning here." Tears began forming. I felt terrible reacting this way. I hugged him, clinging to him as I breathed in his familiar smoky scent.

"It'll be okay. We made it out of the caves once, we'll do it again. Together." He kissed the top of my head.

Zagreus caught our attention as he snorted and stomped his feet, stirring up dust. Moments later, the brothers emerged from the cave. Rafael was supporting Louis as they walked towards us. Louis looked alright... his eyes were open. He was breathing. But as they neared, I realized something was very wrong. His uhra was no longer turquoise, but instead the color of a storming grey ocean—almost no blue to be seen. And his face was drained of color, even his freckles seemed to have faded into his grey skin.

She'd altered his soul. What had she made him do?

As we all gathered around them, Louis shoved us away, separating himself from the group. "I don't want to talk about it," was the only thing he said to me for the rest of the day.

The nervous energy that was present as we began our journey was long gone, but the tension between the brothers remained. As we made our way back, Rafael avoided me, while Louis avoided *everyone*. We were all exhausted and short with each other. All of us, except for Galen, who seemed to be thriving. The prophecy had eased something inside of him and it made me happy for him, *for us*. So I did my best to mimic his enthusiasm, but the truth was, I was feeling... *confused*. Lost.

The blood robbers, the Oracle, the prophecy, Louis... the entire experience had torn me apart. The thing I needed most—to find my shifting form to open the portal—would very likely lead me to my death. How was

I supposed to gain the confidence to find my pneuma, knowing I'd have to return to the witch when I did? What was the point of a prophecy if the witch was going to kill me regardless? She certainly wasn't forcing me back to her cave for a *tea party*.

And then there was Galen—my future—*written in the stars*. And yet, he was still courting Isla... and I didn't know how we were going to get around the obstacles we faced. I was a spooked horse, dangerously close to grabbing the bit by my teeth and making a run for it. Galen's unwavering optimism made me feel even worse. He seemed to have no doubts about any of it. How could he be so sure of us? We were so new... from different worlds. Different Kingdoms. Different species.

It was a lot to consider.

Isla was waiting for us when we walked under the portcullis of Monrovia castle. She ran over to Galen, who was riding ahead of me, and I observed their interaction with barely harnessed rage.

"I missed you," Isla said.

He didn't respond and instead looked back at me. I released a sigh before I heard her whisper, "Come to my room tonight. It's been too long."

I couldn't hear his response as the roaring in my ears became deafening. Permafrost coated me like a second skin and a wave of anger struck like a violent winter storm. Snow whipped around me, while I wheezed and coughed. I'd frozen my lungs, I realized, as I struggled to take in the frigid air that I'd created—air so cold that *I couldn't breathe*.

No one noticed as I held my throat, silently suffocating, absolutely mortified. I hunched over, grasping fistfuls of mane as I tried to stay in the saddle. Hibiscus pranced in place, snorting, then whinnying, as she called attention to us.

"Marigold, what's wrong?" Louis asked, dismounting and rushing to my side. He lowered me off my horse as Galen and Raf appeared seconds later.

"I'm fine. I'm fine," I choked out as I regained control of my magic, sputtering and gasping. Thoroughly humiliated, I shoved through the men and ran towards the castle.

Galen caught me on the stairwell. "She was purposefully trying to rile you. You have to stop letting her get between us," he said in a tone that suggested I was overreacting.

I looked deep into his eyes. I didn't know what was wrong with me, but I didn't believe him. I didn't want to be comforted by him. I couldn't see past the prophecy and the future that I'd never even had a choice in. An invisible string had led me here, which meant I was nothing but a puppet. Free will was all I'd ever wanted and the only thing I'd never have. I needed time alone to process. "I think you should sleep in your own room tonight," I said with a thick voice. "I need some space."

He opened his mouth to speak, then snapped it shut, seeming to reconsider what he was about to say. "Very well. Send for me if you change your mind." He turned on his heels and left without looking back.

THIRTY-FOUR

I'd been dying to talk to Rafael alone—to *finally* discuss all that had transpired on the mountain. The day after returning to the castle, we finally got the chance. We rode out to the grove, staying silent along the way, while my magic itched for release. Small talk didn't interest either of us, not when there was so much to discuss. Nervous energy coursed through me as we dismounted and faced each other.

"Where shall we begin?" Raf's arms were crossed as he stared at the ground. He couldn't have looked less interested in this conversation.

"Louis," I said solemnly. He'd left this morning with a small group of men. I assumed he'd gotten the information he needed and was on a mission to find the missing humans and healers.

Raf nodded curtly. "When you left the caves, Louis asked the Oracle where the Elders are hiding humans. It was a bold choice of words... since we don't have hard evidence linking them to the kidnappings—only what our sources have reported. It could lead to a dead end... but if it doesn't, we'll have an exact location." He met my gaze with a distant glare. "He's on the way to the location as we speak. She gave him coordinates to a place where the Elders are housing humans. We'll find out soon whether the missing people are amongst them."

"Does he need our help?" I asked. *This was it.* We were so close to finding them, to going home. I just needed to find my form and live to tell the tale.

"It would be too risky to bring you, but I'm leaving after our lesson. I'll fly back and forth and deliver news to you as I can. We'll need your eyes and ears here. Are you on board to participate in treasonous activity, keeping all information from your *boyfriend*?"

His attitude was starting to piss me off. It was obvious he had a problem with Galen and I being together. I wanted him to get it over with and *say it to my face.*

I narrowed my eyes. "You should know by now that I'm trustworthy. What was the cost of the question? Is Louis alright?"

"It's his story to tell, but he did the right thing. I think he knows that, deep down."

He wasn't going to tell me? My mind had been going wild, thinking of the possibilities.

"Fine," I said, crossing my arms. "And what was your interpretation of the prophecy?"

"Does it matter? It seems clear enough that you and Galen have already decided what it means. Is a *congratulations* in order? Have you set a wedding date?"

A coward's answer. "Why don't you just come out and say it," I fumed. "You're disappointed in me—because I'm with Galen." Tears sprang to my eyes. I hadn't expected to confront him, but it had just... come out.

His face flashed with surprise, then softened. "I'm not disappointed in you... I just think you're better than Galen." His throat bobbed. "You're better than all of us. I hate to see you with someone like him."

I paused, taking in his carefully vague words. Then I pushed. "What makes me better than him? What makes him so terrible, besides what he's been *forced* to do? Tell me if it's so bad—*make me understand.* You're the one who attacked him, who pretends to be my friend and then ignores me—the one who barges into my room when he feels like it, then disappears when things get hard. So tell me, Rafael, what makes *him* the bad guy?"

He'd completely shut me out since we'd seen the Oracle. He'd hurt my feelings too many times *and I didn't deserve it.* I wanted to slap him—hiss, bite, snarl—*anything* to get a rise out of him. I was sick of this *wall* between us.

He pursed his lips as he stared past me, finally saying, "You are... *good.* In every sense of the word. You treat everyone with respect, while my brother... he has two sides to him. I've seen how he lashes out—how he manipulates. He'll do whatever it takes to keep his power, whoever he has to hurt. You know the role the Elders have him play. He could choose to fight back. Louis and I have never killed for them. Say what you want about me, but I would never work for those purist pieces of shit."

His knuckles were white as he clenched his fists. He was an impenetrable stone wall. Why was this conversation so hard for him? I still didn't understand. *Make me understand, Rafael.*

"Do you think he's not worthy of love, because of what he's done? We all have our demons. He's in a difficult situation, as heir to the throne. He has different pressures than you and Louis. Perhaps a healer is *exactly* what a person like Galen needs—someone who cares, someone who can keep him from becoming one of them. You heard the prophecy, my heart is my strength. And maybe I don't even have a say in any of this. Maybe I'm just a doll for the gods to manipulate as they see fit. Or maybe none of this even matters..."

My cheeks flushed at the rush of emotion, at my outburst. But Raf wasn't riled. He continued to study me with an almost pained expression as he said, "You have a say. Fuck the gods. Fuck the prophecy, if that's how its made you feel." His shadows broke free and began to waft around us; the misty black smoke licked at my skin.

"It's not that simple—I can't abandon my duty. I *won't* abandon those who are depending on me. It's just... I'm not sure I'm ready to promise Galen forever. Please, I need your advice... your honesty."

He ran his fingers through his hair, kicked a rock and sent it sailing, then gave a long sigh. He sounded nearly resigned when he said, "I think you should trust your gut. Maybe the prophecy isn't meant to be fulfilled for another five-hundred years. You have that long—you shouldn't rush such a big decision." He paused, letting out a shaky breath, then pinned me with his eyes. "I *hope* you don't rush that decision. I haven't had nearly enough time... to convince you that you chose the wrong Prince."

I stopped breathing. My heart sputtered to a halt. I tried to suck in air, but my throat was so tight that instead, I wheezed in short, frantic gulps. I forgot how to blink as I peered at my hands, checking to see if I'd turned myself into an ice statue. No... I was just frozen with shock.

The wrong Prince. The words ricocheted against my bones. How could he say such a thing? I loved *Galen*. Raf... he was my friend, *sometimes*, depending on his mercurial moods.

I couldn't deny that he had a sultry kind of charm, a witty intelligence that drove me nuts—or that he was so beautiful, it physically hurt to look at him... But no. *No.* I was with Galen—*fated* to be with *Galen*.

A heavy silence hung between us, while he stood perfectly still with an unreadable expression. "Raf, I-I don't—" I floundered like a fish until he appeared before me, placing two fingers over my mouth, effectively silencing me.

"Are you ready for your flying lesson?" he asked smoothly. It was a peace offering—a chance to divert from what he'd just revealed. I eagerly took it, giving him a shaky smile in answer. It was clear who the real coward was.

Suddenly he was too close, brushing his fingers through my hair. His gaze darkened as a warm palm lingered on my cheek. And then his woodsy scent was everywhere. It was enough to disorient me. I hugged myself, trying to stop the shivers that were threatening to undo me—afraid of what my hands might do if I had to breathe him in for another moment.

Just in time, he severed our connection, striding backwards as he said, "Don't fall off." His mouth curved into a smirk. "And don't forget to grip me with those lovely thighs." I shot him a withering glare and he shrugged. "I'm serious. I don't want to drop you. I've never taken anyone up before."

He transformed into a black pegasus before I got the chance to hit him. I could almost see my reflection in his sleek coat, while his feathered wings stretched wide. They flapped a few times before folding in, and then he was bowing before me, inviting me to climb aboard.

I scrambled on, resting a hand on his withers, while the other reached towards a wing. The nerves I felt were rivaled by my child-like excitement as I lightly trailed a finger along a single feather.

Raf went still, huffing out a breath as I studied his wings. He stamped a foot when I made the mistake of touching him again. *Stop playing around,* I assumed he was saying.

I swallowed hard, wrapping his mane around my fingers. He took off quickly, cantering into a gallop, before snapping out his wings and letting the wind pick us up. We sailed over the pond, almost skimming the water with our feet. Slowly gaining altitude, he flapped hard, creating mighty gusts, as he flew us towards the mountains. We soared higher and higher until the air became frosty, making my magic sing.

Everything looked small and insignificant from up here. As I peered down at the giant, white castle below, I wondered if any of the guards were trying to identify the impossibly large bird in the sky. I laughed with reckless joy as the wind whipped my hair across my cheeks. I never wanted to get down.

I hugged Rafael around his neck for support as he began to turn back towards the grove. We were above the base of the mountains already. I looked down towards the rough trails that had humbled us over the past week. He was a male of much patience, walking a horse up a mountain when he could've been flying. Such a *wondrous* secret he kept. I felt grateful he'd shared it with me. This was my new favorite form of escape; none of our problems could follow us here, as we reached new heights.

We were back on the ground too quickly. His chest was heaving as he slowed down to a trot, eventually coming to a silent stop. I sat paralyzed, not ready to say goodbye to the magic of the moment—or the easy intimacy we shared whenever he was in his animal form.

He stamped his foot. *The ride was over.* I slid off him reluctantly, running my hands along his neck until I was at the side of his face, staring at long, dark lashes and gold-flecked eyes. I scratched the space between his brows—Najma's favorite place to be rubbed. He leaned into it, butting me playfully before I leaned my forehead against his.

"Thank you, Raf," I whispered. He nodded, shifting back, and then we buried the tension, channeling it into training.

"You forgot to use your shields last week, which was my fault as much as yours. We've been focusing too much on offense. From now on, you'll display a shield at all times, anytime we spar."

He shot a tendril of shadow at my wind shield, while I tried to aim a hailstorm at him. He was quick and unpredictable, making it difficult for me to track his movements. Shadow wielders had another huge advantage over the rest of us. They had the ability to transport themselves from one point to another, even *inside* the shield of an opponent, making it nearly impossible to win against him.

I was just glad he was on my side, even if he loved to torture me. He wrapped a vine around my ankle, pulling me to the ground. I noted his grin of satisfaction as the smoke around me cleared.

"Can you see through your shadows?" I asked as I sat on the ground, catching my breath.

"No, but I don't need to. My other senses are strong enough to track an opponent." I caught a gleam in his eye as he purred, "Perhaps I should blindfold you... so you can learn to hone *your* senses." The grove turned into an inky night in seconds and my pulse began to trip over itself.

And then he was gone. His voice bounced and echoed across the field, making it difficult to know where he was as he said, "I can hear your fast little heartbeat. Your shallow breathing. The shuffle of your feet. And then of course... there's your *fucking* scent."

He said it so rudely. "What's wrong with the way I smell?" I scoffed.

"Nothing," he muttered.

My patience was fraying. "I don't like the dark... Come on. This isn't funny—" I gasped as he grabbed me from behind, holding a hand to my throat. I hadn't heard a single footstep. Ice coated my fingertips as I felt his breath tickle my cheek.

"I could've killed you ten times by now, Princess," he whispered. "I think I've found my new favorite way to torture you. We'll practice in the dark from now on." His laugh skittered down my spine as the world began to reappear.

And then I elbowed him in the stomach.

THIRTY-FIVE

G alen had been busy since we'd returned, but he always snuck into my room at the end of the day. He continued to deny that there was anything going on with Isla. I watched them at dinner and my paranoia grew, though I didn't know when he'd have time to be with her, since he spent every night with me. I couldn't keep punishing him for something he most likely hadn't done. I knew I was his choice. But the situation didn't have a solution—he was still publicly courting her. And I was still internally spiraling.

Then there was the conversation I'd been avoiding. Galen still didn't know that I was planning on leaving this world with his brothers, along with as many humans as possible. It wasn't exactly an easy thing to bring up. *"So, your brothers are plotting to overthrow your mother with my help—oh and by the way, we're planning to take all of the humans—as many as we can find—essentially dooming your people. But don't worry, we're going to try and break the curse. Want to join?"*

My pitch still needed some work.

"You've been acting off since we returned to the castle," Galen said one evening while I laid on his chest. We'd just gotten back from dinner and were sipping on wine while we talked in bed. "Exactly how long are you going to be distant with me? And is there something I can do to speed up the process? Because I miss you."

I let out a deep exhale, trying to find my courage. "I don't mean to punish you. The truth is Galen... I still don't fully trust you. And it's kept me from being completely honest with you." My heart began to beat faster and I knew he could hear it. I sat up on my forearms, meeting his gaze.

"You have my attention," he said, eyebrows raised. His pointed ears seemed especially pricked as he studied me in a way that was more feline than man. "I can sense that whatever you're about to say is difficult for you, so let me remind you that there is *nothing* you can say that will scare me away." He gave me an encouraging smile and it looked sincere, but since he'd bitten me at the inn, I could only see *my* uhra around him. No red or blue. Nothing of *him*. It made it more difficult to trust his intentions.

I swallowed, sitting up on the bed and crossing my legs. "I don't want to open a doorway to Erador for your mother or the Elders. In fact, I won't. There's nothing you can say to change my mind." The words tumbled out too quickly. I'd forgotten to take a breath.

His facial features barely moved as he processed what I'd said. He tucked my hands in his and brought them to his lips. "Okay," he said smoothly.

"Okay?" I asked skeptically. "That's it? You're not going to fight me on it? What about—" I was going to bring up what he'd said on the mountain, but instead he cut me off with a kiss that stole the words from my mouth.

On our way to the Oracle he'd said that we didn't have a choice—that I *had* to open the portal for his people. What had changed his mind? The prophecy?

"Oh, were you hoping for a fight?" he asked with a mischievous grin, stoking the flames in the fireplace in a simple gesture of his lethal power. "You said there's nothing I can do to change your mind... so what's the point of arguing?" His eyes narrowed as he gripped my wrists and pulled me towards him. "You better have a plan that involves me though, because even the wrath of all six gods wouldn't be enough to tear us apart. You're mine. Wherever you go, I go."

My eyes were round and wet as he leaned in for another kiss. His lips met teeth because of my wide grin. "Will you go to Erador with me? Without your mother? Without the Elders?"

He swiped his thumb along my cheekbone, wiping away a tear. "I don't want to leave my people, but I know your heart. You wouldn't leave them here to die. So I assume you have a plan..."

I chewed the inside of my lip. I couldn't risk him knowing the details—not when he worked so closely with Sylvia and I'd already been burned by him once. "I can't tell you everything yet," I said. He frowned, but didn't protest as I continued, "Once I can shift, we're leaving to Erador, then we're going to break the curse. When faeries no longer depend on human blood, we can join the worlds, with guidance from my aunt. Ideally, I'd like to see you take your mother's place as King of Nymera as soon as possible."

"Planning a full rebellion, are we?" He gave a low laugh before pouncing on me and pinning me to the bed in one seamless motion. "I shouldn't be surprised. Personally, I'd like to see *you* take my mother's place," he drawled. "By my side. As my Queen."

I squealed as he licked at a sensitive spot beneath my ear and growled, "It's no giggling matter... You're to be the mother of my children. We shall rule two *worlds* together. I'd blood-bond with you right this moment—if you'd let me." His fingers were making their way under my dress, but they stopped as he felt me tense.

"I... don't feel ready for that," I breathed. "But I do love you, Galen."

"I love you more," he whispered, palming my breasts, while scraping his teeth along my throat.

This was a new beginning. Since I'd arrived, we'd experienced trial by fire, but now... now we were on the same team. Anything was possible. A *future* was possible.

He was staring at me like I was the most important thing in the world. No man had ever made me feel this way. I was strong enough to heal his broken parts... and maybe he could heal mine too.

"I want to bite you so badly," he said, tracing a finger up my leg.

"Is there a place less visible?" The last bruise had finally faded on my neck, and it was annoying trying to hide it at training.

"There is." He stood up and pulled my legs to the edge of the bed. His eyes lit up as he admired the many gauzy layers of my pink dress. He took his time unwrapping me, making me feel like an exquisite gift as he kissed up each leg. "There's a spot... right here on your inner thigh," he said in a low rumble, spreading me open and nibbling at the soft flesh. "The blood flow provides me with the magic I crave, gives you the pleasure you crave, *and* it's conveniently located." He smiled as he licked me down my middle, making me gasp.

"Does this sound like something you might be interested in?" he asked, rubbing slippery circles with his thumb, making me squirm.

"Yes," I breathed, laying back in anticipation. Galen flicked his tongue in lavish swirls while he splayed me open with his fingers, until I was throbbing everywhere. Then he stopped. I pulled his hair in desperation. "Please, *more*. Please."

"I want to hear you say it. What do you want?" He kissed my thigh and continued to tease me with his hands.

"Please... *bite me*."

"I love when you ask for it," he said with a low growl of approval. Velvet kisses contrasted with rough stubble, before I felt the prick of his fangs. My magic flowed out of me and into him, taking my mind with it. I trembled with release almost immediately, crying out as I reached for him, needing something, *someone*, to keep me tethered to this world.

He was moaning as he drank, still using those damned fingers to elicit more sensation than I could handle. I was writhing, rolling my head back and forth in exquisite agony, as the rest of the world faded away.

I woke up under him. Had I lost consciousness? I sat up on my elbows, feeling light-headed.

"Are you okay? Did you faint?" he asked. His forehead was wrinkled in worry as he gripped my face in his hands, like he'd been trying to rouse me.

"Perhaps? I think I forgot to breathe," I laughed softly, still spinning. I wiped tears from my eyes as I slowly sat up.

"Are you okay?" He looked down at my thigh. "The bleeding's stopped. I'm sorry if I got carried away."

"I'm fine." I shrugged, then pulled him on top of me. I felt a twinge of unease, but shook it off before it could take root. I was with someone who I loved. It felt good because it was *supposed to* feel good. We were two consenting adults, there was nothing wrong with this. My body was oddly well-suited to handle the occasional blood loss, after all. If he planned on defying his mother, he needed as much magic as I could give him. We'd made it to the other side of something that I hadn't thought we could overcome. He was mine and I was his, and together anything was possible.

THIRTY-SIX

One week later, a silky voice murmured into my ear, "Good morning, beautiful." Galen was already dressed in his royal grey uniform that made his green eyes glitter. He was slowly moving in, leaving clothes in my room, and the intimate step felt sweet... exhilarating. Overall, things felt almost... stable.

"I have a meeting with the Elders today. How would you like me to proceed... in regards to the prophecy? Personally, I'd like to inform them that we've been chosen to unite the realms, so the path is clear for us to be together—so I can stop courting Isla. They can't deny the will of the six almighty gods. Even *they* are not that full of hubris."

It boggled my mind that he still thought them capable of doing the right thing. They wanted to control the narrative and they wouldn't let a little blasphemy stop them. Even if they chose to honor the prophecy, they wouldn't simply hand over their precious power, they'd twist the Oracle's words until it fit their agenda. I held back from lashing out and instead politely smiled. "Can we keep it between us for now? I'm afraid your mother will see it as a threat to her current reign."

"As you wish. You're the brains of this operation, after all." He grinned. "Enjoy your dance lesson. Tell Rafael that if he touches you inappropriately, I'll melt the flesh from his bones." He gave me a soul shaking kiss before he departed, ensuring I'd be covered in his scent while I danced with his brother.

Louis was supposed to be my dance partner for the festival that was now only a few weeks away; however, his current mission had taken precedent and I'd been assigned to a new Prince—a broodier one. The Queen thought Louis was traveling north, crossing through the mountains to Lavinia, but he was actually heading west to Tarragona. And now Raf was being forced to escort me to the dance. I wasn't sure who was more upset, him or Sylvia. They had a long-standing mutual understanding that he didn't attend royal gatherings. He had no interest and she didn't want him there. But this festival was different, because Sylvia felt obligated to announce me properly.

Publicly, nothing less than a royal escort would do for a guest of honor, even if *privately*, she hated us both. A united front, for appearances sake, was important in times of turmoil. Sylvia and the Elders weren't going to miss an opportunity to show off their shiny new world walker at the biggest event of the year.

Meanwhile, Raf had successfully avoided every courtship festival over the last century. But now, thanks to me, he had to go—or at least that's what he said. It wasn't like I had a choice either... I'd dodged one dance just to end up at another—and if I didn't learn how to shift soon, this party would end even worse than my debut.

I'd never seen the Great Hall in the midday sun; the white marble and stained glass ceiling shimmered in the sunshine. As I approached, I spotted Rafael and a well-dressed gentleman, who I could only assume was our dance instructor. A rather short man, for faerie standards, introduced himself as Archibald—Archie for short. He looked dapper in a well-tailored black jacket with a white vest and black breeches to match. He would've fit in at any upper-crest circle in Erador.

"Impeccable style, sir." I smiled. He was balding with thin tufts of slicked back silver hair. He looked old enough to be a grandfather, which meant he must've been ancient.

"Thank you, darling. I have a *passion* for *fashion*. I have since I was a boy. I've seen many trends come and go over the last six hundred years, but if I've learned one thing, it's that a well-tailored black suit *never* goes out of style."

I liked him immediately. He turned to Raf, wearing all black as usual, and said, "It seems you agree, Your Highness. A dashing Prince and an enchanting Princess. You shall make quite a pair on the dance floor." I tried not to laugh as Raf looked increasingly uncomfortable.

"I'm not a Princess, actually," I said, correcting the instructor.

He gave me a quizzical look. "I've lived this long by not questioning the Kings and Queens I've worked under. If Prince Galen says you're a Princess, then you're a Princess." He bowed for emphasis, making me blush.

"Are either of you familiar with the Hyacinth Waltz?" Archie asked. We both shook our heads and his smile dropped.

"What a shame, considering I invented it. It's *the* dance to know at the Hyacinth Festival, naturally. It tells the story of *blossoming love*—the tumultuous courtship dance of faeries. It's rarely a smooth transition from acquaintance to blood-bonded mates amongst our people. And why should it be? Any love worth having deserves a little *dramatic flare*."

Rafael and I exchanged looks; this man was *very* passionate about his craft. I couldn't help but grin... and to my surprise, Raf wasn't able to hide his smile either.

"If you didn't know, Hyacinth flowers are a symbol of young love. Princess Marigold, you'll be the petals. Prince Rafael, the stem. There is no better way to honor the love affair than through the art of dance. Don't you agree?"

This is where he lost me. "I should tell you now, Archie, before you get too invested. Raf is a perpetual spoilsport and I have an *extreme* fear of crowds... and dancing too, actually. We may not be your star pupils. You can just tell us the basics—we don't want to waste your time." I tried to be polite, but he needed to know that it would be a miracle if we showed up at all.

Rafael flashed me a rogue smile. "The only spoilsport here is you, *Princess*. I happen to *like* dancing. It seems you'll have to do your best to keep up."

What was he up to?

That's the spirit!" Archie cheered. "Let's begin."

He arranged Raf and I together, hand in hand... my hips pressed against his. One step at a time, he guided us through the moves. I wasn't completely hopeless; I grew up in a castle after all, but this dance was different than anything I'd ever learned. It was much more *intimate* compared to the upbeat, intricate dances of Aurelius. Rafael picked it up surprisingly fast and I suspected he already knew the steps as I stumbled through each transition... as if he didn't see me embarrass myself enough at training.

"This next part, Princess... you must wrap your leg around the Prince, just so. Yes—that's it! You want to *be* the petals—yes!"

I was mortified as I hooked my leg around Raf and let him lean me back. It was taking all my concentration to not notice his hands. They were *everywhere*: My lower back, my ribs, my hips... my thighs.

If we were in Erador, he would've had to marry me after this dance, because my virtue would've been considered *thoroughly* ruined. I was burning up, trying not to respond to his touch. He was enjoying this, watching me perspire under his piercing gaze. The ice in my veins felt *hot*, like it had melted into boiling liquid and turned to steam. My temples were dewy. I felt feverish. Maybe I was getting sick.

"You're doing great." His dimples were prominent as he grinned down at me.

I glared at him. "You're a *liar*. I know you already know this dance. Can't you just prance me around the floor on the day of the festival and let this be over with. What have I done to deserve this form of cruel and unusual punishment?" I was irrationally angry as the instructor played his fiddle, counting out the beats.

"Is it really *torture*, dancing with me?" His eyes were lit with unabashed amusement.

"Of course not... but it would be for Galen if he saw us right now." I said it quietly, avoiding his gaze. I knew bringing up his brother would weigh down his mood. Raf had to accept my choice. I hadn't told him of my plan to take Galen with us to Erador, but he'd learn soon enough.

"Well then... good thing he's not here," Rafael said, dipping me low to the ground, our noses almost touching. I was trying not to breathe in the heady scent of cedar and rain, but it was impossible when we were this close to each other. It was clinging to me, making me dizzy, almost nauseous. I'd need to take a long, long bath before I saw Galen tonight.

"Has anyone ever told you that you wear too much cologne?" I snapped irritably.

He laughed, quirking a brow at me. "Do I look like the kind of male who wears cologne?" I tripped over my feet and he caught me, leaning me down into another dip with an indecent smile on his lips.

What? *How* could anyone smell like that... *naturally*? I was too embarrassed to ask. It would reveal more than I wanted him to know. So I kept my mouth shut and held my breath.

My heart hammered through the rest of our lesson as I denied the attraction I was feeling. I'd never truly admitted it to myself, but there it was... a gut wrenching thought I couldn't ignore any longer—*if Galen hadn't swept me off my feet so quickly, would Raf and I have grown into something?* Was *this* why he was willing to dance with me? Was he trying to make me acknowledge feelings that I'd been fighting since I met him? Would he be so bold?

He was Rafael; of course he would.

As Archibald wrapped up the lesson, I hardly listened as he talked, lost in thought. I'd already made my choice; the prophecy had spoken to confirm it. Galen and I were *fated*. That should've been enough to settle my pounding heart. And yet... as Raf let go of my hand and said goodbye, I held back tears.

Galen and I had finally gotten to a good place and I seemed hell bent on screwing it up. In the time it took to me to hike upstairs, I'd convinced myself that my feelings were a simple side effect of being forced into close proximity with Raf. Galen had told me that faeries were promiscuous beings... This was just part of who I was. *Lust was natural.* It wasn't *love*—I could easily choose to ignore it.

I asked Lusha to run me a bath when I made it back to my room. She made quick work of it, adding bubbles and oils, before leaving me alone with my treacherous thoughts.

Due to the council meeting, I'd be eating dinner in my room tonight, which suited me just fine. I enjoyed Galen's company, but sometimes I just wanted time to myself. He was insatiable when it came to his carnal desires, and between blood loss and lack of sleep, I was chronically exhausted.

I laid back, submerging my body, while I reflected on my time in Nymera. I'd gone from prisoner to savior, human to hybrid, and now it was apparently my *destiny* to unite the realms, *the worlds.* I wanted none of it. I wanted Galen, but I didn't want the royal titles, the advisors, the backwards rules.

I was bound to my duty; and yet, I grew ill thinking of sitting on either throne. Both Kingdoms were built from bloodshed and exploitation. If my fate was to be Queen, then I'd have to find a way to break the societal chains that had been placed on so many. Wealthy men in Erador and purist faeries in Nymera had both decided that amassing power required stripping it from someone else. Their supremacy was gods' will—passed down through blood, they told themselves, as they let greed consume their souls.

If I rose to power, I'd take care of *everyone*, not just the ones born into fortunate circumstances. I'd demand equality, even if it meant going to war against those who threatened it. This responsibility had landed on my shoulders, and I was finally beginning to accept that no one could bear it for me. I had to let go of the notion that I could escape the life I'd been given.

My mother and Ophelia had raised me to fight for what was right. It rested on me, and it was heavy, but I wouldn't let it break me. I'd claim my gods-given gift, and then the Princes and I would break the curse. Failure was not an option. I didn't *feel* like a heroine, but regardless, I'd been given power and position and I planned to use them for good. I'd find a way to overcome my fears that held me back. I wouldn't be alone; I'd built friendships... I'd found love. *Together*, we'd pave a path that was wide enough to accommodate everyone.

I groaned and dunked my head under the soapy suds that smelled of lavender and chamomile. Perhaps my attraction to Raf represented my desire for escape. He certainly fit the mold with his rebellious nature and bedroom eyes. I'd rise above those feelings too. I took another deep sigh before hearing a bedroom door click. Galen was back.

THIRTY-SEVEN

"Hello?" I called. Galen showed up in the bathroom looking haunted... vacant eyes met my gaze and my heart sank. "What's wrong?" I stood up in the tub and grabbed a towel to wrap around my body. He seemed far away, living out some unknown horror.

"The Elders—they made me execute a couple today. The woman was pregnant with a hybrid." His eyes were glassy, like he'd been drinking or crying. Or both.

I stifled my gasp and asked, "Did you know them?" I stopped breathing... *Melisandre*.

"No," he said sharply. "They were from another village and hiding out in Monrovia. Someone reported them when they noticed she was pregnant."

I was flooded with simultaneous relief and horror. Meli had said that humans and human sympathizers were gathering in Monrovia, awaiting refuge—waiting for *me* to rescue them. I clutched my stomach like I'd been punched in the gut.

"Who would do such a thing? What's in it for them?" I asked, hovering just out of his reach. I didn't want to touch him. It wasn't his fault, but he'd killed those people. I could see the blood on his hands... hear the screams.

Whose fault was it? My heart began to race. What would I have done in that situation? I would've *died* before hurting them.

"The Elders have a new policy... if you report a human-faerie couple, you get to feed from the human before they're executed. Plenty of incentive for someone desperate enough. It's emboldened the whole village to start seeking out improper pairings."

Improper pairings? *He and I* were an *improper pairing,* according to their archaic laws.

Galen's breath smelled of alcohol. He was slurring. I hated when he got this drunk.

"There was nothing you could do?" I asked with a lump in my throat. I didn't want to make him feel worse, but I needed to know that he'd at least *tried* to fight back.

"I didn't know anyone was standing trial until I showed up at the meeting. My mother has been telling me less. And the Elders haven't forgiven me for the death of their last prisoner. I was too outnumbered, I had to comply." His gaze bore into me. "And... they know I care about you. They know I'll do *anything* in exchange for your safety. We're in this together now. Every choice I make is for *us.*"

His words struck like a slap across the face, knocking me to my senses. He'd used *my* magic to kill them. I covered my mouth in horror. He'd murdered innocents. And I... I was tied to it. Their blood was on my hands as well. I braced myself as the truth of it pummeled me over and over.

"I need you," was all he said as he pressed me against the wall of the bathroom and started kissing me with bruising force. His stubble scratched at me like sandpaper. My mind was still reeling. I was in no mood after what he'd just told me. I put my hands on his chest and shoved him back.

"Galen, why don't you lie down... I'll rub your back. You've had a terrible day. Let me take care of you." I wanted to be there for him, even if I was internally imploding.

"That's *not* how I need you right now." His demeanor was demanding as he ripped my towel away and began fumbling between my legs.

I resisted, pushing him away more firmly this time. "Galen—you're drunk. Don't manhandle me." I walked towards the bed to put space between us and he followed.

"I don't mean to take out my foul mood on you. I'm just... struggling. I need you to take away my pain." His expression was pitiful. I hung back before nodding my head. I could do this for him. I'd just compartmentalize... numb myself temporarily.

He didn't hesitate as he arranged me against the bed, facing me away from him as he pressed the top half of my body into the mattress. His usual tenderness was gone as he took me from behind, forcing my head back by gripping my damp curls at the base of my skull. I'd been grabbed by my hair too many times and reacted instinctively, throwing a wave of air at him that knocked him backwards.

"Don't pull my hair," I yelled. "That's what those blood-robbers did. They held me down and tried to—" I was shaking.

"Hey... it's alright. I apologize." His tone softened as he pulled me onto the bed and into his lap. "I didn't mean to scare you. I told you, I'm prone to... moods. And now that you're seeing more of me, they're difficult to hide. Right now, I just need an escape from who I am and what I've done. I can't stand myself."

His head hung low in defeat. I cradled his face between my hands and brought his lips to mine. He hungrily kissed me back, lifting me, until I was straddling him. He situated himself until he'd slid inside me with one long thrust. My breathing hitched as he filled me, moving my hips up and down.

I lost myself to the rhythm and before I knew it, his teeth were in my neck and he was drinking from me. The sudden rush of magic made me spasm uncontrollably, followed shortly by his release. He pulled away from me, lips red, and gave me the first smile I'd seen from him since this morning.

"You're incredible," he murmured.

I shook off the haze from his bite and went to clean myself off. "Galen," I called from the bathing room, putting a towel against my neck. "I need contraception." The last thing we needed was a faerie-human baby for the Elders to butcher. The twisted thought stopped me in my tracks. Would we *ever* be safe to have children? Not in this world. Not with his mother in power.

"I've been drinking a contraceptive tea, but I can bring some for you tomorrow as well," he called back.

I know, but I don't trust you, I mumbled to myself. I'd been careless. I had to start taking myself more seriously. I was giving him too much control. We went to bed in each other's arms, but I laid awake for hours, with a mind too busy for sleep, before finally drifting off.

I was back in the drizzly forest. And I was sick of this dream—of pine trees, of being wet, of running. This time, when I saw my mother's silhouette in the distance, I didn't give chase. Instead, I walked away from her.

My chest ached to follow, but I stayed firm in my decision as I walked the path in the opposite direction. I knew this trail, had walked it every day when I'd lived in a small cabin with my parents. And if my mother wouldn't come to me, then I would go to our home and wait for her.

I stood at the edge of the forest, staring at my childhood home. Smoke billowed from the chimney perched on the thatched roof. Someone was inside. My stomach fluttered uneasily. The impulsive part of me wanted to sprint forward, fling open the door, and shout for my mother. But my feet stayed glued in place, because... what if instead of my mother, I was greeted by my father? I wasn't sure I wanted to face him.

Hesitating, I studied my surroundings. My heart galloped when I took in the small barn and paddock at the far side of the property, tucked behind an apple orchard and my mother's magnificent gardens. I'd spent so much of my youth in that barn with my first horse, Skye. I hadn't thought about her for years and I didn't know how I'd let myself forget her. She'd been my best friend and my protector when... when my mother and father would fight. Sometimes I'd sleep in a pile of hay beside her instead of my bed.

Hazy memories flashed in my mind as I made my way to the barn: the smell of oats and molasses, the tickle of alfalfa dust in my nose, the sharp tang of leather and sweat from the tack room, soft huffs from Skye as I brushed her coat.

Skye. She was grazing in the paddock, flicking her tail back and forth as raindrops rolled off her shaggy Palomino coat. Her ears twitched in my direction and then her eyes locked with mine. I jogged forward excitedly, before slamming into an invisible barrier. The force of it sent me tumbling backwards. It was a barrier of... wind.

Confused, I slowly turned around, then staggered back. My mother stood before me with a sad smile on her face. "I'm sorry, Goldie. But there's no time. You need to follow me. And we need to hurry."

I glared at her, angry beyond reason. "Why? Why do you keep telling me to run? Why are you haunting me?"

"Because he's chasing us. And he won't ever stop. Not until we're dead."

I nearly crumbled to the ground. Tears filled my eyes as I said through gritted teeth, "You're already dead. And I'm sick of running. I'm tired."

"Just a little longer, my love. Just a little longer. Quickly." She held out her hand and I took it, letting her lead me back into the forest.

I found myself more eager than ever for my session with Rafael. Last night, something had changed in me. I was angry. I was formidable. And I was ready to stop being a victim; a victim of my mother's death, my father's abandonment, of my circumstances. I was more than a misfit navigating a new world, trying to keep up with the rules. I wanted to *change* the rules. I wanted to fight. I wanted to *destroy* the systems that prospered by oppression.

Sensing my mood, Raf had us begin with combat. My shields were coming effortlessly these days, making it easier to use both hands for offense. He decided to put his shadows away today and let me fight his earth magic—still a fierce opponent. The earth quaked under my feet as he shot vines at my wrists, but today I was faster.

I hovered above the ground and dodged his vines, throwing ice daggers one after another. They were nearly invisible as they soared through the air, aided by a cold gust of wind. In a series of blurry movements, he blocked them, but the blizzard that followed obscured his senses, giving me enough time to turn his hands into two blocks of ice. He grinned, unable to counter attack.

For a brief moment, I'd won. Then he turned into shadow, breaking from the ice. He popped up behind me to whisper, "Good job," making me jump. "Maybe we should practice our dance. You seem pretty competent in your magic these days."

I gave a half-smile back, stepping away from him. "Sounds like the Prince of Shadows is scared of my ice daggers."

His gaze darkened as he prowled closer. "You know perfectly well that I *love* your ice daggers." The way he said it made my stomach dip. "And I hate to break it to you, but you're not that scary."

I scoffed at him, while my pulse hammered. He was leaning over me now—so close that I had to tilt my head back to look up at him.

"Plus. you're the one who can't seem to control your heart rate when we're together," he said, staring at my lips.

I felt uncomfortably hot under his heavy-lidded gaze. "Fine. Let's dance," I snapped, lacing my fingers with his—not giving myself time to second guess my decision. He placed his other hand on my hip. I was hyper-aware of my heart slamming against my chest.

Pull yourself together, Marigold.

"What's next?" I asked as his breath tickled my forehead.

"Next, you just let go and let me take the lead." He swung me around, marched me backwards, hooked my leg around him with a firm grip, then dipped me back. A laugh bubbled from me as I let him take control.

Magic was simmering beneath my skin, whistling like a tea kettle as it begged for release. This time instead of balking, I was able to let go. Pent up energy erupted from me, mingling with his, in an explosion of golden sparks. I became light-headed as the feeling overwhelmed my senses.

Raf jumped out of the way right in time. Magic took over and transformed me into something *other*. It hadn't hurt. It hadn't felt like much at all, but the sensation of a new body was bewildering.

Rafael's mouth was hanging open in awe, but he recovered quickly. "Come with me." I staggered after him, learning how to pick up my new feet. White legs and golden hooves.

He kept a hand on my neck as he led me to the pond, while I adjusted to my new senses. My ears pricked as they took in more noise than I could process; the crunch of our feet in the grass, Raf's breathing, small creatures burrowing underground, buzzing insects near and far. Layers upon layers of sound. And my vision had been altered too. The trees surrounding the grove were razor sharp, but color had been desaturated, like I was in a dream within a dream.

We stopped at the water's edge and Raf gave me a wide grin, pointing to my reflection. "Take a look, Goldie. You're unbelievable."

Thirty-Eight

I was a... *unicorn*. I looked at Rafael in disbelief before shifting back into my human form and falling to the ground. He scooped me up and spun us around with excitement. "You did it! I'll try not to take it personally—that you shifted for the first time to avoid dancing with me."

"I think I was able to shift because I feel safe with you," I blurted out.

His face dropped into a thoughtful expression and I immediately regretted my choice of words. We sat, staring at the horizon, staying silent as I digested what had just happened. I plucked a flower absent-mindedly, needing something to fidget with. I inhaled sharply, taken aback, when I noticed it wasn't just any wild flower, but an orange Marigold. I turned to Raf in confusion.

He studied me, shrugging as he rubbed at the nape of his neck. "I... uh. It's nothing. I just like them." My heart skipped over itself as I gnawed on my lip, trying to maintain a neutral expression. *Breathe, Marigold.* It was just a flower... well, just a *field* of them. I couldn't let myself go there—I couldn't let myself think about Rafael's feelings and what might inspire him to fill an entire grove with flowers that reminded him of me. If I dug any deeper, I wasn't sure what I might discover. And it terrified me.

I cleared my throat. "So... I'm a unicorn," I said slowly, pulling my knees to my chest. I tried to give a tight smile, but instead I grimaced. I was tired of surprises. I would've preferred to be a normal, boring horse, but the gods had never bothered to ask me what I wanted.

"Unicorns are as rare as world walkers... Myths amongst even magic-wielders. It's said that your horn has the ability to channel wild magic—that it can siphon energy from any source it chooses. A unicorn's power is supposedly *infinite* because of this. I've also heard that unicorn blood has the ability to bring anyone back from near death, which explains your healing magic." This all sounded too good to be true, but Rafael appeared agitated.

He was fidgeting... avoiding my gaze as he continued. "The unicorn horn... it's rumored to work even when its been removed from the body. There have been fables, historical accounts... of corrupt individuals *taking* the horn—wielding it like a wand. If someone was to steal your horn, they'd have access to unlimited power. There are no known horns in existence for this reason—our ancestors destroyed them to keep power out of dangerous hands."

"Oh... I see," I said softly. "So... I'm to be hunted for the rest of my life." What would the Elders do to have that kind of power? What would the Queen do? They'd salivate at the chance to cut out the middleman. *The middleman being me.*

I buried my face into my hands as hot tears clouded my vision, threatening to rain down my cheeks. A sob escaped me, followed by another.

Rafael pulled me into a hug, letting me soak his shirt. "You're not alone. As long as no one knows what you are, we'll be okay. When Louis returns, you'll open the portal before anyone suspects a thing and we'll get you out of this world—away from anyone that would want to hurt you."

He was gentle with his next words. "Don't tell Galen... Don't let him bite you. Your blood would act as the strongest drug in existence to a cursed faerie. He can't find out what you are, what your power is capable of—he's too unpredictable. Do you understand?"

I peeled away from him with wide-eyed remorse. Reluctantly, I moved my hair away from my neck and showed him the swath of swollen marks and bruises dappled across my skin. I could only imagine what it looked like to an outsider... to Raf. Galen had been biting me frequently, perhaps *too* frequently, but I didn't know how to say no. And it was fine. *We* were fine. It was consensual.

For a brief moment, infinite rage flickered behind Raf's eyes. Power rippled across the grove as trees groaned and the ground shuddered. Waves formed on the glassy surface of the pond, lapping at my feet. His face was perfectly blank, but his clenched fists were shaking. What would happen if all that power *erupted*? I swallowed hard, shoulders sagging, while I watched him stand, then pace. He was on the brink of exploding—I'd never seen him like this and *I had caused it.*

"Well shit," he sighed, once he'd composed himself. I hung my head in answer.

He sat back down, taking my hand in his and said, "Don't. Don't be ashamed. This isn't your fault. Galen took advantage of you. I'm sure he didn't tell you how addicting it can be to *both* parties—how he wouldn't be able to stop once he'd tasted your blood. He might not know that you're a unicorn, but he knows how strong your magic is. While I don't fully understand the way cursed faeries react to blood, I know that not all magic is created equal. Yours would be like drinking top-shelf faerie whiskey... like the highest grade of opium. And he's always been one to over-indulge. He should've known better. This isn't on you."

My hackles rose as I came to Galen's defense. "It's not his fault. He *needs* blood to use his magic. I was told that it's natural for faeries to drink from each other—that it's part of the blood-bonding ritual."

Raf curled his lip in disgust as dark shadows spilled from him. "The blood-bond is *sacred*. The curse has made a mockery of it. He can get his blood from the well-stocked supplies in the castle. There's no reason that warrants him biting you, other than he's a *predator*. Have you even considered the possibility that he's using you for your *blood*, for your *power?*"

My heart stopped. If he'd been trying to strike me where I was most vulnerable, then he'd succeeded. But he was *wrong;* I was worthy of love—with or without magic. Galen *loved* me. And none of this was his fault... it was *mine.*

He'd told me from the beginning that my blood had a drug-like effect on him, but I hadn't discouraged him from biting me. Humiliation burned my cheeks and churned my stomach. If he was addicted to my magic, he'd grow increasingly unhinged if I didn't give him access to it.

Something fractured inside my chest as I met Raf's stormy gaze. "Because who could possibly love me for *me*? Certainly not *you*. Your casual cruelty has hurt me in more ways than your brother ever has," I hissed.

His throat bobbed as his mask of anger faded into surprise. "Goldie, I'm sorry. The words came out wrong. My brother's inability to love has nothing to do with you—"

"I'd rather be a fool in love, than a loner who pushes everyone away," I bit back with venom. "Maybe I've had blinders on, maybe I'm in over my head, but at least I'm *trying*. One day, you'll have nothing left but your shadows, with only yourself to blame." My voice cracked as I continued. "And I guess now is as good a time as any to tell you—Galen is coming with us to Erador."

THIRTY-NINE

A mixture of devastation and shock passed over Raf's face before it hardened to stone. We stared at each other, the energy in the air palpable. It felt as if a crack of lightning might strike at any moment. I'd welcome it, if it meant ending this miserable tension.

Wordlessly, Rafael faded into a black fog. When the cloud dissipated, he was across the grove, racing towards the forest in his pooka form. I didn't follow him right away. We both needed time to gather our thoughts. Why did I lack the ability to hold my tongue around him? I hadn't meant what I'd said.

"You chose the wrong prince." His words had echoed through my mind a thousand times. The truth was, he hadn't pushed me away—he'd confessed his feelings, braved rejection. And I'd been a coward, unable to acknowledge what I felt for him—burying it all because what else could I do? I'd already chosen his brother.

I needed to find him and apologize. I was *disgusted* with myself. Rafael was upset... Galen was *addicted* to me. I was a monster who'd come to this world to wreak havoc on everyone and everything.

As I sat there feeling like the victim that I'd just sworn I wouldn't be, my magic shrank from me. How was I supposed to shift in this mental state? My pneuma had revealed itself when I'd been dancing with Raf, in a moment of joy. It was similar to how I'd felt riding through the woods with him, flying above the clouds—a sense of belonging and exhilaration. In each of those moments, my magic had coated my limbs like a second skin. I just hadn't been able to lean in and let go. Until today.

Did my magic surge around him because of how safe he made me feel? Or because of how he made me feel in general? Rolling my eyes, I imagined what smart-ass quip would come out of his mouth if he knew he brought out my inner unicorn.

Galen was the *chosen heir,* the man I loved. So why was Rafael the one who made my magic sing? Was I supposed to just *ignore* what the Oracle had said?

"The Oracle!" I gasped out loud. I had to find Raf; we needed to go to her right away. I pushed my worry aside and visualized myself dancing with Rafael beneath a cloudless night sky. A warm glow bloomed inside of me. It unfurled like a rose, starting in my chest, spreading down my arms and legs. I was capable. I was strong. I was a *unicorn.* And then... I was.

I stared down at the pond's reflective surface and took in my golden mane. Dark brown eyes blinked back at me through charcoal lashes, contrasting with snowy white fur. I had a pink velvety nose and my horn... It was *magnificent.* It shined like solid opal, swirling up in iridescent shades of blush, pearl, and teal before coming to a sharp point. As sharp as any dagger. Let them *try* to take my horn.

Dust clouded around me as I stomped my hooves and used my newly acquired senses to find Rafael. Pricking my ears in the direction he'd gone, I sniffed the air and caught his scent. I felt drunk with power as my legs gathered beneath me and flew through the trees. *This* was the feeling I'd been missing all my life.

I found him in a clearing, grazing in his pooka form. He bobbed his head in my direction before slowly walking towards me. Nose to nose, we rubbed against each other in an equine greeting. Strange and yet... not strange at all.

We shifted back to our faerie forms, close enough that I could feel the heat emanating from him. Thick silence took the place of apologies that suddenly felt unnecessary. His soft, searching eyes told me he forgave me as he rested his forehead against mine. Our breath mingled together while his hands moved along my arms, soothing my goosebumps... creating new ones. His fingers trailed down my spine, causing sparks to explode beneath my skin. And then his mouth was hovering over my parted lips.

I needed to break the trance I was under, but I felt rooted in place. My heart was fluttering frantically, like a butterfly trapped in a jar. I put a hand on his chest to push him away, but then I felt *his* heartbeat. It was racing just as fast. It was difficult to believe that I had this effect on such a powerful male.

His lips met mine and the world stopped. The kiss was a soft whisper... tentative and unhurried. Our lips molded together and I sunk into the painfully tender moment; the minty taste of his tongue, the electricity in his touch, and the heady scent of his warm, solid body crushed against mine.

He pulled back, studying me, staring straight into my soul. My insides were thawing, melting, gushing. His lips dipped back down to brush against mine and I began to tremble. Luxuriously deep and all-consuming, his tongue caressed mine. He tugged at my bottom lip, cupping my face, as he traced my jawline with a feather-light touch.

"Raf..." His name tumbled from my mouth in a desperate bid to stop the gravity that pulled us together. Stronger than any force I'd ever felt. And then I was kissing him back, clutching his shirt to keep from falling to my knees, as we ventured deeper.

A strangled sound escaped me and then his hands were tangled in my hair, gripping the back of my head, pressing into my lower back, tugging me closer. His body was hard and hot and *shaking*. It could've been seconds or a lifetime that we stood entwined, beneath the twisting Black Oak trees.

I finally wrenched away, stumbling back in shock. What had we just done? I held my hands over my lips like he'd branded me—marked me with a permanent vow that couldn't be undone. I didn't know what to say. Words seemed obsolete to the feelings coursing through me. A mistake... just a mistake. I couldn't say the words out loud. It hadn't felt like a mistake.

Raf broke the silence. "Marigold, I need to tell you—" He moved towards me and I extended a stiff arm to keep him from coming any closer.

"No. *Don't*. I'm with—" My voice cracked. "I'm with your brother. I-I can't."

"But I—" He fell silent when he saw my panicked expression.

I chose the coward's path and changed the subject, my voice coming out high and breathless. "The witch. I have to go to her before I can be free from my bargain. Will you come with me?"

He gave me a look that shredded my soul, then shook off the remnants of whatever he was feeling. "Yes... Right now?"

I scoffed at his response and then remembered that in one of his flying forms, we could get there in no time. I looked at the sun approaching midday and lost my nerve. "Tomorrow? Instead of training?"

He nodded. "We can come up with a plan on the way back to the castle."

We transformed back into our animal forms and ran back to the grove, bucking and playing as we ran in circles and relished the feeling of being touched by magic.

We shifted and mounted our horses, which made me bubble over with laughter—at the absurdity of the situation. Hibiscus was extra affectionate with me, rubbing her nose against my cheek. She was grateful there wasn't another dragon shifter to contend with.

"The witch will try to kill you for your horn," Raf said as we rode back.

"I know. Before I knew I was a unicorn, I assumed I was *something* she wanted to add to her collection. Dead or alive."

"I'll be with you every step of the way. You wield infinite power now. You've just undoubtedly become the most powerful being in this world—probably Erador too. If there are other unicorns in existence, they're in hiding. She'll hope you don't know your strength."

"Can she be killed?" I asked. If it came down to me or her, would I be able to end her?

"If anything can kill her, it's a unicorn. And maybe a dragon—that might surprise her enough that she decides to let us go without a fight." He gave me a smile that I knew was meant to comfort me, but after what we'd shared, caused me to ache with a nauseating blend of desire, guilt, and confusion.

"The way she was drooling over you? I can't imagine she'd let you go if she knew you could turn into a dragon. Perhaps we can both be part of her collection of oddities." It was such a morbid thought that we both laughed.

"As long as we're there together..." He lowered his gaze down to my swollen lips, before galloping ahead and leaving me in the dust.

FORTY

I arrived back in my room with Raf's kiss still fresh on my mind. I had to tell Galen, but I was afraid he'd go mad and take it out on his brother. Perhaps it was better if I kept it to myself until I sorted out *why* I'd let it happen.

I couldn't tell him about my newly discovered pneuma either. Lies and secrets were stacking up too quickly. It wasn't just that he was under his mother's influence; it was also that I still didn't trust him. There were too many other lives at stake... and he wasn't the only one I cared for. I reminded myself that our union had been foreseen by the gods themselves—this would sort itself out in time.

I was expected to attend dinner this evening. Lusha arrived right on time to get me ready in a coral gown that looked like a celebration of summer. While life was not ideal right now, I loved that I could spar with Rafael in a shirt and trousers by day and feel feminine in a summer dress by night.

We all had the capability to be multifaceted when we weren't forced to conform to the rigged rules of society. The longer I was in Nymera, the more I knew that to be true. I had spent most of my life in a cage disguised as a castle, but now that I'd experienced flying, I could never go back to the way things were. I had to believe that Ophelia would understand.

I wanted to set others free as well. If I ruled someday, I'd foster communities that felt safe to express themselves through art, hobbies, fashion... I wanted to be part of a world where beings *created* more than they *destroyed*. Leisure wasn't something only aristocrats should be able to afford.

I thought of the faeries and humans who'd risked everything to follow their hearts, just to have it end in tragedy. They were the definition of bravery—standing up for what they believed in, despite the risks.

My mood turned a deep shade of blue as I thought of the people that the Elders, *that Galen*, had killed. Courageous souls who'd chosen *love*, no matter the cost. Those were *my* people. Wearing a bright color felt suddenly crass. I thought about switching gowns, but what would that change? A fashion statement wouldn't help... only action would.

How had we gotten to a place where leaders no longer served the people they were sworn to protect? Did absolute power always lead down a corrosive path? How would I keep myself from making the same mistakes?

Lusha snapped me back to the present when she asked if I'd heard of the recent human attacks in Lavinia. "An entire family was found drained—children too. Evil is spreading. We're doomed if this continues." Lusha didn't hide behind a polite smile as she usually did. Her uhra, typically a bright yellow and blue, was dull tonight. I wasn't the only one reaching the end of my rope in this world.

"They'll pay for what they've done," I said with a cold calm. And I meant it.

I sat at a full table that night. All but Louis were present. I was placed between Rafael and Arnold; cringing at my proximity to the Elder, I slid my chair closer to Raf. Galen noted my behavior and scowled, while Isla glared at Galen. Sylvia arrived and sat down, dumping cold water onto the already frigid atmosphere.

"How was training today?" Galen asked from across the table, looking back and forth between Raf and I.

"Uneventful," we both said in unison. Galen raised a brow.

"The clock is ticking, Marigold. Perhaps your lessons should *become* eventful. No progress in shifting, then?" Sylvia asked with a tight-lipped sneer. Did they suspect something? I was going to be paranoid until I left this world.

"No, still working on it."

"Two more weeks until the festival, then it will be my turn to host you." Arnold gave a malicious laugh and adrenaline shot through me. I was about to send him flying across the dining hall with the force of an icy gale, but Rafael grabbed my hand from under the table and reprimanded me with a stern look. *This was not the moment,* his eyes told me.

Isla spoke next. "Then Galen can wash his hands of you." She hooked her arm possessively around him. He removed it, then swallowed his glass of wine in one gulp. I threw my napkin down on the table and stormed out, leaving a chilly breeze in my wake.

Galen found me in my room, curled up in a chair, staring at the fire. "Marigold, you can't react to Arnold's threats. He's too powerful—you don't want to make an enemy of him. If you don't find your pneuma soon, I'll only be able to do so much. It terrifies me—the idea of you in their possession."

His breath smelled like faerie whiskey. He'd been drinking more. The last round of executions had stolen something vital from him. The tighter I held him, the farther he drifted, like a ship lost at sea. The awful truth was, I hadn't been able to forgive him for it either. He wasn't the only one responsible for the rift that was forming.

"It won't come to that," I promised. Trying to sooth him, I approached, wrapping my arms around his waist, and resting my head on his chest.

He stiffened at my words. "What do you mean? Have you shifted?"

Another fracture formed between us. "No, but Rafael says I'm close. I can *feel* the magic, I just haven't been able to fully let go." I looked down, unable to meet his eyes. My empty stomach twisted uneasily.

"I see. And you aren't worried about what will happen if you don't shift in time?" His tone was skeptical as he gripped my shoulders more tightly.

"I'm getting stronger—and I have you on my side, don't I?" I searched for the love in his eyes, while I lied through my teeth.

He ran hands through his hair, making his auburn tufts stand up. He seemed to be on edge. Or was I the one feeling edgy?

"I won't let them take you," he murmured.

"Why does Isla still act territorial over you? Why is she so confident that you're going to leave me?" It was the worst thing I could've said, at the wrong moment. I was projecting my own guilt onto him.

Flame exploded from the hearth, reaching the chairs that sat nearby—where I'd been sitting moments ago. They licked along the floor until I put them out with a layer of wet snow. I gawked at him, speechless.

His voice rose as he said, "I am *so sick* of you asking about Isla. You really want the truth?"

I stared at a spot on the stone floor, nodding slowly.

"*Very well*. I slept with her. *Once*. The night I found Rafael's rope at your window. I buried myself in her to keep myself from killing him—to keep myself from taking it out on you. It didn't mean anything." He sat on my bed with his head hanging low, anger fizzling into dejection.

The room began to spin and I sunk to the ground. He'd made me feel crazy... and all along, I'd been right. "Why didn't you tell me before?"

"Because... look how you're reacting right now! *It was just sex*. You and I weren't even together. Your human heart is so fragile, you'll hold this over my head—you'll sleep with Rafael to get back at me!" His words slurred, but they still hit their mark.

"That is *not* the kind of person I am. I *am* upset. Because you lied. And not for the first time. My faith in you is growing *fragile*—not my heart." I tried to cool my hot temper with several deep breaths. "Just go. We'll talk when you're sober." I walked towards the door in hopes he'd follow.

I turned around to find him before me, on one knee. He grabbed my hand as my mouth gaped open and he pulled a ring from his pocket. An emerald stone set against a gold band—the jewel was the exact same color as his eyes. He held it up to me, while his hands shook. "Marry me. I can't live without you. I won't lie to you again. I want to be better... for you."

I stayed silent, afraid to respond. This was *not* the moment for a proposal. "Galen, I don't want to rush into marriage. I'm not ready. First, let's get to Erador. Once we're away from the Elders, we can breathe—have a real relationship and see where this leads." I was as honest with him as I could be. I hoped it would be enough to ease his frayed nerves.

He gave no visible reaction. Had he not heard me? He stood up and took my hand, pushing the ring onto my finger.

"Galen, I—"

"Please just wear this as a promise—as a symbol, that you're mine. I've never cared about anything this much. It's driving me crazy. I hate that you spend your days with Rafael. I hate that I can't kill anyone that threatens you. I wanted to *kill* Arnold tonight." He kissed me as he rubbed the ring that was now pinching my finger. I didn't know how to say no... so I kept it on, for him.

Unable to keep my foot out of my mouth, I asked, "Are you addicted to my blood? You told me it felt like a drug in your system. Perhaps that's part of what's making you feel so... out of sorts. I think you should get your blood elsewhere for a while." I braced for his reaction.

He gave me one of his signature charming smiles. "My love, it's not your *blood* that I can't live without... it's *you*. Your magic makes me stronger than I've ever felt—that's exactly what we need right now in these uncertain times. I need to be able to protect you. It's a gift... that I'm so thankful for. Do you not enjoy when I bite you?" He had twisted my words.

"It feels amazing, but—"

Galen silenced me with a kiss before saying, "Good, then it's settled. You're mine and I'm yours. One day we'll be blood-bonded and we'll share each other's blood. There's no shame in being my source until then."

He was so fast, I had no chance to object. Like a lion on an antelope, his mouth was on my neck, drawing blood, before I could even shriek. I tried to push him off as I recovered from shock, but he didn't budge. When the magic took over, I became powerless to the pull of pleasure.

He pulled up my dress and ripped my underwear off in a rough tug. Then he was inside of me with one deep thrust. He lifted me up until he was holding me, his hands braced under my thighs. My legs wrapped around him as he took me, before both of us climaxed together in wave after crashing wave.

FORTY-ONE

Raf and I had planned to leave for the Oracle after first light. Galen left my room at sunrise and Rafael appeared shortly after in a curtain of shadows. I tried to hide the heavy emotions I was feeling from the night before, but he saw right through my glassy-eyed smile.

"What's wrong?" He rushed over to my bedside. Lusha hadn't arrived yet and I hadn't had the energy or will to dress myself. All it took was two words from him before the tears I'd been holding back started to cascade down my cheeks in a torrential waterfall.

He tucked my hair behind my ears and swore when he saw multiple fresh bite marks. They should've healed into bruises by now, but Galen had taken a lot of blood last night. I was still recuperating the loss.

"Did he force himself on you?' Rafael's eyes were dilated, almost completely black. His angry shadows twisted around us before blinking out of sight.

"It's more complicated than that. I think I frightened him into thinking I'd cut him off. It's my fault. It's my blood that did this to him. I pushed him too far last night." I hid my face, flinching as I felt his steady hand on my shoulder. If Galen knew he was in my room...

"We should go. Quickly," I said. "If anyone sees you in here, Galen will lose it. He's not himself right now." I shot out of bed and sat back down as a spell of dizziness washed over me.

"*This* is who he is, Marigold. You aren't safe with him," Rafael growled. "Don't move. I'll get your clothes. What do you want to wear?"

He opened my closet, pushing Galen's clothes out of the way with a growl and leafing through my dresses. He chose a simple gown that I could put on by myself, tossing it to me. He found a bag and began throwing clothes, undergarments, and shoes into it.

"What are you doing? I can't wear *this* to see the Oracle. I need something I can fight in." I watched as he grabbed a brush from my table... ribbons for my hair.

"You aren't staying in this room for another *minute*. And we're not going to the witch today. You can barely stand. I'm taking you to my place until you're stronger, and then—only then—do I want to hear your opinion on the matter." He looked like he was just *daring* me to challenge him. I didn't.

"Turn around while I get dressed." I was too tired, too sad, to throw any sarcasm his way. He faced away from me without a word.

I was wobbly, but able to stand when he gathered me in his arms and turned us into mist. We appeared on castle grounds, a few hundred yards from my window. Apparently that was the limit of how far his shadows could travel in one go. He looked down at me before we were smoke once more. This time we were in the forest and he let go of me.

"I'm going to shift to my pooka form, if you feel strong enough to ride. I don't want to drain my magic unnecessarily. Just in case."

In case Galen tries to stop us, were the words he didn't say.

"I can ride," I insisted, already feeling better with the fresh air, shuddering to think how I'd feel if I didn't have healing magic.

He tossed me a wool cloak from my bag, which felt ridiculous in the heat of the day, but my hair was a dead giveaway to anyone who might see us.

We flew along the forest trail, meeting no resistance. When we arrived in the village, Raf took us to a dark alley, before shadowing us into his room.

"Tell me what happened," Rafael demanded, guiding me to his bed. He pulled up a chair. I thought about holding back information, but it was Raf. I trusted him... more than I trusted Galen. The truth of it made me cringe.

I told him about our argument, then about the proposal. His eyes darted to my hand. "You said yes?" he asked, stunned.

"No. No—I said no."

He looked at the ring, narrowing his eyes in confusion.

"He insisted I wear it... as a promise. I didn't have the heart to take it off. He was a mess. I'm a mess." I looked down at the ring and removed it, setting it on Raf's nightstand. I felt like I was going to vomit. I thought of Galen with Isla and gagged. I *was* going to vomit.

I ran to the bathroom and puked into an empty bucket, wishing for a toilet that flushed. Rafael came in and rubbed my back, adding to my mortification.

"Go away. I don't want you to see me like this," I groaned into the bucket. How had I felt so strong just yesterday? It felt as if Galen had taken more than my blood last night.

"I'm not going anywhere. I live in a brothel. I've seen more than you can imagine."

I laughed in spite of myself. When I was feeling better, he helped me off the floor and we returned to his bed.

"Continue whenever you're ready," he said gently, handing me a glass of water.

"I asked him if he was addicted to my blood—told him that he should get his blood elsewhere. And then he... he essentially told me he needed *my* magic to protect *me*, which doesn't really make sense, now that I've said it out loud. And then he took what he wanted. Once the... *effects* of the bite took over, I didn't even try to stop him when he bit me again. And again." I looked down at my ringless finger.

When Rafael finally responded, his voice came out in a choked whisper. "None of this is your fault," he assured me, clearing his throat. "What Galen did was abusive. I'm no relationship expert, but what he did... it was not from a place of love. He's dangerous. He's *one of them*, whether he wants to be or not. You don't belong with someone that has been groomed to kill people like us—who takes what he wants after you tell him *no*. It's not your job to save him. It's not your duty to stay with him. He doesn't own you. But if you marry him, he will. In the eyes of faerie law, at least."

He moved his chair closer to me and held my hand. I knew what he told me was true, but logic didn't stop my heart from aching. Perhaps if Galen was able to get some distance from his mother, from my magic, from this *world*—he'd go back to being himself.

This was *my* fault, I knew it, even as Raf told me otherwise. If I wasn't there for Galen... who would be? The thought brought a fresh batch of tears. I couldn't give up on him. He needed me.

"I have to go back," I whispered. "He'll come after you if he finds out you took me to your room." Our brown eyes met and I wished... I wished everything had played out differently.

"You truly think that cub can kill me? I'd like to see him try," Rafael scoffed, flexing his biceps as he said it.

I nearly laughed at his ridiculous faerie ego, before I thought of what a fight between them would actually mean—the damage it would cause. Fear stabbed into my chest like a rusty knife.

"He has my magic running through his veins, Raf. And it's no coincidence he trains with a shadow wielder. It would be a mistake to not take him seriously. I don't want to see you, or him, hurt. Especially because of me." I patted the bed, a request for him to come sit beside me. He obliged.

"I don't know what'll become of Galen and me. He's not acting like the male I fell in love with... but I have to face him—I have to do this for myself. And if he doesn't listen, if he tries to hurt me, then I'll have my answer." I spoke freely, knowing Rafael wouldn't react aggressively. He'd let me make my own choices, even if it crushed him.

"I won't stand in your way, but I *loathe* this. You owe him nothing. At least stay here and rest for a few more hours. He'll just think you're at training—then I'll take you back, if you insist... but I'm sending you with this." He held up a key.

"What is that?"

"A key to your room. I should've gotten one to you sooner. I stole it off Robert yesterday—just in case. If they learn what you are—" He paused, collecting himself. "They *can't* find out. *He* can't find out. Do you understand?" He dropped it into my hands and folded his fingers over mine.

"Thank you. And yes. I understand." It should've been Galen who gave me this. Why was his brother treating me with more respect than he was?

Raf got up and left without another word. I thought he'd stormed off, but he appeared several minutes later with a plate of food and a glass of orange juice. "Try to get some sleep, I'll be back soon. I'm going to take advantage of this time and go fly towards Tarragona and see if I can find Louis. I'll be back for you, I promise." He hovered for a moment before leaving me alone in his expansive bed.

It was funny... that I'd found myself in Rafael's bed, before ever seeing Galen's. Perhaps *funny* wasn't the word Galen would've used.

FORTY-TWO

The sound of a door shutting woke me up. Rafael was back. He swallowed hard when he saw me tangled up in his black sheets and I sat up quickly, feeling suddenly shy.

"Did you get some sleep?" he asked, shaking hair out of his eyes. The same lock fell right back into place and I smiled.

He looked windblown, like he'd rushed to get here, glistening with sweat, still in his leather gear. I couldn't help but wonder if he was dying to bathe and lose those layers. I was thinking about it so hard, in fact, that I forgot to respond as I stared at him, slack jawed. He cleared his throat, shifting his feet, as a smirk spread across his face.

"Er, yes, thank you," I blurted out, blushing. "Your bed is surprisingly comfortable... for being in a brothel. You'd think they wouldn't bother with the hourly customers."

He chuckled. "I'm *not* an hourly customer. And I prefer the finer things when it comes to my sleep. I may live in a brothel most of the time, but I'm still a Prince—or have you forgotten that Galen isn't the only heir to the throne?"

I froze. I didn't think of Rafael as an heir, not since he'd told me he had no interest in the throne. Galen was the chosen heir, it was obvious who the prophecy had been about.

"Did you find him?" I was anxious for an update. It had been nearly two weeks since Louis left.

"Yes. It's worse than we could've imagined." He ran his hands through his dark waves and sat beside me. "It's... heavy. And you've already had a day. Do you want to hear this right now?"

My stomach flooded with warmth at his thoughtfulness, but I said, "I want to know everything."

He gave a nod. "We were right—the Elders are behind the kidnappings. Louis staked out a prison with his soldiers. They haven't been seen, but are going to need my help infiltrating it. He's been there for a week now and has witnessed several sets of families brought in—blind-folded and in bad shape. They've also seen bodies being burned outside of the building.

"He thinks they've been experimenting on how to retrieve magic from humans in a more... permanent way. His soldiers found mutilated bodies that were carelessly discarded instead of burned to ash. I'll spare you the more gruesome details, but it's a bad situation. We need to get the prisoners out as quickly as possible. The Elder's retribution will undoubtedly be brutal, so we need to time it right.

"We're finalizing a plan on how to move them under the cover of darkness, so we can get them to Monrovia... and then to your portal. Louis and I know of several safe houses we trust between there and here—friends of friends who are human sympathizers—but we don't know how many people are being held captive and how many are still alive. It could be a dozen, it could be hundreds. We're working on acquiring the resources needed to keep them sheltered and fed as we bring them here."

I was going to vomit again. The Elders had been *experimenting* on humans—mutilating their bodies—to take back magic *permanently*... What kind of dark magic would that even require? It was well beyond anything I'd learned in my few short months here.

"There's more." Rafael took my hand. "There will probably be a lot of wounded people. We'll need healers to get them well enough to travel." I hadn't mastered my healing abilities yet, but perhaps with Meli and Odin's assistance, I could be of some use. Meli would want to help.

"I'm still at the beginning stages of learning how to mend with my hands, but my blood can be used. Meli and Odin will help too."

Rafael sighed. "I can't risk taking you, but we could use Meli and Odin's help."

"What do you mean you can't *risk* taking me? It's my decision, is it not?" My fingers coated with frost. If he meant to leave me behind, I'd never forgive him.

"You are a *unicorn* and our only hope out of this world. If anything happened to you..." He looked apologetically at me.

"It's my decision," I snapped back.

"It's your decision," he agreed begrudgingly. "But let's worry about the Oracle first... We'll head out after sunrise tomorrow. I'll pick you up." He took a long pause. "Are you ready? Are you sure you want to go back?"

His eyes begged me to stay, but I replied firmly, "Yes, it's time."

FORTY-THREE

Galen appeared at my door shortly after I was dropped off. I thanked the gods he hadn't crossed paths with his brother. He was holding a bouquet of yellow marigold flowers when I greeted him. There was a restless energy in the air as we gazed at each other. He had to know what he'd done was wrong. My wary eyes followed him as he set the flowers down on the corner table.

"I've been thinking of you all day. I'm sorry about last night. I-I took it too far. Were you okay to train today after the blood loss?" He looked contrite, but I couldn't bring myself to care as I took in the glow that was illuminating the room. His uhra didn't just float above him, but around him, like a shield. He was *gilded* in gold. I felt primal in my possessiveness over *my* magic. My fists clenched.

"I wasn't able to do much at all today. You took too much of my blood, after I asked you not to. I won't be able to shift or open portals if you continue to take my magic from me," I replied coolly, flashing him a look of steely indignation.

He hovered a few feet from me, hesitating. "I know. I was so angry at myself today. I took a critical day of training from you, because of my own lack of self-control. It wont happen again."

I'd heard that before. "You won't bite me without my permission. I'm not your *source*. I'm your girlfriend."

He closed the space between us, pulling me to him and burying his face in my hair. "You smell like Rafael," he gagged. He held me at arm's length, waiting for an explanation.

"I... borrowed his jacket today. I was cold from training." I almost wanted to tell him the truth. It was *his fault* I had ended up in Raf's bed today.

"*Interesting*. I've never heard you mention feeling cold from your magic before. Did you come close to burn out?" Doubt shadowed his expression.

"No. I-I just pushed myself too hard with the blood loss." I couldn't meet his eyes.

"Would you like to take a bath? I'll wash that gods awful horse smell out of your hair." He smiled down at me and I nodded to avoid further interrogation. He rang the servant's bell to call Lusha in for hot water.

"Galen, you won't bite me again... without my permission. Understood?"

"Yes, of course." He lifted my hair back and kissed each bite mark, making me flinch. "I'll miss seeing these little reminders that you're mine..." He picked up my hand. "But at least you have this now." He went to feel for the ring and I realized it was still on Raf's nightstand.

Shit.

His eyes blazed with fury, while his voice was cold and flat. "Where's your ring?"

"I-I must've misplaced it today at training. Maybe Rafael has it. I'll ask him tomorrow..." I was talking too fast, barely able to hear myself over the pounding in my ears.

"Why would *he* have your ring? That doesn't make sense." As Galen began to pace, the embers in the fireplace fanned into large flames. "I can hear your heart *racing*. What are you not telling me?"

"I-I apologize. I'll find it. You're making me nervous. Your temper... it's been worse lately. I can't help how my body responds to it."

He raised his voice until I began to quiver. "You *reek* of Rafael and you aren't wearing my ring. *You say he has it?* You're lying to me. Are you *sleeping* with him? Is this because of Isla?"

I winced, backing up towards the bed. He followed me with the wrath of a god. "Don't be ridiculous. I train with him—we're friends." I tried to find the confidence I had minutes ago, but instead I felt myself shrinking as I thought of the people he'd murdered—what he was capable of, even if it wasn't fair to him.

"Do you think I'm an idiot? *Something* is going on between you two." His anger simmered into despair.

"He-he was there for me today..." *When you weren't*, I wanted to add. "As a friend, nothing more." I blinked back tears as his face crumbled.

"And you tell him about me? How you don't trust me? I'm sure he's more than happy to console you. It's *pathetic* how he pants after you. He probably tells you of my past mistakes, anything to put a wedge between us," he hissed.

"No, Galen, he doesn't. I'm *yours*. If you feel me growing distant, it's because of your erratic behavior. It isn't him. I feel as if I'm treading on hot coals when I try to talk to you. I don't want this space between us."

Tears filled my puffy eyes as Lusha knocked on the door and entered. She saw my face and gasped, then turned to Galen and balked, backing out quickly.

"Lusha, you can come in. I don't bite," Galen said, before shaking his head in self-loathing. He turned towards the bottle of wine on the table and poured a glass.

"Apologies for interrupting. Is there anything I can do for you?" she asked tentatively, her eyes glued on me.

"We'd like a hot bath drawn. And some dinner... and more wine. Thank you," Galen drawled, dismissing her with a wave of his hand. I wanted to dismiss *him*. I was still recovering from last night. *It shouldn't be this hard.*

We sat in silence as servants came and went. Their presence had halted the conversation at an awkward place. Unspoken words hovered between us. I picked at my dinner, but had lost my appetite. I was drinking wine with Galen while his brothers fought to free enslaved humans and it all felt terribly wrong.

Whose side would Galen be on if he knew what his brothers were up to? How deeply was he involved with the Elders... Did he know about the prison?

Questions were flying through my mind faster than I could catch them. They were pelting me like rocks, but I was too much of a coward to ask outright.

Raf and Louis were risking so much more than Galen. If they were caught, they'd be executed. Galen was the *heir*, surely that gave him some protection from the Elders.

I stared at him as I drank from my glass, feeling increasingly hostile. I'd once thought I could rely on Galen for comfort, but I was beginning to realize that I'd always have to be the strong one. He was too consumed with his own misery to be there for me in the ways I needed him.

Lusha and the others left us alone and my pulse ratcheted back up. Galen broke the silence first, swirling his glass of wine as he began. "I don't want this distance either, Marigold. And the last thing I want is for you to feel unsure about us. I haven't been perfect, but I'm *trying*. I need you to be more understanding to the pressures I'm under. It's not easy balancing a personal life with my other responsibilities. Sometimes a bad day will spill over into our time together."

"You can have bad days... but I won't allow you to take them out on me. You were rough with me last night—you took my blood after I asked you not to. That behavior can't continue... if we're to continue." Heat rose to my face as I stood up for myself, bracing for his response.

He looked up from his wine, concern etched on his face. "You've filled a void in me. And your magic... it's eased a pain in me. It makes it easier for me to fight my demons when I'm filled with *your light*. I can't have you running off to Rafael whenever I make a mistake. He is *poison* to our relationship. I'll take over your training lessons from now on. That's final."

He stood eerily still, like a jack-in-the-box who might spring up at any moment. Did he really think I'd obey him like a trained monkey? Raf wouldn't tolerate Galen taking over my lessons and neither would I.

"I'm not going to stop training with Raf. I've been learning a lot from him."

He flashed me a look that said, *I'm sure you have.* "We can discuss it after your bath. I'd like to make up for last night's poor behavior. First with my hands, then with my tongue..." He gave me a seductive smile and I almost wanted to let it go, to accept his peace offering, but then Raf's words came back to me. *He doesn't own you.*

It was the reminder that I needed to speak my mind. "I don't feel like having sex tonight. After last night, I need comfort. I want to feel loved, but I don't want to make love." I steeled my spine as he got up from his chair and approached me.

"You don't want me to bite you... and now you don't even want me to *touch* you? You *are* sleeping with Rafael. Don't lie to me, damn it." He roared, throwing his wine glass at the wall, causing it to shatter. A splatter of burgundy wine stained the walls, dripping down like blood.

Everything seemed to move in slow motion after that. I peered down at my arm and saw a piece of glass protruding. The liquid sliding down my forearm mirrored the wine on the wall. I pulled the deep shard out with gritted teeth. I stared at the maroon blemish on the wall, my gushing cut, and then at Galen.

"Get out," I said under my breath. So softly, I wasn't sure he'd heard me. He rushed over, inspecting my arm, holding me by the wrists. "Don't touch me." This time, my voice was louder.

We locked eyes and his startled face stared back at me. He let go of me and went in for a hug. My magic reacted to the threat, throwing him back with an icy wind. He slammed against the bedroom door and I could almost feel Beira and Alya smiling down at me with pride. He looked at me in disbelief as he brushed himself off and stood back up.

"Marigold, it was an *accident*." He came towards me and this time I surrounded myself with a shield of ice.

"Get out! We're *done*. You'll never touch me again," I hissed at him.

His eyes flashed with challenge and he collected himself, straightening the lapels of his jacket. "This isn't over." He left, slamming the door on his way out.

The sound rattled me and I ran to lock the door, even if it wouldn't keep him out. Rafael was right. Galen *was* dangerous. Even satiated with my magic, he'd turned into someone, *something*, I didn't recognize. I didn't know what had changed. Had he always had this side and I'd been blinded by lust? Or was I the one who'd changed?

Numbness settled over me, preventing me from feeling much of anything. I climbed into the steaming tub and let the blood from my cut run freely, watching it swirl with the bath oils. It would heal in minutes, but how long would it take for the rest of me to mend? I sank back into the water and decided tonight was my last night in the castle and there was one more thing I needed to do.

I waited until midnight, wondering if Galen would come to my room. The sharp, visceral rage from earlier had faded into a dull sadness. The howling winter wind inside of me thrashed, but I wouldn't let it win. I couldn't afford to break down. Not yet, at least.

I listened outside my door and heard nothing. I tested the door and found it locked. *The cold-hearted bastard.* I couldn't believe I was still being treated like a common criminal. If I was locked in, at least that meant Robert was done standing guard for the evening.

I sent Rafael a silent, *thank you,* for the key and turned the door knob as quietly as possible. An empty hallway met me on the other side of the door. I grabbed the oil lamp that sat on my table and headed towards the Queen's library. I hadn't forgotten what Galen had told me: The library held information about how to break the blood curse—a prophecy scribbled down and forgotten. I couldn't leave to Erador without it.

It was stupid of me—not asking Rafael for help with this—but he'd already done so much for me. Too much. And I couldn't give him anything in return. I didn't deserve his friendship... and whatever else he might feel. We hadn't discussed the kiss and I didn't know if I'd ever be able to bring it up—to face him in the way he deserved. I shook my head, pushing thoughts of him out of my mind, as I padded down the silent corridor towards the Queen's quarters.

To my relief, I arrived at the library without incident. I'd been wanting to come back here ever since my meeting with Sylvia. It appeared well-organized, which gave me a sliver of hope. I looked for anything handwritten instead of printed, like a journal or transcript. I found a box of handwritten notes and began scanning each of them; personal letters, accounts of battles, of policy and trade, of spells, but nothing about the curse.

Something caught my eye. The glare of my lamp had caught a shimmering text. I read the title, *The Mystery of the Unicorn,* and held back a gasp. *A book on unicorns.* I reigned in my excitement, trying to stay silent. I tucked the small square book under my arm and decided I'd have to enlist Raf's help after all. It hadn't been as easy as I'd hoped.

I'd spent too long searching and was beginning to worry that Galen might come back to my room and find me missing. Feeling defeated, I silently tip-toed out of the library, through the Queen's wing, and up the stairs to the guest wing. When I was mere steps from my door, a hand covered my mouth before I could scream.

FORTY-FOUR

"Going somewhere?" Galen whispered with hot, liquor-laced breath. My adrenaline spiked so high that I saw stars. He released me from his grasp and came to stand in front of me.

"Yes, to my room," I said, panting. "You aren't invited." I tried to shake him off, but when I went to open the door, he stopped me, holding the knob.

"You aren't going to your room. You're coming to mine."

I was so frightened that I didn't protest. I had a better chance of this going well if I was agreeable. I let him lead me to a section of the castle that I'd never been to. The Princes' wing. I wondered if Raf even had a room here, if he ever slept in it.

Galen opened a large wooden door and ushered me in. It was dimly lit, but I could see a sprawling four-poster bed and dark walls, nearly black, that contrasted with the rest of the castle's white stone. He had an over-sized leather sofa that faced towards the largest fireplace I'd ever seen.

I scanned the room and saw another set of doors that led out to a balcony. I could see a view of the night-covered mountains out the glass doors. *Why had he never taken me here?* It was undeniably more lavish than my room.

"What were you doing out in the hall? Trying to escape?" His eyes were dilated, glowing like a predator's in the night. But his voice... it was surprisingly gentle.

"No. I went to your mother's library. I was searching for the journal you mentioned—the one with the prophecy about the blood curse."

He scoffed, shaking his head at me. "You would've been better off coming to me, instead of scurrying through the castle, little mouse. I found it already. I hadn't had a chance to give it to you." He softly brushed my cheek with his knuckles before going to his desk and handing me a small book bound in dark, cracked leather.

I couldn't believe it. Instead of berating me for leaving my room, he was giving me a gift. A priceless gift. I suddenly felt guilty that I'd tried to steal it behind his back.

"Thank you..." I said awkwardly. He had me at a disadvantage. I was thoroughly confused by his unpredictable behavior. I hadn't expected him to be kind after what had transpired earlier—after smelling liquor on his breath. But he was *smiling* at me... gently rubbing goosebumps from my arms.

"Let it be a reminder that I'm on your side," he said smoothly. And then his eyes darted to the item I was holding. Before I could stop him, Galen pulled the book from my hand. *The Mystery of the Unicorn.* He read the title and then looked at me with wide-eyes.

"I knew it. I *knew* you'd found your form. You're a unicorn? I should've known with how *different* you taste. Is this why you've been so secretive?" His brows furrowed before melting into an awed expression. "Why didn't you tell me?"

Of course he was in awe. This was the last piece of the puzzle. He could now get everything he wanted.

"You know why..." I eyed him warily. His expression was warm, like the Galen I'd known up until recently.

"You thought I'd tell my mother," he said. "Unicorns are as rare as they come. The last account of one is hundreds of years old. I've never seen this book before..." He flipped through it quickly before setting it on his desk. "The Elders would probably remove your horn the first chance they got. They can't know."

"No... they can't. I now hold my life in your hands." My chest pounded as he tilted his head, studying me, like he was counting every beat, like he could hear the slosh of blood that pumped through my heart.

"When will you understand that I don't want to hurt you? I love you." He touched my cheek and I didn't shove him away.

"You hurt me today. Your moods... I can't keep up with them. Your lies... there have been too many. Sometimes love isn't enough, Galen."

I held my breath, waiting for an explosion. Instead, he led with vulnerability. "If you knew how much I hated myself, you would've never given me a chance in the first place. Do you know *why* my room is so dark? Because I've set every inch of it on fire over the past century. Burn marks coat every wall. And that's how my soul feels. It may have been white once, but now it's an endless dark hole I can't climb out of. From the moment I met you, you've represented a salvation—an escape from my hell. But maybe there is no escape... I sold my soul long ago. I don't want to drag you down with me." He glanced up at me through golden lashes. "But please... give me one more night."

I wished we lived in a reality where I could be all he needed, but I couldn't risk everything I stood for on the chance that he *might* get better. There was also a chance he'd get worse and hurt me beyond repair. Too many were depending on me. I could give him tonight, though. Closure would help us both.

Salty tears coated my lips as I kissed him in answer. He picked me up effortlessly and carried me to his bed. His kisses were patient and loving. If only he could choose to be this person all the time. He stripped before he removed my nightgown, never breaking eye contact. His touch was feather-light, like he was handling a delicate, rare butterfly.

"Can I taste your magic? One last time," he asked softly as his body hovered over mine. I had to tell him. "I have to go to the Oracle tomorrow. I need my magic for the journey."

His eyes narrowed, making my breath catch. "You were planning to go without me?" He went rigid and I felt his biceps flex on either side of me.

"Yes... I decided I couldn't tell *anyone* about my animal form, for my safety."

He was still on top of me, processing what I'd said. "But you told Rafael... You're going to bring him?"

"Only because I shifted for the first time in front of him." My voice shook, even as I tried to stay calm.

Suddenly his large body over mine felt like a cage. He held me down as he whispered, "I'll make sure that was your *last* first with him." Teeth sunk into flesh and I was lost to him... to the magic... to darkness.

FORTY-FIVE

I woke up with a pounding headache. My heavy lids reluctantly cracked open to find that the curtains were drawn. I couldn't tell what time of day it was... how much time had passed.

Assessing my condition, I first noted that I was naked. My neck was throbbing in pain—his bites had never hurt like this before. My throat was dry, my tongue swollen.

Humiliation washed over me as flashes of last night replayed in my head. I could barely remember what had transpired after Galen bit me, but I knew that what had started out gentle had ended roughly. I'd blacked out at some point.

I couldn't believe that I'd let him trick me into thinking he cared about me. It was a cycle that would end in my death. Had any of it been real? I let out a sob as I realized I was *chained* to his bed, with an amber-colored shackle around my wrist. It held firm as I pulled at it. This was lower than anything I could've imagined from him.

What was he planning to do with me? Was this because he'd found out what I was? Panic gripped me around the throat, suffocating me. I sucked in the smoke-tinged air that lingered in his room, gasping as I tried not to let fear shut down my mind.

Slow down your breathing, Marigold. You must figure out how to escape, my mother's voice rang out clearly. I was hallucinating from lack of blood.

I could get myself out of this situation. I peeked around the room to make sure Galen wasn't lurking somewhere in the darkness. The room was empty. Rafael would find me. He'd help me. I didn't deserve him or his help. Galen was who I deserved.

No. I did not deserve this.

There was no excuse that could justify this level of cruelty. Galen had chained me to his bed. He'd... He'd violated me physically and emotionally. I tried to bury the memories of him holding me down—biting me when I'd told him *no*. I had to focus. I needed to move. *Now.*

I tried to shift into my animal form and break the strange stone around my wrist, but the cuff seemed to be impeding my magic. There was a wrongness to it that made my skin crawl. My magic had fallen into a deep slumber and refused to wake. I tried freezing the stone, but my magic didn't respond. He'd somehow completely cut off my power with this devise.

Think, Marigold. Think. I was foggy from blood loss, but I was stronger than I'd once been. I studied how the chain was connected to the bed post. The beam was made of wood... maybe I could break it. I stood on the bed and kicked with all my might. It barely budged. I pulled down on the top of the post, trying to snap it with my body weight. No luck. I looked around Galen's room and saw a knife sticking out of a pair of discarded pants on the floor.

I leapt at it and was hauled back by the chain. But my feet, my legs—they were just long enough. I stretched out my toes and dragged it towards me. I went to work on the bed post, trying to use the pocketknife as a saw. It was tedious work and my heart hammered, waiting for Galen to appear any minute. When the wood had a deep cut in it, I kicked the post again and this time it splintered. A few more kicks and I was free.

The heavy chain still dangled from my wrist. I didn't have time to look for a key. My body was screaming at me to *hurry*. I threw on my nightgown, one of Galen's jackets off the floor, and grabbed the two books sitting on his desk. I checked his door. *Locked*. Of course.

I ran to the balcony and saw that the sun was touching the lake. It was dawn. I peered over the edge, to the gardens below. The room was on the third story and was a long climb down. I could've used one of Raf's vines right now. Instead, I grabbed the silk sheets off Galen's bed and frantically shredded them with the knife, braiding them together to make a long, makeshift rope.

With one last glance at the door, I ran to the balcony and tied the rope to the stone railing. I climbed over and descended as fast as I could. If someone would've seen me, they would've questioned my sanity; half-dressed in a man's jacket, golden waves of hair flowing wildly around me, and a chain hanging from my wrist. Luckily, it was early enough that most were still sleeping. The rope wasn't long enough and I had to drop the last ten feet, hitting hard and rolling an ankle.

What I would've given to shift into a unicorn and run into the woods, but alas, I was to do this without magic. I had to get to Hibiscus. I'd be caught if I tried to walk to the village on foot, so I stayed close to the castle walls, limping, and thanking the gods that I didn't run into any guards.

I made it to the stables undetected and saw a young groom saddling up a horse. I ducked into the tack room before he saw me, grabbing a saddle to cover the chains, before confidently sauntering towards my horse's stall. The groom glanced up at me and was about to speak before his eyes grew large and he thought better of it. I must've looked in a state. I scurried to Hibiscus and threw the saddle on, synching it.

As we exited the stable, I whispered, "Run like the wind, sweet girl. I'm depending on you." She galloped faster than a hailstorm as we raced towards the shelter of the tree-lined trail. I dared a glance back and noticed one guard looking alert as he watched my flaxen curls sail behind me. Galen had forgotten to take me seriously and it would be his decision to regret.

We flew to the brothel and I dove off Hibiscus. "Go get yourself some water and return to the stables. Thank you. *For everything.*" I spoke to her as if she could understand me. I didn't know if I'd see her again. She blinked and then turned around to head towards the water troughs.

I hobbled into the Siren Inn and was greeted by several bewildered women in gauzy scraps of fabric. It appeared that they were still up from the night before. A few men sat nearly unconscious while women straddled them.

"Rafael?" I asked to no one in particular. One of them pointed up the stairs. "Room Six."

I sprinted like a mad woman and knocked on his door. He appeared a moment later, shirtless with pants hanging low, revealing muscles that traveled down in a straight arrow towards his...

My eyes grew round and I looked up. I'd never noticed his tattoos. He had writing scrawled on his tanned arms and chest. I didn't recognize the language. I noticed a set of pegasus wings inked on his shoulder blades as he closed the door behind me. I gawked for a minute before pulling myself together.

"Are you okay? What happened?" He rubbed the sleep from his eyes as he studied me. I watched his face contort from concern to outrage.

I hugged him, burying my face into his hard chest. He saw the chain and shackle and lost his composure. "*What happened*? He chained you? *I'll kill him.*" He made to move towards the door, apparently planning to leave right then.

"Raf, stop. I escaped..." I released a sob as I let the words sink in. I'd made it out of the castle. *I was safe.* "Please don't leave me." I lifted my wrist to him. "Can you help me get this off?" I asked, letting the adrenaline roll off me in waves. Raf took my wrist and looked at the cuff.

"*Jasper.* It's a blend of iron and quartz." He let out a slew of curse words. "Simply touching it is enough to block one from their magic."

"I noticed," I said bitterly.

"Humans used it against faeries in Erador. It's rarely seen here; it goes against everything faeries stand for—to take away another's magic." He snarled. "It's a coward's weapon. It also hasn't been needed since the curse. It's easier to just deny a prisoner access to blood."

He snapped to attention. "You escaped without magic? Where was he keeping you? How did you get away?"

He sat me on his bed and then pulled a lock pick from a drawer and came to sit beside me, working at the cuff as I told him everything. As my story ended, the shackle opened with a click and fell to the floor. My magic responded sluggishly, repairing the various wounds inflicted by Galen and my escape. I'd lost a lot of blood, I realized, feeling suddenly woozy as my body tried to knit back together.

Raf kissed the palm of my hand, tracing a finger lightly around the marks from the cuff. It was too intimate and I yanked my hand away. "I'm so sorry I didn't get there sooner," he whispered. "I'm so sorry for all of it."

He was the last person that should've felt sorry. And I didn't have time to feel sorry for myself. I'd escaped one monster, but it was time to prepare for the next. We were supposed to leave for the Oracle shortly.

Seeming to read my mind, Raf said, "We'll go to her tomorrow. Rest and eat today—you'll need your strength to face her."

I wanted to fight him on it, but I was too tired. "Can I stay with you... if it's not too much of an imposition. I'm afraid he'll find me. And I-I don't want to be alone." Recent events had eviscerated my pride and I wasn't above begging.

Raf's strong arms engulfed me in a tight hug, temporarily shutting the rest of the world out. "There's nowhere safer than right here and you aren't going anywhere. My room is thoroughly warded; no one has ever been able to break in. And if you want to leave for Erador, after the Oracle, we can."

He was offering me a chance to escape before Louis returned, even though it would doom his people if I did. "I won't leave the others behind. I just need to sleep first, then I'll be alright." I yawned, crawling out of his arms and into his bed.

He left for a moment, coming back with a clean towel and a small bowl of water. He hesitated before sitting beside me. His voice grew thick as he said, "You have quite a lot of blood caked on you. Let me help." He dabbed at my neck and the white rag quickly turned red. I hadn't looked in a mirror. Galen had left me bleeding and unable to heal.

I shrank into myself, trying to shield the little girl that had never felt worthy of love after being abandoned. I wanted to protect her from the pain that was lashing at me like a whip. Rafael didn't say a word as he continued to clean me, twisting bloody water from the rag, and dipping it back into the bowl. Once he was done, he brushed my hair with his fingers until I was fast asleep.

FORTY-SIX

The next time I opened my eyes, the room was dark. I'd slept the entire day away. *Again.* My magic was demanding when it was depleted. I could've slept for another day. Another week.

I sat up to find Rafael sitting in a chair at the foot of the bed. The tangerine glow from the fire fell across his face. He was studying something—the unicorn book I'd found in the library. It looked so small in his hands. His gaze turned to me when he noticed me stirring.

"Did you know that unicorns can emit *starlight* from their horns? It has the ability to break some curses and spells—and it can also *blind* enemies. Oh, and also... your horn is capable of channeling *every* form of elemental magic. Looks like you're going to have some new tricks up your sleeve, Goldie. Hopefully I can keep up with you." He gave me a smile that didn't quite meet his eyes. He was trying to appear casual, but I could tell that today had disturbed him.

"Good thing you're skilled at fighting blind." I grinned. "I wonder how your shadows will respond to my light." I rested my head back on his pillow, savoring the feeling of true safety.

"Light and dark... two sides of the same coin. One can't exist without the other." He stood up, while his shadows hovered between us. They swirled towards me before he tugged them back. We laughed and then it grew quiet. Our usual comfortable silence was gone. In its place, a new energy buzzed between us—a product of everything that had transpired in the last few days.

"Have you looked at the journal yet? I've been dying to see what it says about the curse." I scanned the room. It was sitting on Raf's nightstand where I'd left it.

"Not without you."

"No time like the present," I said with a weak smile, before picking it up and opening it. I grew disheartened when I realized I didn't recognize the text.

"What language is this?" I asked Raf, handing it to him. He fanned through the small pages that had yellowed over the years.

"You don't recognize the text of your people? Clearly we've been spending too much time on the physical side of training. This is the ancient language of the Fae. It's still considered something we should all know, even though it's not typically used in everyday conversation anymore. We made Dorish our dominant language when we began interacting more with humans. Most books have been translated over to Dorish now, but you'll still find handwritten texts in Ancient Fae... especially if it's not meant for human eyes."

I must've looked annoyed because he smirked and said, "Don't worry, I can translate." He spent a few minutes flipping through the pages until he landed on something that made him stop.

"Here, this says the curse came from—" He paused, looking confused. *"The Book of Erebus."* Raf rubbed his stubbled jaw in contemplation. "This contradicts what I was told." He looked up to see my blank face and explained, "Erebus is a well-known spell book. It's one of two that were created by the gods, to house the most powerful spells. Its opposite is the book of Chrysus, a book of creation, while Erebus is a book of destruction. Our people lost track of both of them centuries ago.

"If the curse came from Erebus... it means a magical being must've cast the spell—it changes everything." He swore and loosed a long breath. "It's always been assumed that Chrysus was the source of the curse. Anyone can cast spells from it... It can be used by humans. The magic used for creation spells is pulled directly from the land. The accepted belief amongst our people is that a human created the blood curse—this challenges that theory. Erebus can only be wielded with true magic."

He furrowed his brows before musing, "Why isn't this common knowledge? Someone with significant sway must've purposefully kept this information from going public... Someone who knew the truth." We both looked at each other.

Sylvia.

But why?

Raf flipped to a new page. There was a name written on top it. *Aides Ruhn.* "This was a prophecy given to my Uncle Aides. He died in Erador. It almost seems connected to yours... Let me translate."

Rafael got a piece of pen and paper and began writing:

Two books united, Six Chosen souls
By horn and feathers, claws, and bones
The cost of magic will be steep
Bonded-blood must spiral deep
The black book's spell demands a fee
Destruction has no empathy
Next an ancient spell that mends
Only then will the blood curse end
A war rages across the land
Chosen heirs must take a stand
The curse may start once more anew
If the caster is allowed to do
What they intend with hate and scorn
They'll rule both worlds with blood and horn

We locked eyes when we finished reading. The chosen heirs had been mentioned again. Two spell books and six chosen souls... This left me with more questions than answers.

The prophecy appeared to cover more than just how to break the curse, but how the war between worlds might play out. *Chosen heirs.* My heart sank. Was I truly meant to be with Galen? My body seized up at the idea. Would the fates be so cruel? Was I supposed to blood-bond with a monster?

"What do you make of it?" I asked, shivering as I hugged myself.

Raf saw my crestfallen face and took my hands in his. "Don't give up now. This is information that will only help us. It tells us exactly what we need to do, once we figure out what it means... This doesn't mean you have to go back to Galen," he assured me. "Don't spend another moment worrying about him, about the chosen heirs. Let's get to Erador before we try to decipher the prophecies. They'll only distract us from what we have to accomplish in the next two weeks."

"How can you say that? I can't ignore such vital information. What if I'm meant to bring him to Erador?" Were Raf's feelings for his brother preventing him from seeing the situation clearly?

"Maybe you misinterpreted it. Maybe there's more information waiting for us in Aurelius. Please, don't worry, all will be explained in time." He was avoiding eye contact.

"There's something you aren't telling me," I said skeptically.

"Let it be for now. *Please.*" His pleading eyes met mine and I dropped it, turning back to the book. The next several pages were ripped out and the rest were blank.

"I guess that's all the information we're getting." I sighed, disappointed.

Rafael stayed silent as he closed the book, tucking it away. "I'm going to go get us some food. Any requests? The chef here is surprisingly talented." He stood quickly, seeming eager to put distance between us.

"Everything on the menu," I joked. Raf gave a tight smile before leaving, locking the door behind him.

What was he hiding? I wasn't going to push him for information. After everything he'd done for me, I'd let him keep his secrets. For now.

While Raf was gone, I watched the window and the door, folding my knees to my chest and hugging them as I tried to self-sooth, rocking back and forth.

My partner—someone who I loved, who'd said he loved me—had violated me last night. I tried to block out the bits I remembered—that threatened to undo me. Just as I thought I might fall into a hole of despair so deep that I'd never be able to climb out, I heard the twist of the door knob.

I shielded myself, readying for a fight, before Raf appeared with several maids in tow, each of them carrying multiple trays of food. "Your wish is my command," he said with an exaggerated bow. I let out a long sigh.

We laid out all the plated food on a thick rug that covered shabby hardwood floor, sitting in front of the fireplace as we ate. I was pulled into a dark, haunted corner of my mind as I watched the flickering amber flames.

I heard Raf's voice, but it felt far away, like I was underwater and trying to swim my way back to the surface. My lungs burned as I realized I'd been holding my breath.

"You're safe," he whispered, moving closer, wrapping an arm around me. I shied from his touch, before accepting his words and leaning into his warmth.

"I'm not sure I'll ever recover," I said quietly.

"Give yourself some time. You've been through a lot. It'll take a while to realize that you've escaped." One large hand was on my shoulder, while the other offered me a piece of warm bread. Tears formed and I let them fall in fat drops on Raf's oversized shirt that I was currently wearing. How many of his shirts had I soaked in tears over the last few days?

"Eat. You'll recuperate faster if you do," he said gently.

I took the buttered toast from him and took a bite. "Do you... do you think he ever loved me? Or did he just want my magic?"

He scooted towards me, curling an arm around my back. It felt natural to settle against his chest. "You're so much more than your magic. I'm sure Galen knew that. It doesn't mean he deserved you."

"I-I'm sorry," I said, hoping he knew all that I was apologizing for.

"Don't apologize to me, you've done nothing wrong." He rested his cheek on the top of my head as we both stared at the fire.

"You aren't the only one that made the mistake of trusting Galen," Rafael said into the silent night. It took him a long time to speak again and I patiently waited.

"When I was a child, I looked up to him. He's forty-five years older than me—he was an adult when I was born. I didn't know why he didn't like me, until I learned we had different mothers. Sylvia loved using him to torment me—to put me in my place.

"He ignored me when I was a child, but when I became a teenager and he saw that I could use magic without needing blood... he was jealous. Threatened. He'd challenge me to duels before I knew how to use my magic, under the guise of training. I thought it was a chance to bond with him, but he used it as a way to torture me. He'd kick my ass and then... he'd use his flames to show me that he was stronger than me. I still have nightmares of being held down and burned. I have scars, even with the healing powers granted to all faeries. You can imagine how deep some of the burns were." He pointed to patches of shiny, uneven skin on his arms, under the tattoos. He lifted his shirt to show me the hard lines of his stomach with burn marks slashed across.

"That's when I began staying here. He didn't care about me enough to wonder where I went, he just wanted me to know that he had the power. Galen likes to control his environment; probably because Sylvia keeps him leashed and muzzled most of the time.

"My father reprimanded him once, when he caught him holding me down and putting flame to my face. I thought he was going to permanently disfigure me. Our father was so angry that he threatened to kill him if it ever happened again. Galen stopped bullying me after that. And I got stronger. The animosity between us has never really subsided. Sometimes we're forced to work together, of course. I still hung around the castle for Louis's sake. I didn't want him to grow up with only Galen and Sylvia as influences, especially after our father died. Luckily, Galen has never seen Louis as a threat."

Raf paused, taking a swig of a beer, before adding, "And then more recently... when you arrived... I began spending more time at the castle again." He sighed.

"Why didn't you tell me sooner?"

"It's been eighty years since then. I thought you might think I was just trying to find a way to get between you and Galen. But I watched over you from afar... I had to make sure he and Sylvia were treating you alright.

"I often take the form of a black cat in the castle... they don't notice me, since there are cats everywhere. I followed you to the library... the day Sylvia brought you in for a meeting. I also spent some time as a crow, watching you train with Louis. I should've told you sooner."

I thought of all the times I'd curled up with that black cat on my bed—how sad I'd been when it stopped visiting. And then I remembered... the cat had been there that day at the library when Raf had attacked Galen. That's how he'd appeared so quickly. I sat speechless for a moment.

"I can't believe that was you. I might die of embarrassment. Did I ever undress in front of you?" I asked through slitted lids.

"Don't be embarrassed... I shouldn't have invaded your privacy. I stopped visiting once you seemed to be doing fine without me. And no... you never undressed in front of me." He couldn't hold back a smirk. "But you did give excellent back scratches..."

My cheeks grew hot and I gave him a playful shove, suddenly feeling grateful for the dimly lit room. "Thank you, for watching over me, even when I didn't deserve it."

"Yes, you did."

Our gazes met. There was so much depth behind his honey-glazed eyes. It was easy to get lost in them.

"I'm sorry—for what Galen did to you," I said, putting my hand over his. "And that you had to watch me get close to him, knowing what you knew."

"And I'm sorry that I wasted so much time distancing myself from you. I'm an idiot." He fed me a piece of cantaloupe wrapped in prosciutto. The emotion in his eyes mirrored the regret I felt. It was too late to go back in time and change the way things played out; we had to suffer the consequences. I'd be haunted by Galen forever... just as Rafael was.

"Why *did* it take me so long to win you over?" I asked, nudging him.

He grew contemplative as he said, "I try to stay away from anything that Galen's claimed ownership over. It's easier that way."

I wondered what else Galen had claimed in the last century. The throne was the first thing to come to mind. "How does succession typically work in faerie society? I know it's assumed that Galen will take the throne, but who decides?"

"Usually it's the eldest son, but if another sibling is magically stronger, they can make a claim for it," he explained, growing dour. "I've never been interested in the throne. In fact, I've spent most of my life actively rebelling against anything having to do with it."

His posture had been relaxed until I'd brought up the throne. Now he was sitting up straight, scowling at the fire. Did he feel unworthy? He was a born leader, though I admittedly hadn't thought so when we'd first met.

He let Galen march around like *he* was the strong one, the brave one, the kind one. And I'd been naive enough to fall for it. My body temperature dropped as another wave of bitter anger washed over me. If anyone was unworthy, it was me.

"Let's figure out how we're going to approach the witch tomorrow," I said, needing to change the subject.

"I think we should try to flush her out of her lair."

"How?"

He flashed a devilish grin. "You're going to find your flames tomorrow."

"You want me to flush her out with *fire*? Have you lost your mind?"

"And wind."

"I can't! You know that I don't know how to wield fire." I wouldn't have an opportunity to practice if we were to leave before sunrise. He couldn't expect me to channel a new element just because a book said I could.

"Your magic won't challenge you in your unicorn form. I believe in you. And... if you can't produce fire, we'll improvise."

I sighed, resigned. "Fine... I'll try. But don't get your hopes up. Either way, tomorrow we shall show the witch what happens when you try to snare a unicorn." I spoke more confidently than I felt, but what other choice did I have? It was a death sentence to not face her. It was probably a death sentence either way. At least I'd have Raf by my side.

Once we'd both stuffed our faces, lying splayed out on the floor, bellies distended like two lazy leopards, Raf yawned and said, "We should go to bed. You need as much rest as possible before the Oracle. I'll sleep on the floor."

I made a snort of protest. "No way, this is your room. You can shift into a cat if you're too chaste to sleep beside me in your faerie form."

"Hmm... there's an idea. Am I more likely to get back scratches in my feline form?" He arched a brow at me and my stomach gave a nervous flip. I loved how he teased me. With so much tension between us, so much uncertainty ahead, it was a miracle that he could make me smile.

"Sorry to burst your bubble, but I've decided I'm more of a dog person." It had been meant as a joke, but suddenly there was a lion-shaped elephant in the room.

"Ah... fair enough. Well, I promise to behave myself." A long silence filled the room as Raf helped me off the floor and into his bed. I crawled under the covers, facing away, as I heard layers of clothing drop to the floor. The bed sagged when he climbed in beside me. I tried to ignore the clean cedar scent that enveloped me.

As I was beginning to drift off, Raf broke the silence. "Did I mention I've been working on a wolf form?"

I smiled into my pillow. "Big wet nose? Fluffy tail? I bet you're adorable."

The bed rocked with laughter. "Big sharp teeth too. And if you scratch *just* the right spot, I might let you leash me. Fetch a ball... Destroy your enemies."

I swatted him with my pillow. "*Go to bed*, you dirty dog." I didn't turn to look at him, but I could feel him smiling.

FORTY-SEVEN

R af and I fumbled to get our clothes on in the dim light of a dying fire. The cold bit at my nose as he launched us into the air in his pegasus form and we sailed towards the mountains under a blanket of stars.

The first glimmer of dawn nearly brought me to tears with its beauty. Once the sun was peering over the lake, we were already soaring over lilac mountains, surrounded by the most glorious sunrise I'd ever seen. We were in the middle of a peachy pink oil painting, full of colors and textures that I hadn't known existed until this moment.

As we began to descend, cold wind whipped at my face, making me grateful for the fur-lined coat I was wearing. Even with the ice that ran through my veins, my limbs were numb by the time we landed in a thinning patch of forest.

Rafael was all business, immediately barking orders at me once we'd touched ground. "You can change into your animal form now. We want her spies to tell her you're on your way—that you're alone. I'll shift into a bird and be by your side the entire time. If there's any hint of danger, I'll be ready."

I nodded, trying to find my courage. My body hesitated, still traumatized from the events of yesterday. I took a few deep breaths, closed my eyes, and imagined myself back in the sky with Raf, far from anything that could hurt us.

I blinked and took in my surroundings through the eyes of a unicorn. Rafael had shifted as well and sat high in a tree, tracking me as I began walking towards the witch's lair. The birds stopped singing as trees grew scarce and a glittering purple cavern came into view.

Sentinels spotted me, standing guard in the depthless black eyes of the skull-shaped rock. As they came down to greet me, I noticed they were different than the last set of men—though they had the same sunken eyes and dull, sagging skin.

My instincts were screaming at me to run, but an even stronger impulse told me to *fight*. To destroy this place. Dark magic had reigned here long enough.

"She's ready to see you. Please follow us." Their hollow voices rang out in unison. I didn't budge.

They gaped at me, repeating themselves. "You must follow us if you want to see the Oracle." I stood my ground. They reached out to touch my neck and I reared up, pointing my horn at them in warning.

"What's your game? Do you wish to see her or not?" They hissed, shielding themselves when my head lowered in their direction.

Out of morbid curiosity, or perhaps some primal instinct, I commanded my magic to break the spell they were under. A white light shot from my horn, hitting one of them square in the chest. I reeled back, surprised at how responsive my magic had been. Pure energy shot from me like a bolt of lightning.

He screamed, shriveling and decaying before my eyes. His sockets caved in first, his nose followed. Fingers turned to bone, then dust. He'd rotted into... *nothing*. The only trace left of him was a pile of white sand and a few scraps of clothing. I should've been appalled, and yet I could almost feel his soul thanking me as it floated away on an invisible wind. Finally free.

"You think destroying my creations will get me to come out? The only thing you've succeeded at is making me angry. You shall meet me in my lair or *die* waiting!" The witch's voice rang out from her sentinel, now retreating back into the cave.

"*What a time for experimentation, Goldie.*" Raf's laugh echoed between my ears. He'd told me Fae could speak mind to mind in their animal forms, but I still wasn't prepared when I heard his silky voice inside my head, like he was whispering in my ear.

I concentrated as I sent my thoughts back to him. "*I don't think we'll be able to flush her out of her lair. She knows I only have a few more days to visit her before I must pay the cost or die.*"

"Let's at least try to smoke her out. Fire should clear out anything else living in there too." The last thing I wanted to do was summon fire. I gave a shaky breath and began walking towards the cave entrance. *"You'll want to use your wind magic as well,"* he continued. *"Fan the flames into the cave as far as you can. Use an ice shield to protect yourself."*

"You're very bossy." I resisted looking back at him, but felt his answering grin.

I tried to summon what I knew of fire. It was mesmerizing, unpredictable... *dangerous.* There were many parallels between the element and the male who wielded it. I opened a small door within my mind that I'd locked all thoughts of Galen in. Compartmentalizing was the only thing keeping me upright, but I had to pull from my knowledge of fire magic.

I was pummeled with pain as I let myself think of him—how *easy* I'd made it for him. I'd been a doe-eyed fool caught in his crossfire, forgetting even the most basic of survival lessons. *Play with fire, get burned.*

I stood paralyzed at the mouth of the cave as feelings of Galen rendered me useless. I aimed my horn at the tunnel, put up a shield of ice, and willed my magic to send out flame. I'd watched Galen do it a thousand times.

The tiniest ember sparked in front of me before sputtering to the ground. The witch's cackle reverberated through the cave, making me dance like a dressage horse as I resisted the urge to bolt.

Crushed velvet brushed against my mind as Raf said, *"Instead of thinking about magic, think about the element. What does fire mean to you, beyond my brother? Nights where it kept you warm, kept your loneliness company, illuminated the pages of a dirty book..."*

I choked back a laugh, shaking my head. *"I can't. He's ruined fire for me."*

"No. He's already taken enough from you. You and the flame that lives inside of you are one in the same—both bringers of light. Darkness cannot contain you or claim you—just like he couldn't. Take back your light. Burn it down, Goldie. You can do this."

I wanted to reject his words, but instead I exhaled and let them sink in. Rafael was right. Galen hadn't wanted a partner, he'd wanted a fix. No amount of love, no amount of magic, would ever be enough. I couldn't save him; he had to save himself.

He'd done his best to snuff out my flame, but I could still feel it burning, deep inside my chest. I let that small ember grow until it consumed me... until I remembered my greater purpose, beyond Galen. I had people to save and a witch to kill. I had a home to return to.

It was me or her—and I would not cower. *Ever again*. Maybe once I'd been easy prey, but not anymore. I turned around and walked away from the entrance. Once I was far enough back, I sprinted forward, screaming at my magic to blaze.

Flame shot from my horn in shades of indigo and white. It streamed out in a monstrous wave aimed right at the mouth of the cave. I knew it was burning hotter than any natural fire, by the color alone. The skull seemed to shrink from the flames as I burned through its belly. I came to a sliding stop at the entrance and sent wind after the fire, pushing it farther and farther down the cave.

First I heard screaming. The shrieking rang in my ears, making me grit my teeth as I held the flame as long as I could. Then I felt movement. Pebbles on the ground began to vibrate. A herd of *something* was racing towards me.

I broke off the flame and raced back towards Raf—towards a thin line of pine trees that seemed to reach for me with outstretched arms. The screaming got louder, and then too many spiders to count were crawling out of the cavern's many orifices.

They completely covered the rock with their scuttling legs. Each one was the size of a large dog with shiny, sharp fangs bared, ready to give their life for their master. Some were on fire, but still running at full speed. There must've been *hundreds* of them.

"*Flame, now!*" Rafael shouted.

I panicked and created an icy wind instead. Some froze solid and bounced back, while others continued towards us, unscathed. Rafael shifted into his Fae form and ran to my side, sending a tornado of shadow at them. Where darkness touched, they disintegrated into nothing.

They were close enough that I could see them in detail now. Some were black with shiny round abdomens and long, stilt-like legs. Others were burnt orange and brown, covered in fine hair, creeping low to the ground.

As they approached, they reared up on their back legs, fangs glistening. We threw up our shields simultaneously. Two spheres of ice and shadow encompassed us, while a living carpet of arachnids swarmed us. Tapping their legs on our shields, they searched for any weak points.

Spider silk clung to branches as they dangled from the trees, finding new angles to terrorize us. Rafael's shadows weren't eliminating them fast enough.

"Close your eyes," I shouted through our mental bond. Starlight erupted from my horn, cracking like lightning and illuminating the top of the mountain in a brilliant glow. It radiated out in waves of pure energy, before a new round of screaming began.

A chorus of shrieking spiders formed a haunting melody as they began to roll over onto their backs, curling in on themselves. One by one, they turned to piles of sand. If starlight broke curses and spells, then the entire herd of spiders must've been created by the Oracle's dark magic. And *holy gods,* my magic. I could feel it in my chest, my veins... pumping through my heart. I felt electrified—*invincible.*

Raf and I exchanged a look of disbelief. "I know you don't want to be a savior, but you aren't helping your case with magic like that," he said, panting.

The witch's voice called out from the caves. *"A powerful form, indeed. You may have destroyed my children, but once your horn is mine, I'll make an entire army. I look forward to tasting that magic of yours. It's been a long while since I've tasted sunshine. You're not worthy of the power you wield, human filth."*

Rafael placed a hand on my cheek. "She's lashing out because she's nervous. I won't leave your side."

A shadow dragon *was* a convenient bodyguard. Our best chance of survival relied heavily on him killing her as fast as possible. What business did I have even showing up to this fight—besides the fact that I had to. I was not a fighter, but I would become one if that's what the world needed from me. And this horn *did* give me a boost of confidence. I might not know how to wield a sword, but my magic... it was unstoppable. And Galen had known it. The thought made me stumble over my feet as we made our way into the cave.

"Watch yourself, Princess," Raf murmured, keeping a hand on my back.

Most of the debris we'd passed in the cave during our first visit was now blackened or nothing but ash. Some items were still on fire. I spotted a small toy unicorn burning and used my ice to douse it.

"Superstitious?" Raf asked, picking it up and putting it in his pocket. I snorted in response.

"Personally, I'll take luck wherever I can find it," he said with a dimpled grin.

We moved carefully as we made our way deeper into the cave, leaving a trail of ice and vines along the walls. All I had to do was see her in my unicorn form and the cost would be fulfilled. I wasn't above running if it meant staying alive.

I started to breathe in short, shallow gasps as claustrophobia set in. Raf kept a steady hand on my back in an attempt to comfort me. Once it was too dark to see in front of us, I emitted a soft light from my horn and the purple walls of the cave lit up. We were surrounded by glittering, crystal-like rock that twinkled in shades of lavender and violet as the light refracted through it. It would've been beautiful, had I not been so petrified.

When we began running into thick webbing, I knew we were close. It stuck to my face, my horn, and legs, causing me to trip over my feet. Raf made us stop several times while he methodically removed the silk that clung to me.

It was so dark that we couldn't see more than a few feet in front of us and I was afraid to shine my light any brighter and draw attention. He sent his shadows into crevices and corners, making sure we couldn't be ambushed. Panic squeezed at my ribs, making me light-headed. I was too large to maneuver quickly through the narrow walkways that we now stood in. I could barely turn around. This was suicide. We needed to move, *now*.

I sprinted forward in a frantic instinct for survival as Rafael raced after me. I began to slide on loose rock and screamed, surprised to hear the whinny that erupted from me instead. Unable to find a foothold, I continued to careen down the steep path. This was a trap. *We were going to die.* I somersaulted forward, preparing to topple off a sheer cliff and into the dark abyss below.

Just as I was beginning to accept my fate, Raf lassoed a vine around my neck, lunged for me, and turned us into shadow.

FORTY-EIGHT

We landed in a large, hollowed-out den. Sunlight trickled through cracks in the rock, illuminating the Kunzite ceilings. Icicle-shaped formations hung down precariously. As we caught our breath, I pushed my fear aside and grounded myself. There was no room for doubt. *She would be the one who died today.*

"That's more like it," Rafael replied. Apparently that thought had been loud enough for him to hear. An endless network of spider silk surrounded us. They all led to a single, massive web in the center of the room.

I could sense her before I heard her. Ice crystals formed in my blood as she approached. Ancient, dark power pulsed around us. Something wet dripped onto my head and I grimaced, apprehensively peering up.

An enormous spider hung suspended in the air, slowly spinning as she moved spindly legs towards us, unhurriedly assessing.

She was a shade of bruised violet, blending in with the rock walls that surrounded her. The Kunzite was unpolished and rough compared to her glossy exoskeleton. Everything about her screamed huntress, including the bright white hourglass that flashed along her abdomen.

Startled, I reared up on my hind legs, nearly falling backwards. The glow from my horn reflected on something bone white in the distance and my blood went cold. Countless lumps were trapped in her web, wrapped tightly in white silk, lifelessly hanging. *Bodies.* Dozens of bodies.

I caught a glimpse of a hand, a foot... some looked partially decayed, others freshly killed. Nausea roiled through me. I backed up slowly, blind with panic. I had seen her... now we just needed to leave with our lives.

She dropped to the ground with a loud thud. Moving at the speed of light, she forced us to leap out of the way, effectively separating us. She came after me first and I acted on instinct, sending out ice arrows that bounced off her impenetrable shell or shattered on impact.

Raf struck with his shadows next. He lassoed her legs with his dark magic, intending to disable her—instead he enraged her. She swung towards him, coming down hard on his shield with dagger-like fangs. They sliced into his shield and he jumped out of the way, inches from getting pierced.

I heard her laugh rattle through my brain and it was enough to cause temporary paralysis. *"You thought bringing your Prince along would save you? Who should I eat first? He smells nearly as good as you."*

Her eight legs scrambled forward as she tried to corner me. My horn exploded with light and she backed up a step, but didn't disintegrate like the others had. It had given her pause, though. Raf looped a vine around one of her legs and pulled her away from me.

She whirled, charging towards him with lethal velocity. The sound that escaped me was a bleating cry for him to watch out. He disappeared, then reappeared behind her, sending spears of shadow at her. They ricocheted, hitting the walls of the cave, before turning into smoke. She scrambled up the side of the wall onto the ceiling and flew towards us, preparing to drop on top of us.

Raf threw out a shield that stopped her fall momentarily, but her fangs tore through it like it was made of paper. Her heavy body shook the cavern as she landed, causing rubble to rain from the ceiling.

They moved impossibly fast. All my eyes could catch were blurry streaks of black and purple in the dim light of the cave as they danced circles around each other. He shadowed himself on top of her, preparing to drive his sword into her head, but she reared up and sent him flying.

He turned to mist, before nearly hitting a wall, and then he was under her, trying to stab her hourglass with the blade. He swung with the strength of a god, but the obsidian steel hit an even stronger material, shattering on impact. She side stepped him and sliced his back with one of the spikes along her legs. My heart stopped when I saw his blood spill, but he was gone before she could get her fangs in him.

"Aim for the hourglass. She's trying to protect her abdomen—it's her vulnerable spot," Raf yelled.

I ran towards her and angled my horn at her belly, but she was too quick. She charged and I skirted out of the way, missing her fangs by inches. I felt fear roll off her when my horn was close. Raf was right—my horn would be strong enough to break through her exoskeleton—but how was I going to get close enough to stab her?

Each time she dropped from the ceiling, she slammed hard onto the ground, shaking the entire cave. Rocks fell around us, adding to the chaos. She wanted us rattled and ripe with fear.

Rafael erupted into his dragon form, snapping razor-sharp teeth at her, aiming for her belly. She scuttled up the wall, away from his jaws. He was so large that I had little room to maneuver as his tail thrashed in frustration. He blew violet fire at her, warming the air around us, but she emerged from the flames unscathed.

She dropped to the ground, preparing to bite Rafael, but he shifted into a bird and flew out of the way. She jumped towards him and knocked him out of the air. He hit the cave wall and my heart nearly imploded at the sight. I didn't know if he was alive, *but I knew she was dead.*

My rage was a spitting volcano that could turn entire worlds to ash. She lunged for me and I had just enough time to wheel around and charge her. Reeling back, she screamed as she retreated. Raf's body had shifted back to his faerie form, but he appeared unconscious. Every fiber in my being wanted to go to him, give him my blood, *heal him,* but I couldn't lose focus.

I was on my own. I couldn't run—I *wouldn't* run without Raf. I stood guard over his body, holding my head low as I kept my horn directed at her. Indigo flames roared around me and she crawled back to the ceiling.

"An immortal witch, scared of a unicorn?" I said mockingly.

"Just choosing the right moment to strike," she purred back. *"I enjoy playing with my food, you see."*

"Then come play." I held steady as she scuttled towards me and reared up in an attack stance. As she lifted her front legs, I galloped forward, sliding under her. I drove my head up with everything I had. My horn perforated through her hard shell with a deafening crunch as she landed on me, fangs extended.

We both fell to the ground. My legs collapsed under me as the white-hot sting of her fangs sunk into my haunches. The burn from her venom sliced through me, hotter than a freshly forged blade.

My horn was wedged deep inside of her, so I did the only thing I could; I poured all my light into her belly, melting her from the inside out. I couldn't escape the screaming that reverberated against my skull as a silver, syrupy substance oozed from her, onto me, searing my skin.

As her poison entered my blood stream, my veins caught fire. I writhed and struggled to breathe as blinding pain consumed me. My magic sang a war cry as it battled against her venom.

She curled and twitched as she fought the true death. Her heart pulsed around me as it slowed, then sluggishly halted to a stop. As her body relaxed, the full weight of it crushed me, constricting my ability to breathe. My heart thumped slower and slower, while venom continued to spread. My lungs grew heavy with fluid and I started to convulse. I closed my eyes, too tired to fight any longer.

FORTY-NINE

I blinked as the world around me came into focus. I was laying outside the cave entrance, under the blood-red glow of the setting sun. Rafael... where... where was he? I frantically tried to stand, tripping over my feet and gracefully face planting. My horn stabbed into the ground before I toppled onto my side.

"Hey, hey... Goldie, it's okay. We're okay." Raf's voice was calm and steady and an instant salve. His face came into my line of vision as I panted, sides heaving, struggling to breathe. My lungs burned. My head was pounding. My chest throbbed.

The only thing that didn't hurt were my toes and I was pretty confident that I didn't have toes in my current form. Raf's dimpled smile was enough to slow my heart and clear my mind. I closed my eyes and concentrated until I felt magic coat me like a warm, tingling blanket.

I held my hands up towards the sky, squinting as I counted my fingers. Ten. *My toes hurt too.*

Rafael's face lit up with relief as he pulled me into a hug and kissed me on the temple. "I didn't know what her venom was made of, if your body would be strong enough to fight it. I could hear your heart beating faintly, but you haven't budged in hours. I moved us out of the cave, but I was afraid to take you any further."

I exhaled slowly, trying not to puke. "Sorry... for scaring you," I said in a cracked voice, needing water. Before I'd finished the thought, a canteen of water was resting on my parched lips. I choked down a few mouthfuls before pushing it away.

I was disoriented and queasy, but I was alive. *Raf was alive.* "Is she dead?" I asked tentatively.

"Yes. Thanks to you, witch-slayer. And you saved my life... I'm sorry I let you down when you needed me most," he said, offering me a hand. I took it, standing up with a groan.

"You didn't let me down," I replied with a tired smile. "You would've had her, if you had a horn... but a Prince I know—who's *occasionally* right—told me they're rare. And it was high time I returned the favor. Can we go home? I feel like a five-hundred-pound arachnid sat on me."

"She was probably closer to one thousand pounds—and that's exactly what happened. I found you crushed beneath her, your horn buried in her abdomen. Not a sight I ever want to see again."

I laughed. "I'd be happy to never see another spider again."

"I don't know... I think you were born for this, Princess."

I raised a brow. "Born for what?"

"Saving the world... and the occasional Prince."

I snorted. "An *occasional* Prince who is a *constant* pain in the ass."

He pinched my side and I screamed with laughter, before we made our way home.

Rafael's room was a welcome sanctuary after what we'd faced today. I looked at his bed and wanted nothing more than to crawl into it... but we needed to go to Louis. They were waiting for Raf before making their move and infiltrating the prison.

"You should rest before we head out," I said. He looked as tired as I felt, with purple circles under his eyes.

"*We?* Please Marigold... stay here. I'll fly back to you as soon as the fighting is over and the prisoners are free. Louis can lead them to Monrovia without me. I won't be able to leave your side out there... and they *need* my help. I can't imagine the amount of people that are out searching for you on Galen's orders. It's not safe."

I contemplated what he said. Wherever Raf was, that's where I felt safest, but I didn't want to be selfish. I knew he was needed. I didn't want to be a distraction. The truth was, I did want to sleep... forever. My depression was pulling me down. Even *standing* felt like an energy drain that I couldn't muster. But what if they needed my help?

"You think I'm safest in Monrovia... so close to Galen?" I sat on the bed, trying to think beyond the fog of exhaustion.

"This room is the most warded and protected place in Monrovia. The women downstairs can bring you meals throughout the day. You can rest and build your strength for what's ahead. Of course I want you to come; I hate the idea of leaving you behind, but I'll be able to travel faster and fight more effectively, if you stay here. I don't know what threats will be waiting at the prison, but I know I don't want you near any of them. However, it's your decision."

I let my weariness decide. "I'll stay. You'll come back as soon as you can? If there are people who need my blood to heal, I want to be there to help."

"I'll race back as soon as possible. I won't abandon you. I promise."

As soon as Raf left, I fell into a deep pit of loneliness—like I was grieving the loss of my parents again. I regretted my decision to stay almost immediately. Being in Rafael's room, with only my thoughts, was *not* what I needed right now.

I saw Galen in the crackling fire, Raf in the shadows, my mother in the bathroom mirror's reflection. I couldn't summon any strength... any hope. The mixture of fatigue and depression *did* allow me to sleep for almost two days straight, at least. The Oracle's venom had been strong. I was sure it would've killed me in my human form.

By the third day, my blood was alive with magic and I finally felt recovered. Rafael should've been back by now. I dared a look out the window and was disheartened to see heavy rain flooding the cobblestone streets below. The creek that ran through the city was overflowing.

He wouldn't be able to fly in this weather. It was difficult to know if the storm would help or hinder their rescue mission. If they had hundreds of humans with them, the rain and mud would significantly slow them down, but maybe the rain would also keep them hidden; surely it would be difficult to track anything in this.

Realizing I might be alone for several more days, I became increasingly restless and agitated... There were plenty of books to read, but I couldn't
focus. My mind was only capable of descending deeper into darkness.
Rafael had been holding me together more than I wanted to admit. Without him, I felt like a shipwreck slowly sinking into a deep abyss. I began
to obsess over worst-case scenarios. What if Rafael and Louis had been
captured? What if they were dead? How long should I stay here before I
went to find them?

By the fourth day, I was itching to leave the room and search for them.
Raf's scent was probably lost to the storm, especially since he'd flown, but
something told me I'd still be able to find him.

My spiraling was disrupted when a flicker of magic pulsed down
my spine. Frost formed on my fingers as I sensed danger. Someone was
approaching. My ears pricked when I heard footsteps down the hallway,
and then my eyes darted to the rattling doorknob.

Rafael? I braced myself as the bedroom door swung open and a
silhouette appeared before me. My heart leapt, before it crashed to the
ground.

FIFTY

G *alen*. I stumbled backwards in disbelief, nearly falling to the floor as he prowled towards me. He was still shining bright with my magic, but as I studied his twisting, shifting soul, the gold burn away, until only a dark red glow remained. His mask was off. And he was *angry*.

"Did you really think I wouldn't find you? You are mine. We're *fated*, Marigold." He spoke like a snake charmer, continuing to stalk closer. Pausing, his eyes fell upon the emerald ring sitting on Rafael's nightstand.

By the time his focus was back on me, I was ready. He darted towards me, but I'd already slammed a wind shield between us. I sent ice towards his feet, freezing him in place as I scrambled past him, out the door—only to meet Robert and Alaric blocking my exit to the stairs.

"We don't want to hurt you, Lady. Don't resist," Robert said, having the gall to look guilty. I whipped wind at them and they both tumbled down the stairs. They hadn't bothered to shield themselves against me. I was getting used to being underestimated. I raced after them, using wind to propel me over their somersaulting bodies, landing on the ground floor below. I looked back to see Galen sauntering down the stairs, curling his lip in disgust at his two guards laying in a heap.

I ran towards the front door, past screaming prostitutes. There were only a few scattered customers left. I readied to shift into my animal form, but was stopped by Galen's shadow-wielding trainer, Frederick, blocking the exit. Before I had time to strategize, he'd shadowed *inside* my shield—like Rafael so often did during our training—restraining me with little effort.

I fought back; jabbing him with my elbow, stomping on his feet, then sending out frozen wind that swirled through the room, knocking over furniture and people. He was too strong, too quick, as he pinned my hands firmly behind my back. He stayed in a state of partial shadow that made my attacks as useful as an arrow trying to pierce mist.

Galen took measured strides towards me with a satisfied smile on his face. "Well, this was easier than I expected. Where's my brother? Did he already grow bored of you?" Galen gripped my chin in his hands, looking into my eyes. I lurched away from his touch and refused to answer him.

"Fine, keep his secrets. He'll come looking for you eventually and then I'll get my revenge. I'll teach him to take things that belong to me." He pulled out a pair of stone cuffs and the magic in my veins shuddered.

"Please don't, Galen. I'll come willingly. Please, don't cuff me." I sobbed, terrified of the numbing feeling that came with losing access to my magic.

"It's just temporary, little dove. Once you submit to me—once you're my blood-bonded—this chapter can be buried in the past. I don't want to hurt you more than necessary, so don't make this more difficult than it has to be."

I bucked and screamed as Galen passed the cuffs to his shadow wielder, continuing to thrash even as they clicked around my wrists. I felt the eternal light inside in me blink out. The ice in my veins dissolved into *nothing;* my restless wind grew stagnant. I was hollow. Everything that had blossomed within me shriveled and died. I wanted to crumple to the ground and cry, but I couldn't give him the satisfaction.

He was a *monster*. He'd burned Rafael—his own brother... *What would he do to me?* The male that I thought I knew was ash in the wind. Our love had been a beautiful illusion, like the moon on the water—all it had taken was a few storm clouds to show me that it had never been real.

The shock of my predicament made me complacent as he gripped me by the arm and led me to the carriage that waited for us. Once he'd shoved me in, I sat in silence, drenched from the short walk, while he sat across from me. The rain clung to my clothes and a chill settled over my skin, penetrating deep into my bones.

"Rafael was stupid to leave you alone," Galen drawled. "I suppose he didn't know Robert was a bloodhound shifter, capable of finding anyone, anywhere. Especially *your* scent that he's studied for months.

"My brother must've grown too comfortable, assuming he's still the most powerful faerie in this world. Fortunately, for me, *your magic*—soon to be *my magic*—is flowing through me. And it appears it outranks his. His wards crumbled under my flames once Robert found out where you were. Not many can track past wards so strong, but Robert is *exceptionally* gifted. Did you think I kept him around for the conversation?" He laughed and I began shivering with a deep loathing. It was a laugh that I'd adored until recently. I didn't know that heartbreak and grief were one in the same until now. Every word spoken was another shovel of dirt, burying the male I'd cared for, killing the love we'd created.

"You'll learn to forgive me with time. We're well-matched. We'll breed powerful children and be capable rulers. The sooner you accept this, the sooner you'll gain your freedom back." He stroked my cheek with the back of his hand and I jerked away. He sighed and pulled out a flask of something—whiskey, by the smell of it. He took a swig before offering me some. I refused.

"Drink," he ordered. A flame appeared in his other hand. He weaved it between his fingers, taunting me, while bringing the flask to my mouth.

I took a sip, glaring at him. And another. And another. Until I was sputtering and coughing. "To the death of any affection I once held for you," I said, spitting the words.

He caught the whiskey trailing down my chin with his thumb and chuckled. "I'm going to teach you manners. Soon you'll be begging for *anything* I offer you, including my *affection*."

The alcohol quickly warmed my limbs and I fell back in silence. I settled my head against the carriage window as it bounced along. It was heart-wrenching to look at him and remember what we'd shared—how much I'd thought he cared. We'd shattered so quickly, so spectacularly.

Galen peered out the window before announcing that we were almost to the castle gates. "It'd best if my mother doesn't find out I have you. As cruel as you might find me, I promise you, I'm the closest thing you have to a friend now. My brothers will not rescue you, so behave yourself or things will get much worse."

He cloaked me before leading me to a familiar door towards the back of the castle. We were going to the dungeons. I began trembling as we descended. Instead of turning towards the open arena where he trained, he took me down a narrow hallway, into a small room that flickered with soft light from a single candle.

I spied something across the hall in the adjacent room. It appeared to be the innards of a dead animal, encased in a large glass tube. It hung from the ceiling like dry-aged meat, making my stomach churn uneasily.

My chest pounded with a deep primal fear. Whatever it was, it was unnatural. I could feel magic oozing from it like thick tar. Galen slammed the door when he noticed me staring. "Wha-what was that?" I stammered. The remains of something—*someone?*

"A project the Elders have been working on. You're right to be scared. Humans will soon be obsolete in Nymera. The Elders have found a way to harvest magic from human hearts. The blood continues to pump, even when their souls are gone. They plan to kill every last human and make countless devices like that. Soon the Kingdom will control the entire magic supply. We'll have total and complete power—and enough blood to take care of all *loyal* citizens." He looked smug, but I saw fear in the whites of his eyes.

I tried to grasp what he was telling me, still reeling from the horror of it. "I just saw... a human heart, contained in some kind of vessel? You're collecting magic from a dead person's harvested organ? An abomination! They're monsters—*you're a monster.*" I kicked and screamed... trying to knock him down. He sighed as he pulled me to him with a hard tug.

"Don't worry, love. I won't let *that* happen to you. I don't plan on sharing. You taste too good." He shoved me to the bed and I took stock of my surroundings.

I was in a small room with stone walls and floors. No windows—and definitely no fireplace or bath. Just a bed, a chamber pot, and a small desk with several metal tools sitting on it. My eyes widened when I identified small knives, hooks, scissors, and saws... *torture devices.*

Galen followed my gaze. "I've used this room for interrogation before. I don't plan to use any of those on you—as long as you don't do anything stupid. Yield to me. Once you blood-bond with me, this will all go away."

Silent tears began to fall, despite the strength I wanted to show.

"You poor, gentle-hearted creature. Always crying, always trying to save someone. It must be exhausting, always trying to do the right thing." My eyes narrowed at him as he continued. "There must be a part of you that wants to give in... to let me take control. I'm your destiny, after all." He tried to brush back my hair and I scrambled away from him.

"We'll undoubtedly be great together. We *have* been great together. I'll eventually forgive you for running off to Rafael. After all, I've been letting Isla lick my wounds. I'll teach you how I like to be licked... perhaps she can show you. Monogamy gets boring. You're young... you don't understand the larger picture, but you'll learn in time. I don't expect perfection from you, but I do expect *obedience*." He took the engagement ring out of his pocket and held it up to me. "What do you say?"

I spat at him in answer. That proposal had somehow been even worse than the last. He had the audacity to look outraged as he wiped spittle from his face. "That was uncalled for, *pet*." He huffed, before sending me flying as he backhanded me.

The pain was instant, searing, and somehow stung more than the spider venom that had burned like acid. My cheek throbbed as I sat hunched on the floor in disbelief, holding my face, completely gutted. He'd continue to hurt me if I didn't obey. His flames would be next. I clamored towards the corner of the room and curled into a tight ball.

"Your willfulness is tiresome." Galen sighed. "I gave you patience and protection, and in return you ran to my brother. Just remember, this is all your doing. We could've done this the easy way, but you decided to become disobedient." He stood up straight and smoothed down his green velvet tunic. He nodded to the guards and they gripped me by the arms, securing me to the wall.

Prisoner—that's what I'd been to him all along. I'd made it so *easy* for him, but now my blinders were off and I planned on fighting like hell.

He couldn't force me to blood-bond. Could he?

"I'll leave you here to mull over your choices. Don't make me wait too long..." He glanced at the desk, before methodically gathering up the tools, one at a time, and handing them to Robert. I laid on the bed in shock, rubbing my swollen cheek.

My Prince Charming had been a villain all along.

FIFTY-ONE

I stared into eternal darkness, eyes glazed over and unfocused. Time was a winter night, stretching on and on. My candle had gone out and I no longer knew if it was night or day. My stomach grumbled angrily at me. How long would it take Rafael and Louis to find me? What if they'd been captured too?

My mouth was parched, my lips chapped. I tried to ignore the relentless thirst as dread crept in. With no magic, no light, I felt completely upside down. I inhaled faster and faster until I had to lay my cheek against the cold stone floor to avoid the spins. Hours passed and still no one came. I faded in and out of consciousness, wondering how long it would take for me to die.

I heard my mother's voice. "*Stay strong, Goldie. You're not alone.*"

I repeated her words over and over. *I am not alone. I am not alone.*

I am not alone. And yet, I felt more alone than I ever had. I was beginning to recall memories of my father, who I hadn't been able to picture clearly for years. Dream and reality began to blur together as fragments of another time came back to me. It was like trying to put a smudged and shredded letter back together.

His blonde hair hung over my mother's limp body as he shook her lifeless form, telling her to wake up. He seemed almost convinced that she'd be able to. Ophelia leaned down and whispered something in his ear, and then he'd simply... left. What had she said to him? I watched him walk away, not knowing it was the last time I'd see him. He hadn't said goodbye.

I remembered gardening with my mother with soil-covered hands. My father teaching me to ride a horse. Playing hide and seek in the loft of the barn. My mother's bruised cheek after a fall down the stairs. Blood. So much blood... soaking into the hardwood. My mother's pale, lifeless hand. Her hunched body as she scrubbed at the stained floors.

A bright light blinded me as someone entered the room. I breathed in Galen's smoky scent and squinted up to find him staring at me with a dead expression on his face. He set down a plate of food and water before lighting my candle with the snap of a finger. I didn't bother to peel myself off the floor.

"I've been thinking of you down here... cold and alone. This isn't easy for me. Are you ready to forgive me?" he asked softly. I could hear the internal conflict in his voice. Some part of me felt bad for him and his warped mind.

"Don't do this, Galen. I know you want to be good—I've seen it, felt it. Marry Isla and let me return to Erador. Respect what we shared and let me go. *Please.*" I pleaded and knelt at his feet, bowing from exhaustion rather than a desire to grovel. He stayed quiet for a moment.

"I can't," he said in a clipped tone. "Your magic is too powerful, and I know what you are. Only an imbecile would give that up. You are *mine* to claim, the Oracle said as much. Blood-bond with me. Give me your magic, open a portal for my people, *then* I'll let you go." He squatted beside me, offering me a cup of water. I didn't respond, afraid he might hit me or worse if I outright refused him.

"Very well." His voice turned flat again. "Then I'll take what I need and give you more time to consider your options, or lack thereof." He pulled me up by my arms and I struggled against him, attempting to knee him in the groin.

He turned me, holding me firmly, as I flailed in his arms. He pressed against my backside and I panicked, becoming frantic in my efforts to evade him. "Be still. I'm not going to force myself on you," he said gruffly as I continued to fight. "Well... I'm going to take your blood, but I won't touch you beyond that... if that's your wish."

"It's my wish," I sobbed. "Don't touch me!" I yelled, twisting, trying to bite anywhere I could. "Help! Someone help me," I cried out to the void.

He gave an exasperated sigh and walked me forward until I was pushed against the stone of the wall. "You used to *love* when I took you this way," he whispered into my ear. "And you will again. Once my brother's *poison* has left you. But for now, this will be enough." He brushed my hair back—kissing my shoulder, my neck. I froze, rigid with fear, as he took a sharp intake of breath and bit down.

To my relief, it didn't hurt. To my alarm, it made me go supine, relaxing into the rush of euphoria as I let out a humiliating moan. The bridge linking us took away the hollow ache in my veins, allowing me to *feel* my magic. I tried to call upon it as he drank from me, but it hovered just out of reach. There was a small comfort in knowing that it was right there, waiting for me—because he couldn't keep me cuffed forever. I'd strike hard and fast when I got the chance. He pulled away and left without another word and I slumped against the bed, depleted and dejected.

"Goldie," my mother's voice was urgent as it attempted to rouse me.

"What?" I groaned.

"We need to go. He's coming."

"Who's coming? We've been at this for weeks. I'm tired. Even in my dreams, I'm not allowed to rest," I snapped irritably.

"Quickly, get up. Now." She sounded so frantic that I opened an eye. We were in the loft of the barn, surrounded by blankets and piles of hay. I had a toy unicorn clutched in my hands—the one Rafael had rescued from the cave.

I sat up groggily. "Who is—"

"Quiet," Mama hushed me with a sharp whisper. "He's here."

All it took was a glance in her direction to know that she was absolutely terrified. It was enough to sober me. She was trembling, gripping my shoulders protectively with both hands. I attempted to speak again and she covered my mouth.

"Eliana..." A male's voice echoed across the barn, causing my pulse to soar. Slow, deliberate footsteps hung in the air as he sauntered directly below us. I couldn't see him, but his voice made the hairs on the back of my neck stand up. My father. We were hiding from my father.

I tried to count the days, but it was impossible without the sun and moon's guidance. I was almost certain that Galen had been bringing me food twice a day and taking my magic once a day. I kept a small kernel of hope that I'd see Raf at the door, but Galen was always the one who appeared. I was in such a dark place that I began to look forward to his visits, knowing his bite would take me to oblivion, if only for a moment.

"You've been here a week now," Galen announced, jarring me from a dream of Rafael and I flying through an onyx sky. "Only three more nights until the festival. I'll be announcing you as my future bride at the party. It would be convenient if you came around before then. I don't need you making a scene, especially with how hard Isla has been working to make this festival an occasion to remember. She'll be disappointed enough when she hears the news."

He was a sociopath.

"Your mother did a number on you," I said through gritted teeth.

He contemplated, rubbing his jaw. "Yes... she did. But she also taught me how to get what I want. And since love doesn't come easily to me, power shall be my beacon. Let me remind you of the power that I wield." He lifted two orbs of fire into the air. They started out amber in color before reshaping and changing hue as he juggled them back and forth.

"Orange and red flames are more than capable of burning flesh in seconds, but thanks to *your* magic, I now have a rainbow to choose from. I have a theory about the purple flames—I think they can leave even a healer scarred. Which body part do you like the least? We can start there. A pinky toe, perhaps? I hate to mutilate a delicate flower unnecessarily... I'm going to be looking at you for the next millennia, after all." He flashed white teeth at me and I almost vomited at the beauty in his smile. *He was a fraud. An imposter.*

"How could you burn someone that you claim to care for?" I rasped. I was terrified, but I'd withstand it. I wouldn't let him scare me into submission.

"You can make this all go away if you stop denying me what I want. I don't *want* to burn you, love. But I will. You need to learn your place, just as I had to learn mine."

His mother had successfully ruined him—beaten him into obedience. Like an abused animal, he'd learned to bite anyone who got too close. He broke the things he loved, before they could break him. Somewhere along the way, he must've decided that relationships were always conditional and that if he wasn't on top, then he was on the bottom. I hated Sylvia with my entire heart.

"You know nothing of love, so stop calling me *love*," I said, baring my teeth.

He gave a dark laugh. "To be fair, I preferred seduction... over *this*. We had some fun, didn't we? Bow to me or burn. Last chance, my obstinate little pony. Just say *yes*."

I lunged at him in answer, before hitting the ground as chains yanked me back.

"Very well then," he said stiffly. "This is a *taste* of what you can expect if you make a scene at the party."

"Robert, Alaric. Get in here!" he yelled. I shrunk into the corner of the room, trying to make myself small as possible.

"Restrain her," Galen commanded. I begged them to leave me alone. The guards looked apologetic, with drawn brows and sunken shoulders. They pulled me from the floor, each taking an arm.

"Turn her around. Take off her dress."

They hesitated and I felt the heat from his flames roar in response, making them startle and comply. They unfastened my buttons until the top of my body was exposed. I didn't let the shame hit me. I'd already burrowed deep within myself and was too far away to reach, flying through a starry sky.

While Galen sent a whip of flame at my back, I prayed Raf and Louis had gotten the humans out. I visualized them walking through the forest towards Monrovia. They would come for me. *We'd go home.*

He sent another lick of flame towards bare skin, making me scream as my body involuntarily arched, snapping me back to the present. He was making thin, precise lines on either side of my spine. Slash after slash, he burned over the same patch of skin in sadistic repetition.

I lost my footing and then Robert and Alaric were keeping me upright as Galen continued his assault. Each lash destroyed another sliver of my soul, while I waited for the one that would finish me off.

The smell of burnt flesh, blood, and salty tears made my stomach roil and I began to heave up bile. This was more painful than anything I had ever known and would ever know, because this went beyond torture, this was *personal*. This was a loss of faith and the deepest kind of heart break—the ultimate betrayal from someone I'd trusted and loved.

He'd broken me, but not in the way he hoped. I'd never be his, nor would I ever be the same. Forevermore, I'd walk hand in hand with the ghost of the woman I'd almost been—someone who believed in love, someone who believed in happy endings. It was devastating that *Galen*, of all people, had been the one to teach me what romantic love was. My naivety had been his opportunity. He'd helped me transform into a butterfly, only to burn my wings before I could take flight.

"Eliana... I just want to talk. You're only making things worse for yourself—for Marigold. I know you're in the loft. I can smell your fear. Come down now and I won't hurt you."

My mother had stopped breathing, but her grip around me remained firm.

"I'm only going to repeat myself one more time. Come down willingly and I won't hurt Marigold," he said with lethal calm.

Silent tears fell down my mother's face as she slowly detached herself from me with a shaky sigh. "Promise to leave her out of this, Fallon," my mother said softly.

It was quiet enough that her voice traveled through the rafters—quiet enough that I could hear his steady breathing before he answered, "I promise."

I shook my head furiously. No. No... she was so scared. I wouldn't let her go. Together, we could fight him. Together, we could get away.

She moved away from me, towards the ladder, and I lunged for her. "No—you can't," I hissed. "Let me come with you, let me help."

Her head hung low. "The only thing that matters is keeping you safe. Please, stay here—no matter what happens. I'll draw him out, and then you must run, Goldie. Far from here, far from him. Take Skye and go to Ophelia. I'll join you when I can." Her chocolate eyes held endless depth, endless love.

"No... stop." My voice cracked as she descended the ladder. I clung to the sleeves of her white cotton dress, refusing to let her leave.

"Let me go, sweetheart," she said with determination. "It'll be okay."

I refused, but with a burst of magic, she sent me into a pile of hay. By the time I scrambled back to the ledge, my father was holding her by the shoulders, shaking her like a rag doll.

"You stupid, useless female," he growled. "Why can't you just obey your husband, for once?" He roared and shoved her down. She slid across the dirty ground as golden tendrils spilled across her face. It reminded me of the night I'd watched her take her last breaths.

"You bring this on yourself," he seethed. "Every time you run away. It's like you want me to punish you. What will it take to teach you that you're mine?" He kicked her in the ribs and I screamed.

Before I knew what I was doing, I'd climbed down the ladder and was standing beside him, tugging him back by his shirt, trying to make him stop. He kicked her again and she curled into herself.

"Stop," I said with a throat clogged with tears. Neither of them registered me as I continued to yell and scratch at him. Ice coated my fingers as fury consumed me. I was desperate to help her.

"Father," I cried. "Stop! You're going to kill her."

He finally turned, facing me with a detached expression. Rage simmered underneath his dead stare. His blonde hair was unkempt, hanging around his face, around his pointed ears. Faerie ears. My father was Fae. And he was drunk, I realized. The familiar, anxiety-inducing scent of faerie whisky rolled off his tongue as he said, "So what if I do? Are you going to stop me, love?"

His face was ruddier than I remembered. Cold terror trickled down my spine as his blue eyes began to morph, changing shape and color. Then emerald eyes, flickering with hellfire, met mine. Galen's eyes.

I gasped, stumbling back as he flashed a cheshire grin. Flame danced in his open palm. "I thought your mother told you to run," he purred. "You should've listened."

With bared fangs, he lunged for me. I leapt out of the way as he struck. When he spun back around, I was ready. I didn't hesitate as I plunged an ice dagger deep into his chest, right into his black heart. And twisted.

He took a step back in disbelief. Something like devastation spread across his face as he stared at me. When he collapsed to the ground, I was already at my mother's side, helping her up.

And then we ran.

Pain radiated down my spine. I'd escaped Galen in my dreams, but I was still very much captive in this living nightmare. The burns down my back were so severe, I wasn't sure I *could* run, even if I had the chance.

My father had abused my mother. And unknowingly, I'd repeated the cycle, finding a male just like him. How had I forgotten the terror I'd felt, hiding from my father as a child? Nausea gripped my stomach as I stared at my candle's pulsing flame. If I became afraid of fire, then he'd win. Galen had burned me with *my* magic.

A blurry figure came into view. I wasn't alone. I'd been fading in and out of lucidity since Galen had left me in a heap on the floor.

"Lusha…" I rasped when I recognized her strawberry blonde hair. I tried to sit up before lightning shot down my spine, causing me to hunch back down.

"Stay still," she said. "You've been sleeping for nearly a day. I'm here to help. Your back isn't healing because of the jasper." She choked back a sob as she removed a strip of wet linen that had adhered to my skin, making me cry out.

"He expects me to go to the festival like this?"

She nodded. "Aye. Is there anything I can do? Beyond dressing your wounds." The way she was staring at me… she wanted to help. But what could she do? *Find Raf*, was my first thought. But if he could easily be found, he'd be here. I tried to think through the fog of pain… and then I latched onto something that had a low probability of working.

"I have an idea… though it's not a great one." I told her the plan and she promised to do what she could before applying a cooling balm that helped numb the pain. And then I was alone, lost in my misery.

The door opened and I didn't bother lifting my head. *Lusha.* "Your message has been delivered, Your Grace. I brought your gown for this evening. I've been instructed to give you a sponge bath and make you presentable."

I gave her an assaulted look. "*Your Grace*? Lusha, please... call me Marigold. Look at me." I was covered in bandages. My hair hadn't been washed in over a week and was coated in blood and sweat. I was so tired. How did Galen expect me to stand tonight when I could barely move? Every muscle in my back protested as I sat up.

"Alright, Marigold. Take it easy," Lusha hushed, carefully checking my wounds. I felt a surge of hope when I thought about my dance partner. Raf would show if he could, if he was alive, but Galen would be prepared for that.

I was going to be bait for a trap. A new wave of pain had me clutching my stomach. If anything happened to Rafael because of me, I'd never forgive myself.

Lusha worked her magic; brushing tangles out of my hair, taking away small bruises, smoothing my hair, and cleaning my nails. Next came the dress. It was a white satin, off-the-shoulder gown, embroidered with lace flowers. Galen had a sick sense of humor. It was almost a replica of my debut dress, except tailored to faerie fashion. It was simple and elegant and I *hated it*. Which was good, since I'd bleed through it within the hour.

After much effort, Lusha helped me into it, spoon fed me, then forced water down my throat, like I was a helpless baby. This entire experience was demoralizing, but I'd be forever grateful for her kindness. When it was time for her to go, I clung to her. "Please, don't leave me," I begged.

Her face crumpled. "I must. Prince Galen will be coming to collect you soon. I'll keep an eye out for his brothers. Be brave, sweet one." She touched my cheek, but as she moved to leave, I gripped her wrist.

"Throw a shield around us," I hissed. We were alone in the room but there were guards outside in the hall. She didn't hesitate though, shielding us in a thin layer of water.

"Raf and Louis found the abducted humans," I said in a low murmur. "They're planning to bring them here. If I get out, I'm going to try and help them escape to Erador. I've been cut off from any more updates, but this is important..."

Lusha nodded, staring at me with round eyes as I continued, "The Elders, Sylvia, and Galen are exterminating humans—they've found a way to steal their magic and plan to hoard it, giving the Crown complete control. You need to warn as many people as you can and build a resistance. If I make it back to Erador, we're going to break the curse and then we're coming back to fight. I won't abandon you here. I promise."

Her eyes were cartoonishly large as she exited the room without another word. Even if I died tonight, at least someone knew what was happening. I did all I could. Now it was time to wait.

I sat on the bed, staring at the door. Panic slithered its way through me—squeezing my heart, clawing into my stomach. Galen was going to burst in any moment and then I'd be on display, surrounded by crowds and chaos. I was so weak. Would I get the chance to beg a stranger for help? I had to try.

Before I could strategize any further, the door opened. I held my breath, expecting to see Galen, but instead a pair of bright blue eyes stared back at me.

FIFTY-TWO

"We don't have much time," Isla said, already dressed for the festival in an evergreen gown that shimmered as she flitted around me. She pulled a set of keys from her cleavage, fumbling with them, then testing them on my cuffs.

"You-you retrieved the key... I didn't have high hopes of you helping me," I breathed.

"All of his keys, actually," she chirped smugly. "I'm here, aren't I? I want the crown and I believe what your maid told me—that he plans to propose to you. I've never trusted him, and lately he's been even more erratic. I need you out of the picture. If he doesn't propose to me, my father will assume it's my fault." She scowled, then met my gaze. "Will you leave us for good?" she asked, pausing her progress on the lock.

"Yes," I promised. "I'll leave as soon as these shackles are off my wrist. I never want to see Galen again. Please, be quick. He's due to come any moment." I heard the click of a cuff and then one wrist was free.

"Obviously, I know that. He'd be here already if it wasn't for me. It wasn't easy to retrieve these," she said, holding up the keys. "First, I had to get him drunk, which wasn't difficult. Then I had to lay with him until he was so thoroughly exhausted that he passed out. His valet will wake him soon, though."

The second shackle dropped and I felt magic surge through me. My back tingled and itched as flayed, charred skin began to heal itself. "Thank you, Isla. I owe you my life." She'd already turned around.

"Don't forget it," she said, looking back with a grin before rushing out.

My legs wobbled as I walked to the door and peered out the hallway. Only a few dim sconces lit the way. I turned towards the staircase, but the steady thud of a phantom heart beat drew me back. The heavy drumming shook my bones as it pulled me in.

Dark magic, seductive and sweet, called to me as I moved towards the Elder's evil creation. I approached it cautiously, studying the mechanics. An encased, blackened heart sat suspended in the air, pumping on its own. Blood funneled from a network of arteries into a large vat in steady, gushing bursts. I hissed at it with disgust.

Its magic brushed against me in soft, soothing strokes, but it had no power over me. I'd already been to hell and back, and I'd learned a thing or two. *The best way to defeat darkness was to let in the light.*

With no time to waste, I shifted into a unicorn and sent wave after crashing wave at the heart. The dark magic curled and writhed as it flooded out of the pulsing organ. It tried to escape, but there was nowhere to hide as starlight lit up the room and disintegrated every evil thing in its path. Glass shattered, blood boiled, and the heart splintered, until the only thing left was a pile of white sand. Then I ran for my life.

It took all my willpower to not stay in my pneuma form. I knew I couldn't be seen, but the impulse to protect myself was difficult to ignore. I let out a steady breath before shifting back into my fragile human body, feeling instantly vulnerable. I raced up the stairs, two at a time, until I arrived at a door. I cracked it slowly and then stepped through.

Fresh air engulfed me and I sucked it down with gratitude. The position of the sun told me it was late afternoon and guests would be arriving soon. I backed up against the castle's white stone walls, trying to camouflage myself as I reigned in my frantic desire to *run*.

I began to slowly scoot along the building until I came to a corner and cautiously peered around it. Before I could so much as yelp, someone grabbed me from behind... and everything went dark.

FIFTY-THREE

I registered the smell of cedar and rain and relief washed over me. *Raf.* He took me to the forest in several quick spurts and then he was hugging me, burying his face into the curve of my neck, like my scent was a comfort to him too.

"Marigold, I-I'm so sorry. I shouldn't have left you. I've been out of my mind with worry. I haven't slept since I came back to my room and you weren't there." He pulled back to meet my gaze.

"What took you so long?" I asked, laying my head on his chest and squeezing him as hard as I could. His chest was pounding wildly and after feeling the pull of the phantom heart, I found it hilarious that I'd ever thought Rafael capable of dark magic. He radiated light, even if he produced shadows. He was real. Solid. Safe. *He was in my arms.*

"Fucking *Galen.* He must've used your magic to make wards around his training den—stronger than any I've ever come across. I knew where you were—it wasn't difficult to assume where he would've taken you, *but I couldn't get to you,* no matter what I tried. He hid the entire castle from me.

"And then today, some of the wards lifted... like he's just daring me to come to the festival. I've been pacing the perimeter for a week in different forms, searching for a way in and then... there you were. Here you are." He kissed my forehead, making me go rigid as frost coated down my spine. I didn't know how to tell my body that he wasn't the enemy. I pushed away from him, needing space.

"What did he do to you?" His eyes were feral as they looked me over. He was panting, nostrils flared. I began to shiver as I felt anger radiate from him.

Gods, I was not okay. He would never hurt me.

"I'm alright. I've been chained in jasper since he took me from the brothel... He was trying to force me to blood-bond with him. But Isla, of all people, rescued me." I played with my necklace that finally felt warm again. I didn't want to discuss what I'd been through. Not now, maybe not ever. Before he could respond I asked, "Louis, the prisoners—what happened? Did you save them? Where are they?"

He studied me with a pensive expression. "I have a lot to fill you in on, but it was a successful mission. I brought Meli and Odin with me in my dragon form. Louis and his team were waiting for us. Kaya and Leon were there as well—you'll meet them soon. They're my real family."

"Meli mentioned them once," I replied. I held back from asking why he hadn't brought them up before now. What other secrets did he have? Maybe I wasn't as important to him as I thought.

He gave me a tight smile. "Together, we infiltrated the prison and killed over forty guards. We kept a few of the workers alive to interrogate them. They... were healers."

I gasped. The missing healers.

"*Corrupt* healers," he corrected himself. "Most of them, anyway; some had been forced into it. They were experimenting on humans—" He paused, gazing at me with heavy, tired eyes. "Removing their hearts. They used their healing abilities to pin-point the source of magic in the human body. They somehow spelled hearts to pump blood separate from the body, to continuously produce magic. The prison was a death sentence to all who entered. People had been mutilated, left to bleed out..." He cleared his throat. "It was awful, Goldie."

I squeezed his hand, even though touching was hard for me right now. "They had one of the spelled hearts here, in the dungeon. Galen told me that the Elders plan to *exterminate* humans and monopolize magic." We wore equally bleak expressions as we stared at each other.

"It's not all bad news..." Raf said. "We saved over a hundred people. Thanks to Meli and Odin, all are healed and on their way to recovering from the horrors they experienced. The group was planning to cross into the Whispering Woods under the cover of darkness tonight, but I haven't connected with them since I came back for you last week. Now that I've found you, we need to make sure they're on track to arrive by midnight. If they are, we'll need the Queen's sentinels diverted to the castle. It'll take a big distraction to clear the watchtower. I was planning on causing a scene at the festival. You can stay with Louis and the others while I go—"

"You idiot," I interrupted. I punched him in the shoulder—hard enough that he stumbled back. "Did you learn *nothing* over the last week? We're stronger *together*. I'm not letting you face them alone. Plus, I want to pay Galen back for what he did to me. I'm much more capable when I'm not chained in jasper."

"I didn't want to assume that you'd be willing to face Galen... after everything. But you're right; we're a good team. I won't leave you behind—ever, if that's your wish."

"It is. I don't want to be parted from you ever again," I whispered. An electric current passed between us as I met his gaze. Once again, I'd put my foot in my mouth. And once again, Raf brushed it off.

"Looks like we're crashing a party."

I grinned back and asked, "Can we spike the punch?"

After we'd formed a plan, it was time to reunite with Louis and the others. Raf flew us high above the clouds in his Pegasus form. He dipped low when we were close to the designated meeting point. I couldn't see anything, but Rafael had said they'd be warded. We bee-lined for the edge of the forest, shooting through the sky like an arrow. I could feel the bite of magic as we passed through the wards and saw a crowd mingling below, waving and pointing.

I spotted Louis's red-hair and then Meli's black curls. Beyond them were hundreds of unfamiliar faces—survivors from the prison. They'd been through so much more than I had. If they could be strong, so could I.

We landed and were immediately swarmed. "We've been so worried!" Meli cried. "What took you so long?"

"Galen," I said through a blur of tears. *She was safe.* Something in my chest relaxed and I could breathe easier. "It's a long story and I know we don't have much time."

She grabbed my hands and immediately absorbed the heaviest of my emotions, giving me a gentle hug, taking care not to touch my back. "Thank gods you're safe now." She smiled.

I gave her a tight smile back, not ready to talk about it. The night was far from over. I had to stay sharp, even if I felt dull, rusted, and broken.

"Long time no see," Louis said. "Nice dress." He looked me over with a smirk. "I'm having deja vu from when we first met." His grin didn't meet his eyes. "Thank you for killing her," he murmured under his breath. I hugged him, feeling the weight of how much we'd sacrificed to get to this point. Soon we'd have time to discuss all of it.

"Marigold and I are going to the festival to make a scene, distract the sentinels, and rile up Sylvia... and kill Galen," Raf growled, staring at Louis with a clenched jaw. They exchanged a look and my heart began to race.

"We're coming along." A petite, dark-haired woman pushed through the crowd. She looked me up and down with wary moss green eyes. "You're *the* Marigold, I presume?"

She didn't introduce herself, but the boisterous man that appeared behind her made up for her tepid greeting. "I'm Leon. The rude one is Kaya. We've been looking forward to meeting you. We're Raf's friends—his only friends," he teased, jabbing Rafael in the ribs.

Raf shoved him back. "Hit me again and I'll have one less friend." Raf flashed his fangs.

"Rafael never told me about you two, but I'm not surprised. He likes his secrets... I'm sure it's a lot of work to keep up the tough guy persona," I joked.

Leon gave me a warm grin back. "Definitely, but he's a big ol' softie, deep down. Aren't you, sweetie?"

Raf shot him a glare that would shake most people, but Leon continued unfazed. "Don't mind Kaya. She's another tough nut to crack, so don't take anything she says to heart."

He was giant... with muscles stacked on top of muscles. His long, blonde hair was so thoroughly tangled, I couldn't imagine anyone but Lusha being able to tame it.

"Wait until you hear what else he hasn't told you..." Kaya pursed her lips at me and narrowed her upturned eyes, as if she was sucking on something sour.

"Enough, Kaya," Raf said sharply. She lifted her hands in apology, rolling her eyes. I watched their dynamic in fascination, trying to figure it out. Was she a past lover? A current one? I felt an absurd twinge of jealousy, even knowing I had no claim over him.

"Can we shadow in tonight?" Kaya asked, crossing her arms.

"Yes," Raf replied. "The wards over the Great Hall have been lifted. They're going to set some type of trap for me, so I'll need both of you staying vigilante, while Marigold and I create chaos." They nodded in unison.

"Louis, do you have your plan in place? We'll meet at the portal at midnight. Don't hesitate to incapacitate anybody you come across, even if you're familiar with them. We can't take any risks tonight. Understood?"

Louis mumbled, "Yes," in the same way any little brother might and it made me laugh. We were all a little broken, but together we were fighting for a better world, for *two* better worlds. As we combed over the plan one more time, I felt my chest swell with a glimmer of hope. And if I was still capable of feeling hope, then perhaps Galen hadn't taken everything from me, after all.

As we flew towards the castle, my magic sung, ecstatic to be under the night stars with Raf. If I died tonight, at least I got to experience flying with him one last time. After so much solitude, so much fear and pain, I had a better read on what was important to me, *who* was important to me.

Rafael was who I'd clung to when I was alone in the dark. He'd been my light. I cared for him more than he knew, but I had no intention of telling him. His friendship was something I wouldn't risk. I was shattered, beyond repair, and he deserved... *everything*. He deserved someone who hadn't chosen his brother over him.

I shifted my thoughts back to our mission as we drew near. He was going to shadow us inside when the bells of Monrovia Castle's clock tower chimed eleven—the time slot we were originally scheduled for. We had no idea what we'd be walking into, but our main goal was simple; steal the show and stay alive.

"It's time to dance again, Goldie." I heard my mother's voice in my head, thick with pride.

The clock tower rang.

ding, dong, ding, dong.

ding, dong, ding, dong.

ding, dong, ding.

And on the eleventh chime, we turned to mist.

FIFTY-FOUR

My eyes blinked as they adjusted to the bright ballroom. Black tendrils of smoke spilled off of us, contrasting against my moon-white gown. An opulent party surrounded us, but my focus was solely on Rafael.

We arranged ourselves into position. Someone gasped. A glass shattered. And then I heard our dance instructor, Archibald, cheering. "Bravo! What an entrance! We were told you weren't coming, but this arrival was well worth the suspense!" He clapped his hands enthusiastically. I tried to keep a straight face as the musicians gawked at each other in confusion, fumbled with their instruments, and began to play at his instruction.

Archie turned to the crowd, as rehearsed. "Ladies and Gentle Fae, may I present Prince Rafael Ruhn and our very own world walker, Princess Marigold of Aurelius!" He beamed as the crowd cheered.

Raf locked eyes with me and we began to spin around the floor, bending and twirling. I dared a quick glance around the room and spotted Galen's auburn hair as he stood next to Isla. They both wore matching green formal wear—a gold crown glittered atop Galen's head.

I'd never seen him in a crown. I pulled my lips back in a silent snarl. Raf should be the one wearing a crown. He'd make a better King than his brother, in every way that mattered.

Galen and Isla's mouths were gaping open so wide, it was nearly comical. I'd taken his surprise reveal from him. I was supposed to be standing where she stood. He looked as if he might turn into a raging ball of fire and combust.

If I let my fear rise to the surface, I'd crumble to the floor. I reminded myself that I was safe in Raf's arms. Sylvia sat on her throne, unimpressed and aloof, in a royal blue gown. But I *knew* she was steaming inside. They'd lost the world walker and now here she was, on her own terms.

The Elders were salivating as they sat in a neat row at the edge of the dance floor. They looked a little too comfortable and it made me uneasy. Had Galen told them what I was? We were taking such a big risk—we were in the enemy's territory with only blind faith and minimal backup to save us.

I faltered. This was all too much, too soon. I struggled to breathe, taking shallow, short gasps. My lungs were burning, my chest felt tight and heavy. We were using ourselves as live bait.

So many faces blurred together in an endless sea of faeries, all watching us. I saw a flash of my mother's pale, limp hand on the floor. Her golden hair strewn across her face. I stumbled a step as stars danced across my vision. *I was going to faint.*

Raf leaned in close. "Look at me." My eyes were unblinking as they scanned the room frantically. "Goldie, look at me," he said more sternly. My gaze found his and I focused on the golden flecks in his irises. An entire galaxy of stars stared back at me.

"There you are." He smiled. "Let the rest fade away. Slow your breathing—that's it. We're almost done. Say the word and we can leave and never return."

If he was worried, it didn't show on his face. I took a deep breath, letting my anxiety roll off of me. It was just him and I; training in the grove, galloping through forests, fighting side by side, flying through the stars. *It was just us.* This was nothing compared to what we'd accomplished together. I touched nose to nose with him as he dipped me one last time and *kissed me* in front of everyone.

Even though he'd warned me that he was going to kiss me for dramatic effect, I was still unprepared when his lips met mine. Moonlight filled my soul as our mouths melded together in perfect synchronicity. Chills shot down my spine and fire licked through my core. The combination melted me into a sopping puddle. For one magical moment, the crowd faded and it was just Raf and I, locked in a romantic embrace that rearranged the cosmos.

And then Galen exploded. "Get your hands off her! *She's mine.*" He spewed his words like a hissing tomcat, hurrying towards us, flames in hand. Before he could reach us, Raf and I had our shields up.

Shadows swirled around us as Rafael released a low growl. "Never again will you lay a finger on her, because once I'm through with you, *you won't have any left.*" The power emanating from him reminded me that a dragon slept dormant under his skin. I shivered as the room was swallowed in darkness. The terrified crowd of faeries faded from view, until it was just us and Galen.

Rafael kept his magic reeled in most of the time. He didn't usually want the attention, didn't want his title. That version of him was absent tonight as he let the court size him up in all his glory. Perhaps the first whispers of whether Galen was truly the best fit for successor would start this very evening.

"I will dance on your ashes," Galen seethed, sending fire towards us. I flinched as the flames ricocheted off our combined shields.

While Sylvia's guards rushed around her, attempting to clear the Ballroom of the thick black smoke emanating from Raf, the Queen's voice pierced the air. "Galen, let the whore make her way through the entire Ruhn family tree before she brings us to Erador, if that's her wish. She's here, be glad of that. You're promised to another."

As the fog cleared, I took her in. She had the lethal stare of a reptile that had gone too long without a meal. "Dance, Prince Galen. Show off your betrothed to the court," she commanded. Isla smiled triumphantly. Galen looked ready to murder his mother.

The veins in his neck bulged as he walked over to Isla and took her hand. We exited the dance floor as they shouldered past us. "This isn't over," Galen snapped, swinging Isla to face him.

Isla looked down her nose at me. "Human trash," she said convincingly. I bit my lip to keep from laughing.

While they danced, we watched the Elders whisper to each other. Would they try to attack us in the open, in front of the party guests? It didn't seem their style, preferring to have their dirty work done for them. They were all glowing with magic that had probably been collected from the dead. I wanted to shift into my unicorn form and rattle them, *end them*, but we had people depending on us. I wondered if their souls were as shriveled as the Oracle's, if starlight would be enough to kill them.

"Don't drink the wine," Raf whispered to me. "They could easily slip poison or powdered jasper into it." He looked past me and smiled.

"More guards just arrived... and some of them are sentinels that should be patrolling the forest. So far, so good."

He gave me a quizzical look as I stared at him. "Do I have something on my face?" he asked, diligently scanning the crowd.

"No. I'm just happy to be standing next to you, instead of *him*. Galen was going to propose to me in front of everyone tonight. I feel like I just dodged a cross-bow bolt to the chest." He was barely listening, focused on a scuffle in the crowd, and I couldn't help asking, "Do you think we created enough of a stir with our kiss?"

His head turned sharply and I felt the full weight of his gaze settle over me, making my stomach flip. "If we didn't, I'm willing to give it another shot." He pulled me to him, closing the space between us. I grimaced when he touched my back.

He gave me a look edged with concern. "What's wrong? Are you hurt?"

Damn. I'd been avoiding telling him. "Galen burned my back. I haven't fully healed yet, because of the jasper."

Shadows exploded as he started towards Galen, who was still occupied on the dance floor. I clung to his arm, holding him back. He began to drag me across the floor and I huffed, "Stop, Raf..."

"Let me finish this—for all the times he's hurt you. I can't let it stand. *Please*," he begged, like my pain was his to bear.

"We'll get our revenge when the time is right. Don't turn *broody-brute* on me now. I need you to keep your head." I put a hand to his cheek. He slowly relaxed, taking long, deep breaths.

"If I get the chance, I'm taking it. He deserves to die for what he did to you. And I want to be the one to end him."

I needed to change the subject quickly. "Would you like to walk me around and introduce me to your peers?"

"My peers?" he scoffed. "No, but I will. Prepare to be amazed by the vapid nature of ancient creatures." Sighing, he rolled his shoulders, as we made a wide circle around the room, trying to keep the attention on us. His shield surrounded me as we mingled, unsettling the guests. I could feel eyes on us as soldiers continued to pour in. We were surrounded. Great for Louis and the rest of the group, hopefully not fatal for us.

We pushed past bodies, while I took in my first faerie festival. Most people were dressed in jewel-toned formal attire, showing off indecent amounts of skin. Some were completely naked and strategically painted. Many embellished their features with glitter and makeup. Elements of nature adorned both sexes: Feathers, shells, leaves, fur, antlers and flowers. Many faeries didn't bother to conform to a gender at all. The crowd as a whole seemed utterly free of societal constraints, comfortable expressing themselves however they wished.

Candles floated in the air above us, casting a dusty rose-gold glow on the party below. The full moon illuminated the space further, filtering through the domed stained-glass ceiling. Gauzy curtains, tied back with thorny roses, draped over tall windows, running the length of the walls. Tables held elaborate centerpieces with perfectly pruned bonsai trees, rare orchids, and vases full of the glowing yellow flowers I'd seen on my first day here. Every type of food imaginable was laid out in gluttonous quantities: Roasted meats, vegetables cut into intricate shapes, bowls of ripe berries and cream, loaves of bread and wedges of countless types of cheese.

All elements were represented in the decor. There were rocky waterfalls, torches of fire, and a sweet-smelling breeze that blew through the entire party, keeping temperatures pleasant. Ice sculptures of faeries entwined in provocative poses were scattered throughout. Shadows darkened corners of the room for anyone seeking privacy. How I wished I could go hide in one of those corners.

Most faeries were trickling onto the dance floor. Some gyrated together, as if they were having sex with their clothes on, while others danced in free-spirited glee, kicking their legs up and spinning in circles. Some had already coupled up, passionately kissing against pillars. They were uninhibited in a way I couldn't imagine Aurelians ever being.

As we passed one of the refreshment tables, I noticed a three-tiered chocolate fountain cascading into foaming waves. I reeled back when I realized it was *blood*. Human blood. I shouldn't have been shocked after what I'd seen and experienced the last few months, but the brazen self-indulgence, the mockery of human life... it made my veins turn cold.

My skin crawled with a deep loathing for the gluttonous celebration that surrounded us, while so many others suffered. The disgust kept my panic at bay as we made our way to the dance floor. The Elders were gone. We looked at each other and moved back-to-back as we scanned the crowd, circling slowly.

I spotted Kaya against a wall, subtly nodding her head at us. "This way, Raf!" I pulled him towards her.

"The Elders left several minutes ago, through the main doors. Leon is trailing them. Sylvia is still at her throne, but something isn't right. We need to leave," Kaya said under her breath. Louis and the others should be close to their destination now... if they hadn't been caught.

I looked up just in time to see Galen blazing a trail towards us. I turned to the Queen, who was sitting up straight in her seat, tracking him. "How did you escape?" he asked with ire. I ducked behind Raf as my back prickled with pain.

"One more step and you're *dust*," Rafael said, flashing his teeth. They both had their shields up; shadow and flame hovered between them. I stood beside Rafael and lifted my hands, readying an ice dagger for Galen's heart if he struck. The music stopped as people began to notice us. Isla hung back, glaring. I *did* feel bad for ruining her party. She was the reason I wasn't in chains right now.

Galen dropped his hands to his sides when the Elders strode back into the room. "Let them have you," he said, cursing us as he stepped back and they approached. It was time for us to go. Leon was anxiously bee-lining towards us, pushing through throngs of flustered faeries.

Radley greeted us first, flanked by the five other advisors. A burgundy cloud, the color of rotten wine, followed them. Theirs souls still appeared to be fused together unnaturally. "What a marvelous entrance you two made. Thank you for delivering her to us, Rafael. As the clock strikes midnight, a new day will be upon us. It's time for you to come into our custody, Marigold. The Queen has given us permission to take you."

Rafael stood protectively in front of me. "If you want her, you'll have to go through me," he said with a face made of stone.

"Move aside. We just want the girl. We won't kill her, we just need to make sure she stays close until her shifting form is found."

Galen hadn't told them. He wanted my power for himself.

Raf took my hand and went to shadow us out, but his magic balked. There was something blocking our exit. He turned to me with wide eyes. Kaya and Leon were now standing at our sides, hissing at the Elders.

"What did you do?" Rafael snarled.

Arnold smirked maliciously. "Our wards can now keep people *in*, as well as out. An invisible cage, if you will. Your magic is outranked, *Prince.*

It's no match against the book of *Erebus*." Raf's eyes flashed with surprise. "That's right, the book has been with us all this time. Now that we finally have an *infinite* supply of magic, it yields to us. Together, the six of us command the most powerful spells in existence—as one. Your shadows won't be making a quick exit tonight. Now... give us the girl."

Rafael, Leon, Kaya, and I wordlessly threw up our shields, creating a protective cocoon as we figured out our next move.

Leon whispered, "I'm sorry... by the time I saw what they were doing, it was too late. I came as fast as I could. What's the call, boss?"

FIFTY-FIVE

"**S** tay close. Follow my lead," Rafael said. The Elders struck at those words. Harkin attacked first, creating an avalanche of large stones that rained down on us, causing small fissures in our combined shield. She was *strong*.

Galen struck at the same time as Radley, both releasing deep crimson hellfire onto us. Faeries began screaming and tripping over themselves as they fled for safety. Some hid behind tables and chairs as they continued watching from a distance.

"Get ready," Raf whispered to us. "As soon as this wave of fire ends, we're leaving. Hold onto my back."

We each placed a hand on him. As the flames receded, Rafael's form *exploded*, breaking our shields, filling the room, and scattering the Elders. I was dangling off the back of a black dragon, gripping a long, curved spike. Kaya took my other hand and pulled me up as we all scrambled to climb onto him. His body was so wide that it was difficult to latch on. I held on wherever I could.

I'd never forget the expression on Galen's face as he realized his little brother had managed to conceal this secret from him for one-hundred years. There was a flash of wonder, before his eyes narrowed into fiery slits.

Rafael gave a blood-curdling screech as he turned his massive head towards the advisors and released violet flame onto them. Several were too slow to shield and caught fire, screaming as skin melted from their faces, their bodies. He roared again and it reverberated through me. He swung his spiked tail towards the Queen, still sitting in her throne.

She threw out vines around his feet and head simultaneously, while her guards sent a typhoon of rain and wind at us, trying to knock us from his back. Raf whirled towards them, scorching them with dragon fire. I began to slide off his back and Kaya lunged for me, clutching my dress, and pulling me to her.

The Queen sneered at us, refusing to look bothered, as her shield began to disintegrate under the flames. A few more seconds and his fire would burn through her. Only a lunatic was that fearless.

"Raf, let's go!" yelled Leon. Rafael snapped back into himself, unfolding his wings as he began flapping, trying to gain air. I pushed wind under his wings and we began to rise. Arrows were flying at us, bouncing off his impenetrable scales and our shields. I kept my body low, holding him tightly.

His back reared up vertically as he lifted higher. We all hung on, white knuckles gripping. It felt as if I was dangling off the side of a cliff. I refused to fall… I *refused* to go back to Galen. I just needed to hold on a little longer. Raf blew another round of fire down at the vines that restrained him as he began to inch higher. My legs shook as I used all my strength to cling to him.

Even the bravest of observers were running for the door now, creating pandemonium as they all tried to exit at the same time. Raf smashed his head through the top of the glass dome, causing the chandelier to plummet down on the royal families below. I watched it crash onto Radley, severing his legs from the rest of his body. Galen hovered over Isla, protecting her from the impact. The shards from the window pelted our shields like a hailstorm, and then I was breathing fresh air.

Raf hit a barrier and roared in anger, flapping along the edge of an invisible wall. He blew fire at the wards and they flickered under his power. Leon sent wind blowing at gale speeds as Kaya shot bolts of shadow in wave after wave.

I knew what I need to do, but I couldn't shift into a unicorn on the back of a dragon. I let the chaos fade as I tried to summon starlight. It came so effortless in my pneuma form—*I had to do this*.

I released my pent up fury as I sent raw magic towards the spelled wards in a force of power that knocked me backwards. Kaya caught me as beaming *starlight* answered my call. The wards rippled and shuttered before crumbling under light that radiated in bright, pulsing waves. Sand rained down on the faeries below as Rafael bellowed in triumph and flew us out. *Freedom.*

We whooped and cheered as we flew to the garden, cold air nipping at my beaming cheeks. The only sound in the silent sky was Raf's wings pumping up and down—until he let out an ear-splitting *roar*, alerting Louis we were on our way.

We were so close.

The night wind pulled tears from my eyes as we began to circle and land. The first face I saw was Meli's. I shook with relief as I jumped from Raf and ran to give her a hug. Hundreds of petrified people crowded against the walls, watching, waiting.

"You made it." I grinned at Meli and Odin.

"So did you! We brought some friends."

"Just a few," I laughed.

"There are more hidden outside of the garden. We'll bring them through once the portal is open."

I hugged Rafael who had shifted back into his Fae form. "You were incredible... Thank you," I whispered.

He cradled my head against his chest, murmuring into my hair, "Let's go home." We held hands as we walked to the wall in a full circle moment. I gave him one last smile as I shifted into a unicorn.

The glow from my horn shimmered across the garden. The warm light washed over clumps of fuchsia snapdragons, white lilies, and goldenrod. Fireflies bumbled through the air, twinkling against the shadows of night. The smell of jasmine brought me back to the night I'd come here with Raf. He was the first one I'd ever shared it with and it felt fitting that we should be here together now, in this moment.

I looked upon countless bewildered faces, all staring at me. Louis covered his mouth in shock. Meli beamed at me with pride, while Odin wrapped himself protectively around her. Raf rested his hand on my shoulder and said, "You've got this, world walker."

I bobbed my head at him and then stared at the wall. After months of wondering if I'd ever get the chance to go home, the only obstacle that remained was *me*. There was no one to hide behind and nowhere to run. If I didn't open this portal, then no one would.

Why had this task fallen on my shoulders? Why had I, out of everyone, been given the gifts of a unicorn? And how had I even arrived here in the first place? I could stand here, forming new questions and never finding answers, or I could simply *try* and see where it led.

I sauntered over to the wall, running my opal horn along jagged stone. *"Take me home,"* I said, willing my magic to transform a wall into a door—a door that would lead to a new *world*. A seed of light appeared in a small pocket of stone. It grew as I concentrated on Erador and the people waiting for me on the other side.

I closed my eyes, visualizing the towering castle, the rolling green grass, the manicured gardens. The secret hideout that sheltered me as I grieved my mother, the aunt who loved me like her own, the horse that taught me how to fly, and the stable hand who'd given me endless patience. The Lady's maid who taught me humility and the best friend who never laughed at my dreams, but instead dared to dream with me.

When I opened my eyes, the groove had grown into a golden, luminescent door. It flickered and faded, but I knew what I needed to do. I had to channel *everything* I had to give. I had to transform darkness into light.

I willed more magic into the wall, letting myself feel the rage, grief, lust, joy, loneliness, fear, love, and loss that I'd experienced since arriving here. This world had destroyed me. This world had forged me into something new. Raw power flowed from me as my horn siphoned energy from the air, from the earth. The ground vibrated and stone walls tremored as the door demanded *more*. Rafael sounded far away as he shouted, telling people to close their eyes as my magic lit up the garden, the forest, the sky.

I was panting as I opened my eyes and saw a translucent golden doorway. I could see the garden waiting for me on the other side. *Erador.* I pushed my nose through the shimmering veil that separated the two worlds, smelling crisp, cool Aurelian air on the other side.

I'd done it.

People cheered as I reared up in triumph, shifting back. I studied the arched door more closely, noticing scribbles of Ancient Fae etched along the frame. A six-pointed star sat atop the door frame like a crown. "What does it say?" I asked Raf.

He squatted in front of the portal, quickly running his fingers along each word.

"I don't think we have time to translate it all right now, but it looks like instructions... a guide of some sort. Maybe this is what the last world walker used to find Nymera."

I nodded, knowing every minute counted. "Let's start moving people through."

Rafael immediately began to delegate. "Form a steady line. We need to be quick. Louis, I want you and your men on the other side, helping people through and keeping them organized. Marigold and I will come through last."

The doorway was only wide enough to fit a few people through at a time. A long line switched back on itself before spilling outside of the garden gates. My heart was pounding; this was taking too long. How fast could Galen get here in his lion form? We needed to *hurry*.

"Quickly, everyone," Meli shouted as people brought through horses, small carts, and personal items.

With just a trickle of people left in line, my worst fear was realized as I heard Galen's voice. "You thought you could just leave us behind? Some savior you are." He prowled towards us as his mother followed behind him, guards flanking them. His shadow wielder was also present. My lips curled into a snarl, noting the jasper chain he held.

"We should've gotten here faster, but your garden proved difficult to find—and I see that you're stealing magic on your way out." He clicked his tongue as he watched people run through the portal. "After all I've done for you..."

"You mean *saving* humans? Let us be, Galen. You know what their fate is if they stay here. I refuse to believe you want innocent blood on your hands. I saw how tortured you were after you were forced to kill. This is your chance for redemption," I reasoned, taking a step towards him to protect Meli and the others behind me.

"Sweet Marigold... worried about my soul, even after what you've seen me capable of. The problem is, love... the Elders *will* win. They have *Erebus*, which means the only feasible option is to join them. It will be better for my people when they don't have to rely on humans. We've found a way to take back what is ours. And now I'll take back what is *mine*." His temper flared and flames erupted.

Raf and I shielded on instinct, but Galen's shadow-wielder had gone for Meli. She was in Galen's arms with flame licking at her neck in seconds.

"Now we shall see just how righteous you really are. Will you trade yourself to save your friend?" His eyes were so cruel, so different than the one that had once looked at me with reverence and affection. I opened my mouth to speak, but stopped when I saw Odin running for Meli.

"No," I gasped, reaching out my hands in a desperate bid to stop him, but the Queen was too quick. She wrapped Odin in her vines and pulled him to her with the flick of her wrist. She held him by his throat as Meli screamed.

"Stop," I cried. "I'll go with you. Please, let them go."

Rafael's head was swiveling between me, Odin, and Meli. "Don't," Rafael said firmly, putting a shield between me and them.

Sylvia put her red lips to Odin's neck. "You have one more second before I drain him."

Meli was screaming, sobbing as Odin rasped, "Don't let them win. I love you, Meli."

"One," Sylvia said, rolling her eyes, before biting him. Meli's agonized sobs pierced my ears—I couldn't think, couldn't act.

My heart was pounding throughout my whole body and there were too many things happening at once.

"Take me! Take me," I choked. "Don't hurt anyone else."

"No," Rafael said, but I blocked him with a shield and ran to Galen. The terror in his eye felt like an arrow through the heart.

Galen pulled me towards him with bruising force and tossed Meli to the side. He held me by the nape of my neck, fisting clumps of curls. I stifled a cry as he wrapped a jasper chain around my neck. "I dare you to move," he murmured into my ear. I trembled as my magic sputtered out.

"Let him go," I snapped at the Queen. "I've cooperated."

Sylvia pulled away from Odin, her teeth stained red. "I don't think I will. His existence is an insult to the gods. I can taste it in his blood—they're blood-bonded." She pointed to Meli with a menacing finger. "She's given this human gifts meant only for faeries."

Rafael attacked, but she dodged him with surprising speed, still holding Odin by the neck. He was nearly unconscious now.

"Just for that... Give him the true death, Galen. He's nearly drained and has fulfilled his pathetic purpose," Sylvia sneered.

I clawed at Galen, struggling against the chain, as he jerked me back.

"Please, no! No, no, no," Meli howled in haunting repetition, gripping her belly and falling to her knees.

"Galen. I beg you. Let him go. I'll do whatever you want. *I'll marry you*," I pleaded. Meli was bowing, begging for mercy.

The Queen snapped Odin's neck in one quick motion and threw him to Galen's feet. *To my feet.* I turned away, nearly vomiting. Galen hesitated and I whimpered, pleading to him.

Rafael struck for Galen, appearing inside his shield. At the same time, Galen released a stream of fire onto Odin as Meli dove forward.

"Meli," I cried. Raf changed course, shadowing to Meli and knocking her out of the way.

My teeth chattered as Meli's tortured wailing filled the air. Odin's body was no longer there. All that remained was a pile of ash. It had only taken seconds to disintegrate his body and Meli had barely escaped with her life.

Kaya and Leon were hurrying the last of the people through on Raf's orders. Wordlessly, Kaya shadowed to Meli, and then to the wall. She ran Meli through the portal before Sylvia could strike. And then Rafael was behind the Queen, holding a knife to her throat.

FIFTY-SIX

It was a family standoff. Galen held me against his chest, while Rafael's knife sat snug against Sylvia's throat. "Let her go," Raf growled between gritted teeth.

Galen gripped me tighter. "Never."

The Queen's Guard swarmed around Raf and Sylvia like angry hornets, trying in vain to break his shield. Magic ricocheted back at the soldiers as they attacked, then *poof*—they were gone. He'd reduced all six men to dust without moving a muscle. Rafael pressed the knife tighter into Sylvia's neck, drawing blood, and then... it was her turn to disappear.

She'd shifted into her animal form, I realized, as I spotted a striped black and tan cobra coiled on the ground. Sylvia lifted her body in the air, swaying as she exposed her hooded head and fangs.

Rafael struck, but she was nimble. She lunged at his ankle and he let out a surprised yelp. It was the first time I'd ever seen true fear in his eyes. Leon was instantly at his side. He threw up a shield of wind and supported Raf as he crumbled to the ground.

I didn't realize I was screaming until Galen covered my mouth. I bit him and he snapped back his hand, bleeding.

"Raf!" I wailed. "Let me go to him—let me heal him. Then I'll go with you. I promise." Tears stung my eyes as my world began to shatter.

Sylvia shifted back and smiled as she stood between us and freedom. Everyone was through now besides Raf, Leon, and I. We'd been so close. And now I was watching Rafael *die* in front of me.

I pulled at the chain until my hands bled. I wrenched and twisted in Galen's arms, but he was as unmoving as an oak tree as he held me captive. We needed Louis—we needed help.

"You have *no idea* how long I've been waiting to sink my fangs into you," Sylvia said to Raf. "King Cobras leave more than a nasty bite, I'm afraid. My venom kills quickly, even a faerie of *your caliber* should stop breathing within minutes." Sylvia gave a mocking grin. "Oh, and while you're still conscious..."

Raf looked up at her with burning hatred as he began to convulse in Leon's arms. "*This* is how I killed your mother. A small dose to make it as slow and painful as possible. The *whore*—flaunting her relationship with your father in front of me. She blood-bonded with him, *with my husband.* Then she dared to ask me to spare you. And I did. For Randall, not her. For one-hundred years I've let you live and how have you thanked me? By being a thorn in my side and an ever-present reminder of your father's betrayal."

Rafael sent shadow straight at her chest, but she blocked him with a shield that he would've normally been able to destroy. In his weakened state, his magic was fading. Leon was frozen in place, waiting for Rafael to give him a command.

"Leon, get him through the wall to Meli. She'll heal him," I said, before Galen covered my mouth again. Leon supported Raf in his arms, shielding them both, as he began to hobble towards the wall.

"One more step and I drain Marigold. The portal is open. We don't need her anymore," the Queen warned. Leon continued walking.

"Bring me the girl, Galen," Sylvia ordered. Leon paused as Galen hesitated, before dragging me to her. "I've been wanting to sample you for so long. Galen tells me you're *special.*"

"Mother, don't do this," Galen said with a low rumble in his throat.

"*Just a taste.* Good boy." He let me go reluctantly and her lips hovered at my throat. I held my breath as teeth sank into flesh.

I screamed as sharp pain tore through me, ripping away any chance of stoicism. There was no euphoria, no oblivion, only searing agony as her fangs sank deeper. I could hear Galen in the background shouting, "Stop! You'll kill her. She's mine."

Rafael was pleading with his last breaths, "Fight her, Goldie. Help her, brother!"

I could feel my pulse beating beneath her canines. Hot tears fell down my cheeks as I held onto Raf's words.

Sylvia pulled back, hissing at Galen to stay back. "What *is* she? She's *mine* now." She bit down again, drawing fresh blood as I screamed for someone—*anyone*.

Magic was *rushing* out of me too quickly. I was useless. I'd been so close to making it home, and yet here I stood, a few feet from freedom. But *Raf*... I couldn't let him die. I roared in frustration, refusing to accept this fate. I clawed at her face, tore at her hair until she was forced to loosen her grip that had become slippery with blood.

Galen lunged between us and pulled the chain from my neck. Sylvia shoved him back, lost in blood-lust, but I felt my magic crash back into me. An angry tidal wave growing into a tsunami. With rage as deep and cold as an arctic sea, I screamed, "I BELONG TO NO ONE."

Sylvia's fangs ripped from my throat as I transformed and whirled around to face her. Her face grew pallid against her red lips as her jaw fell open. I glared back at her, furious. I wanted revenge. She'd murdered Odin. Raf was dying. She'd nearly drained me. I was going to *kill* her.

I backed up before sprinting forward, blinding her with brilliant light. Running at a full gallop, I gored her in the chest, slicing through flesh, muscle, and bone. I arched towards Leon and Raf, the Queen still impaled on my horn.

Rearing up, I threw her into the stone wall, with a loud bone-crunching splat. Leon, Raf, and I flew through the doorway together before I twisted around and faced the portal.

Galen's dark silhouette waited on the other side. He made no move to follow us. In our last moments together, he'd saved me, showed me a glimmer of the male I thought I knew. It shredded the last tattered scraps of my soul. I knew who he'd become with *them*. And yet, I wouldn't help him.

Never again would I let him hurt me. We stared at each other in a silent goodbye as I sealed the portal.

Fifty-Seven

S printing to Rafael, I shifted back, slitting my hand with Leon's dagger.
I dropped to my knees, dripping healing magic into his mouth and
over his swollen ankle. I waited, watching his unmoving purple lips.

He wasn't breathing—it wasn't working. Was I too late? No, I refused to accept it. Leon began doing compressions. Kaya was on his other
side. She held his hand as silent tears slid down her cheeks. I tried to rouse
him, gripping his face and forcing blood into his mouth. He couldn't
swallow—he wasn't *breathing*. I'd slay all the gods if they let this happen.
I'd steal him back from Aku's hell if I had to.

I felt wind on my face and looked up. A scarlet bird with long golden
tail feathers hovered over us, landing beside Rafael. I was dumbstruck,
making no move to stop it as it bent over his ankle. I didn't know who it
was, but I had no choice but to trust them.

Hunching protectively over Raf's body, I sobbed, pushing his dark
locks out of his face. "Raf, come back to me. *Please*. I can't do this without
you."

I pleaded to the gods, offering them *anything* in exchange for his life,
then resorted to threatening them. Their silence was deafening as I leaned
down and put my forehead against his. I felt a puff of breath against my
cheek and pulled back. His eyelids flickered. I gulped down air as I realized
he was *alive*. We all turned to the red bird in disbelief.

Rafael turned his head to me, eyes half-closed. "Are we dead or alive?"
he asked weakly.

Stifling my sobs, I responded, "Alive, somehow. We're in Erador. We
made it."

I looked over at the bird as it flapped away from us. It shifted and I fell back in disbelief when I saw *my mother* standing in front of me.

"Mama?" I gasped. "Are you a ghost? How is this possible?"

She came over to me, hesitating, then dropped to her knees and hugged me. "It's a long story... but I've always been near, waiting until I could hold you again. When you were born, we knew what you were right away. You had the birth mark on your forehead that my mother had spoken of. Our family had been waiting for you."

In a daze, I touched my forehead. "What birth mark?"

"It's under your hair now. You have a white circle above your forehead. Your grandmother had one too when she was born. *The mark of a unicorn*. I went to the Oracle and asked how I could keep you safe—keep you from being hunted. Unicorns are vulnerable to predators the moment they enter this world. The witch told me I had to die on your tenth birthday and let my sister raise you. She instructed Ophelia to erase all memories of you from your father's mind. He wasn't worthy of them anyways. She destroyed any evidence that could lead him or anyone else to you.

"You were protected in the castle—raised to know nothing of magic or the curse. And we didn't want others to know of you. Aurelius was scrubbed of all magic and faeries long before you were born, but when you arrived, we doubled down on our efforts. The Oracle said on your twenty-first birthday, the gods would lead you to your fated mate—that I'd be allowed to follow and help you, as long as you didn't see me.

"The price of keeping you safe was steep, a cost I willingly bore. I had to remain hidden until you returned to Erador. The penalty for letting you know who I was before then was true death. I've been so proud to be your mother—every day of your life. I-I know this is a lot to process."

She reached out and touched my necklace. "This is a tracker. I have one too. Each of the original Chosen Six were gifted one from the gods and they've been passed down ever since. It helps us stay connected. This is how I kept close in Nymera."

I tried to take in all that she told me, but I simply couldn't. I fidgeted with the pendant of my necklace. "How did you come back to life after the poison? Are... are you a phoenix?" I asked, thinking of the statue I'd seen so many times in the throne room.

"Yes. The poison stopped my heart, but phoenix's have the ability to come back from the dead—to rise from the ashes. We also have the antidote for all poisons and venom in our tears. It came in handy today." She smiled at Rafael.

"Thank you," he said softly, sitting up and resting a hand on my shoulder.

"I've tried to help you, even though it might not seem that way after all that you've faced. I kept as close as I could... I knocked quite a few guards unconscious over the last few months. You have a propensity for trouble, just like your mother." She grinned. "Luckily, faerie pride kept most of them from reporting anything. Galen's valet didn't know what hit him this evening, but it did buy you some time to escape.

"I followed the group of humans through the portal tonight, so I wouldn't be spotted, and then anxiously waited for you to come through. *You did it*, Goldie. You made it back to Erador." She hugged me and it felt like hugging a ghost, except that she was warm and I was cold. She smelled like soil and sunshine.

"We have much to catch up on. Perhaps we should save the rest for a more private setting. I'm looking forward to being the mother you deserve... now that I've paid the cost," she said, choking back emotion. I didn't respond as exhaustion, adrenaline, and shock worked their way through me. "I'm going to fly ahead to Ophelia and let her know you've arrived. Bring everyone to the castle. We'll take care of them until we can get them settled into their new lives."

I watched her fly towards the castle I thought I'd never see again, before searching for Meli in the crowd. She was with Louis, just a few feet away. I'd been so focused on Rafael and my mother, I hadn't seen them. I held her tightly as we cried. Their child was safe, but there were no words for her loss. Her mate, the father of her unborn child, was dead. I wouldn't let her face this alone. Taking her hand, we led the group to the castle.

"I love you, Meli. He died protecting his soulmate and his daughter and none of it's fair. I'll be here for you in whatever capacity you need me, please know that."

She responded with a squeeze to my hand.

Fifty-Eight

I was in such a fog of adrenaline and blood loss, I barely registered arriving at the castle. As servants swarmed around us, ushering people to and fro, I saw Queen Ophelia, beaming brilliantly at me through the parted crowd. She looked radiant as usual in a flowing teal gown. Her glow was also coming from... *magic.*

I pulled away from our hug to look at her through a new lens, one that knew of magic. The tips of her ears were round, but every other feature was pure Fae. She was waif-like with large, glittering eyes—and wrinkle-free, despite her silver hair. She must've been old. Very old, indeed, to have so much silver. We looked at each other with a new understanding, and yet I didn't really know her at all.

"We have much to discuss," she murmured. "Do you have the energy to come with me now?"

"Yes, but I need to let Rafael know—I'll be right back." She waited for me as I found him in the sea of people and pulled him aside. "I need to talk with my aunt in private. I'll come find you later."

He managed to show off a dimple with a tired crooked smile. "I have plenty to keep me busy here. I'll see you soon."

I exited the Great Hall with Ophelia and spotted my mother a moment later, following us discreetly. Once we were safely tucked away in one of the Queen's private parlors, she turned to us. "The guards, the advisors... they know very little of what's going on. It seems that current events have become too large to simply put them back in Pandora's box now. We'll have to tell them some truths, while still keeping our most precious secrets safe—secrets I'm sure you're eager to hear, Marigold."

I stared at my mother, unable to look anywhere else. "I want to know everything. But I'm feeling quite overwhelmed, and I've lost a lot of blood…" They led me to a small floral-patterned love seat. I had endless questions, but didn't have endless energy. I was slowly coming apart at the seams.

"How are you feeling, sweetie? Should we ring a doctor? Do you need some food?" My mother gave me a warm smile. I shook my head, feeling… *shy* around my own mother.

Ophelia cleared her throat. "I'm sorry we kept so much from you. I hope you know that our hands were tied. Your safety was our top priority. It has been, since before you were born. You're part of a prophecy—"

"I know of the prophecies, but I *refuse*. I-I won't blood-bond with Prince Galen, even if he's the chosen heir," I said with a lump in my throat.

"Have something to drink." My mother poured me a glass of water from a dew-covered pitcher and I took a slow sip.

"Perhaps it would be easier to *show* you what transpired one-hundred years after the blood curse. There was a meeting between the Chosen Six—we tried to reverse the curse, unfortunately not all of the pieces were in place. We've had to wait over two-hundred years for the stars to align again," Ophelia said.

"Show me?" I asked, staring down at my blood-splattered dress. White was really *not* my color. I laughed out loud, feeling a bit hysterical.

They exchanged glances. "Yes. I'm a sphinx, Marigold. I have the gift of mind manipulation. Not only can I read minds; I can alter the memories and thoughts of others. I can show you my own memories, even someone else's, if I've seen inside their mind. I'd like to share one of mine with you." She sat beside me. "It won't hurt. I just need to hold your hands and I'll be able to bring you into a memory. You won't be able to interact with what unfolds around you, but you'll be able to see it as clearly as I did."

"Alright…" I took one more sip of water and set down my glass. "I'm ready."

As soon as Ophelia held my hands and I closed my eyes, I found myself at a table with four other people, my mother included. We appeared to be in a royal meeting room that I didn't recognize, sitting at a round marble table. Everyone looked as restless as I—as *Ophelia*—felt.

This meeting had been postponed too many times. Why was it so difficult to get six people together? War was upon us—tensions had escalated to new levels as the effects of the blood-curse rooted itself deeper into Fae and human society. Watching our people become blood-thirsty as vampires these last few months had disturbed me greatly. It was a reminder that anyone was capable of great evil under the right circumstances. We needed to act swiftly before war tore this entire world apart.

Five of us were here and ready to discuss the prophecy. Where was Aides? He should've been the first one here with his shadow magic. I rolled my eyes impatiently as I sat with my mother, my sister, Dario, and Nicos. The Unicorn, The Phoenix, The Dragon, The Hydra, and The Sphinx, waiting on The Pooka, as usual.

The door opened and I expected to see Aides, but instead we were greeted with a messenger. "Urgent news from Aurelius, Queen Astra," the man said, handing my golden-haired mother a letter with a green wax seal. I bit my tongue so hard that it bled, as I watched her scan the contents of the note. Before she'd even finished reading it, I knew something was terribly wrong.

"Aides," my mother said, staring at me. "He's dead. So are Jorand and Persephone. A group of assassins murdered them in the middle of the night. They used jasper chains and killed the entire family in their sleep. Randall is the only one who escaped—he was just named King."

"What?" I stood, my hands on the table. We all began talking over each other in an outburst of fear and anger. Aides was my betrothed—we were the two heirs that were promised—the Chosen Heirs. We were to be blood-bonded this very day... I felt my world crashing around me. Pain seeped into every crevice.

We weren't in love... yet, but he was to be my partner for eternity. And now he was just... gone? Before I let fresh feelings befuddle my mind, I tucked them away. This changed everything. The prophecy... had we gotten it wrong? Or perhaps, we'd been too late. No, it must've not been meant for us after all.

"The curse can't be broken until a new Pooka is born, until we can once again unite the Six. There won't be another born for a hundred years, with the rate the Fae have been breeding. Humans won't last another decade, let alone a century, if this war continues. We must separate the Kingdoms. We

must act quickly." I spoke with false bravado, like my entire purpose hadn't just been pulled out from under me. I was a sphinx... I was supposed to be the wisest one here. They needed my guidance and we were running out of time.

"And how do you suggest we do that? Build a new Aurelius? The Fae don't want to be in hiding anymore. They're angry and out for blood," Dario muttered, glowering. He looked as if he was about to burst into his dragon form at any moment.

"Keep it together, Dario," Nico drawled. "We have a world walker amongst us. And she happens to be a Queen. We've been preparing for this, right Astra?" Nico looked to my mother.

"As a last resort," she said curtly. "I don't take the decision lightly—to send our own people to a new world with little to no magic in their veins—it may lead to the extinction of our race. I don't want faerie blood on my hands." She stared at Nico with an emotion I couldn't quite read.

"With the rate we're killing humans, there will be a mass extinction for both species if we don't betray the faeries," I said. We had to separate the two species until the blood-curse could be broken. If we didn't fix this, no one would.

The gods gave faeries magic and power from their own blood, while they blessed humans with fertility and ingenuity. Together, we coexisted in Erador for a millennium, but the gods knew the balance was off. Faeries were too strong. The gods created the Chosen Six to right their wrongs. We were strong and sworn to protect the humans, to whatever end.

"We can send them with humans—humans that are willing to go—who have relationships with faeries. They do exist, as rare as they are. And we know that blood-bonding with humans breaks the curse, as does breeding human with Fae. We can encourage this amongst the faeries, perhaps they'll break the curse by uniting with humans on their own accord. They may not have another choice," Eliana, always the optimist, suggested.

My mother looked between Eliana and I, and sighed. "Very well. I've already found the perfect world. It's beautiful—hospitable. Erador's food will grow in the soil. The water is potable. There is native flora and fauna that they can nurture and cultivate. Perhaps this is the best course of action. If it prevents blood shed, then I'll do what must be done."

"They won't go willingly," Dario huffed.

"So we'll trick them." Nico gave a resolved twitch of the mouth. "For the greater good."

"How?" breathed Eliana.

"We'll tell them the blood curse will be lifted in the new world—that they are only bound to it on Erador. We'll tell them that they can travel between worlds, then seal them out of Erador, until the curse is lifted," I said impassively, hating myself.

Everyone grew contemplative. No one could think of a better idea. Poor Aides. He'd fought to keep the peace, encouraged his family to befriend humans and work with them. And he'd still been killed. In his sleep. Faerie retribution would be a blood bath. We needed to act fast.

"Eliana and Dario, you must fly to Aurelius and find King Randall—tell him that we've found a habitable world where Faeries can live in peace—where the curse can be broken. Tell him what you must of the Six, but the less he knows, the better."

I turned to my mother. "You need to find a portal that can be accessed from Aurelius. We need the faeries out as quickly as possible. The more time they have to think about this plan, the less chance it has of working." I met my mother's warm chocolate eyes. They were heavy with guilt. She hadn't even acted yet, and was already tormented.

"Sometimes, you're too clever for your own good, Ophelia. If this will save lives, then we must do it, and face the consequences. When a new Pooka is born, we'll unite the Six and break the curse—only then will I reopen the gateway between worlds. And pray to the gods for forgiveness," she sighed.

"All who agree to this plan, raise your hand," I said.

All five of us raised our hands.

The memory faded to black and then I was back in Ophelia's parlor. "Raf is a pooka. H-he's the Chosen Heir? All along he was the one I was fated to find?"

I wanted to scream. I wanted to cry. I needed to find him.

"Yes. He's the one we've been waiting for." My mother smiled. "Does he know?" I asked, covering my mouth in horror. I chugged my water, but my throat still felt like sandpaper.

Gods, if he knew... and I'd chosen his brother...

"I'm not sure... Randall knew that his brother was part of the Chosen Six. It's possible he told Rafael."

He would've told me. He wouldn't have kept such important information from me.

"How did Astra die?" I asked. "She was Queen?"

I'd never met my grandmother. She'd been the last unicorn... before *me*. I'd never even heard her name spoken. Or perhaps I had... and Ophelia had erased the memory. I felt a stab of betrayal. It was my family that had exiled the faeries. And we *were* from a royal blood line... I'd always been told that Ophelia had married into royalty. They'd lied about *everything*. Was I cursed to spend my life surrounded by liars?

"A group of faeries that stayed behind in Erador found out what we did, and who was responsible. I wiped as many minds as possible—I tried to make sure that the Chosen Six remained a secret, that the world walker stayed anonymous. But I failed; she was hunted from the moment she closed that portal. Eventually, she was cornered and butchered—her horn stolen. We've been waiting for someone to reveal themselves for almost two-hundred years, but there hasn't even been a whisper of her horn. No sign of its power." Ophelia's face was drawn into a soft sadness.

"Her body was found... her heart and horn gone, so we know it exists somewhere. There's a rebel group called the *Ruhn Rebellion*. We think they're the ones responsible. Their loyalty lies with King Randall and his descendants." My mother's face was distraught. I'd forgotten how she wore her heart on her sleeve, for the world to see.

"I've never been able to have children, so when Eliana became pregnant, we all prayed you'd be a Chosen—either a pooka or unicorn. And then you were born and became the biggest blessing of our lives. Keeping you alive has been our entire purpose. You're the heir that was promised. And the gods led you to a Pooka. We can finally break the curse once the others come out of hiding. Please forgive us," Ophelia whispered. All three of us were teary-eyed, squished together on the love seat. They had worked towards this moment for two-hundred years.

"I forgive you." The words came out flat, because it wasn't completely true. "So... how long have you been on the throne? How many husbands have you gone through?"

She laughed. "You're putting together the pieces quickly. Mind manipulation has come in handy over the years. I've been Queen since our mother died almost two-hundred years ago. We moved the human King-dom of Corinthia to Aurelius when faeries left to Nymera. It took time for people to move into the city, which allowed me to mold minds as they arrived. The magic capital of the world was flushed of all magic quite quickly, with the aid of wards, spells, and my gift.

"We gave humans a refuge here. Faeries had built the most advanced city in the world, and we capitalized on it once they left. We became a cultural and economical epicenter, which gave us the power we needed to keep our family safe—to keep humans that supported our reign safe. I control much of the power in the world, while hiding in plain sight. I let the humans guide our rule, even when their views differ from mine. The Chosen's job is to protect humanity, not control it, which is why I let the council have so much say."

"But I still don't understand how you've gotten away with being the Queen of Aurelius for two centuries."

"Women aren't taken seriously in Aurelius. It's been easier than you might think. People don't care who sits on the throne in times of peace. As long as they have enough food on the table, they're content. Over the centuries, I've manipulated Princes from different realms into thinking that they're the rightful heir and I'm simply a consort... over and over. My inability to bear children made things less complicated. Fake portraits of false Queens hang in the gallery. This is the longest I've gone without a King. I won't choose another now that I have an heir. It will be your turn to rule soon, Marigold."

As Ophelia and my mother beamed down at me with hundreds of years of knowledge between them, I decided this was all the information I could handle today. I didn't want to think about being Queen just now.

"Thank you for everything you've both sacrificed," I said, meaning it. My heart was full of hope, and yet I felt a deep sadness for all that had happened and all that was to come. I needed to see Raf. I had so much to tell him. "I know there's more, but I need to rest." The sun would be rising in a few short hours. I hugged them goodbye, after insisting that I could make it back to my room on my own, even though that's not where I planned on going.

Before I could leave, my mother stopped me. "One more thing, sweetie," she said. Ophelia made a quick exit, seeming to understand that my mother wanted a moment alone.

My heart sped up as I turned to her. It was difficult to look directly into her eyes. She'd been nothing but a ghost for years—a figment of my imagination that I'd been desperate to have a few more minutes with. Now that she was here in the flesh, I'd lost the words that had hovered at the tip of my tongue for so long.

Trepidation flashed across my mother's face and I knew—I just knew—who she was about to bring up. "Is this about Father?" I asked, meeting her gaze. Her face crumbled and I patiently waited while she struggled to compose herself. She tucked her hair behind her ears and took a deep breath.

With a weak smile she asked, "How did you know?"

"I've been having dreams... and my childhood memories have been resurfacing." Memories that Ophelia had erased. "As things began to spiral in my relationship with Galen, you kept coming to me in a recurring dream. We were at our cottage, in the woods. You were running from something... *someone.* Eventually he appeared."

Mama nodded. "Ophelia thought it would be best if you didn't remember your father. For your safety and your... peace of mind. He was a nightmare. We had an arranged marriage that started out happy—passionate, even—but he became abusive.

"Your father was, *is,* very powerful. His entire family is. Leaving him wasn't an option, at least while I was *alive.* He's not the reason I faked my death, but the silver-lining from this entire ordeal, was getting rid of him. I believe he's still around, but since he thinks I'm dead—since Ophelia erased his memories of you and I—he won't come looking for either of us."

I'd already deduced most of what she told me from the fragments I'd recovered. "What happened the night he found us in the loft?"

She put a hand on my shoulder and took a deep breath. "Im not surprised that you were haunted by that night. I am too. What do you remember?"

"He was hurting you. In my dream, he... he turned into Galen. I stabbed him and we ran."

She gave a sad smile. "Unfortunately that's not quite what happened. You didn't stab anyone—you were only five. And... he knew I was a phoenix. He knew he could—" She swallowed hard. "That he could beat me... *kill me.* And I'd always come back. He was angry because I'd gone to the Oracle without telling him and left you with Ophelia. He couldn't be trusted to know what you are, so I hid the truth from him. When we returned home, he'd been stewing in his own drunken rage for quite some time, convinced I was leaving him and taking you with me, even though I promised we'd return. I planned to hide you in the loft while I faced him in the cottage, but he found us and took out his fury in front of you. You were never quite the same after that. You were wary of him, of men in general. I'm so sorry, Goldie. I wish I could've shielded you from that experience. It's one of my deepest regrets—I should've found a way to leave him sooner."

"Why didn't you fight back?" I asked quietly, staring down at my fingers that were now coated in frost.

"Because I didn't want him to take out his anger on his young, defenseless daughter. It was my most important job—keeping you safe. It still is. And because... some small part of me thought he was right—that I deserved it."

I choked back a sob. I felt simultaneously lighter and heavier. A sense of understanding and acceptance washed over me, while a heavy stone sat in my stomach, knowing what my mother and I had both gone through.

I wasn't sure Ophelia had done me a favor, erasing him. She may have blocked out the memories, but the feelings had stayed. No wonder I'd spent so much of my life not believing in romantic love. If I'd remembered him and what he was, would I have been able to see Galen's true character sooner? Would I have made the same decisions?

"Please, don't be sorry. You sacrificed everything for me. I'm so glad you're free of him. And that we're together again. I love you, Mama." I hugged her tightly, sinking into her embrace.

"I love you more than you'll ever know. A mother's love is endless. *You* are the best part of me. And I'm so glad that you left Galen in Nymera—that you didn't marry him and tie yourself to an abuser. You've always been wiser than me," she said, wiping tears from my lashes with a handkerchief.

"I had a support system. I had Rafael. You were alone in the forest, raising a child with your husband. You did your best. And now you're free, Mama. We're both free."

"You're my hero, Goldie." Mama smiled with tears in her eyes.

"And you're mine."

FIFTY-NINE

After my mother and I parted ways, I wandered to the bachelor's wing, which women were strictly prohibited from entering, *especially* unwed women. But after everything we'd just faced, I was in no mood for useless rules. I followed Raf's scent and found myself at his door.

Rafael opened the door quickly, making me startle. My jaw dropped as I drank him in. He was shirtless, and must've been wearing borrowed trousers, because they were too big, hanging low on his hips, yet comically short. I strolled in like a walking corpse and he closed the door behind me. He looked at me in my blood-soaked gown and motioned for me to turn around, so he could help take it off.

"You shouldn't be here," he said with hitched breath as my dress fell to the floor.

I grumbled at him, stepping out of my dress and kicking off my shoes. His eyes wandered as he stared at me in silky undergarments, selected by Galen, for his dungeon bride.

I sucked in a breath, feeling the unspoken tension between us, but I honestly couldn't tell if he was staring at my body or the blood. I needed a bath. I also needed to tell him who he was... *my destiny.* I swallowed hard. I was so tired. And so was he. It could wait.

"For gods sakes, can't the savior of our people do what she wants?" I asked with feigned annoyance.

"Perhaps, but I'm pretty sure Princesses can't... at least in Erador," he teased.

"Good thing I'm not a Princess." My smile died on my lips. "Actually, I think I just found out that I am, in fact, a Princess," I groaned, leaning into his chest.

Rafael huffed a low laugh. "*Finally*, you're worthy of my time." He wrapped me in his arms and I let him hold me momentarily, before pushing away. He grinned down at me as I shot him a dirty look. His tone turned serious. "We both had close calls tonight. How are you feeling?"

"Like I've escaped death too many times since I met you." I rested my cheek on his chest, listening to his solid heartbeat. "And... I'm grateful you're here. I don't want to exist in *any* world, if you aren't in it." I breathed in his scent, needing a temporary reprieve from trying to keep him at a distance. In this moment, I couldn't deny that we fit like two puzzle pieces.

There was so much more I wanted to say. But the words wouldn't come.

"Watching Sylvia drain you will be the image that haunts me for the rest of my days," Raf confessed. "I should've ended her when I had the chance. I hope you killed her. That was a great shot, by the way. A ten out of ten as far as gorings go." We both laughed.

"Let's get some sleep," Raf yawned. He took my hand and led me to the bed. He lifted the covers, scooped me up and placed me in, then crawled in beside me. We laid together nose to nose, breathing shared air.

Tomorrow we'd worry about breaking the blood-curse. Tomorrow, we'd find a way to unite both worlds and defeat the Elders. Tomorrow... everything would change. But today... today we'd sleep the day away in each other's arms. Today we'd cherish the friendship we'd found. Today, good had prevailed over evil.

I snuggled into Rafael and he pulled me closer. "Goldie?" he whispered.

"Yes?" I yawned back, almost asleep.

"I'm glad you stumbled into my world."

I grinned, eyes closed. "I'm glad you followed me back to mine."

"Ours," he corrected.

"Ours."

SIXTY

SYLVIA

So this was Erador. In my snake form, I couldn't see much beyond the woods. It was difficult to enjoy anything with a gaping hole through my chest, but I'd heal soon enough. I had the blood of two healers in my veins and an entire world of humans to drain at my leisure... I'd enjoy reaping the riches of war. Erador owed me. It would pay in blood.

She was a unicorn. The little bitch had been in my grasp and I'd let her slip away. If my son hadn't been such a moron, perhaps I'd already be wielding her horn upon my throne with *infinite* power.

The first order of business, once I acquired the horn, would be to kill Arnold. His grand ideas and thirst for power had gone too far. The book had made him too bold. He needed to be reminded *who* was in charge. *They all did*. Dahlia would be angry, but if I gave my son to her daughter, she'd forgive me in time. She was nearly as thirsty for power as her soon-to-be late husband. And the others would bow before me and *beg* for me to spare them, once the horn was mine.

But first, I needed a plan, along with money, clothing, and protection. I could acquire those things easily enough. It would be difficult to get to the girl, now that she was guarded in her castle built by *my* ancestors. I couldn't just slither in and bite her. I needed her in her unicorn form. I'd have to coax her into a trap. And her mother was a phoenix, that complicated things. She held anti-venom in her tears. I'd need to find powerful allies.

Why had the gods bestowed her family with so much power? No matter... Soon I'd rule both worlds. Perhaps I'd enlist help from the Oracle of Erador. If she knew Marigold had killed her sister, would that sway her to my side? The mountain spies had been eager to inform me of the Oracle's demise, yet no one had told me *what* had killed her—only who. They'd all suffer for their insolence.

I snaked my way through a patch of ferns, leaving a crimson trail in my wake. I'd cover this whole world in blood soon enough. The humans would pay. Marigold would pay. The shadow-wielding bastard would pay most of all. I'd kill her in front of him... make him beg. Then perhaps I'd bring him back to Galen as a gift. I flicked my tongue, scenting the air around me. Victory was so close, I could taste it.

The End

Want more?

Sign up for my newsletter
to receive a Bonus Chapter
from Rafael's POV.

www.authorkristencari.com

About the Author

Kristen Cari is a debut indie author. She's a mother, wife, and photographer living in Milwaukee, WI. Kristen plans on writing the next installment of *The Forgotten Fae* series in Summer 2025. You can find the latest news on her website. www.authorkristencari.com or on instagram @authorkristencari

Acknowledgements

They say it takes a village to raise a child, and this book often felt like a second child—taking up my time, taking over my mind, and contributing to my ever-fluctuating emotional state. So first off, I'd like to thank my husband, my daughter, and our dogs. Thank you for putting up with my late nights, my distracted daydreaming, and the missed walks. Thank you for encouraging me to pursue my passions and for your eternal patience.

Alan, thank you for teaching me what real love feels like—what *healthy* love feels like—for being my best friend and my Shadow Daddy. I would never have had the clarity to write a book like this, if I didn't have you; my muse, my anchor, my baby daddy, and my mate.

Winnie, thank you for giving me more drive than I know what to do with. You are my reason, my inspiration, and my mirror. I want to be the best version of me for you.

Thank you to my mom, who has been my biggest cheerleader throughout this entire process. Learning how to become an indie author is a big endeavor, but you always support my tenacity, never questioning whether I'm capable of reaching my dreams. Your love for reading and writing nurtured my creativity, while your unconditional love helped me find my voice. Every little girl should be so lucky, to have a mother who supports her dreams and emboldens her to speak her truth.

To Michelle and Shannon, thank you for being the first people to read In the Blood. YOU READ MY FIRST DRAFT. I could die of embarrassment—but also, thanks for encouraging me, even when the book was in its infancy.

To J, thank you for always making me feel like an ethereal goddess, no matter what my current ADHD hyper-fixation hobby is. Thanks for knowing this was more than a hobby. Thanks for always making me feel seen. Thank you for showing me what it means to be a strong female in so many ways.

To Taylor Swift, thank you for being an inspiration and writing the soundtrack to my life and this book. ITB was written and plotted while listening to TTPD on repeat.

To SJM, thank you for making me fall in love with reading again. Thank you for your wonderful mind. Thank you for Feyre and Rhysand.

To Kaven Hirning, thank you for being my gateway into the booktok world, even though I still suck at tiktok. I've loved following your writing journey and I hope we get to meet someday because I have a girl crush on you.

Thank you to my ARC readers who took the time to read a debut novel from an indie author.

To the SPA podcast ladies, thank you for teaching me so much about the industry and making me feel less afraid and alone.

To Gabby, my editor and beta reader, I truly didn't know if I was going to publish it until you read my work and were so encouraging, so a huge thank you to you!

To AOC, thanks for being such an inspiration in these dark times. Thanks for standing up to the the Elders and fighting for all of us.

To Daenerys Targaryen, Mother of Dragons, thank you for helping me find my dragon fire. The writers did you dirty. You'll always be my Khaleesi. *Dracarys*.

www.ingramcontent.com/pod-product-compliance
Lightning Source LLC
Chambersburg PA
CBHW020542120726
47903CB00001B/85